The Wrath of Kings

By

Philip Photiou

This book is dedicated to my family, and to the thousands who fought and died at Towton.

To Michele

Enjoy the best / regards

[signature]

Acknowledgements

I would like to personally thank the people and institutions listed below for their invaluable help in getting this book to press. Without their generosity and understanding I would never have done it.

Philippa Gregory, who explained the difficult task of transforming myself from a writer of non fiction to a writer of fiction

Graham Turner for designing and painting the cover

Louis Hampson, York minster archives

Dr David Edge and Dr Tobias Capwell, The Wallace collection

Dr John Clark, Museum of London

Dr Richard Mortimer Westminster Abbey library

Mrs E Thirst, Islington

Dr Nichola McDonald Centre for medieval studies, York

Mrs Carole Powell

Julie Snelling Windsor Castle archives

Lambeth Palace library

York minster library

Oxford archives

Tewkesbury Abbey

St Pauls cathedral library

The Tower of London

Mrs Joan Dunn St Michael's parish church, Alnwick

Bamburgh Castle

Newcastle city library

And many others, too numerous to name who have helped me research and interpret this important period in English history

Prologue

The deaths of Richard; Duke of York, his son Edmund, and his brother-in-law Richard Neville, Earl of Salisbury, at the Battle of Wakefield in December 1460, was a devastating blow to the Yorkist cause. The heads of all three were cut off and impaled on the spikes above Micklegate, in York, and a paper crown was stuck on Richard's head; a reminder of his ambition to be king.

In the months after Wakefield, York's eldest son and heir, Edward, smashed a Lancastrian army at Mortimer's Cross, but his cousin Warwick came to grief at the second battle of St Albans, leaving Queen Margaret a day's march from London. Having pillaged and burned her way south, Margaret found the city gates closed to her, and hesitated, giving Warwick and Edward time to meet and slip into the capital. Infuriated, she retreated north with Edward in pursuit. Moving quickly, he caught up with the Lancastrian rearguard at Ferrybridge, near Pontefract. After bitter fighting, in which Warwick was wounded, the Yorkists forced their way over the river. By 29 March Edward was only four miles from the royal army, at Tadcaster.

Chapter 1

Ferrybridge, Yorkshire. Saturday evening: 28 March 1461.

A bitterly cold wind skimmed over the surface of the swirling River Aire and sang soulfully through the tall grass swaying along its marshy banks. The planks, used to repair the damaged stone bridge, were coated in a thin layer of opaque ice, making them hazardous. Philip Neville, a manorial knight in the service of his cousin, Richard Earl of Warwick, coaxed his nervous horse off the treacherous bridge and onto the boggy north bank.

"Wait!" he barked, jerking back the reins and raising a hand to emphasis the order.

Thomas Markham, his teenage esquire, brought the rest of the company to a halt several yards from the end of the bridge. Resting his hands on the high pommel of his saddle, Philip sniffed the contents of his nose back into his throat and spat. The sun had set more than six hours before, and his quilted crimson doublet and fur-edged woollen cloak failed to keep out the unseasonable cold. While he struggled to make sense of the dark, unfamiliar terrain ahead, his horse pawed the mud with its hooves. Suddenly the moon broke through the cloud and the Great North Road was lit up, like a long, twisting length of silver ribbon, tapering off in the distance. Philip hated travelling on unfamiliar roads at night and had contemplated returning to Pontefract, but the scent of blood was in the air and he decided to press on.

The human detritus of the day's fighting still speckled the waterlogged ground on both sides of the road. Many of the dead lay in shallow pools, their stripped bodies covered with a dusting of frost that made them glisten in the moonlight. Philip had witnessed many similar sights during his eight years of knightly service and showed little emotion as he snapped the reins.

"Move on," he whispered, clicking his tongue against the roof of his mouth and indicating the road.

Clovis, Philip's eleven-hundred pound, chestnut palfrey - a mist of smoky white vapour billowing from its dilated nostrils - trotted on.

The three men-at-arms, six archers and three servants of Philip's retinue, slithered their horses off the bridge and followed him along the road to Tadcaster, thirteen miles away. Commanded to escort the baggage wagons from Doncaster to Pontefract, Philip had missed the fighting at Ferrybridge and was anxious to rejoin the army before its next encounter. Aggravated by his lethargic retainers, he turned in the saddle and glared back at the dark indistinguishable shadows, bobbing along in his wake.

"Hurry!" he hissed, digging his spurs in and forcing Clovis into a half canter.

Dragging an overloaded wagon and extra mounts prevented the others from keeping up and a gap quickly opened. When Philip failed to respond to their diminishing cries they gave up and followed at a less punishing pace. With one of his men already missing, Philip ordered the rest to stay together and meet him in the Earl of Warwick's camp, if they become separated. When dense cloud moved to cut off the moonlight, Philip once again, found himself plunged into a strange landscape of uniform blackness.

As Clovis clattered blindly along the old Roman road, Philip dabbed his badly cracked lips on the back of his glove, leaving a bloody stain on the calfskin.

"Let's go horse," he said, urging the animal into a half gallop, his body tingling with fear as he strained to make sense of his shadowy, distorted surroundings.

At twenty-six, Philip Neville was in his prime. His lightly tanned, oval face was dominated by dark, arching brows and a set of cold, piercing eyes. Conscious of his slightly oversized nose, which came from his father, and a mop of dark wavy hair, inherited from his mother, he was impetuous and lacked tolerance. Philip kept his romantic emotions locked away, but could not control his volatile temper. When he blew, anger flashed from his eyes and he would spit obscenities at the object of his wrath. Any wrong against him or his kin could lie dormant for years, until the right moment.

Arriving at Warwick's camp scattered around the village of Lead, four miles south of Tadcaster, Philip dismounted. Removing his gloves he entered his cousin's hectic pavilion and presented himself. Sir Richard Neville, Earl of Warwick, was seated in a high chair having his wounded thigh redressed while a bevy of messengers came and went.

"Where are my wagons?" he demanded in an aggressive tone, his lobe-length hair slick with sweat.

"Pontefract, my lord, as you commanded." Philip answered with a weary bow, the throbbing in his lower back symptomatic of a long day in the saddle.

"Pontefract," he huffed, the whites of his eyes red from the agony of his wound, which rose to an unbearable level as the bandage was tightened. "We are commanded to join the king before dawn."

Philip waited while Warwick gripped the arms of his chair to counter a fresh wave of pain.

"Henry is close…" he hissed through his teeth, unable to finish the sentence.

"Good." Philip smirked.

"We'll talk later, get some rest," Warwick groaned, while a servant placed a cold, wet towel on his fevered brow to ease his agony. "Now leave me, all of you."

The physician stood up, bowed and backed out, followed by others. As he left the warmth of the marquee, rest was the last thing on Philip Neville's mind. Agitated after his long ride and curt reception, he needed a drink. When his retinue arrived, Philip ordered his esquire to feed and secure the horses, and bed the men down, before he went in search of the village's only tavern.

Sometime after midnight Philip fell out of the bawdy, overcrowded alehouse and zigzagged blindly toward a stone barn, but he was not drunk he told himself. Opening the door as quietly as he could, Philip carelessly stepped over a carpet of slumbering bodies, until he found a space to lie down. Removing his cloak and boots he belched loudly and collapsed on the damp straw.

"Pardon," he apologised, before snatching a blanket off a sleeping soldier.

With so much wine gushing through his veins, Philip's eyelids dropped shut and he moaned contentedly.

Hours later he was woken by a loud rasping sound coming from the flapping lips of a pot-bellied soldier, grunting and wheezing unconsciously. An acrid tinge of tallow furred Philips tongue and he spat, but the bitter tang clung to his throat. No matter how hard he tried to go back to sleep, the snorting warrior kept him awake. He cursed, he threatened, and he threw a boot at the cause of his aggravation, to no avail; the boot bounced off his quivering stomach, but he never woke.

Lead village, before dawn 29 March 1461, Palm Sunday.

The solitary tallow candle burned low, its tremulous flame fighting for life. Mesmerized by the candles muted, yellow glow, Philip knew it was time to get up. Releasing a tense growl, he pulled the woollen blanket up under his chin, rubbed crusted muck from his eyes and muttered at the irritating concerto produced by more than a dozen snoring men-at-arms. Observing the black silhouettes dancing on the wall, an apparition caused by the dying candlelight, Philip knew that before this day was over he could be fighting for his life. A chilling sense of doom crept up his spine and gripped his neck, causing him to shiver.

Glancing at the candle, Philip noticed the flame drowning in a puddle of its own fatty residue. As he watched the stuttering light, his chest felt heavy and his breathing became difficult. Sitting up, he gulped in air and calmed down. When the candle finally hissed into oblivion, the amorphous dancing shadows vanished. Throwing off the blanket, Philip pulled on his boots and hurled a stream of abuse at the rousing soldier who had caused him such a restless night.

"Good morning," the overweight warrior mumbled, stirring from hibernation.

"Take your good morning and stick it up your fat arse!" he spat, drawing the damp cloak around his shoulders before leaving.

The Earl of Warwick's sprawling camp came to life long before dawn, and its hundreds of colourful tents bustled with frenetic energy. While he crunched over the frosty ground this Sabbath morning, Philip Neville yawned heavily and cursed his lack of sleep. Insensitive to the familiar stench of a military encampment, choking wood smoke, stale sweat and shit, he ignored the sergeants and centenars bellowing orders at sluggish, hungry soldiers, while their wives stood by sniggering. For most there would be no breakfast, as the supply wagons were still bogged down somewhere between Pontefract and Ferrybridge.

Philip's retainers and servants were camped behind a marquee, near St Mary's Church. With the first grey splashes of dawn in the sky, Philip stopped at the church. Standing before the oak door, he grabbed the cold iron ring and pushed. Unable to force the door open, he slammed the sole of his boot hard against its weathered surface. With a grating yawn, the swollen wood gave way and he stepped into the dark interior.

Closing the door, he crept along the narrow aisle between parallel rows of roughly hewn benches, removing his gloves as he went. Unable to see, he stretched his hands out and continued blindly towards the stone altar, which he knew to be at the far end. The damp, stale air filled his nostrils and the rustle of something scurrying across the reed-covered floor, caught his ear. Outside, the clouds parted and a shaft of milky moonlight shone through one of the windows. The bright beam hit the altar, highlighting a large silver cross and two candlesticks. The spiritual implication drew a gasp from Philip's throat, and he traced the Trinity on his chest. Before he could make sense of the phenomenon, the moon disappeared and the

5

tiny church was plunged back into darkness. Philip edged forward until his fingertips made contact with the frontal, a silk edged cloth that covered the altar. Drawing his thick, fur-lined cloak back he dropped to his knees.

With a deep-rooted aversion for the Church, Philip struggled to understand why he was drawn to the building. While escorting the baggage train from Doncaster to Pontefract, he was tormented by a bout of pessimism. His esquire advised him to seek divine consolation, but Philip scoffed at that idea. Glancing over his shoulder, hoping no one saw him enter, he lowered his head. Quietly he mumbled a prayer taught to him by his Latin master at Sheriff Hutton.

"Mea culpa, ideo precor beatam mariam simper virgini et te pater orare pro me ad dominus deum nostrum."

Philip repeated the incantation until a scraping noise outside forced him to stop.

"Lord, help me fight manfully this day," he added quickly. "And if I survive, I will attend church every Sunday."

Even as he offered the oath he knew he would not honour his side of the bargain, and such barefaced deceitfulness irritated.

"One in four," he appended; a deal he felt more comfortable with.

"Amen," he ended, crossing himself and rising to his feet.

As he left the church, he slammed the door harder than was necessary, an action that made him cringe. Looking up he saw a group of soldiers sharpening their swords on the cornerstones.

"Show some respect you pigs!" he barked, pulling on his gloves.

The swordsmen sheathed their weapons and slouched away, jeering at his comment.

"Sheep fuckers," he snarled.

Philip found his retainers and servants lying on the ground, fast asleep.

"Get up!" he bellowed, kicking the nearest blanket-covered body and resenting their ability to sleep. "Get up, damn you!"

Coughs, curses and a series of bodily noises erupted from the damp coverings, but slowly they emerged, rubbing their eyes and scratching themselves.

"Lazy dogs!" he snapped, shivering.

Philip joined his esquire and page in a small hemp tent, set up behind Warwick's grand pavilion. After a frugal breakfast of barley bread and bacon, he commented on Thomas's sour disposition.

"Why so glum?"

"'Tis Lent and I am eating meat," he whined, eyeing the lump of greasy bread between his fingers and crossing his chest.

"So?" Philip scoffed. "Fear not, I'll ask the Pope for a dispensation."

"You should not mock the Church, my lord."

"Eat your food."

With his hunger satisfied, Philip instructed Thomas to join their men with Lord Warwick's, before turning to Ashley Dean, the youngest member of his retinue.

"Fetch Hotspur."

"My lord!" His young page yelped, scampering from the tent on all fours.

Philip licked fresh blood from his badly chapped lips and indicated for his esquire to help him dress.

Wiping his greasy fingers on a napkin, Thomas sidled over to a long, wooden chest at the back of the tent.

"Is that Scot here?" Philip asked, referring to his missing retainer, Arbroth, last seen in Pontefract.

"No my lord," Thomas frowned, opening the chest to reveal a suit of armour wrapped in an oily sheet. "He'll turn up."

Growling his frustration, Philip stood, grunting at the effort.

Twenty minutes later he was encased from neck to toe in a suit of highly polished plate armour. Leaving the

cramped tent, Philip released his arming sword from its
scabbard and performed a series of exercises to test the
armour's flexibility. Satisfied, he re-housed the blade and
waited for his horse.

"Where is that boy?" he whinged, impatiently punching
his gauntlets together.

His retainers slowly appeared. His armourer arrived
first and set about checking Philip's steel suit.

"That'll do," he nodded, tugging every leather strap and
buckle, making sure there were no gaps, "Yes, that'll
do…"

"Hotspur is in fine spirits this morning, my lord!" his
page panted excitedly, dragging the huge fourteen-hundred
pound courser by its bridle.

"You took your time," Philip complained, snatching the
reins from the nineyear old and shooing him away.

"My lord, he would not obey me," his groom groused,
holding the stirrup steady. "I dunno what's got into im?"

"Have you fed him?" Philip asked, stroking his
courser's soft face.

"E's had the best oats."

"Then he's eaten better than I have," he scoffed, turning
to his page. "You stay in camp when we march." He
added, stabbing a finger at the boy to emphasis his order.

The disillusioned youngster sloped away and Walter
thumped the breastplate hard.

"You're tighter than a virgin's cunt," he grinned.

Unsure of his meaning, Philip slipped a foot through
the stirrup, pulled himself up with the aid of pommel and
cantle, and wedged his backside in the high chair. With his
stomach churning from too much wine, he let out a lengthy
breath.

Winding the reins around his steel fingers for better
control, he stroked Hotspur's soft neck with the leather
underside of his gauntlet. Closing his eyes he breathed
deeply until his stomach settled. Flicking its head from
side to side, Hotspur champed on the iron bit behind his
teeth for comfort, before allowing Philip to steer him

around to the front of his cousin's grand marquee.

"Keep the men together!" he commanded as an afterthought.

"Yes, my lord!" Thomas answered, waving him away.

Easily identified by its central position and the sixteen-foot, red tapering standard flying above, Warwick's magnificent pavilion was the focal point of the camp. Inside the colourful tent, the earl slept, ate, prayed and held council. Trotting around to the well-lit entrance, Philip acknowledged several captains he knew and waited. They were already late for their rendezvous with King Edward.

"Make haste, my lords!" he urged, as his cousin and uncle strolled from the tent, the unseasonable cold shaving his patience.

William Lord Fauconberg, an elderly, hard-cursing veteran of the French war, ignored his nephew's impertinence and continued to converse with Warwick.

While they talked, a portly, well-dressed figure hurried from the marquee with two companions. Light from inside the tent lit up Philip's face, and the nobleman stopped and stared at him. Taking several steps forward, the fat man silently scrutinized Philip's features. Suddenly he spat in disgust and walked away. Confused by the unprovoked insult, Philip swore at the fellow's lack of breeding and deliberately rattled his armour, until Fauconberg glowered up at him.

"Patience!" he barked; his thick, white beard sprouting from his helmet like weeds from a wall. "The king will wait."

"Ignore him Uncle," Warwick smiled smugly, while an esquire straightened the heraldic tabard over his breastplate, "for he cannot hold his drink."

"'Tis not the drink, I have been kept awake all night by the snorting of a pig."

"Yes," Fauconberg mused, "I hear you have offended Sir Edmund?"

"Who?" He frowned trying to put a face to the name.

"Sir Edmund Grey... you shared his quarters last night and cursed him for his charity." Fauconberg reiterated, pointing at the disappearing figure.

"Why, I took him for a common soldier."

"Your mouth will lead you to the gallows," Warwick warned.

"Go to him and apologise," Fauconberg suggested.

"I will not, I care nothing for that Lancastrian traitor."

"You forget your training?" Fauconberg roared. "Etiquette, courtesy, humility!"

Warwick's smirk turned into a grin and Philip rolled his eyes. It was fortunate his uncle was too busy struggling to mount his horse to notice.

"What's this world coming too?" Fauconberg grunted, hauling himself into the saddle.

As dawn's early light filtered through the dark, cloud-lined sky, the three knights rode to King Edward's camp. Despite wearing a satin-lined, leather arming doublet beneath his armour, Philip felt the raw wind penetrate every crack in his steel shell. When he glanced up at the sky, he felt specks of ice prickling his face.

"Snow?" he gasped.

Disorientated by lines of dying torches, illuminating the route to the king's camp, the three Nevilles drew up beside a group of soldiers and Fauconberg asked directions. Their slurred responses irritated the old warrior and his face turned purple.

"Get off the road you damned codheads!" he roared, lashing out with a foot.

"Patience, my lord," Philip smiled.

Incensed by his nephew's impertinence, Fauconberg galloped ahead of his companions. With his armour clanking metrically in time with Hotspur's canter, Philip reflected on the events that brought him here.

Philip Neville was an unruly child, whose youthful indiscipline quickly spiralled out of control. With her husband in France, another young son to care for, and a baby on the way, his mother asked her brother-in-law, the Earl of Salisbury, for help. He promised to take the boy and train him for knighthood. On his eighth birthday, Philip was packed off to Sheriff Hutton Castle, to learn the art of becoming a page. Life with his uncle was hard, but the mind-numbing chores of serving wine, grooming horses, polishing armour and studying languages, kept him too busy to complain. Four years later, Philip was made an esquire and his training stepped up. Now he learned how to don armour and was taught to fight with a variety of weapons. To strengthen his body he ran three miles a day in full armour, and in all weather. During his time at Sheriff Hutton, he fell under the influence of Salisbury's son, Richard, the future Earl of Warwick, and his brothers.

For his candid opinion of King Henry's bad councillors, Philip's father, Sir George Neville, was recalled to England. On the way to London he was foully murdered. Word that the Duke of Somerset was involved oozed into every Neville household. Though he rarely saw his father, his murder fuelled Philip's nascent hostility against the Beauforts, an emotion nourished by his cousins. When Philip's brother came to train for knighthood, he tried to indoctrinate him with his bête-noire of the Beaufort's, but Michael was too young to understand. Two years younger and five inches shorter than Philip, Michael loathed discipline. Disillusioned he returned home eight months later and found his mother married to Somerset's younger brother, William.

With the war in France going badly for England, Philip and Michael joined Lord Talbot's army. At the disastrous battle of Castillon in 1453, the boys hacked their way through the French army and escaped by the skin of their teeth. Despite receiving a Knighthood for his service, Philip was far from content. Brooding over the defeat and distressed by his stepfather's kinship with the Duke of Somerset, he refused to live in the same house. Bidding his mother adieu, he left to visit the two manors bequeathed him by his late father. These humble holdings, North

Marston in Buckinghamshire and Stratton Audley in Oxfordshire, provided him with enough income to maintain a small band of retainers. Life away from his cousins soon proved dull and he returned to Yorkshire.

Philip enjoyed his time with his cousins, hunting, hawking and jousting. At a tournament in Coventry he was knocked out of the saddle by Sir Ralph Percy. Landing awkwardly, he broke several fingers, his left elbow and wrist. As he was carried from the field, Percy's blustering incensed him, and he vowed to get even. In May 1455, the enmity between the Beauforts and their new allies the Percys, and Richard of York, and the Nevilles, exploded at St Albans. Here Philip fought beside Warwick as he smashed through the Lancastrian defences. After serving, on and off, in Calais, he returned to England, and at Northampton, in July 1460, he followed Edward through the rain to victory.

Seven months later, Warwick was beaten at the St Albans refight, and Philip again tasted defeat. When a visit to his family ended in a quarrel with Michael, who received his spurs for his part in the second battle of St Albans, he left. Infuriated by his brother's misguided loyalty, and envious of his knighthood, Philip rode to London. En-route he bore witness to the destruction wrought by Queen Margaret's army during its march south. When he saw the blackened ruins of Stratton Audley and was told North Marston had suffered a similar fate, he flew into a rage. With his source of income gone, he had no option but to indenture himself to his cousin Warwick, for sixty marks a year.

In the village of Saxton, a mile east of Lead, a dozen Yorkist nobles were gathered outside a huge marquee, beside which the quartered, red and blue banner of England, twisted and snapped against its juddering pole. Sheltering from the worsening weather, beneath the bare branches of a creaking oak, they slapped their sides for warmth. A tall, well-dressed figure attended by several fussing varlets, eventually emerged from the pavilion.

"My lords!" the young King Edward yelled, above the trenchant wind, as he joined them, "Henry marches against us!"

"Then we must make haste, sire!" one of the quivering nobles declared.

"We are greatly outnumbered," another added woefully. "We must wait for Norfolk."

"No, we cannot wait," Edward insisted. "Fetch every man able to bear arms... the army will march at once!"

The shivering nobles acknowledged his command with a concerted bow, and dispersed. As they left, Edward's ears pricked up at the sound of horses approaching from the west. Looking at the line of torches marking the way to his camp, he spotted several dark shadows on the narrow road. Squinting, he stared until they were close enough to recognise his cousin, Richard Earl of Warwick. Behind him rode his uncle, sixty-year-old, short stocky and heavily bearded, Lord Fauconberg, while another relative, Philip Neville, brought up the rear.

Dismounting tentatively, Warwick pulled off his gauntlets and limped toward the king still suffering from the wound he received at Ferrybridge. Edward removed his black velvet cap and tossed it on a nearby drum, muttering as it blew off, to be plucked from the ground by a quick-thinking servant.

"Good morning, my lord, 'tis good to see you, and your horse?" Edward smiled, making a reference to the previous day's fighting, when Warwick bragged he would slaughter his warhorse to stimulate his soldiers. Fortunately for the animal, he failed to carry out his boast.

"Your Grace is in good humour on such a cold morning," Warwick replied bowing graciously.

"I am not, Mass took too long, as a consequence I was forced to gobble my breakfast," he frowned, patting his stomach. "And I shall suffer for my gluttony."

"At least you have eaten, sire," Warwick sniffed, glaring at Philip. "Today most of our men march on empty stomachs."

"We were fortunate yesterday," Edward said, ignoring Richard's blatant plea for sympathy. "Today we must be more cautious."

Much shorter than his cousin Edward, Warwick was a proud man with an unquenchable thirst for power. Married to Anne Beauchamp, heiress of the vast Warwick estates, Richard's fortune had grown in tandem with his flamboyant lifestyle, until he believed his position and influence second only to the king, if not higher. Philip spent much of his early life in Richard's shadow and found him to be arrogant, sinister and greedy, but he was also generous, courageous and polite. Well loved by his retainers and tenants, Warwick was an obsessive perfectionist. Before offering battle, every eventuality had to be planned out.

Shifting his attention to the diminutive knight shuffling uneasily behind Warwick, Edward smiled. "Listen to that wind my lord Fauconberg; are your archers in good spirit?"

Buoyant after his role in the victory at Ferrybridge, Fauconberg removed a gauntlet and poked a finger in the air to gauge the speed and direction of the wind.

"Aye nephew," he answered gruffly. "The wind is with us."

"Then, my lord, join your men, for today, they will lead the advance."

"No, I must stay with you, your father…"

"Dear Uncle, when I was thirteen I stood beside my father on St Albans field," he said proudly. "Since that day I have led armies to victory at Northampton and Mortimer's Cross" "So you see, I am well versed in the art of war. But I thank thee for thy concern."

"But, Your Grace, you are…" the red-faced Fauconberg blurted, only to be restrained by his unruffled nephews raised hand.

Sitting on his horse listening, Philip smiled, half expecting his uncle to explode out of his armour.

Disconcerted by Edward's self-assurance, Fauconberg nodded sharply, and remounted with the aid of an attendant. The muttering servant cursed at the excessive amount of oil coating the old man's armour, as he forced his arse into the saddle. While his uncle cantered away complaining to the trees, Edward turned to the third member of the triumvirate.

"He's as mad as a March hare," Edward joked, "but he's a tough nut to crack."

"Since his release from a French prison, he is not the man he once was," Warwick said, referring to Sir William's capture in Normandy. "He has no patience."

"Yes, the old man has suffered much," Edward sighed, turning to Philip, "Cousin?"

"Sire," he sniffed, bowing from the saddle, and admiring the confident way his teenage cousin dealt with his strong-minded kinsmen.

"We fight a battle this day that will decide once and for all who wears the crown. How shall we fare?"

"His reputation is worth a company, my lord," Warwick interjected, attempting to ease the pain in his thigh by senselessly rubbing the steel cuisse protecting it.

"Then I pray your reputation serves us well," Edward smiled, looking north. "I doubt cousin Henry is with his army today?"

"When this day is over I will seek him out and take the crown off his head."

"You will not," Edward warned. "No king should suffer such an indignity."

Philip twisted his torso from side to side, testing his armoured joints and sniffing at Edward's droll reply, though he did not care for the reprimand.

"Somerset will pay for your father's murder," he announced.

"They will ask for mercy," Edward said, evoking an image of his father's death at Wakefield. "But they'll not receive it."

"Sire?" Philip questioned.

15

"No quarter - if Somerset is taken I want his head on a spike. But you will bring Andrew Trollope to me alive," he simmered, "He will die slowly for betraying my father."

Philip nodded his understanding and Edward continued, "What of your brother? Was it not Michael who addressed Henry's parliament at Coventry and swore to die before a Yorkist took the throne?"

"My brother is a fool," Philip said, glaring at Warwick, who, by his dubious expression, was responsible for passing this piece of news on to Edward.

The king glanced at the snow beginning to speckle his boots.

"This will cause problems."

"It'll be worse for them," Philip said, impatiently flipping his reins over his courser's ears to annoy the animal.

"They've been moving through Tadcaster all night," Edward revealed.

"Then we won't have long to wait," Warwick announced looking north.

As the conversation tailed away, Philip tried to rid his nose of an aggravating whistle by blocking first one nostril then the other. But the shrill noise continued to annoy him every time he breathed in. While Edward spoke to one of his heralds, Philip wondered how his young cousin would cope in the coming battle.

Yet to reach his nineteenth year, Edward of York stood a massive six feet four inches tall. This firm-jawed, chestnut-haired fusion of physical strength, handsome features, intelligence and courage, believed the crown was his by birthright. The opportunity for an historic victory lay in his open palm; all he need do was stay focused, reach out and close his fingers.

Lifting a hand to protect his eyes from the irritating snow blowing into his face, Philip watched three esquires and a fresh-faced page arrive, bearing the king's armour on red velvet cushions. Skilfully and swiftly they helped Edward out of his fur-lined cloak and into a suit of black, plate-armour. Squatting on a nearby barrel, Edward spread his legs and an esquire secured the steel, pointed sabatons to his feet. As snowflakes danced in the air, Philip sensed the wind increasing and glanced up at the dark clouds rolling across the sky.

Driven by vengeance and inspired by a vision of the crown on his cousin's head, Philip felt they were on the threshold of a battle, which, if successful, would give the House of York its ultimate triumph. Victory this day would allow the hostile knight to appease a malevolent streak, which, over the past twelve weeks had burned deep into his restless soul. The deaths of his uncle Richard and two cousins, Edmund and Thomas, at Wakefield, and the ghastly murder of his mentor and uncle, Richard Earl of Salisbury, turned Philip's blood to ice.

While Warwick chatted with Edward's herald, Philip blew the contents of his nose onto the grass. Turning back he watched as the red and blue quartered royal tabard, emblazoned with the golden lions of England and the lilies of France, was lowered over Edward's head. Securing the tabard to his breastplate, the senior esquire carefully checked every strap and buckle. William Hastings, Edward's chamberlain, now came forward carrying the king's padded helmet on a golden cushion. Breaking from his fussing esquire, Edward took several steps forward, crushing the cold, crisp grass beneath his feet.

During the king's harnessing, twenty thousand Yorkist soldiers filtered out of their camps and headed north. Catching the martial beat of trumpet and drum on the wind, Edward signalled for his courser and mounted. Irritated by the acute whistle in his nose, Philip watched as Edward was handed his padded armet. Drawing the steel helmet down over his head, the young King muttered something unintelligible while Hastings stood on a stool and strapped the helmet to its bevor, a high steel collar protecting the neck and chin.

"Heralds!" Edward shouted. "Stay close."

"Yes, Your Grace!" they answered smartly.

Tugging the reins to the right, Edward dragged his white caparisoned warhorse round to face his cousins.

"My father's father was executed for treason by Henry's father," he announced, lifting his visor. "Today I shall wash that stain away forever!"

"I have no doubt of it sire," Warwick responded, preparing to mount. "God protect you, most gracious majesty!"

Edward made the sign of the cross and rode away.

The king and his escort were swallowed up by the deteriorating weather, leaving Will Hastings to bid Philip and Richard adieu.

"What kind of armour is that for the king of England?" Philip asked, "'Tis as black as coal."

"He's not happy," the chamberlain revealed. "Some fool has left his best suit in Pontefract, yet no one will confess."

"Then someone will be in the shit," Philip grinned, before following Warwick back to Lead. "Fare thee well!"

"By sunset we'll all be in the shit," Hastings muttered, acknowledging their departure with a raised hand.

Within an hour of Warwick's return, his scattered encampment was deserted, except for the wounded of the previous days fighting and the camp followers. Snow fell ad infinitum and a driving wind threw it hard against the backs of the Yorkists as they marched north to meet more than twenty-five thousand Lancastrians, reported less than a league away. Before setting off Philip and the rest of Warwick's knights dismounted and removed their spurs, indicating they would fight on foot. Warwick's quartered banner, bearing his family colours, was brought to the front. Many of the earl's retainers wore new scarlet surcoats with his emblem of a standing white bear next to a ragged staff over the left breast, but the material was thin and they would suffer for their pride.

As he marched, the effects of wearing close fitting armour over a padded doublet, forced Philip's body temperature up until sweat bled from every pore.

"This wind is the work of the devil," Warwick gasped, his injured leg causing him considerable pain as he urged his men on.

"Look at it as a good omen, for it will blow the crown from Henry's deranged head!" Philip prophesied, the leather soles of his armoured shoes slipping on the damp grass.

Philip's frustration turned to relief when he discovered the whistling in his nose had ceased.

"Is your brother with them?" Warwick asked, limping on.

"Have no doubt of it, my lord," he panted, wiping perspiration from his face with the palm of his gauntlet. "Michael is a fool, but if he is taken, he must not be harmed."

"What if the king demands his execution?"

"Edward is not yet King."

"He is King and is so called," he puffed.

"He has not taken the crown."

"A crown does not make a king!"

Refusing to be drawn into an argument, Philip blew hard at the exertion of walking over ground littered with concealed lumps and hollows.

Struggling up a low ridge less than a mile from Lead, Philip saw the army bunching up and fanning out along the crest.

"Why have we stopped?" he wondered aloud, bending forward to fill his lungs with cold air.

Warwick waved at one of his liegeman, directing him to lead his retinue to the far right of the line.

"Look!" a partly-armoured centenar cried, thumping the base of his poleaxe at the hard ground and pointing off in the distance. "There is the enemy! By God, see how boldly they stand."

Straining to see, the Yorkists narrowed their eyes and could just about see the Lancastrian army, arrayed in lines along the top of a second ridge, less than four-hundred paces away. The fast-flowing River Cock covered the enemy right flank and boggy marshland protected their left.

"Get out of the way!" Philip yelled, pushing a way through the crowd, the stench of stale sweat and alcohol forcing him to hold his breath.

Annoyed at the strength of the enemy position, he drew his lips back and exhaled sharply through clenched teeth, while Richard hobbled up beside him.

"There are too many of them," Philip hissed, irritably scratching his wet hair and staring through a curtain of falling snow at the Lancastrian banners spaced out along the far ridge.

"We have waited too long!" Warwick spluttered, "They hold the best ground. Now we will go forward and be slaughtered!"

"Why nephew?"

"Uncle," Warwick gasped, surprised to see the old man still mounted, "they have the advantage my lord; they will not come to us."

"They won't?" Fauconberg questioned in a calm voice, fighting to control his excited steed, "Steady."

"They'll stay on that god-damned hill all day. We will have to go forward or withdraw."

"Wait and see," Fauconberg scoffed, tugging his reins to the right and wheeling his courser away. "My archers will start this dance and we'll see how long they can stand it!"

"Dance...?" Philip huffed, unimpressed by his uncle's inane euphemism.

Warwick opened his mouth, but before he could speak the command, 'Horses to the rear' boomed out, and those still in the saddle, dismounted. Edward's knights, sergeants, esquires and centenars began forming their men into the three traditional battle lines. While complaining soldiers were pushed and prodded into line, a number of boys brought up skins of cider and ale. Philip shared a cup of wine with his cousin Richard and watched the trembling warriors, many already on the road to intoxication, vying for the ladles. Fortified by strong liquor, they began yelling abuse at the distant foe.

With the wind increasing and snow thickening, the Yorkist commanders struggled to sort out their ragged lines. As officers threatened and beat cursing men-at-arms with gauntlet and sword, thousands of belligerent archers filtered through them to a point twenty paces in front of the army. Dressed in colourful livery and wearing a small, round sallet on their heads, each bowman carried a three-finger thick, seven-foot yew bow and several sheaves of arrows. While they unsheathed their bows, Lord Fauconberg and his standard bearer weaved their horses between them. The bearer held the quartered flag against the wind so its two rampant lions, in diagonal corners, were clear for all to see.

Philip watched amused, as his uncle's courser flounced conceitedly in front of the archers, its heavy leather trapper, decorated with Sir William's coatofarms. Yawning loudly, he cursed Edmund Grey for his lack of sleep and observed the archers going about their business. Philip held the bowmen of England in high regard, and often went along to the butts in York Castle, after Mass on Sunday, to watch them practice. Under Fauconberg's leadership these men were about to earn their 6d a day.

The order to 'String bows!' was suddenly relayed down the line by dozens of centenars: trusted men commanding the independent companies. Blowing to defrost numb fingers, the bowmen removed the strings from beneath their helmets and strung their war bows. Twenty paces behind the archers, the men-at-arms stood checking buckles and straps. The expectation of battle now swept through the army, as men from England, Scotland and Wales hugged their weapons close.

To ease his own apprehension, Philip chatted with Warwick's flat-headed, talkative herald. Suddenly a hush descended over the Yorkist ridge, and the whole army dropped to its knees. Warwick's youngest brother, George, Bishop of Exeter, solemnly led a clutch of chaplains to the front. Standing behind a portable altar, overlaid with white cloth, the bishop raised his wooden staff topped with a gold crucifix. Dressed in a sleeveless, deep purple chasuble over white robes, the young bishop prayed loudly for success and offered a mass absolution. After his final words, 'Benedicat vos omnipotons deus pater, et filius, et spiritus sanctus. Amen!', the soldiers crossed themselves. Those with a sword kissed its symbolic crossbar; others touched their lips to the ground, or made the sign of the cross in the soil. After a coordinated 'Amen' they stood up.

Accompanied by his nobles and knights, King Edward walked back through the men-at-arms to take private communion with his cousin, the bishop. Impatient to get at the enemy, Philip stood alone between the men-at-arms and the archers. With his chin stuck out defiantly and arms folded across his breastplate, he was an object of curiosity for those who failed to comprehend his behaviour. Moments later, hundreds of Yorkist standards were brought forward. These multicoloured banners, stiffened with buckram, were planted at intervals behind the archers so the men-at-arms could find their commander during the fighting.

Having strung their bows, Fauconberg's archers watched him edge his horse slowly forward, until he was out in front alone. Leaning back, his left hand resting on the high cantle of his saddle, the old man stared across the snow-blown area between the two armies. Drawing his sword from its scabbard with a loud scraping sound, he held the blade down at his side.

"God forgive me for doing battle on this most holiest of days." He whispered, staring up at the sky and crossing his face.

Fauconberg's centenars, standing in front of their men, backs to the enemy, shielded their faces from the driving snow and waited. William Neville stroked his white, feral beard and playfully rubbed his horse's twitching ears, while Philip, agitated by the delay, gnawed his lower lip.

Suddenly Fauconberg's right arm shot up and the tip of his sword pointed to heaven.

"Notch!" his centenars yelled.

Philip held his breath, as adrenaline sent the blood rushing through his veins.

Thousands of ash arrows were pulled from the ground and laid against thousands of bow staves.

"Draw!"

The archers responded by slotting the delicate, grey goose feathers onto the hemp and stretching the strings back to their chins, before aiming the arrows skywards.

"Send the dogs to hell!" Fauconberg roared, glancing over his shoulder as far as arthritis allowed, and dropping his sword arm sharply.

"Loose!" his centenars roared, snapping their arms down.

The two fingers of the archer's right hands sprang open and the hemp strings whipped down the hard, leather bracers protecting their forearms, before shuddering against vibrating bows. Thousands of steel-tipped, wooden shafts arched into the sky and homed in on the tightly-packed Lancastrians in the distance. The unique hissing sound of arrows in flight never ceased to amaze Philip. His mouth unconsciously fell open as his contracting eyes traced the dark, sinister shelf winging its way across the valley.

Though he couldn't see the effect, he knew what the enemy could expect when that deadly shadow fell from the sky. The lethal rain would hit with such force that steel bodkin and broadhead tips would penetrate light armour, leather and flesh, like a knife cutting into a ripe pear.

Viewing the contest from the right of the Yorkist line, Philip treated the returning arrows with contempt. The strong wind, which helped the Yorkist shafts on their way, caused the Lancastrian arrows to fall short.

"We may not have to fight at all today," Warwick mused, conscious of his throbbing thigh, as he was handed his helmet.

"All I want is Somerset," Philip said ominously.

"Calm yourself cousin; or this burning hatred you nurture will consume you."

Philip huffed at his words and sneered as he imagined the mayhem spreading through the Lancastrian army. "Look, the antelope of the usurper!" he declared, pointing across the valley.

"Where?"

"There, my lord!" he insisted, shooting a steel finger across the vale.

"I see only the blue lion of Northumberland," Warwick said, straining to see. "Henry is not here; Margaret will keep him in York."

"Then harken to my words, cousin! When the fighting is done, I'll ride to York and tear that cowardly prince from the arms of his French harlot…."

"I know not from where this passion of yours has taken root," Warwick said, grabbing the oily gardbrace covering Philip's left shoulder, and looking into his dark eyes. "But if you cannot put it aside, you will fight this battle with one eye closed."

"I want vengeance for my murdered father!" he answered, shrugging Warwick's hand off.

"Somerset is dead," Warwick growled.

"Yes but his son is here."

One of Fauconberg's archers suddenly lowered his bow and turned to the waiting men-at-arms.

"They're coming!"

"What?" Warwick gasped. "Why?"

Leaning forward Philip squinted, but falling snow obscured almost everything beyond a hundred paces. "I see nothing," he frowned, his confidence cracking. "What's happening?"

"They're coming out!" someone echoed.

Warwick ordered his captains to make ready, while King Edward and his standard bearer cantered down the line. Drawing back on the reins, Edward brought his courser to a slithering halt and the royal coat of arms, embroidered on the linen trapper was sprayed with mud.

"Stay together, my lords!" he warned, pointing north, the ecstasy of battle stimulating his senses. "They will be on us soon!"

"We'll give them a welcome they won't forget!" Philip vowed, banging a fist against his armoured hip, while those in earshot echoed his sentiment.

"Is every man ready to do his duty?" Edward cried dramatically, lifting his visor.

"Aye!" the unified response came back.

Trotting his skittish courser around his standard bearer's more composed palfrey, Edward examined the ground between the two armies.

"We'll meet them halfway!" he announced.

"Let them come to us!" Warwick advised.

"Your Grace, they will blow themselves out and we'll still be fresh," Philip added, coughing harshly and spitting a bubble of yellow phlegm.

Edward studied the wraithlike figures, advancing towards him through gaps in the snow, his eyes flickering as he ran an armoured finger thoughtfully up and down the bridge of his nose.

"Somerset commands their right."

"And Northumberland has charge of their centre!" Philip shouted excitedly, catching sight of the red and blue standard of the Percys.

"Then he will die as his father died on St Albans field!" Edward prophesied, before wheeling his horse and galloping away to assume leadership of the left battle. "Remember... no quarter!"

Riding across the front of his troops, Edward waved and shouted encouragement.

Philip covered his eyes with a hand and tried to observe the Lancastrians marching torpidly down from their ridge through fields of spent Yorkist arrows. Their colourful flags appeared endless and when they began ascending the Yorkist ridge, the rhythmic thump of their feet made the very ground tremble. Eager to get at the enemy, Edward's men-at-arms gripped their weapons and edged forward. Standing beside Warwick and his close friend, John, Lord Scrope of Bolton, Philip silently watched the quartered royal banner of King Henry coming ever closer.

King Edward cantered down the line again, this time carrying his personal murrey and blue standard. Halting in front of Warwick's retainers, he raised the flag high so all could see its sable bull and ten white roses set against bursting suns.

"My children, you ask that I be your king!" he shouted, his voice full of passion as he pointed at the enemy. "Bolingbroke stole the crown from an anointed king. Will you help me to take back that which is mine by birth?"

"York! York! York!" they roared, shaking their weapons in the air.

"Remember, God is on our side!" Edward bellowed so loud his voice broke up, as he thrust a finger at the enemy. "Not theirs!"

Philip watched his regal cousin, who looked much taller than his six foot four inches, and his eyes drifted to the Latin text 'Dieu et Mon Droit' embroidered in gold on the royal standard. A sense of familial pride surged through his body and he couldn't help adding his voice to the chorus.

"To the death!" Edward spat, his eyes wide with excitement, as his sixteen-foot banner coiled in the wind.

"To the death!" they screamed, and the name of York was chanted more passionately.

Handing the tapering standard to his bearer, Edward dismounted, drew his heavy bastard sword and battle-axe and waited for a varlet to remove his spurs.

"Axe or blade?" he asked the nearest men.

"Axe!" they roared.

"Blade!" he grinned, handing the battle-axe to a varlet.

"Soldiers, today I fight with you," he vowed, his words accompanied by a generous shower of spittle. "Stand together and we will triumph!"

The king's highly charged broadcast was followed by a

reflective silence, as the men lowered their heads in a final personal prayer. Snapping down the visor of his armet, Edward walked away waving his sword at the cheering soldiers. The Lancastrian army was closing fast, their mantra of 'King Henry, King Henry!' and the tramp of twenty thousand marching feet rising to a deafening crescendo. Philip glanced to the right at the enemy looming out of the snow, less than a sixty paces away, and sweeping towards the exposed Yorkist flank.

"Pray for Norfolk," Warwick said nervously, regretting his decision to fight afoot. "Shift over John!" he barked, angrily urging Lord Scrope to block the threat.

"Forget Norfolk, my lord," Philip answered, captivated by the approaching wall of humanity.

"God help us," Warwick gasped, as ethereal images materialised in front of his eyes and the ground vibrated beneath his feet.

"God will not be here today," Philip said, drawing his arming sword from its scabbard and fingering the tight steel gorget circling his neck. "Whether we live or die is up to us."

"I was told that when death is close we see those who have gone before," Warwick revealed.

"I too have heard this, my lord," Philip replied pensively. "They say they bear no wounds and appear at peace."

Richard looked at Philip and both men burst out laughing, but it was the humour of despair.

Harnessed from neck to toe in highly polished, well-oiled plate-armour, the Latin phrase 'Fides et honor' etched in gold along the top of his breastplate, Philip Neville chose to fight without head protection. A helmet limited visibility, kept in the heat and gave him an overpowering sense of fear. To guard his vulnerable neck, he preferred an old-fashioned narrow gorget to the restrictive bevor. As a sign of his allegiance, he wore a crimson linen tabard over his armour, the Warwick coat of arms blazoned across the front.

With the enemy so close, Lord Fauconberg withdrew his archers back through the waiting men-at-arms.

"It's up to you now, you miserable bastards!" he shouted, cantering after his bowmen. "Kill every last mother's son!"

On the left of the Yorkist line, Edward raised his sword above his head and held it poised.

"Forward!" he commanded, lowering his blade until the tip pointed directly at the enemy. "Forward for the crown of St Edward!

The pent-up emotion of ten thousand Yorkist men-at-arms exploded in their throats as they bounded forward.

"Sir," Thomas Markham said, offering Philip his helmet.

"You will be a target for every jackanapes out to make a name for himself," Warwick cautioned.

"Take it away!" Philip barked, knocking the helm from his esquire's hand.

"It will be your own fault if your noggin is struck off," Warwick warned, as his own sallet was strapped to its bevor. "Perhaps it'll knock some sense into you!"

Philip muttered an incoherent response, as his cousin unsheathed his sword and led the Yorkist right forward, and Thomas retrieved the helmet.

Gripping the hilt of his blade with both hands, Philip turned it upside down and made sure no one saw his trembling lips touch the crossbar.

"Keep your miserable servant safe today, merciful Lord," he whispered, before righting the weapon and resting it on his shoulder.

As the Yorkists moved forward, Philip found himself forced away from Warwick. With the enemy almost upon him, a sickly sensation churned in the pit of his stomach and he clenched his buttocks to prevent shitting his braies. Perspiring heavily, yet shivering violently, his teeth began to tingle and the urge to flee became overwhelming. A strange sense of loneliness froze the blood in his veins and he failed to stop the wind trumpeting out of his arse. It was the same distressing emotions before every fight.

Chapter 2

Philip Neville braced himself as the two armies collided with a loud, clattering crunch and thousands of yelling knights, and men-at-arms began their deadly work. Philip was so close to the enemy he could smell the fear on their warm fetid breath, and with his features contorted into a fearsome scowl, he lunged into melee. A teenager armed with a scythe blade looped over a crude pole was his first victim. The youngster's terrified expression and poorly aimed strokes boosted Philip's confidence. Easily avoiding the homemade halberd, he swung his arming sword up and brought its heavy blade in from the side. The honed steel tip sliced into the lad's unprotected neck and almost severed his head. Blood and splintered bone sprayed out and he dropped to his knees. Attached by a single tendon, the head bobbled against the front of his leather jerkin and a fountain of steaming blood gushed into the air. Before his body hit the ground it was trampled into the mud. Kicked free the head bounced around like a football and disappeared underfoot.

"Sweet Jesus," Philip spluttered, crossing himself quickly and shaking his blade at the Lancastrians, who yelled, stabbed and sliced their way forward. "Is this all you have to offer?"

Encouraged by such an easy kill, a yearning to live replaced Philip's earlier apprehension. If killing the enemy was the key to survival, he would kill them without mercy. Two more quickly fell to his raging bloodlust, and as they dropped others took their place, until Philip's vision became distorted by so many angry faces and waving weapons. One Lancastrian, armed with an axe, bore such a perverse grimace it reminded him of the gargoyles perched on the walls of York Minster. Utilising the point and pommel of his sword, his elbows, fists, and pointed, steel sabatons, Philip found himself trapped in a nightmare scenario of chaos, confusion and self-preservation.

Melting snow, blood and scattered entrails quickly

transformed the ground to a greasy crimson mush. Heads, ears, noses, arms and legs, everything that could be hacked off was. Men fell by the score, their blood meandering down the slope in hundreds of dark red rivulets. For thirty minutes York and Lancaster slaughtered each other, and the cries of the dying were carried on the wind all the way to Tadcaster.

Fatigue and dehydration soon set in and Philip found himself struggling to stay on his feet. Having fought a faceless knight to a standstill, he acknowledged his skill with a curt nod and both men drew apart.

"By Christ's blood," he gasped, as sweat poured down his face and his body ached from a barrage of blows.

Unable to breathe properly, he staggered out of the front line, and was joined by others. Passing a vibrantly-attired herald, standing behind the lines with quill and parchment, noting the battle prowess of the Yorkist nobles, Philip glared at him.

"Paper soldier," he sneered.

The herald and his pursuivant ignored the insult and continued their work; they were used to such abuse.

Irritated by the chafing steel gorget Philip's hands shook as he tried to remove his sweaty, plate-covered leather gauntlets.

"Come on!" he hissed, the tight gloves refusing to release his swollen hands.

Once free his fingers tore feverishly at the gorget straps, to eliminate the cause of his torment. Finally liberating his sore swollen neck, he let out a relieved gasp and stumbled toward a cart, twenty paces behind the line. Plunging his bloody sword into the hard ground, Philip fell to his knees, folded his hands over its rounded pommel and allowed his head to flop forward. He remained in this position for some time, catching his breath, while the chaotic battle symphony resonated inside his head.

Scattered around the empty cart were several hundred wounded and exhausted soldiers, with more arriving. Having cast aside their weapons and helmets, they lay on the wet ground panting for breath while women passed among them with skins of ale and cider. Raising his head, Philip gulped in cold air, but his close-fitting armour and posture restricted the intake. Looking around he offered a lopsided grin to a bearded veteran, propped against the cart.

"This fight will last all day," the old hand managed, utilizing a large wheel for support and slavering uncontrollably.

Philip noticed a deep tear running diagonally across his blue and purple jack and released a low groan to relieve the pain in his ribs.

"You're lucky to be alive," he coughed, focusing on the horsehair stuffing and mangled steel plates protruding from his ripped jack.

"A spear point did that, but I can be fast, even at my age," he managed, spraying bloody spittle through the damaged, brown stumps of his remaining teeth, as he observed Philips shredded tabard. "Are ye Lord Warwick's man?"

Philip responded with a feeble nod. Grabbing a ladle of ale from a passing boy, he poured the liquid between his lips, an action that made his scabby mouth sting and bleed.

Unable to stand any longer, the bearded soldier, his face a network of healed scars from some long ago fight, slid down the wheel. When his arse hit the grass, the ale lodged in his rusty, brown beard, showered out.

Twisting his head, Philip saw his cousin, Richard, limping toward him and wondered why his jaw ached. The unconscious act of grinding their teeth together during combat caused many soldiers to suffer from jaw ache and fractured teeth. Removing his helmet, with the help of an anxious page, Warwick reprimanded the boy through his visor.

"You useless knave!" his voice echoed inside the helmet as he lashed out with his injured leg, only to miss and howl in agony.

Once relieved of his sallet, Warwick dabbed his bloated

red face with a wet towel and spoke to a French officer, sent to Warwick by the Dauphin Louis. Jean d'Estuer, Lord de la Barde, commanded a detachment of Burgundians and fought under the banner of the Virgin Mary. With his expensive blue and white velvet-covered armour, tainted with English blood, the Frenchie put a hand to his ear and tried to listen through his helmet. Finally nodding, he rejoined his troops, while Richard stumbled over to the cart.

"Water, for pity's sake," he croaked, blood streaming from his nostrils. "We make no headway here!" he snorted, wiping bloody sweat from his face.

"If you say so, my lord," Philip replied, "What did the frog want?"

"Jean is a brave soldier; he asks that he be allowed to fight under his own flag."

"You mean his 'rag'; is it his wish that the French take the glory from this field," Philip scoffed, "Have you seen the king?"

"Yes," Richard panted, ignoring his hostility. "He fights with more passion than his father ever did!"

"Does he not have good reason?"

"The devil takes his reasons," he spluttered, pouring the contents of a ladle down his throat and over his head.

The shock of cold liquid took the earl's breath away and he shivered.

"Where are your men?"

"I've no idea," Philip said, scowling at the elderly Sir John Wenlock, who stood in reserve, with his white liveried retainers.

Though a close friend of Warwick's, John Wenlock's previous service to Queen Margaret did not sit well with Philip.

"Leave him be," Richard growled, sensing his antipathy.

"There are many here who served Henry. Have you forgotten Wakefield?"

"Forget Wakefield?" Richard moaned.

"How can I," he scoffed contemptuously. "Can you?"

The weight of Lancastrian numbers steadily pushed the Yorkist front line back up to the crest of the ridge. Alarmed by the retrograde movement, Philip knew he must rejoin the fight and gestured for an attendant to come and secure his gorget.

"Yes," Warwick said, replacing his padded helmet and lifting the visor, while a fussing varlet strapped it to the bevor, "we'd better go back!"

Philips stomach knotted, as the skulking spectre of mortality returned. Looking up at the leaden sky, Warwick raised his blade dramatically.

"Send us Norfolk, Heavenly Father, before we are undone."

Fingering the cold, steel gorget gripping his neck, Philip smirked at Warwick's theatrical riposte.

"That's enough," he snapped, shooing the attendant away and pulling on his gauntlets.

With a final nod at the veteran sprawled beside the wheel, Philip yanked his sword from the soil and followed Warwick back into battle, twisting his neck for comfort.

The wind continued to pelt both armies with prickly sleet, but many were too busy killing each other to notice. Lords, knights and men-at-arms relentlessly hacked off body parts and ripped arteries open in pursuit of victory. The clash of steel against steel and the ear-splitting cacophony of desperate men filled the air as more reserves fuelled the maelstrom.

Philip Neville fought several aggressive opponents bent on hacking off his unprotected head, before finding himself hemmed in by his own men and unable to swing his sword with any impetus.

"Get out of the way you fools!" he cursed, pushing his elbows out to make room.

Suddenly his face was awash with blood and he turned aside in disgust.

"For fuck sake!" he spat, wiping the warm, sticky fluid from his face with the underside of his gauntlet.

A loud swishing sound made him snap his head up, and he was baffled at the sight of a long poleaxe blade, rising behind the enemy ranks, and moving towards him. Those Lancastrians in the front line stepped aside, allowing their man through. The rotating axe-blade, secured to a seven-foot pole and spiked at the end, was a dreadful weapon in the hands of an expert. A number of Yorkist soldiers wearing only padded brigandines, fell over themselves to avoid its honed edge. Spotting a knight without his helmet, the poleaxeman bargained on an easy kill.

Watching the blade cut invisible circles in the air, Philip was rapt by the concentration blazing from the half-closed eyes of the determined warrior. Twitching his face at the aggravating snow, the red-faced Lancastrian began to tire. Still snorting blood from his nostrils, Philip divided his attention between the whirling blade and the Lancastrians flickering eyes. The hatless, heavy-set warrior, dressed in a faded green surcoat, forced him to backtrack. A barely discernible whimper and slight drop in momentum alerted Philip to his fatigue, and in one mad moment he attacked. Bending low he bit into his bottom lip and thrust his sword arm forward. Waiting for just such a move, the Lancastrian jerked his torso sharply, like some exotic dancer, and the deadly sword point struck air.

With a wide-eyed sneer, the attacker twisted his wrists and the ghastly weapon changed its angle of flight. Cutting acutely downwards the steel blade hit the surprised knight hard, and with a nauseating crack he was knocked to the ground. A series of narrow, steel ribs covering the pauldron protecting his left shoulder, buckled and flew off. The power behind the strike split the pauldron beneath, ripped through the mail covering the shoulder of his arming doublet and tore the satin-lined leather doublet before gashing into soft flesh.

"Bastard!" Philip cried, dropping his sword and scrambling back.

The wild-eyed Lancastrian swung the weapon above his head and altered the slant of the blade, to slice off his unprotected head.

Unable to help, Warwick's men screamed obscenities and waited for the deathblow. Kicking and scraping to grip the slippery ground, Philip yelled, but no sound came from his mouth, yet in his mind it was deafening. Raising his right arm defensively, everything around him seemed to slow down. Oblivious to the blood belching from his injured shoulder, he saw the triumphant leer on his assailant's face and thought he could hear his companions goading him on. Releasing a guttural hiss in horrified expectation of death, Philip remembered the words of those who had come close to dying. Then at the last moment, as all sound was muted and blurred, faceless figures flashed before his distressed eyes, his opponent arched backwards. It was only when he heard the cheering from his own men as they grabbed his shoulders and helped him up, that Philip's hearing returned.

"God be praised," he blubbered. "Thank you Lord, thank you."

Retaining their bows against orders, a pair of archers hovered near the front waiting for an opportunity. When Philip was knocked down, they saw their chance. Looking along the aspen shafts, they took deliberate aim at the poleaxeman and let loose. The first arrow hit him in the left eye, went through the skull and came out the back, the jellied remnant of an eyeball dangling from its barb. The second arrow caught him in the throat and penetrated to the goose feathers. When he hit the ground, bloody foam bubbled from his mouth, and his arms and legs thrashed wildly. The unfortunate wretch lived briefly in terrible torment before being trampled by his own men in their enthusiasm to wreak vengeance on those who had killed their champion.

Hauled to his feet, Philip thanked the archers and stumbled away in search of a surgeon. Now the pain kicked in and he felt warm blood trickling down his left arm and into his gauntlet. Delicately he raised the injured limb, which only increased his agony but allowed the blood to pour from the cuff, and he vomited.

Finding several large tents, used by the surgeons, Philip stumbled inside the first one and sat on a stool. Detaching the damaged pauldron and breastplate from his shredded shoulder caused him considerable anguish, and he cursed the surgeon's unsympathetic assistant.

"You enjoy your work," he gnashed through a liberal stream of spittle.

The assistant grinned as he wrenched Philip's breastplate off.

"Ouch!"

Using a pair of tweezers, the surgeon removed strands of satin and bone splinters embedded in the six-inch gash. The poleaxe blade had cut deep and the wound ran from the top of his pectoral joint to below the armpit, exposing torn muscle and bloody bone.

"You are fortunate the arm is not broken," the surgeon explained, rotating the joint, fascinated by the open wound's resemblance to raw pork.

"My God..." Philip moaned, closing his eyes to the torture, "you cunt-"

"I've been called worse," he grinned, deliberately jerking Philip's arm down. "You'll live."

Once the shoulder was cleaned and sutured, Philip swallowed a cocktail of alcohol, vinegar, hemlock juice, opium and boar's gallbladder, before falling asleep in the back of a tent.

While he slept the wind dropped, but snow continued to fall, and the battle went on as morning passed into afternoon. By mutual consent, both armies broke off and drew apart to catch their breath and clear away the mounds of dead and wounded obstructing the fighting. When combat resumed, the pendulum of success swung first to the Lancastrians, then to the Yorkists, and back again. The nerve-racking cries of a badly wounded knight brought Philip out of his much needed slumber. Being helped into his hastily repaired armour produced a bout of excruciating agony and vomiting, and he swore liberally.

Positioning his injured limb across his stomach, Philip took a second dose of medicine and headed back to the front.

His return to battle was preceded by rumours of disaster filtering down from the left of the Yorkist line. Hard-pressed, Warwick was unable to send help or withdraw. Catching sight of his cousin toiling up the ridge, he raised his visor.

"What are you doing here?" Warwick asked, concerned by Philip's awkward posture and blood-splattered armour.

"I have nowhere else to go."

"Then stay out of the way!"

Philip gave a disapproving grunt and remained behind the front line. Casting a worried eye over his shoulder, he waited in distress planning a way out, should the day be lost.

The bad news from the left was sparked by an aggressive Lancastrian assault. Unfortunately the Earl of Northumberland, commanding the centre of Somerset's line, failed to press forward at this critical juncture, and the Yorkists beat off the attack. Several boys, perched in the trees behind the fighting, shouted the news to a herald, who spread the word, and a relieved Philip Neville put all thought of retreat from his mind.

"There!" he warned, as an armoured Lancastrian breached the line and rammed his spear into the neck of a surprised esquire.

Warwick casually thrust his sword under the assailant's vulnerable armpit, while one of his men brought the head of a lead-lined mallet down, crumpling his helmet. The Lancastrian fell and the mallet struck his sallet again and again, crushing the steel and pulverising the soft head inside.

Philip Neville gathered a dozen men-at-arms and used them to reinforce any threatened point within his sphere of vision. By mid-afternoon the wind had ceased and both sides were fully committed. With no reserves, and his flank bending back, Warwick rallied his jaded Spartans and prayed for Norfolk. Bandaged and bleeding, they held; just. Skulking in the rear, a wounded Burgundian hand-gunner, whose unstable weapon had exploded in his hand, anxiously watched a column snaking its way up the road from Ferrybridge. Using a handful of snow to wipe his powder-burned face, the Burgundian held his breath until he recognised Norfolk's orange and blue flag flying at the fore. Barging a way through to Warwick, who was busy finishing off an opponent, the gunner grabbed him by the arm. Twisting the earl around, he pointed his mutilated left hand at the approaching column.

"The white lion, my lord, Norfolk is here!" he cried in broken English, crossing his chest. "We are saved!"

Sir John Mowbray, Duke of Norfolk, cousin to the king, Warwick and Philip, was a sick man. Forced to rest at Pontefract, he sent his five thousand soldiers on to Towton under his cousin, John Howard. The sight of Norfolk's eighteen foot long, four foot tall, swallow-tailed standard, injected fresh energy into fatigued limbs. When his men, in their blue and orange livery coats, surged onto the field, they extended the Yorkist right and overlapped the Lancastrian left.

Mowbray's herald and Norfolk's standard-bearer rode to the top of the ridge, in search of Warwick. With his throbbing left arm useless, Philip was gathering his men to plug a potential gap, when he spotted Norfolk's banner floating gracefully along the crest. Hurrying to join Warwick, he found his cousin surrounded by dead and dying men, one foot resting on a folded corpse.

"At last," Warwick gasped, raising his visor.

"You have arrived at a most opportune moment," Philip said, rubbing his bloodshot eyes. "Now we can win the day."

Curling his gauntlet into a fist, Warwick shook it triumphantly at Norfolk's gorgeous standard. When news of the reinforcements spread among the embattled Yorkists, an almighty roar erupted from the hilltop. The enemy faltered at the sight of Norfolk's flag, its rampant white lion taunting them, and ripples of disaster filtered through their ranks.

Philip removed his gauntlets, stuffed them through his belt and snatched Warwick's standard from his surprised bearer. Hoisting the unwieldy flag high, he rested its pole against the short metal skirt protecting his abdomen and turned to those nearby.

"Charge on," he yelled, "remember Wakefield!"

Most of Warwick's men looked at him as if he was mad, but pushing through them were Norfolk's fresh troops, eager to get into the fight. It was to them that Philip repeated his appeal.

"Forward!" he cried. "Charge on!"

Still there was no movement, a few of the more daring bounded forward, but when the rest held back, they bashfully withdrew.

"What are you waiting for?" Warwick bellowed, twirling his sword above his head, "Charge on!"

With a loud uncoordinated cheer the Yorkist right poured down the shallow slope with renewed verve and broke over the Lancastrians like a wave. Unable to stem the tide, enemy resistance crumbled.

Enthusiasm overcame injury and Philip shuffled forward, but as he tried to hold the flag, the hemp sutures binding his wound, snapped and the pain returned. The unwieldy banner trembled in his hands and he prayed for strength, but God wasn't listening. Screwing his face up to counter the fresh agony, his armoured toe struck something buried in the mud and his tired legs folded. As he fell forward, the standard flew from his grasp and he hit the ground face down.

"By St George," he coughed, the shock taking his breath away.

With his entire body wracked by pain, Philip closed his eyes and pressed his right hand down for leverage. Opening his eyes he found himself face to face with a gutted body half submerged in the mud. The outstretched arms and saintly demeanour reminded Philip of Christ's crucifixion. Repulsed by the foul wetness in his throat, he spat and retched. Suddenly his hand slipped out and his face dropped back into the exposed stomach.

Releasing an animalistic roar, Philip wrenched his head up and wiped away the bloody viscera clogging his nostrils and mouth. Struggling to contain the vomit racing up his gullet, he made a fresh attempt to rise. Leaning on the dead man's chest and drooling uncontrollably, he jerked to his knees in staggered stages, but the sharp crack of ribs breaking under pressure, forced him to cry out.

"God help me!"

Drawing on the last of his strength, he made one final superhuman effort. Fearing a collapse back into the quagmire, Philip laid his good hand on the dead man's sternum and pushed. Suddenly his fingers slipped down into the open stomach and blood, and soft entrails oozed over his quivering digits. The din of battle, echoing like a thousand blade-smiths hammering their anvils, almost shattered his sanity. With his right arm shaking uncontrollably, he yelled against the pain and his determination brought him through. Once on his feet, Philip blew his nose and spat out tiny pieces of unpleasant gore. Wiping his tacky fingers on the remnants of his shredded tabard, he stared down at the dead man's glazed eyes and shuddered.

"Sweet Jesus," he hissed, cradling his useless left arm and stumbling away.

The agony of his wound, loss of blood and dehydration made Philip's armour feel heavy, and he had great difficulty going on, but he persevered. Spotting his cousin Warwick, he staggered towards him. Unable to continue, the earl drove his sword into the ground and flopped down on a pile of bodies. A servant removed his helmet and he rested his neck against a headless corpse.

"My lord," Philip groaned, nursing his injured arm.

"Cousin," Warwick managed, his face flushed with the effort of breathing. "Join me."

"But they are on the run," he declared, puzzled by his

kinsman's macabre banquette.

The excessive amount of vile flesh clinging to Philip's bloody face, hair and armour brought an amused grin to Warwick's mouth.

"It will soon be over," he announced, drowsily, watching a group of soldiers robbing the dead and murdering the wounded. "The men are out of control; they are killing everyone. Are you in pain?"

Philip gritted his teeth and closed his eyes, as his shoulder wound flared angrily.

"Yes," he moaned, "Are you coming?"

"No… but you go," Warwick coughed, tearing a piece of cloth from the nearest corpse and wiping bloody sweat from his face, "Find Somerset and have your God damned requital."

"I'll find him," Philip promised, unsheathing his sword and tripping his way over the body-strewn field. "And cut off his head!"

Every step distributed a fresh jolt of torment through Philip's weakening body, but he pressed on. As he dragged himself over the uneven ground, a numbing sense of surrealism misted his vision. He saw archers discard their bows and walk among the wounded, executing them in the king's name. Those with minor injuries were forced to their knees and killed by a blow to the head; others had their throats cut by blood-splattered soldier's crazy with battle fever. For the nobles who died on the field, death was not the end; their bodies were stripped and mutilated.

The ground Philip traversed was strewn with broken bodies, smashed weapons and a blend of blood, brains, severed limbs and intestines. Where the fighting was hardest these had been trodden into the mud to such an extent that large areas had the consistency of a thick, dark red stew. A stink of death pervaded the very air and Philip could taste it with every breath. He had witnessed many terrible sights during his service, but today would stay in his memory forever. As he looked at the countless dead and dying, littering the fields, a sublime sadness replaced all thought of retribution.

"Pie Jesu Domine dona eis requiem," he mumbled over and over, 'Blessed Jesus Lord grant them rest.'

Forced ever backwards, the enemy conducted a fighting retreat. Many of Somerset's nobles and knights were dead, others had fled, but he fought on, withdrawing steadily towards the woods above the River Cock. All the while the Yorkists kept up the pressure, allowing him no chance to disengage.

The exhausted Earl of Warwick, his thigh throbbing from infection, refused to move from his grisly, but comfortable seat.

"Tired old man?" a stentorian voice boomed out.

With tremendous effort Warwick craned his neck and saw his uncle, Fauconberg, standing behind him, his white hair flat against his head and beard blown every which way.

"Hello," he managed.

"It's as if some force had lifted our two armies up and thrown them down," the ancient warrior observed solemnly. "One bloody mess. Where's Philip?"

"Somewhere out there," Warwick indicated with a casual wave, opening his mouth to catch a few flakes of snow. "This is a great day for the Nevilles."

"Yes, but its finished... we are doing murder now, killing to satisfy a king's vanity. This is not the way; if we refuse them mercy they will show us none the next time we meet," Fauconberg warned, glancing down at the scratched and dented sallet nestled under his arm.

"What mercy did they show my father, your own brother, at Wakefield?" Warwick scoffed, watching a group of soldiers rounding up prisoners for execution. "They dragged him out and killed him like a dog... No, Uncle, the days of chivalry are over."

"Why?" Fauconberg frowned, shaking his head.

"Because the king says so."

"Don't lay this on Edward," he growled. "What they are doing now is for greed."

"They've earned the right."

"I must stop it."

"Then I wish you well."

"Nephew," he nodded, strutting away in an attempt to save lives.

"Good luck," Warwick muttered, downing a cup of red wine, to the unconcealed sniggers of his servants. "Quiet you dogs!"

Somerset's centre and right folded back towards the River Cock and held, but only until Edward brought up a body of mounted spearmen. When this mass of steel and horseflesh charged in, resistance withered. Somerset's men broke and fled down the steep slope toward the swollen river. It was here that disaster awaited them, for the duke had destroyed the bridge before the battle. With no way across many jumped into the fast flowing water, pursued by the Yorkists. Some made it to the north bank, but Edward's cavalry was hard on their heels, and the slaughter continued through Tadcaster and beyond.

Philip followed the trail of blood down to the body-choked river and squelched along its flooded bank in a state of incoherent stupor. Occasionally he stopped to stare at one of the bodies littering the riverbank, and speculate on the manner of death. Shivering from the cold he shuffled on, to where he wasn't sure. With darkness descending, torches were lit and soldiers walked among the dead and wounded seeking friend or fortune. Spotting a gang of women winding their way down to the river, totting poles, Philip's curiosity got the better of him and he followed them. Despite the mud and blood, they pulled up their skirts and used the poles to drag bodies to the bank. Hauling the corpses from the water they stripped them, before callously rolling them back into the river.

"You God damned harpies!" he screamed, viciously kicking a discarded helmet in their direction.

The women jeered at his condemnation and continued their perverse work. Cradling his left arm, Philip stumbled on, their demonic laughter echoing in his ears.

When dusk finally lowered its enigmatic mantle over the battlefield, the killing frenzy petered out. Total exhaustion after a day of continuous combat, and a scattered army, prevented any organised pursuit. The victors constructed hundreds of bonfires, and soon a myriad of fiery orange tongues were leaping into the night sky. Edward's army flocked around these welcome beacons to eat, drink and boast of daring deeds. Drawn to the nearest fire, Philip was offered a cup of cider by a soldier, whose forehead and left eye were swathed in a bloody rag.

"Thank you," he croaked, snatching the bowl and slurping down the refreshing liquid.

Wiping the back of his hand across his cracked lips, Philip returned the bowl and nodded his gratitude. Suddenly his attention was drawn to a loud-mouthed archer wearing Fauconberg's blue and white livery. Picking up a severed hand, the bowman craftily drew his own up into his floppy cuff, before offering the hand of friendship to a passing billman. When the unsuspecting warrior grasped the proffered limb, the archer released the hand and jerked his arm back, leaving his startled billman holding the ghastly relic. The victim's horrified expression's had the archer and his companions howling with laughter. Standing closer to the fire, Philip chuckled at their morbid sense of humour and shivered violently.

One of Warwick's esquires, sent to find Philip, found him questioning a captured Lancastrian knight for news of his brother, Michael. The esquire waited patiently for him to finish his futile interrogation before relaying his master's request that he attend the king. Learning nothing from the prisoner, Philip moodily accompanied the esquire to the royal pavilion. Passing a large, open marquee, a bandaged red pole, and a line of wounded waiting beside the entrance, indicating it belonged to a barber surgeon; he pushed to the front of the queuing knights and esquires. Kicking aside several amputated limbs dumped on the ground, he entered the illuminated field hospital.

"But the king-" the esquire whined.

"Don't worry," he said.

Discarding his upper body armour, with the esquire's reluctant help, Philip called for someone to attend him.

"Wait your turn!" a barber surgeon snapped, brushing his long, wet hair away from his sweaty face, while he struggled to cauterise the shredded stump of a thrashing warrior's amputated leg.

"But I'm bleeding like a pig!" Philip complained; the screams of a knight under the knife, unnerving.

"So," the surgeon spat, as perspiration dripped freely off his blotchy chin. "Keep him still!" he yelled, as the four men tried to keep their master in the chair.

"I can pay!" Philip flared, glancing at the next in line, who waited calmly, holding his bloody face together.

"I need more hands, not money!"

Angered by his attitude, Philip grabbed a jug from a sideboard and took a long swig of bitter wine, most of which went down the front of his stained arming doublet.

"Forget it!" he barked, throwing the jug on the ground and pushing the esquire out.

"I'm nearly finished..." the physician called after him, his tone less abrasive.

"Don't bother!" Philip snapped. "I'll be back for my armour."

"Then go to hell," the barber surgeon growled, returning to his tormented patient. "Hold him, hold him!!"

Philip Neville joined the king in his lavishly furnished pavilion, its cluttered interior lit by candles and lamps, and warmed by several braziers. Buoyant after doling out knighthoods by the bucketful, Edward sat flaccidly in his high-backed chair, wrapped in a robe of blue tussu bordered with marten fur. The king's long neck rested against a soft, red velvet cushion and his knees jutted out, making him look too big for the seat. Except for Warwick and Fauconberg, his nobles had removed their armour and changed. Slumped on chairs and stools, they supped wine and tried to stay awake.

When Philip arrived, Edward was listening to a fawning herald, gleefully revealing the names of those who fought valiantly and those who did not. Raising his eyes at the bloodied, partly armoured latecomer, Edward signalled for his herald to stop and motioned for Philip to sit. As he bowed painfully, the stench of blood, urine, and sweat emanating from his clothes offended Sir John Howard, who was sat near the entrance. Holding his injured arm, Philip delicately eased his backside down on the damp ground, and Howard offered him a snooty nod.

"Your Grace, I haven't had time to change," he apologised, glaring at Howard.

"A most remarkable triumph sire," William Hastings offered, warming his skeletal fingers over a hot brazier.

"Yes," Edward sighed reflectively, rising from his chair and pacing slowly.

"God has blessed you with another great victory sire," the Bishop of Exeter announced.

"Yes," Warwick added, seated on a low chair, and smiling at his devout younger brother, George. "But he left it late."

"My King…," Fauconberg interrupted, his aged body yearning for rest.

"Not yet Uncle," Edward cut him off. "As long as Henry is free that title eludes me."

Fauconberg released a rumble of displeasure into his beard and exchanged eye contact with Warwick.

"Lancaster must be destroyed before I can truly be called King," Edward confessed. "We must catch him soon or Somerset will raise a new army and all we have achieved today will count for nothing."

Edward stopped pacing and flopped down into his ornately carved chair, facing his nobles.

"What of Andrew Trollope?"

"Dead, Your Grace," the herald interjected.

"Good," he smiled smugly, comparing the three grimy Nevilles to his more pristine nobles. Running his fingers down the cold blade of the bastard sword resting against his chair, he huffed at the jagged burs. "Tomorrow we ride to York."

"Why wait?" Philip moaned his concentration blurred by constant pain, "Henry will not tarry in York."

"We've waited for you," Fauconberg growled, noisily sucking a beef bone.

"What is to be done with the prisoners, my lord?" Howard interrupted.

"Execute every last mother's son, I'll make these northerners pay for their loyalty to Lancaster," Edward said coldly, turning to his uncle and grinning at his manners. "How are your archers, my lord?"

"Those who are not dead are dead drunk," he slurped, using a bone splinter to clean his teeth. "We should ride on to York now."

"This army is exhausted, hungry, and in no condition," Edward explained, the state of his recently arrived cousin, confirming his statement.

"Henry will be long gone by now," Warwick added, his injured leg resting on a stool.

"He'll head for Scotland," the softly-spoken Will Hastings offered, tugging his wispy chin hair. "The queen has friends there."

"Who cares?" Warwick sighed irritated by Hastings' voice.

"No one," Howard yawned, taking a goblet of wine from an obliging server.

Leaning against a wardrobe, Fauconberg's irascibility increased as the futile conversation rambled on. When Howard deliberately prolonged the inane dialogue, he clamped his teeth together and glared at him.

"No one Jack, are you sure?" Edward questioned, calling Howard by his nickname and watching amused as his uncle looked for a voider, before giving up and tossing the bone out of the tent.

"No one," Philip echoed, the grinding in his shoulder and the cold forcing him to sidle close to the brazier.

"My lords, you need sleep," Edward announced, tickled

by the strands of dark meat embedded in his uncle's white beard. "Go to your beds, for tomorrow we ride to York."

With outstretched arms and voluble yawns, the council rose, bowed to the king, and filed out. Fauconberg was about to speak, but changed his mind and left muttering to himself. Refusing Howard's hand, Philip struggled to his feet and urged the king to keep a strong guard outside his tent.

"Don't worry about me," Edward smiled, frowning at his cousin's ashen face and darkly-rimmed red eyes. "Is your wound corrupted?"

"I fear it is so, Your Grace."

"Then I shall send my physician to you," he promised, placing a hand on his good shoulder and directing him out.

"Thank you, sire," he smiled weakly, the sweat of infection glistening on his forehead as he withdrew.

Leaving the royal pavilion, Philip stumbled over to the nearest bonfire, wondering why he'd been summoned to the council. He had no idea where his retainers were, or if any had survived. He was cold, hungry and alone, and his wound throbbed remorselessly. Several hundred exhausted soldiers lay huddled in circles around the bonfire, fast asleep. Finding a space, Philip slumped down and pushed his swollen-jointed fingers toward the fire. The mass of snoring soldiery gave him security and the hypnotic flames offered comfort, but the post-battle adrenalin fall depressed him.

The welcoming heat anaesthetized Philip's battered body, and he gradually succumbed to overwhelming drowsiness. His eyes flickered, he drooled excessively but finally, he fell asleep. With his head slumped forward he began dreaming, but the images flashing through his mind were not pleasant. Waking with a jolt, he sat up and saw someone watching him from the trees, but couldn't make out the face. The featureless figure left the trees and moved towards him, a hand covering the lower part of his face. When he was close enough for the crackling flames to light up his face, Philip wiped saliva from his prickly chin and blinked rapidly.

"What do you want?" he hissed, not sure if he was dreaming.

The mysterious figure lowered his hand, to show a bloody gap where the lower jaw should have been. Shocked at the ghastly sight, Philip attempted to stand, but the leather soles of his sabatons slipped on the damp ground, and he fell back heavily against a tree.

"What in hell's name…?" he gasped, slapping a hand to his injured shoulder.

The stranger extended a hand, to reveal the severed part of his jaw wrapped in a bloody rag.

Placing thumb and forefinger to his eyes, Philip shook his head, and when he looked up, there was no one. Taking a deep breath, he stared hard into the night and moved closer to the fire. Drawing his sword he lay down, tucked the handle under his chin and watched the flames until he fell asleep.

Chapter 3

Harnessed in a silver suit of the finest Milanese armour, King Edward cantered along the tree-lined road from Tadcaster to York: a highway littered with the debris of a defeated foe. Philip Neville, his clean doublet and hose shrouded by a heavy cloak, rode several horse lengths behind the king as part of his escort. Philip's drawn ashen face and deeply furrowed brow were symptomatic of his fragile condition. The weak, pale sun shining from a cloudless sky, made a welcome change from the cold of the previous day. As the head of the column cleared the trees, York's off-white, manganese limestone walls shone brightly in the distance. When Philip saw the countless church spires rising beyond the walls, a balmy sense of gratification blew over him.

Trotting up to Micklegate Bar – the gateway into York from the west – Edward pushed his feet forward and pulled back on the reins drawing his horse to a halt. Wiping his nose in a handcoverchief, offered by William Hastings, he looked up at the rusted iron spikes crowning the merlons of the gatehouse and shuddered. While the city's church bells clanged a doleful requiem for the defeated King Henry, Edward's eyes became transfixed on the decomposing heads of his father, his brother and his uncle, impaled on the barbs. Philip experienced a moment of profound sadness at the sight of his relatives' putrefying heads and shared his cousin's grief. The protruding teeth, black eyeless sockets and lacerated flesh, torn to pieces by birds, were an insult he would never forget. The three wide open mouths, though silent, seemed to cry out for vengeance. Gripping the reins, Philips mouth trembled in a melange of anger and distress as he crossed himself and fought to hold his temper. Clenching his fists to suppress the rage rising within, he received a comforting nod from Fauconberg, which helped to cap his anguish. When Edward saw the paper crown stuck on his father's head, he stood in the stirrups and thrust a gloved forefinger at the ornamental gateway.

"Remove that, that abomination!" he spat, "I'll burn York to the ground for-!"

"Sire, this was Somerset's doing… destroy York and you destroy your future," Warwick warned, looking wretchedly at his own father's rotting head.

Warwick's impulsive younger brother, John, Lord Montague, a prisoner in York since the second battle of St Albans, had been released by the Lancastrians after Towton. Riding out to the Yorkist camp, he met Edward on the road and joined him.

"Most gracious cousin," Montague began, nudging his horse close to Edward's. "Your father held great affection for York."

"Yes, but the people are for Henry," he growled angrily.

"People are sheep," Philip added, "they would follow a turd if it wore the crown."

"Where are the sheriffs?" Edward pouted, turning to his uncle.

"Hiding under their beds, Your Grace," he scoffed; annoyed the traditional welcome for an arriving monarch was not being observed.

"Sire," Hastings intervened, "we should go on."

"What will you do?" Montague asked.

"I don't know," the young king frowned, his rage softening, as he eased his backside down into the curve of his saddle.

At a signal from Fauconberg, three men manoeuvred their horses out of line and lashed them through the open gates, to remove the heads.

Philip stared at the spikes until the skulls were taken down before following Edward. Trotting over the paved, wooden drawbridge and through the inner gates, he glanced right and left, wondering if an assassin might be lurking in the shadows. Edward and his standard bearer led the way through the quiet street and down the slope, towards Ouze Bridge.

Riding alongside his cousin, John Neville, Philip sneered distrustfully at those who came out to watch their progress.

"Look at their stupid faces," he scoffed, "York is full of traitors."

"We should hang all men between fourteen and forty," John nodded, glaring at those who dared to meet his stare. "Remember Castleton? How many of Percy men were from here?"

"Yes," Philip mused, recalling a hot July day in 1457, when the Nevilles confronted the Percys. "We beat the shit out of you!" he bragged, pointing at an unassuming bystander.

"'Twas a grand day," Montague smirked, as the poor fellow fled at Philip's gratuitous outburst.

"Did they treat you well?"

"Yes. But they watched me so close I couldn't take a shit without looking over my shoulder," he admitted, catching Philip's faraway stare. "What is it?"

"Oh nothing, I had a strange dream last night," he recalled. "At least, I think it was a dream."

Clattering over the narrow, humpbacked, Ouse Bridge, Edward led his escort up the hill and into a city cloaked in fear. The only sound audible was the clanking of armour, the rhythmic clip-clop of horse shoes and the fluttering of Edward's standards.

Near the High Minster Gates of St Peters, the gothic cathedral dominating the city, Archbishop William Booth stood alone. Draped in a dark purple cope and mitre – the traditional colour for Holy Week – and richly decorated with gold thread and glittering jewels, the Archbishop of York waited anxiously. In the shadow of the great church, the clergy and a host of city officials gathered beside the Dean of St Peters, as he nervously shifted his processional cross staff from one hand to the other.

Dismounting before the gates, Edward passed the reins to his groom and walked toward the elderly archbishop. Philip stayed in the saddle and watched his cousin kneel for a blessing. Booth placed a wrinkled hand over the young king's head and appeared to hesitate, before offering a short prayer.

"Dominus Vobiscum!" he ended; his aged voice croaking as he made the sign of the cross and Edward rose.

The diminutive dean now led his relieved flock forward to give fealty. This demonstration of deference by ecclesiastic and civic leaders was followed by the commonalty flooding into the streets. Satisfied with his reception Edward turned to face the burgeoning crowd.

"I am not here for revenge," he began, the words sticking in his throat, "but to pray for the souls of my father, Richard of York, and my brother Edmund, murdered at Wakefield!"

Philip examined the shiny leather fingers of his riding gloves and sneered at the obsequious faces of the clergy.

"The old archbishop is as sharp as a razor," he whispered to Montague.

"We'll take the edge off him," he grinned, before dismounting.

The king rose to his full height and announced he would be staying in the city for several weeks, a gesture the sycophantic churchmen appeared keen to encourage. Archbishop Booth invited Edward into the Minster for a mass. Curious to get a look at the young king, the crowd tried to follow, but the church guards kept them outside.

"It appears Edward is much loved," Montague pondered, stroking his horse's neck.

"Yes, but these dogs would be baying for his blood if we lost yesterday," Philip countered.

Exhausted after a protracted battle, weak from blood loss and preoccupied by the unremitting pain in his shoulder, Philip was anxious to go home. While the king's men dismounted and filed into the Minster, Fauconberg spoke privately to his nephew and pointed at Philip.

"You may take your leave," Edward said.

"Your Grace," Philip nodded thankfully, turning his horse in the direction of Claremont Hall: the family town house in St Saviour's parish.

With his mother and young brother in the city, Philip's concern for their safety was paramount.

As he rode through the streets, Philip's physical pain was supplanted by an emotional fever and he perspired heavily, for he had not been home for twelve months. Following several horse lengths behind, riding a sorry-looking hackney, was Philip's thirty-five-year-old retainer, Arbroth. Short, wiry and round-faced, Arbroth was a Scot with shifty eyes and a prominent broken nose, framed by a mass of wild curly hair.

Philip and his brother, Michael, first met Arbroth in France. Arrested for pilfering silver from a Cathedral in Bordeaux, and sentenced to hang, the wily Scot dropped to his knees before the army commander. He wept; he wrung his hands, and he protested his innocence so hard, he was released. Caught selling the silver back to the Church, he was re-arrested and publicly whipped. Tickled by his impudence, the Neville boys took him in. Grateful for their indulgence, Arbroth remained loyal to the brothers until they went their separate ways. Forced to choose, he stuck with Philip.

Ordered to stay with the baggage on the march from Pontefract, Arbroth disappeared, only to surface the morning after Towton with a cart, a sack full of booty and an old horse. The Scot found his master having his wound examined by the royal physician. Used to his wayward behaviour, Philip stared at him for an explanation. Evading his accusing eyes, he revealed news of Thomas Markham's death. Philip and Arbroth left for York, leaving the rest of his retainers to pack and join them later.

Dismounting outside Claremont Hall with painful deliberation, Philip handed his reins to the family smith, who greeted him with a huge grin.

"Welcome home master."

"It's good to be home," he said, arching his back, and

ordering the smith to brush down his horse. "Take a look at my armour," he added, touching his injured shoulder and groaning. "See what you can do."

Unable to find his own armourer before leaving Towton, Philip hoped the smith could make a provisional repair to the pauldron, which was in a sack tied on Arbroth's nag. A second sack slung over the animal's dusty rump contained an assortment of salvaged booty, which the Scot hoped to sell.

"Yes sir," he nodded, untying the wrong sack and receiving a grunt of disapproval from Arbroth.

"Is my mother at home?"

"Yes m'lord," he answered, reaching for the second bag and scowling back at the Scot.

"Good," Philip sighed, using the hem of his cloak to dab feverish sweat from his face.

A two-storey stone and timber house hidden behind a row of shops in St Saviourgate, Claremont Hall had been part of Lady Joan's dowry when she married George Neville. Philip spent most of his early years here before leaving to train for knighthood.

As he approached the door the cloak slipped from his shoulders. Pulling it back in place, he snatched the cap off his greasy hair and straightened his blue velvet doublet. Spotting fresh blood seeping through, he moaned and pushed the front door open. Stepping over the threshold, the homesick knight glanced round the dimly lit hall and his stomach knotted. The house seemed more compact than the last time he was home and a smell of damp hung in the air. Several new screens divided the hall from the kitchen and pantry, making the place look smaller. The uninviting dark wood panels lining the walls, timbered whitewashed ceiling and narrow windows, made him wish he hadn't come. Spotting a familiar tapestry depicting a colourful hunting scene, he stepped closer and yearned for a sense of nostalgia, but, like the house, its charm had faded and Claremont Hall no longer felt like home.

"Philip?"

"Thomas!" he chirped, grateful for the distraction.

"Thank God you're alive, mother will be pleased."

"Not as pleased as I am, where is she?"

"In the garden, I'm glad you have come," Thomas said, anxiously biting his fingernails. "Most of our friends have left the city, and we hear…"

"Have you been listening to rumours?" he scowled dropping his cloak, cap and gloves onto a table, and unbuckling his sword belt with one hand. "How is she?" he asked, wrenching the scabbard free and tossing the bundle at Thomas, wincing as the effort made his injury flare.

"She worries about everyone and everything," he chuckled, noting the expanding dark patch staining Philip's doublet. "You're hurt."

"'Tis nothing," he insisted, walking toward the low, ticking fire and stretching his right hand towards its heat. "The only pain I feel is that Henry and his jackals have escaped us; but we'll catch him soon."

Seventeen-year-old Thomas Neville was the youngest and tallest of the Neville brothers. His passion for the eldest daughter of Mr Henry Champney of Oxford was the only thing on his itinerary. Since his stepfather arranged the marriage, Tom had been fixated on the day Sarah Champney, along with two manors in Lincolnshire and a sizable income, would be his. Lanky and thin with long, brown limp hair and a prominent moustache that underlined his sharp nose, Thomas was home on leave from Michael House, Cambridge. Apathetic to the study of law, 'Long Tom' as he was known, received regular beatings for his lack of motivation.

Since his engagement, Philip considered Thomas a lost cause, and called him a fool for desiring wedlock at such a young age. Whenever the three brothers met, Philip and Michael teased him with warnings of a future full of drudgery. 'You are doomed to go from one breast to another.' Michael would say. 'When you wed Sarah Champney, you will also wed her mother,' Philip appended. Thomas's response to such abuse was a throaty grunt, followed by moody silence.

"You're not going to start on that again are you?" Thomas moaned.

"You should have joined the Church..." Philip responded sarcastically.

"So, the prodigal son has returned," an austere feminine voice interjected, as Thomas placed Philip's sword on a small table next to the stairs.

"Mother," Philip replied cheerfully, his right arm ready to envelop her.

Joan Beaufort was short and plump, with watery grey eyes, faint brows and light hair shrouded by a fitted wimple. Her thin lips and firm chin denoted a stubborn streak, but her sons knew how to get around her.

Without relaxing her strict posture, Lady Joan failed to react as he hoped and simply offered her cheek. Smiling at this show of false displeasure, Philip bent and kissed her warm face.

"Your boyish charm is wasted on me," she huffed, the roughness of his cracked lips harsh against her soft skin. "So you have decided to pay us a visit?"

"Oh, don't ride that old horse again," he blew, broadening his smile in an attempt to soften her frown.

Drawn to the dark, expanding stain blotting his doublet, her rigid scowl vanished and she quickly handed the flat basket of wort, cradled in the crook of her arm, to a maid.

"Boil some water and fetch my ointments," she snapped, rolling back her funnel sleeves.

"Stop fussing, it's only a flesh wound, all I want is some hot soup and a bed."

"You use this house as nothing more than an inn," she admonished, touching the moist patch on his tunic gingerly.

"Is Michael safe?" he asked.

"Yes," she confirmed, examining the fresh blood on her fingertips.

"And, your husband?"

"Do you care?"

"Forgive me," he said, lowering his head meekly.

"Why do you hate William?"

"I don't…" he lied, wincing as she used her scissors to cut through the seam of his doublet and the linen shirt beneath, to reveal the crudely repaired wound.

"Butchers," she rasped, pulling the material apart and motioning for Thomas to fetch a stool.

"That should have been seared with a hot iron," Thomas volunteered, lowering the stool and craning his neck out of morbid curiosity.

"The surgeon wanted to cut off my arm!" Philip yelped, as the rough fibres of his doublet snagged on the crude stitches. "I told him if he took my arm, I would cut off his bollocks!" he snarled through the pain.

"Sit!" she commanded, angry with his choice of words. "And take off your jack."

Tom sniggered at Philip's vulgarity and his mother's brooding countenance; both boys knew she hated such language.

Carefully removing his doublet, Philip sat on the stool and braced himself, as she sliced open the sutures. Not renowned for her gentility, Lady Joan drew out the hemp stitching and roughly washed the black, crusted wound with a mixture of warm water and wine. When fresh blood and foul-smelling fluid oozed from the gaping cut, she pressed the inflamed flesh hard, forcing him to grit his teeth.

"You need a bath," she commented, turning her nose up at the foul odour of his unwashed body.

"We fought from dawn till dusk yesterday…" he hissed, licking salty sweat from his lips, and closing his eyes to stifle the pain, "We did not have the time to bathe."

Despite three surviving children, one dead husband and the pressure of being married to a Beaufort in a family full of Nevilles, Lady Joan retained her sanity and her dignity. Sincere and sympathetic, she spent much of her time

Arbroth's smile disappeared and he skulked away, trailing the blade through the damp grass.

"Lift it," Philip growled.

Swinging the arming sword up onto his shoulder, he sloped away, muttering something about the English under his breath.

Grabbing Alexander by his threadbare woollen cloak, Philip threw him down hard in the mud. Dropping to one knee, he drew a narrow stiletto dagger from his belt, wrenched the man's head back by his hair and pushed the sharp point into his taut, stubbly throat. Frazer looked terrified, but took a moment to notice the beautiful jewel embedded in the handle.

"Forgive me I did not know you," Philip whispered, his face so close to Alexander's he could count the faint hairs sprouting from his bulbous nose.

"It must be done, mah Lord," he grunted, squealing as Philip purposely drew a thin line of blood from his exposed neck.

"I must see thy mistress."

"Mercy!" he gasped, before replying, "mah lady desires to see you too."

"Praise be. When?"

"Twenty days hence."

"Twenty days," he groaned, "each day will be as a year. Where?"

"You say," Frazer coughed, the guards gruff laughter resonating in his ears.

"I'll wait by the riven oak at Breckles Miln, before the morning mist disperses."

Frazer indicated his understanding by blinking rapidly. Both knew the place, a secluded spot less than six miles from York.

"I want to tell your mistress—"

"She knows," Alexander interrupted.

"Praise be, now, do you have an aversion to cold water my Scottish conspirator?"

"Cold water?"

sorting out the problems of others. Such was her prestige that within two years of her husband's death, she had been courted and wed by the wealthy William Beaufort, uncle to the third Duke of Somerset.

No one understood her reason for marrying a Beaufort and she never spoke of it, but the rumour at the time was that George Neville had left her with a mountain of debt. King Henry approved the marriage, hoping such a union would reconcile the Nevilles and Beauforts – he was wrong. Whatever her motives and regardless of the ramifications, she married Sir William. Despite Lady Joan's entreaties, her three young sons refused to call him 'father'. Whenever he was at home, Philip went to live with his cousin, Richard Neville, or his uncle, Richard of York.

Philip's fellowship with the Yorkist faction often led to bitter arguments with Sir William whenever they met. Lady Joan tried hard to reconcile her husband and eldest son, but it was not to be. When Michael began leaning toward the Lancastrian cause, he despaired and left home for good. Philip was convinced that William Beaufort had pushed his brother into Lancaster's camp, but Michael insisted his mind was his own. Lady Joan found herself pulled both ways; on one side was her husband, his powerful family and her second son. On the other, her first born and the relatives of her dead husband, and she was in between trying to stop them killing each other.

Dabbing the unsightly wound with a piece of rabbit fur dipped in egg white to slow the bleeding, Lady Joan stepped back. Satisfied the cut was clean, she sewed the shredded flesh back together.

"Ouch!"

"Baby," she snapped. "Alice, fetch me a cobweb from the garden, if you can find one… but be careful."

Mesmerised by her mistress's surgical skill, the young girl, dressed in a plain linen apron and cap, snapped out of her trance and hurried to obey.

"Cobweb?" Philip questioned.

"'Tis good for setting the blood."

"What nonsense," he mocked.

"Mother is a witch," Thomas laughed.

"There is only one witch in England," Philip announced, "Margaret of Anjou!"

When his mother failed to respond to his taunt, he exchanged a smirk with Thomas.

Having neatly stitched the weeping wound with fresh white hemp, Joan Beaufort laid the gossamer thread of the spider delicately over the ugly mess. Pouring honey onto the cut, she covered it with a woollen wad, soaked in a weak solution of henbane and briony and bandaged the shoulder up. Proud of her handiwork, she stepped back and nodded approvingly.

"Are you trying to succeed where the Duke of Somerset failed?" he moaned, stretching the lower part of the damaged limb to ease the taut stitching.

"Infant," she scowled. "Are we safe, here?"

"Yes mother," he grunted, carefully pulling his ruined shirt back together. "Edward and Richard are your nephews, why would you even ask such a thing?"

Ignoring his sarcasm, she washed her bloody fingers in a bowl of water, brought over by a servant. Noting the girl's sweet face, Philip tried to attract her attention, but she refused to be drawn. Wiping her hands on a towel, Lady Joan frowned at his palpable attempt to flirt and eased the girl's discomfort with a smile before waving her away.

"Don't run," she commanded, as water sloshed over the rim of the bowl and splashed onto the floor.

"Where are the rest of the servants?" Philip asked, while Thomas helped him with his doublet.

"Seward House," she replied, referring to the family home ten miles from York. "Thomas and I are spending Easter there; the Champney's are coming for a visit."

"Huh," he sneered, struggling to button his tunic.

"Was it so bad?" she asked, having heard terrible tales

from the survivors who fled to York the previous day.

"Eight thousand dead and still counting," he said; his voice fading as he gazed into space, a sense of sadness darkening his cheerless eyes. "'Twas a good hunt nevertheless." He smiled, coming out of his preoccupation.

"A good hunt," she gasped, "you men think war is a game?"

Philip recalled the mass grave being excavated as he left Towton that morning.

"We suffer," his mother continued, "yet you go on killing each other without a thought for us."

"I fight to put the rightful King on the throne," he responded proudly.

"No, you fight for pleasure; your heart has turned to stone."

"My heart was turned to stone by Henry of Lancaster and the Duke of Somerset."

"Yes my son, believe what you wish to believe."

Philip looked at his brother and caught a look of concern between him and one of the servants.

"What's wrong Thomas?"

"Nothing, we are apprehensive," he answered, "The heads of our uncles and cousin looks down from the Micklegate…"

"Those poor men," Lady Joan lamented, using a finger to stretch the wimple circling her face away from her cheeks. "Edmund was only a boy."

"What will happen…?" Tom asked.

"You have nothing to fear; Edward will not murder and pillage as Margaret did on her way to London. That bitch destroyed my manors," he said, grinding out the final sentence. "Henry and Somerset are on the run, but we'll catch them soon, and then…"

"Have the people of England not suffered enough?" his mother whined, clasping the wooden cross round her neck.

"This will go on until Henry and Somerset are dead, and the nobility accepts the House of York as the true royal line."

"I know you have lost everything, but William offers you-"

"I want nothing from the Beauforts," he pouted, trying hard not to raise his voice. "Where is *Sir William*?"

"With King Henry."

"Huh."

"The Duke of Somerset arrived here last night and urged the king to leave, but he refused to travel on a Sunday," Thomas revealed. "It was past midnight before they went from here."

"Your cousin John; is he safe?" Lady Joan asked, breaking in before Philip went rambling off on one of his superfluous pro-Yorkist sermons. "I visited him several times during his incarceration."

"'Twas a relief when he met us on the road, we half expected to see his head on a spike," Philip explained, the thought of Henry's panicky departure bringing a smile to his sickly features, which gradually faded as he continued. "Thomas Markham is dead; he would have made a fine knight. Now I must beg my cousin for another... for I cannot afford one."

"We can help," his mother offered.

"No," he said firmly.

"What of Richard?"

"Richard is in good health."

"Praise God you are all safe."

"Yes mother, let us rejoice in his compassion," he mocked; the thousands of bodies littering the Yorkshire countryside shaking what little faith he had.

"Oh Philip..." she gasped flinching at his blasphemy.

"They say many were put to death, after the battle," Thomas interrupted.

"Don't listen to gossip, brother, the good duke would have cut all our heads off had he won the day," he cautioned, trying to justify the post-battle slaughter.

Joan Beaufort shook her head at her son's implacable hostility and Philip was about to apologise, when the floorboards overhead creaked and groaned. Snapping his head up, his eyes followed the sound as it moved across the ceiling and towards the stairwell. The sound of a door, opening and closing, confused him, and when his brother appeared at the top of the stairs his mouth fell open. Forgetting the pain in his shoulder, he leapt at the table, extracted his blade from its scabbard and assumed a defensive stance.

At Towton, Michael Neville fought with the Duke of Somerset until Edward's cavalry broke his line. In the confused rout which followed, a spear point tore his cheek open, from below the left eye to his upper lip. Fortunately his steel bevor prevented serious injury, but the wound looked ghastly. When Somerset abandoned the army, Michael sought a way out. Spotting a tethered hackney, belonging to a priest, he leapt on its back. Struggling to control the obdurate beast, he snapped the leathers and kicked until it moved. Steering a way out of the chaos, he rode to York holding his flapping cheek together.

Michael found the city in turmoil; those loyal to King Henry were heading for the exits, watched apathetically by others with no interest in who wore the crown. Wounded soldiers from the battle collapsed in the streets, and were offered bread and ale by the monks of St Mary's Abbey. Discarding his decrepit hackney near Pavement, Michael limped home. Removing his armour, he allowed his mother to sew up his face before falling into bed. When he woke next morning, it was too late to leave.

As Michael stomped heavily down the wooden stairs, Philip edged backwards, lowering his sword.

"What in God's name are you doing here?" he gasped. "The king has ordered all Lancastrians arrested if you're caught here…"

Dressed in a plain cream coloured jack, his short, thick bull neck concealing the white collar of a shirt, he continued slowly down the stairs; his closed, swollen left eye and stitched ugly red scar, evidence of his presence at

Towton. With his good eye fixed on the sword in Philip's hand, Michael was strangely silent. His closely cropped hair, unshaven chin and dark flickering right eye were intimidating.

"The king?" he scoffed. "You mean the Duke of York."

Thankful he was alive, Philip suppressed his relief, but Lady Joan observed his reaction and knew their kinship was strong.

"Better a Duke who fights for England than a king who fights for France," Philip retaliated.

"Henry *is* our King, anointed so by God, not that towering streak of piss you follow."

"Henry's grandfather murdered the true King and stole his crown. Edward has merely taken back that which belongs to him by right."

While the brothers argued, the household servants withdrew into the kitchen.

"You're a fool to stay loyal to a turd who gave away our French lands on a whim from his royal whore," Philip continued, squeezing the wooden handle of his arming sword; an action that sent pain shooting up his left arm.

Joan Beaufort shook her head in despair and Thomas curled a protective arm around her shoulder. When these two bulls locked horns, she was powerless to intervene.

"Stop!" she pled. "I weary of this senseless brawling every time you two meet."

"With him here, you are all in danger!" Philip warned, nudging his chin at Michael. "If he's caught he'll be tried for treason... I cannot protect him!" the intensity in his voice highlighting his concern.

"You would not defend your own brother?" Thomas said.

"You know Thomas, you talk shit!"

"Why are you so angry?" Lady Joan gasped, as Thomas pouted in humiliation.

"Because I am angry!" he snapped, knuckling his forehead.

"He's been like that since he went off to live with our

cousins," Michael scoffed, annoyed with his mother for having not woken him in time to get out of York. "I don't need advice from you. Go. Join Edward and bathe in his glory while you can."

"I took their side after Edmund Beaufort murdered our father, and his brother climbed into our mother's bed!"

"Lies!" Michael hissed, banging his fist against the wall while his mother turned away shamefully.

"Don't worry, I'll go," Philip sneered, "but get out of York, before your head ends up on a spike."

Deeply wounded by her son's pejorative remark regarding her fidelity, Lady Joan tried to shrug off the slur.

"How is Edward?" she quivered.

"Edward will make a great King," Philip said, mortified by his callous criticism, but too embarrassed to apologise.

"Hah," Michael scoffed.

Lady Joan's distractive comment had no effect; both boys were tired and poised to react at the slightest provocation.

"Did Somerset come here last night?" Philip demanded, without taking his eyes off Michael.

"He arrived in the city late," Thomas offered, "but he did not come here."

"And William went with them, when they left," Lady Joan said touching her cheek, and recalling her husband's parting kiss.

"Do you know the gallant duke abandoned his army and left his men to die…?"

"To be murdered by our merciful cousins, after they surrendered," Michael countered, aware Philip was right, but refusing to admit it.

"Did you expect mercy after Wakefield?"

"Only the leaders were executed."

"They were our uncles and cousins!"

"They were traitors!" Michael snapped, "I was not at Wakefield."

"How would we have fared brother, had we lost yesterday?"

Michael failed to respond, but his blinking right eye gave Philip his answer. Both knew Somerset would have shown little mercy, had he won.

The two brothers continued to glare at each other across several feet of hostile air, the trauma of Towton etched deeply on their haggard faces. Fatigue, irritability and pig-headedness fuelled the tension.

After a momentary respite, Philip savaged the reputations of King Henry and his lapdog.

"The most Somerset can do in battle is fart and Henry will run behind holding a bag under his arse to collect it!"

"And Edward is the bastard son of a common archer!" Michael countered with venomous invective.

"Where did you hear that shit?" Philip scoffed, "From that codhead Somerset, whose own father is father to Henry's bastard?"

Michael tensed his facial muscles, drew his sword and raised it sharply above his head. Philip reacted in a split second. Crossing his own blade in front of his face, he parried the downward strike and forced Michael's weapon aside. Changing the angle of attack, Michael slashed in from the side. The two weapons clashed and Philip's sword screeched down his opponent's blade to the crossbar. Circling the point of his sword, Philip deftly flipped Michael's blade from his hand and used his weight to push him off balance.

"Philip!" his mother screamed pulling away from Thomas, as he raised his sword with both hands for the coup de grâce, and Michael's weapon clattered across the floor.

"You see!" Philip crowed triumphantly, as the flat of his sword came down hard and stopped barely an inch from Michael's hair. "This is what I trained for!"

Lady Joan's terrified outburst had an instant effect and both boys knew they had gone too far. Unable to comprehend what happened, Philip lowered his sword and rubbed his face vigorously.

"Forgive me," he apologised to his mother, stooping in

stuttered stages to retrieve his scabbard. "I must leave."

"Now?" she gasped.

"Yes, we must catch Henry before he can reach the coast," he lied, re-housing his blade.

"You won't catch him," Michael growled from his perch on the bottom step, humiliated by his poor swordsmanship.

"Get out of York soon," Philip warned. "Join your friend Somerset... the dog whose father murdered our father, or have you forgotten?"

"I forget nothing, nor do I believe Neville lies."

"You're a Neville!" Philip hissed, kissing his mother goodbye. "Or have you become so enchanted with the name 'Beaufort' that you deny your birthright?"

"Just go," he sighed.

As he walked to the door, struggling to buckle on his sword belt, Philip shook his head at Thomas.

"Take this," Lady Joan offered, handing him a small phial, "'tis a balm to heal your lips."

"Thank you... I will call on you soon?"

"God bless you," she said, shaking her head at Michael, who buried his face in his hands at her maudlin comment.

Snatching his cloak, gloves and cap from a servant, Philip scowled at Michael, before leaving.

Impatiently pacing the cobbled courtyard outside, Philip huffed at the delay. Having listened discreetly from a window behind the smith's forge, Arbroth had wisely re-saddled Clovis.

"Make haste," Philip hissed, irritated by his retainers' obtuse sluggishness.

Throwing the cloak around his body, Philip massaged his injured shoulder, which thumped aggressively due to his mother's surgery and the scuffle with Michael.

"Take off the harness, put on the harness," Arbroth griped, tugging the long sleeves of his ill-fitting tunic back from his fingers and dragging Clovis by the bridle. "Make yer mind up mon."

Mounting slowly failed to prevent a fresh wave of pain

from tearing through Philip's shoulder and he moaned deeply. Once the agony receded to a bearable level, he nudged Clovis out of the courtyard. Before departing, Philip pulled on his riding gloves, bent as far as his wound permitted and whispered to the old man holding the gate open for him.

"I'll be at Neville's Inn. Have a set of clothes sent there and keep an eye on my brother."

Loathing Sir William Beaufort, Old Arthur remained in Lady Joan's service at Philip's behest, keeping him informed of events. The gangly, sallow-faced servant glanced back at the house, to make sure no one saw him, and passed his master a toothless grin.

Philip rode to Neville's Inn, his cousin's town house near Walmsgate. Falling onto a bed fully dressed he slept soundly. In the street outside, Yorkist soldiers went around ransacking the houses of known Lancastrians. Many arrests were made in the post-battle euphoria and numerous executions carried out; the heads of the most prominent being cut off and skewered above Micklegate.

Chapter 4

During a late luncheon next day, Philip Neville received a visit from Arthur. The bow-legged servant brought him a set of clean clothes and news that Michael had escaped from the city through the ancient sewers. After a restful day, in which he bathed, shaved, ate and played cards, Philip was commanded to attend the king at a meeting scheduled for the following morning. At the appointed time, he made his way to the council chamber, on the western end of Ouze Bridge.

When he entered the striking, two-storey building, Philip found himself in the midst of a storm. Angry citizens shouted obscenities, as their condemned Lancastrian relatives were led to the prison below. Wounded Yorkist soldiers and weeping widows, several with babies attached to bare breasts, harried the guards mercilessly, while waiting to petition the king for relief. Up on the first floor, Edward tried to ignore the racket resonating up the stairs.

Wearing the distinctive red livery of the Earl of Warwick, Philip held a linen handcoverchief to his nose and pushed a way through the odorous mass of humanity. Convinced he was queue-jumping, the crowd grew ugly and hurled abuse at the officers at mace, as they forced an opening for him. Once clear, Philip, furious that someone had rammed into his injured shoulder, gripped the hilt of his dagger and gnashed his teeth. When the pain abated, he climbed the stone steps and came face to face with two esquires of mace and sword.

"Do you have business here?" one of the esquires demanded, barring the open door with his body.

Philip was set to explode, when John Neville signalled for the guard to let him pass. As he entered the chamber, Warwick offered his testy cousin a nod of recognition and he responded with a curt bow.

The Yorkist high command had requisitioned the upper floor of the city council chamber for its inaugural assembly, but the hastily improvised cabinet looked more like a county fair than a royal congress. The smell of stale breath and rancid perspiration, filtering up the stairwell from below, permeated the green and white upper chamber, fouling the air. The king was seated in the sheriff's chair, at the midpoint of a long, narrow table. On either side of him were the Earl of Warwick; Lord Fauconberg; Edward's close friend and chamberlain, the immaculately attired Sir William Hastings, Sir William Herbert, the sickly Duke of Norfolk and 'Jack' Howard. All spoke simultaneously, each competing to out-talk the other, with the exception of Warwick's brother.

Seated in the mayoral chair away from the rest, John Neville conversed privately with several city aldermen. A handful of petitioners congregated near the windows, waiting to be called by the king. Despite a roaring fire, Edward was bundled up in his thick, heavily furred cloak, sipping wine from a silver chalice.

"Sire!" Philip shouted above the noise, dropping spectacularly to one knee.

Startled by his dramatic entrance, Edward raised a hand, bidding his councillors to cease. Leaning back in his chair, the young king placed a forefinger between his teeth and smiled.

"Rise cousin, you have no need to kneel before me, I am only half a king."

"A fraction of a Yorkist King is worth more than the entire Lancastrian dynasty," he retorted, struggling to conceal his pain.

As he rose, flinching at the effort, a murmur of agreement trailed his statement.

"Henry's father was—" Fauconberg began.

"Where are the sergeants?" Edward demanded, unintentionally cutting him off.

"They have disappeared sire," Hastings revealed, rubbing his chin on the back of his gloved hand. "Like rain in the desert."

"Tosspot," Fauconberg muttered under his breath,

sneering at his poetic phraseology.

"Clear the room!" Edward commanded placing his massive hands firmly on the table and easing his body out of his chair.

The two esquires of mace and sword used their weapons to push and prod until the upper chamber was devoid of all petitioners. Once they were back at their posts– one on either side of the door– Edward slumped down in his seat. Yanking an annoying cushion out from under his arse, he tossed it at a servant and casually cocked a leg over one of the arms. The council immediately broke into fresh argument. With a meaningful sigh, Edward pushed away a candle to avoid setting fire to his sleeve, and spoke quietly to Warwick.

"You see how easily men turn from merciless killers to squabbling washerwomen. I had hoped this would end after Sunday."

Warwick tutted and shook his head, while Edward rested his chin on the thumb and forefinger of his left hand.

"Enough my lords," he groaned. "Can we not agree on one course of action?"

Hastings rolled the gaudy, blood-red, ruby glove ring set in gold on his right forefinger, and sighed.

Despite his towering strength, Edward was only nineteen years of age and a novice head of state. Rather than allow his youth to be exploited, he cloaked his inexperience by pretending to take advice from his elders.

"Let us put our argument to one who cares nothing for personal profit," he announced, satirically. "What do you say Philip? Our Uncle Fauconberg promotes raising a fresh army and pursuing Henry. Our dear cousin Richard insists we rest here."

With each member of the council looking at him, and well aware of their personal ambitions, Philip decided to play devil's Advocate.

"Sire," he began, respectfully to Edward, "my lords," mockingly to the rest, "may I speak plainly?"

Edward nodded.

"When the game has broken cover, pursue and corner the beast, then kill it... but make sure it is truly dead." Lowering his voice and narrowing his eyes, he added portentously, "As we should have done at St Albans."

For a moment no one spoke then the quarrelling broke out afresh. Only Hastings remained detached and signalled his apathy by staring at the ceiling and exhaling slowly. Irritated by the endless bickering, Fauconberg banged his clenched fist down hard on the table. Everyone in the room jumped, especially Hastings, but there was quiet, except for the muffled din from below.

"He's right!" the old man roared, "we must capture Henry soon or all the blood spilled at Towton will have been for nothing!"

"If we march north our enemies will gather behind us and move on London, we must rest and rebuild the army," Herbert warned.

A rugged-face veteran of the French wars, William Herbert had served Edward's father faithfully, but behind his back he was branded a Welsh upstart by the English nobility.

Habitually sceptical of Herbert's reasoning Warwick found himself in agreement for once. Jerking his eyebrows up and down he rolled his eyes, causing Philip to smirk at the juvenile antics of such powerful lords.

Agitated by his council's lack of harmony, Edward frowned and drummed the table with his fingertips.

"Your Grace, today is the first of April," Philip said conscious of his irritation.

"And the significance of that is...?" Edward scowled.

"All Fool's Day."

Tickled by his brazen inference, Edward sniggered like a naughty chorister.

"Sire," Philip continued. "The longer we remain in dispute, the harder it will be to catch up with Henry."

"He's right," Edward snapped, leaning across to the Duke of Norfolk and accidentally knocking over a goblet of red wine. "A decision will be made now! What say you, Your Grace?"

Sir John Mowbray, Duke of Norfolk and Earl Marshal of England, was a lukewarm Yorkist. Despite his tentative fidelity, Mowbray's time was running out. His once handsome face was drawn, pallid and unshaven, his greying hair was unkempt and his darkly ringed eyes blinked aimlessly. The bleak journey to Towton almost killed him, but he kept going and arrived on the field late that night.

During the conference, Norfolk constantly pulled the thick, ermine-lined coat close to his wasting body to keep the cold at bay, but he said very little.

"Rest here, sire," he mumbled, insensible to the spilt wine dripping on his hose. "Do not offend the archbishop."

"A pox on the archbishop!" Fauconberg bellowed, waving a hand at his sick nephew.

Sir William's rejoinder brought a smirk to Philip's face.

"Archbishop Booth will change his allegiance quicker than I can shit," Fauconberg growled angrily. "As for that snake in the grass dean…"

Warwick whispered in the royal ear and both smiled at their uncle's surliness.

"Calm yourself, my lord," Edward grinned. "Our gentle cousin Norfolk is right; we must coerce the Church not attack it. We can learn from the clergy, but I will watch the good archbishop closely. If treason is found, I'll fill the prisons of England with priests."

Aggrieved by the king's opposition, Fauconberg leaned back in his chair, scratched his bushy white beard and muttered to himself. Warwick gloated at his uncle's mild reprimand, but it was to him that the king now turned.

"My lord, you will pursue Henry," he commanded, adding ominously, "try to catch him before he can get across the border."

The confused earl stared incredulously at Edward and saw something in his smooth, young face, something he had not seen before: strength and determination.

"Cousin?" Edward said, puzzled by his silence.

Expecting to stay with Edward, Warwick was stunned, and it was all he could do to control his temper.

"Hound the dogs, my lord; allow them no time to rest," Edward urged, making the most of Warwick's discomposure.

"Will you be joining the hunt sire?" Hastings asked, his soft voice drawing a glare from Fauconberg, who saw through his transparent fawning.

"No, I shall remain here in York, for now," he explained, laying a supportive hand on Warwick's arm to ease his evident distress.

"Henry was never the threat," Fauconberg scoffed, just loud enough for Edward to hear.

"What do you say, my lord?" he asked.

"Henry's mind is too far gone; his wife, Margaret, is the one we should be concerned with. Her uncle is King of France."

"France has her own problems," Jack Howard revealed, referring to the rift between Charles VII and his son, Louis.

"What of London?" Herbert intervened.

"London is in no danger."

"Grant me leave to pursue Henry," Fauconberg offered.

"No Uncle, I have a special task for you. The men of Beverly fought against us at Towton. Go there and bring them to heel," Edward urged, releasing Warwick's arm. "Have no doubt my lord, Henry and Somerset are gathering men as we speak; the end is not yet in sight." Turning to Herbert, "Can you raise more from Gloucester and Hereford?"

Dressed all in black, to match his hair and beard, the king's newly appointed Commissioner of Array for those counties, contemplated.

"Yes sire," he nodded firmly.

"Good!"

"What if Somerset slips in behind us and marches on London?" Herbert repeated.

"London is safe," Edward reiterated. "Thanks to Lord Warwick," he added, smiling at his uninterested cousin.

"There is no one in the south capable of raising an army against us now, my lord," Philip confirmed, massaging his injured arm.

"Many of our best soldiers lie rotting on Towton Moor," the longhaired eagle-eyed William Herbert declared, looking down his pitted nose at the king's faith in such a lowly knight. "It would be better to withdraw to Nottingham and recruit."

Aggravated by Herbert's resentment, Philip stared at the floor and compressed his cheeks until they pulsated.

"Welsh bastard," he muttered, well aware Herbert was yet another who had grovelled before Henry VI at some point in his career.

"These Lancastrians come out of their holes whenever their king appears," Hastings warned.

"Sire," Herbert mused, stroking the green material of his chair with his coarse fingers, "Henry will seek help from Scotland. We will be better placed at Nottingham, to counter insurrection in the south, or invasion from Scotland."

"Mary will not oppose me."

"Mary does not know you," Fauconberg huffed peevishly, meaning the Dowager Queen of Scots.

"That may be Uncle, but she will rue the day she gives aid to my enemies."

"Sire, diplomacy could stop Lancaster from seeking sanctuary in Scotland," Hastings suggested.

"Yes," Herbert added, leaning forward as if it were a secret. "Mary's Uncle Burgundy desires an alliance with England. You might… um, offer… marriage?"

"My God sir, what are you thinking, she has borne seven children!" Edward gasped, shocked by the proposal.

"But she is not yet thirty," the Welshman revealed.

"She is a sick woman," Jack Howard added, his long, dark hair streaked with grey, "and may not live long?"

"I'll think on it," Edward shuddered.

"Marriage will guarantee an alliance with Scotland and Burgundy," Hastings appended.

"With such an alliance, and the French monarchy at odds, we might re-conquer our lost lands there," Howard pressed.

"'Tis worth considering, sire," Herbert confirmed. "A treaty with the Scots?"

"There must be another way," Edward trembled, glancing at Warwick, who seemed to be in a world of his own. "Mary would not dare cross swords with me."

"The Bishop of St Andrews will persuade her otherwise," Fauconberg warned. "His hold over the queen is strong."

"I will think on the matter," Edward repeated, tracing a deep split in the table with his thumbnail, hoping Warwick might offer an alternative.

Richard Neville remained strangely quiet. He had known Edward's father intimately, but with his old friend dead these four months, he was sceptical of how far he could manipulate his son.

"Will you join me?" he announced, suddenly snapping out of his gloomy silence and aiming his question at Philip.

There was nothing Philip enjoyed more than a good hunt. He loved the exhilaration of chasing down a quarry and dispatching it with dagger or bow. Putting the anguish of his injury aside, he was about to accept when Edward spoke out to deny him.

"No."

"Sire?" Warwick questioned, surprised by the king's refusal.

"Philip will stay here with Lord Norfolk. I want this city purged of Henry's influence. I will kill every man in York to keep my crown," Edward declared. "This place is a hotbed of Lancastrianism; I need someone here who is not cultivated by the rattle of gold coins. Do you agree?"

With the exception of Warwick, the council agreed, and Edward allowed himself a triumphal smirk.

Unable to accept the way the king went against him, Warwick stood up. Taking a deep breathe, he straightened his crimson doublet and calmly begged permission to leave. Edward nodded and the indignant earl picked up his cloak and limped heavily to the door. As an afterthought he turned and bowed.

"Sire, Lord Warwick would be of better service at sea," Herbert advised, cupping a hand to his mouth, so Fauconberg and Montague should not hear.

"On the deck of a ship, my cousin is unsurpassed, but his politics could damage our cause," Edward warned, remembering when Warwick was 'Keeper of the Seas', sailing in and out of Calais and attacking ships regardless of nationality. "I want him on dry land where I can keep an eye on him."

"My lord," Philip whined, deaf to the conversation between Edward and Herbert. "Let me go with Lord Warwick, his wound is not healed."

"Has yours?" Edward parried, mindful of the way Philip held his arm across his midriff.

"But…"

"By God's teeth, have I taken the crown to be defied?" he roared, ramming his empty goblet down and denting its rim.

Edward suddenly stood up, intimidating everyone with his towering persona.

"I will be obeyed!" he bellowed, pointing at Philip. "You stay in York!"

"Yes sire," he bowed submissively.

The council looked sympathetically at the mournful object of Edward's wrath, with the exception of the slimy Herbert. Pleased with himself, Edward sat down and released a grunt of satisfaction. Philip knew the reason behind the royal outburst, and the fleeting eye contact between him and his liege lord assured him the rebuke was aimed solely at the departed Earl. Edward merely confirmed that he was going to rule England, not his scheming kinsman.

Edward left York for Newcastle in mid- April, leaving Philip champing on the bit, at having to babysit his sickly cousin. Slowly his shoulder healed and his strength returned. To clear his mind he walked the streets of York, carrying out the Duke of Norfolk's inane order to round up those suspected of being sympathetic to Henry of Lancaster. The ailing duke attempted to rule mutually with the council and church, but it was an uphill struggle for one so ill. The Archbishop of York took advantage of Edward's absence, by persuading Norfolk to release a number of prisoners.

Early one morning Philip, much more dynamic than his ailing kinsman, had had enough. Accompanied by armed guards he marched swiftly up Lop Lane and through the High Minster Gates. Bursting into the cathedral he ranted until the stout, elderly dean appeared urging restraint. Gloating over the way the old man cowered before him, Philip suddenly turned and left. Norfolk's captains failed to comprehend his surly disposition, but when they saw him sitting on the crumbling remains of a Roman wall, nursing his shoulder, they blamed it on his wound. In truth it was Philip's inability to pay even a brief visit to his beloved Elizabeth that brought about such irrational behaviour.

Despite many offers of marriage, Philip's heart was set on Elizabeth Percy, the nineteen-year-old offspring of the late Sir Thomas Percy, Lord Egremont, brother of the Earl of Northumberland. Unfortunately inter-family rivalry condemned the relationship to a world of secrecy and deceit, but Philip cherished his fragile happiness and hoped one day to marry the daughter of his enemy. The couple courted for over a year, corresponding in coded letters and meeting at secluded locations. Unfortunately Philip had not heard from Elizabeth since her father's death, and believed she held him liable.

Several of the Percy estates lay tantalizingly close to York, but Philip couldn't trust Norfolk to counteract the archbishop's scheming during his absence. He was also conscious of Elizabeth's distress over the loss of her father. One of King Henry's more brutal supporters, Egremont, had been killed at the battle of Northampton. In his letters Philip explained that he had no part in Egremont's death, but there was no response. He knew Elizabeth was staying with a relative, but which one? To make matters worse he had not heard from her in over twelve months.

On a balmy spring afternoon, while the city cleared up after its May Day festivities, a Scot arrived before the Micklegate and did his utmost to get himself arrested; it wasn't difficult in such suspicious times. Denied access, due to his lack of a pass, the tall long-haired gangly Scotsman let out a cheer for King Henry and was promptly arrested. Roughly searched and threatened with hanging, he convinced the guards he had vital information for the Earl of Warwick. With Sir Richard away and Norfolk unwell, he was frogmarched to Philip Neville, who was busy exercising his horses in a field outside the walls of St Mary's Abbey, close to the River Ouze. Shoved, dragged and kicked before Warwick's cousin, the Scot dropped to his knees. With bony fingers clasped together before his face and forced tears streaming through whiskered cheeks, he wailed uncontrollably.

"Oh, Mah Lord, do no kill me! I am no spy, ah am true to King Edward. Take me to Lord Warwick, he'll vouch for me, this cousin's war o' yourn is no for us Scots!"

Philip knew immediately who he was by the last part of his sentence, for this was the code used whenever Elizabeth wished to communicate with him. A servant of the late Lord Egremont, Alexander Frazer was now the devoted confidant of his daughter. The shifty look in the eyes of this scraggly-haired, black-robed Caledonian confirmed his suspicion. When Arbroth approached grinning and bearing his master's sword, Philip glanced at the two laughing guards and thrust a hand out.

"Stay with the horses. I want this miserable dog to beg for his life."

"Good," Philip smiled, standing up, "Guards!"

Philip's three men-at-arms advanced on the bewildered Scot before he knew what was happening.

"Throw him in," Philip commanded.

Alexander was dragged away yelling, his heels shredding the lush, green sward as he fought to break free. Arbroth brought the horses over, a sardonic smile playing on his lips.

"Next time save your cheers for the right King!" one of the soldiers laughed, as they lifted the Scot off the ground, counted to three and tossed him into the slow-flowing River Ouze.

The flaying bundle disappeared under the cold, murky water before bubbled to the surface, spluttering for breath. Swimming to the north shore, Alexander scrambled out of the river, scooping handfuls of mud from the riverbank as he hauled his waterlogged body up the slippery slope. Laying on his back, arms and legs outstretched, hacking up river water, he felt something annoying in his boot. Fumbling to relieve the irritation, he found Philip's jewelled dagger. Jumping to his feet, he hurled insults across the river at the hysterical soldiers before stumbling away.

"What language," Philip tutted, shaking his head and mounting his palfrey, "and in front of such a holy place."

Dragging his master's stubborn courser, and several rouncies, Arbroth scratched his head, curiosity pleating his brow.

"Mathew!" Philip shouted at one of his laughing men-at-arms, nudging Clovis up the slope in the direction of Bootham Bar.

"My lord?"

"I'll wager I reach the gatehouse before you!" he laughed, breaking into a canter.

On foot and weighed down by brigandine, helmet and sword, the sergeant shook his head at the ridiculous boast and gave up the chase after only a few paces. Alexander Frazer's fortuitous news sparked a warm glow in Philip's breast and the nagging pain in his shoulder had disappeared. He now believed there was a numinous reason why he had been left in York, but events elsewhere were already conspiring to shatter his euphoria.

King Edward had left Newcastle early in May and rode west to Middleham Castle, Warwick's home in Richmondshire, where he graciously accepted an apology from his errant kinsman. Before leaving the north, Edward learned that Henry and Margaret had ceded the English town of Berwick to the Scots for their help. Infuriated, he made up his mind to return to London and take the crown, thus validating his title. The Earl of Warwick, his brother John, and Lord Fauconberg were to continue the suppression of the northern Lancastrians.

As Earl Marshal, the Duke of Norfolk was required to organise the coronation, and was summoned to join Edward. Several days after Norfolk's departure, a furious Philip Neville bade his mother an angry farewell. During supper the previous evening, a message was delivered to Claremont Hall commanding him to assemble the remaining mounted troops and join Edward near Warwick. As he read the missive, Philip's temper boiled and he crushed the letter in his palm. In utter frustration, he banged the table so hard he knocked over a table jug of red wine, which toppled into a silver salter, ruining the salt. Philip apologised to his mother, and though he could not disobey the king, he refused to reveal the reason for his tantrum.

Leaving York through the Micklegate, its battlements festooned with the rotting heads of executed Lancastrian nobles, Philip Neville rode in front of the mounted column, keeping his own company. Sporting a handsome red jack, furred with squirrel, which he acquired from selling his share of the Towton plunder, Arbroth weighed up his master's mood. Gauging Philip's temperament by his rigid posture and intense brooding eyes, he drew his rouncey back several lengths and warned the others. To broach a conversation when he bore that narrow-eyed, tight-lipped expression would be a mistake that could lead to a cuff across the face. The canny Scot whispered his advice to the rest, and the journey began in sombre silence.

Within days the sun vanished behind ever darkening clouds and a strong north wind blew. When the windstorm eased off, rain would fall in sheets, washing mud onto the Great North Road and turning the ancient highway into a slippery morass. By the time they reached the town of Warwick, the king was ten miles further on. When Philip's detachment joined up with the main army, the rain stopped and the sun burst forth. Sliding his horsemen into a gap in the long, drawn-out column, Philip removed his sopping cloak and tossed it at Arbroth, before sending his young page ahead to announce his arrival.

Edward rode at the head of his extensive entourage, escorted by a body of nobles and knights. Behind him marched the foot companies from Kent and Lincoln, and bands of archers from Cheshire. These were followed by creaking wagons, helped through thousand-year-old ruts by carping men-at-arms. The Duke of Norfolk, too sick to sit on his horse, rode in a coach and the rest of the army brought up the rear. Accompanied by one of Norfolk's esquires, Ashley Dean was soon cantering back down the line, his probing eyes searching every face. Spotting a lone rider slouched in the saddle, his crimson doublet soaked through and his head bobbing loosely, the young page pointed.

"There," he said, leaving the esquire and rejoining his companions.

Swinging his mount to the left, the esquire cut in front of the solitary horseman and stopped.

"Philip Neville?" he asked, crinkling his nose at the bedraggled knight.

Philip looked up and nodded wearily at the fresh-face, expensively dressed teenager.

"The king craves your company," he announced; his demeanour offensive.

"I am content here," Philip sighed.

"'The king's command is not open for discussion."

"The Duke of York is not yet King!" he snapped, fighting to hold his temper.

"I shall convey thy repudiation to his majesty…"

With his affaire d'amour shrouded in secrecy, Philip had been unable to send a message to Elizabeth, and the thought of her waiting for him at Breckles Miln stoked his ire. Cold rain lashing down day and night nurtured his breeding resentment, and he unleashed all his pent up hostility at the pompous youngster before him.

"You little shit!" he roared, drawing his sword.

"Stay thy hand Philip Neville!" a voice boomed.

The unexpected directive from somewhere in the rear, caused the bemused soldiers behind to look around. Seeing his chance, the shocked esquire turned and galloped away. Shoving his sword back into its scabbard, Philip pushed his feet against the iron stirrups and stood in the saddle. Glaring at the puzzled faces of the mounted archers behind, he spat in disgust. Failing to recognise anyone who would dare speak to him in such a manner, he dropped his damp arse back into the curve and urged his horse on.

Closing his eyes, Philip angled his cold, pallid face up at the sun and bathed in its fragile warmth. While he brooded on his capricious romance, a hefty clout on the back sent a bolt of pain shooting through his injured shoulder.

"I'll cut your head off you turd!" he yelled, gripping the hilt of his sword and turning angrily. "Will?"

"A turd I may be, but I am a turd that has been handsomely rewarded," William Hastings grinned, edging his horse level.

"Forgive me, my lord," he apologised, eying his garish clothes and beautifully caparisoned horse.

"'Tis not your fault dear friend," he smirked, "I expect no less from a Neville."

"You're a schemer, my lord. I know of the rewards you received from Henry after your plea for mercy, at Ludlow," Philip growled, his affront to the Nevilles rubbing him the wrong way. "Phew, you smell like a French whore, and so does your horse!"

"And you smell like shit, but you should not judge me on one act of desperation."

"Shouldn't I?" Philip sniffed, fingering the soft silk cuff of Hastings' shirt, poking out from his gold-embroidered, blue velvet doublet, envious of his new-found favour. "Lovely."

"Then you must also remember how your gallant uncles and cousins abandoned the army that same day and fled overseas… to save their own skins."

"I was in Calais with my uncle, Fauconberg. I know nothing of their motives for leaving the army at Ludlow, but they must have been good," he said, defending the family reputation.

"Hogwash," Hastings scoffed, confounded by his blinkered loyalty.

"By God's teeth how did you escape the axe?" he gasped, shaking his head, while the throbbing in his shoulder eased.

Hastings responded with a meaningful nod and Philip huffed. By simply looking at his clinical companion, he felt dirty. His clothes were wet and stained, his boots and hose were splattered with mud, and rain had penetrated to his very bones.

"I believe you are boiling away," Hastings satirised, resting a gloved hand on his hip and observing a faint cloud of steam misting off Philips doublet; an apparition caused by the sun evaporating water from his clothes.

Philip was in no mood for levity and he snorted heavily through his nose.

"What troubles thee?" Hastings asked; his voice as soft as a maiden's.

"My shoulder, tis taking forever to heal and my disposition suffers for it."

"When we make camp this night, I'll send my own physician to examine your wound. He spent eight years learning his trade in the east and is not given to bleeding," he explained, raising his almost invisible eyebrows. "My barber and tailor will also attend thee."

Philip nodded his gratitude and the chamberlain continued:

"Methinks there is something else on thy mind... a woman perhaps?"

"Perhaps, where have you come from?" he pressed, aggravated by his accurate postulation.

"It was my misfortune to be delayed in Coventry last night, where an angel appeared at my lodgings. 'Begone fair maiden' I commanded, but it was her wish to remain, so I wined and dined her, then I beat her wool not once, not twice, but thrice."

"What a pile of horseshit," Philip sneered, scratching the abrasive stubble on his chin. "Three times eh?"

"'Tis the truth," he grinned, crossing himself and kissing his thumb, "I swear it."

Despite the eleven years difference between Hastings and his King, Sir William was destined to become Edward's most devoted companion. Squire Hastings was wiry in body and thin of face, with steel-blue eyes and a prominent Romanesque nose. Whether attending church or going into battle, Will Hastings came well groomed. 'The best dressed man on the field' Richard of York once said of him. Possessing a soft, almost effeminate voice, William spoke with such eloquence it was said he could talk the devil out of his domain.

As they rode on, a beaming ear-to-ear grin slowly brightened Hastings' face.

"When we reach London I shall find you all the women you'll need and we'll drink and fornicate for a week."

Philip threw his head back and laughed boisterously. He loathed Hastings' rapid hike in status and envied his intimacy with Edward, but he knew he was a man of his word.

"I believe you will corrupt our young King," Philip grinned, massaging his left wrist to alleviate the dull ache brought on by damp weather.

"Corruption is considered righteous at court; why our most popular Kings were more than a little praetorian, besides, Edward needs no help from me, he is insatiable."

The two friends continued to converse until Norfolk's esquire cantered down the column a second time, accompanied by two unarmoured knights and a herald.

"Trouble's afoot," Philip whispered out of the corner of his mouth, wrapping the reins in his left hand and crossing his right over the handle of his blade.

"Trouble? Hath thee offended someone?"

"Only this baby-faced esquire."

The royal messenger and his party angled sharply across the road, forcing Philip and Hastings to jerk back on the reins to avoid a collision. The mounted men behind concertinaed to a halt and pressed forward, to listen.

"My lord Chamberlain," the esquire offered, bowing respectfully as he recognised Sir William by the gold chain of office beneath his open coat.

Hastings nudged his chin in response and waited for Philip's reaction. After an elongated silence, Philip placed a hand on his hip and spoke with impatience borne out of irritation.

"Move out of the road damn you!"

"I am here on the king's business," the esquire announced, sitting straight in the saddle and staring defiantly at Philip.

Hastings twisted his neck from side to side and peevishly rubbed the nape.

"The king invites you to join him," the youngster declared. "Or stay here and eat his dust."

Philip glanced at Hastings and saw the exasperation on his face. Exhaling submissively he turned his palm up, an indication for the messenger to lead on. Surprised by this unexpected turnaround, the esquire responded with a nod and rode away.

"Plucky son of a bitch," Philip huffed.

"Dear friend, you must cultivate the king's good graces," Hastings warned, placing a hand on his arm.

"Edward is not as tolerant as his father, to those who do not conform."

Without a word, Philip lashed the reins and followed the esquire, trailed by his pristine companion. With a tinny clanking of horse furniture, the rear half of the column set off to close the gap.

Sir John Wenlock was the first to acknowledge the two knights when they arrived at the front of the column, followed by the king, who greeted them with hearty affection.

"William, was she that good that you appear before me so late... and cousin, you deign to grace us with your presence, we are honoured," Edward bowed sardonically. "Not content with insulting the Dean of St Peters, and in his holy sanctum, you go out of your way to offend your King. What are we to do with you?"

Perceiving satire and sarcasm in his voice, Philip bowed from the saddle.

"Sire, no slight was intended. Archbishop Booth and the Dean of St Peters are a brace of knaves who would undo all we have accomplished."

"You set yourself on a path to excommunication," Wenlock warned.

"I don't give a fig for such nonsense, my lord," he growled, remembering his grandfather's excommunication for treason, during Henry V's reign.

Wenlock frowned at his discourteous response, but Edward was sympathetic; he knew Philip would rather be hunting down his enemies than escorting him to London.

"Moderate your hostility to the Church or you will suffer eternal damnation," he advised, smirking at Hastings' dazzling persona. "Will, Lord Wenlock and I have been discussing what rewards to bestow upon my most faithful companions."

"It would be better to consider the loss of Berwick," Philip intruded, forcing Clovis in between Wenlock and Hastings, "than compensate those who do no more than their duty."

Philip detested Wenlock; this one-time chamberlain to Queen Margaret had been dismissed by her for conniving with the Duke of York. After the first battle of St Albans, Wenlock managed to charm his way into the Earl of Warwick's intimate circle, but Philip disliked him.

Disapproving of Philip's candid retort, the cheeriness drained from Edward's face. Sensing the king's agitation, Hastings slowed his horse.

"Why is everyone concerned with Berwick?" Edward snapped, loud enough for all to hear, but aiming his comment at Philip. "Forget it!"

Conscious his remark had antagonised, Philip lowered his eyes in the form of an apology.

"What of Northumberland's estates, Your Grace?" Wenlock interrupted.

"And who is to have them my ambitious friend?" Edward asked ominously.

Philip presented Wenlock with a scathing glare, but the grey-haired veteran, in his late fifties, refused to look at him.

"The Percys will pay a high price for their allegiance to Henry," Edward promised, ignoring Wenlock's transparent implication.

Philip knew Edward was no fool despite his youthful inexperience, and believed he intended to rule as his own master. Edward was secretly planning to coax the Lancastrian nobility away from Henry with promises of clemency, land and status. If Warwick knew his cousin's mind he would have none of it. The earl intended to control Edward, and with his great wealth behind him, the young King would be hard put to protest. But, with his enterprising kinsman far away, Edward hoped to initiate his strategy without opposition.

"Your Grace," his herald, interrupted; riding up and bowing from the saddle, "the horses need fresh oats. Shall I order the wagons to Banbury?"

Edward nodded, set his sights on the road ahead and increased his horse's gait, a sign that all conversation was at an end.

Mindful of his argumentative nature, Philip bowed and drew back, hostility blazing from his eyes at the sycophantic faces of those close to the king. As the column continued south, he rode alone, engrossed in his own world of prejudice and jealousy. The weather gradually improved, but an invisible cloud of ambiguity hovered over the temperamental knight.

Chapter 5

It was late June, 1461, by the time London finally blossomed into glorious summer. After a miserably wet spring, the city echoed to the delightful resonance of thousands of excited people pouring in from the suburbs and funnelling through the streets. They were coming to express their fealty to Edward Plantagenet.

The young King had arrived in London two weeks earlier and rode through the cheering crowds lining his route to the Thames. On that day the people were ecstatic, for they loved the charismatic son of Richard of York. Appointed captain of the royal bodyguard, Philip Neville was stunned by the reception, and he struggled to keep pace with his energetic cousin. The pageantry of that day brought Edward's youthful high spirits to the fore and he waved and smiled at every beautiful woman who caught his nomadic eye. Reaching the river, he stepped aboard the royal barge, lavishly adorned with a gold canopy, colourful bunting and garlands of fragrant flowers. The blare of trumpets accompanying his progress, faded as the gaily-decorated barge was rowed upriver.

Disembarking at Westminster Palace, Edward was forced to wait while an armada of vessels pulled in behind the royal barge. A cornucopia of knights, barons, earls, esquires, princes and bishops, struggled to disembark without tipping the boats. One of the first ashore, Philip tapped his foot impatiently and glanced up at the heraldic banners, planted at intervals along the river wall. As he studied the various coats of arms, a slip by William Hastings distracted him. Losing his footing Hastings slithered along the wet dock, his arms waving to prevent him falling into the river. Out of the corner of his eye, Edward saw his cousin turn aside and put both hands over his mouth to suppress his mirth. Philip's red face and streaming eyes made it difficult for Edward to stay focused. The king's mother, Cecily, Grand Duchess of

York, glowered at her nephew's puerile behaviour and a cutting stare was enough to reprimand him.

Now, two weeks on, Edward was back; more popular, more confident and ready to take the crown. To foil any assassination plot, Philip advised a shift to the royal palace of Sheen, seven miles upriver from Westminster. Unhappy with the palace security, he suggested Hastings should urge Edward to move again. The chamberlain laughed at his concerns, but when Philip insisted, he grew irritable and stormed away, censuring him for such obsessive fears. The following morning a grumbling royal household packed up and transferred to Lambeth Palace, the Archbishop of Canterbury's London residence, across the river from Westminster. While Philip and a dozen guards searched the palace and interrogated staff, Edward mentally prepared himself for the coronation.

Edward had come to Westminster after the second battle of St Albans, to accept the title of 'King'. On 4 March he took the oath, put on the royal robes and sat on the marble King's Bench, but he refused a full coronation until Henry was defeated. Towton convinced him the time was right.

The three-day ceremony began on Friday 26 June when the mayor and aldermen of London, and four hundred commoners, arrived at Lambeth Palace to escort Edward to the Tower of London. Philip Neville and William Hastings, dressed in their finest clothes, walked the king through the cloisters and into the Great Hall.

"Why the sour face?" Edward asked, adjusting the ornate leather belt chaffing his hips.

"Sire, I shall breathe easier once the crown is set firmly on your head," Philip answered, glaring at every passer-by who failed to show proper respect.

"Surely you do not suspect…?"

"Your Grace, I do not trust my own shadow," he declared, anxiously gripping and releasing the handle of his arming sword.

"'Tis not so, sire," Hastings interrupted. "His heart is burdened with envy."

"Envy, what dost thou covet that causes thee such concern?"

"He covets that which you have given to others, Your Grace: title and reward."

Edward stopped abruptly near the door, leading from the Great Hall to the courtyard, and placed a hand on his shoulder.

"Good cousin, honour has been bestowed on those whose wealth I need to secure the throne. Were it in my power I would shower gold upon every soldier who fought with us on Towton field. T'was the common men of England who won that fight, and by so doing will this day place the crown of King Edward on my head," he explained, lowering an imaginary coronet onto his hair.

Philip was tired; the clammy heat of the season and his failure to meet with Elizabeth Percy rankled, while the strain of protecting his sovereign from his own conjured intrigues piled on the pressure. The anxiety of the past month showed in his darkly-circled eyes and drawn face, but he was in no mood for monarchical justification.

"Come sire," he half smiled, urging him on, "put such thoughts from your mind. I care little for reward or position. Lord Hastings is toying with you."

"Good, I have enough to worry about," Edward said, continuing through to the porch and out into the crowded hall courtyard, where an elegantly dressed page held his white horse.

"You there!" Philip snapped drawing his sword and aiming its point at a shadow lurking in a doorway. "Come out."

A thin, red-faced, chicken-necked figure emerged from hiding.

"Who are you?"

"I am steward here," he answered; his face twitching nervously.

Detesting any disruption to the running of his

household, the steward awaited the royal departure with unbridled irritation.

"Why do you skulk in the shadows?" Philip demanded, re-housing his blade.

"Your Grace," he stammered, looking at Edward and bowing, "I have the same affection for you as I had for your father."

"Then go about your duties," Edward said, waving him away and exchanging eye contact with Hastings.

"Slimy toad," Philip muttered as he hurried off.

Dressed in a suit of plush blue and crimson velvet, overlaid with jewels and gold thread, and edged in white ermine, Edward mounted his brightly caparisoned horse. The highly-strung courser wore a heavy leather cover, decorated with a white cloth trapper bearing the golden arms of England and France. With Sir John Wenlock, and a number of his most trusted knights and esquires in tow, he led the procession out through the cream ragstone gate. A band of royal trumpeters preceded him to announce the king's coming with a noisy fanfare. Clearing the palace, the lengthy cavalcade wound its way along the dirt road running through the Lambeth marshes. Behind the royal entourage rode the middle-aged mayor of London and his aldermen, dressed in scarlet robes. They were followed by the commoners in green raiments.

"The mayor doesn't look too happy," Philip commented, trotting alongside one of the aldermen.

"'Tis no wonder, he promised to open the city gates for Queen Margaret after St Albans, but the people shouted him down," the alderman explained. "When King Edward arrived he grovelled before him like a dog."

"Cowardly knave," Philip sneered, cantering to the front of the line.

The intense sun cast a golden aura over the city, which many took as a good omen. Passing the two arenas, for bull and bear baiting, and Winchester Palace, Philip dabbed his sweaty chin on the back of his glove. At the priory church of St Marie Overie, near the Southwark end of London Bridge, the royal progress came to a halt. The aged prior and his black-robed monks silently shuffled out of the church and joined the column as it prepared to cross the river. Meanwhile, Philip Neville, Sir John Wenlock and the royal bodyguards eased their horses onto the bridge. Trotting through the Stonegate, its battlements decorated with colourful flags, Philip dismounted and turned to Wenlock.

"My lord, set your guards at intervals along that side!"

Wenlock assigned his men to their positions, while Philip sprinkled his on the opposite side of the crowded bridge. Aware of his antipathy, Sir John refused to speak to Philip unless it was necessary.

Using a sleeve to mop a sheet of moisture from his face, Philip drew in a deep breath of warm air. The oppressive heat held in by the one hundred and forty shops and houses lining both sides of London Bridge, unravelled his nerves. Aggravated by the pressing mob, he rubbed his wet neck to alleviate an irritating itch and shook the sweat from his hair. Several thousand spectators were on the bridge, many hanging precariously from wooden scaffold poles.

"Press them back, my lord!" Philip yelled at Wenlock, as his men were jostled by the crowd. "Use your swords!"

At that moment Edward rode onto the bridge, and was overwhelmed by the adoration.

"Put your weapons away," Hastings yelled, countermanding Philip's order. "They only wish to pay homage to their King!"

Philip threw his arms up in baffled submission. Every building on the nine-hundred-foot span was jammed with cheering Londoners, beckoning the king to acknowledge them. Thrilled by the enthusiasm, Edward waved and returned their kindness with nods, smiles and handshakes. Reaching the drawbridge, a third of the way across, Philip rested against a beam propping up the jettied upper story of a draper's shop. Grateful for a light breeze wafting along the river and cooling the perspiration on his face, he led his horse over the drawbridge and through the narrow gatehouse.

"This is a nightmare," he growled, tugging the wet collar away from his neck.

Halfway along the bridge, Edward dismounted and entered the chapel dedicated to St Thomas à Becket. All with the exception of Philip, his guards followed him inside. After a short prayer, the colourful cavalcade left the chapel, remounted and cantered on to the north bank. At the church of St Magnus the Martyr, the royal party left the bridge, swung east along Thames Street and headed for the Tower of London. When they arrived before the D-shaped Lion Tower, housing the royal menagerie, an armoured knight rode out and challenged anyone to deny Edward the right to take the crown. Philip surveyed the crowd for signs of dissention, and a lion roared angrily from the somewhere in the bowels of the tower. Edward saw this as another good omen and cheerfully nudged his horse toward the Middle Tower.

Crossing the wide moat, the party entered the fortress through the Byward Tower. Dismounting they walked on to the Great Hall, between the Wakefield and Lanhorn Towers. The rancid odour of the moat, accentuated by the heat, forced the guests to cover their noses and move quickly. Inside the hall, the mayor took the sword of justice and presented it to Edward. Gripping its handle firmly, he stared at the blade before passing it to a knight standing behind him. After a sumptuous dinner of wild boar, venison, peacock, calf meat, fish and other delicacies, washed down with pipes of wine, Edward took the sword a second time. Handing it to back to the mayor, he swayed slightly.

"My Lord Mayor, I command thee to dispense justice fairly and guard the rights of merchants and commoners alike," he slurred.

"Our goodly mayor wriggles like a fish on a hook," Philip smiled at Hastings.

"He has good reason," Wenlock added.

"As do many," Philip scoffed.

Philip Neville enjoyed the feast, downing quantities of Bordeaux red and Syrian white wine, and matching Hastings and Wenlock cup for cup. With glazed eyes and dulled senses, he watched all who approached the king, but always kept one eye on Lord Wenlock.

Keeping with tradition, Edward created thirty-two Knights of the Bath over the weekend, and rode in their company to Westminster Abbey on Saturday afternoon. Early next morning, Sir John Mowbray, his seventeen-year old son, and Philip, left the Tower of London and rode along Tower Street, Eastcheap and Watling Street towards the abbey three miles away. Passing St Paul's, Philip mopped his sweaty brow and looked up at its fire-damaged spire before moving on to Ludgate.

"Are you well, Your Grace?" he asked of Sir John, the muggy weather causing a layer of sweat to coat his pale face.

The sickly duke answered with a nod and Philip massaged his forehead to rid his mind of the effects of far too much wine. The exertions of the previous days had exhausted Norfolk, but as Earl Marshal he was determined to oversee his responsibilities.

Rattling under the Ludgate arch, they slithered down the slope towards the Fleet River, passing between the moated Fleet Prison on the right, and the Blackfriars Monastery on the left. Once over the Fleet Bridge, they proceeded on along Fleet Street via Salisbury Inn and Whitefriars, leaving London by way of Temple Bar. Trotting along the Strand, through the Liberty of the Savoy, they passed a host of walled, high-status ecclesiastic mansions, interspersed with town houses, bawdy taverns, misshapen hovels and patches of wasteland. Bypassing the extensive ruins of the once magnificent Savoy Palace, they urged their mounts into a canter. At Charing Cross the party turned south and followed King Street to Westminster. The ride cleared Philip's head, but his shoulder wound began to irritate.

Entering the extensive abbey grounds through its lofty ragstone gateway, Philip dismounted and rotated his left arm to relieve the nagging ache. Still exercising the limb, he followed the Duke of Norfolk and twenty-two liveried men-at-arms through the great west doors. The church's cavernous interior was lit by thousands of candles; a sight which overawed Philip. As Earl Marshal, Norfolk was charged with organising Edward's coronation, but when he dipped his trembling fingers into the stoup near the door, he felt faint. Struggling to go down on one knee, he managed to make the sign of the cross before collapsing. Norfolk's son, John, rushed to his side, loosened his coat and signalled for his steward to pour a cup of Metheglin.

"Leave this to me, Your Grace," Philip offered compassionately, as the painfully thin duke laboured to raise the spiced mead to his lips. "I'll secure the abbey."

Barely able to sit up, the sallow-faced duke lowered his head feebly, and his young son, John, one of those newly ennobled with the Order of the Bath, validated his consent with a nod. Bowing confidently, Philip dispersed the guards to sweep the nave, quire and the sacrarium. Left alone, he glanced up at the opulent magnificence of the massive cross shaped building; its towering gothic arches and painted, glass windows, making him giddy. Dozens of workmen were busy draping red and blue cloth over the rails of a stepped wooden platform, specially erected for those guests standing at the back to have a better view.

"What is the meaning of this?" a rasping voice demanded.

Turning his head, Philip came face to face with Edmund Kirton, Abbot of Westminster. Attired in a gold-embroidered beige cope and mitre, elaborately bejewelled for the king's investiture, Kirton was accompanied by a clutch of curious monks.

"I am here on the Earl Marshal's business!" Philip shouted above the hammering, pointing his chin at the distressed Duke of Norfolk.

"His Grace would not allow this," the abbot gasped,

shaking his head at the armed intruders thumping around his abbey. "Who are you?"

"Philip Neville, my lord Abbot," he answered, his tone laced with insolence as he turned his back on Kirton. "Captain of the king's bodyguard."

The hurried search revealed nothing, but with Edward's imminent arrival, Philip was not satisfied. Shaking his head, he left his men and headed for the quire, shadowed by Kirton and his entourage of fussing monks. With their shuffling, sandaled feet echoing in his ears, his frustration rose and he spun like a cornered animal, and barked a warning at them not to follow. The crumple-jawed octogenarian refused to be cowed in his own house. Breathing heavily he pursued the knight out of the quire, along the east cloister and down to the Chapter House.

"Stop," he wheezed.

Philip ignored Kirton's plea as he turned a corner and stepped into the Chapter House. Suddenly he was bathed in a fountain of warm, hazy sunlight, beaming in through seven tall, colourful stained glass windows. Strutting over the red and orange tiled floor, he belched quietly and swore under his revolting breath. Standing in the centre of the octagonal room, Philip rubbed his stomach to relieve the burning sensation, and stared at the beautiful painting of The Last Judgment, running along the wall above the stone seats. Lowering his gaze to the base of the wall and the strange beasts and birds painted there, he wondered what some of them were. His train of thought was suddenly broken by the high-pitched voice of the abbey bailiff.

"You are not permitted in here," the chubby little monk squawked.

"Shush," Kirton hissed, putting a finger to his thin lips.

"But…" the bailiff implored, only to be mutely rebuked by the abbot's raised shaggy eyebrows.

"I am here by order of His Grace, the Duke of Norfolk, Earl Marshal of England," Philip repeated, pushing his chest out and standing straight, but keeping his back to the

Benedictines.

"There are no conspirators here, sir knight," Kirton protested, while several inquisitive monks poked their tonsured heads into the Chapter House, to see what all the commotion was about.

"But my lord," the bailiff implored, "Henry is our anointed King. This is a travesty against God's law."

"Your Grace," Philip erupted, turning to face Kirton and forcing the bailiff to duck behind the abbot. "Let me to do my duty."

"I know you, Philip Neville," Kirton cut in, leaning on his silver crozier, "your father was a chivalrous man and a generous benefactor to this abbey."

"My father was a generous benefactor to the Church, in order to redeem his father's excommunicated soul, and by doing so he left my mother in great debt," he struck back; his voice distorted by the acoustics, "and forced her to marry a man not fit to wipe my arse."

William Kirton was tall and thin, with high prominent cheekbones and short grey hair that stuck out at the sides, making him look younger than his four score years. Dark hostile eyes and a frigid mouth, devoid of all but a few teeth, gave the impression that he was not a man to take abuse lightly.

"Sir William Beaufort is an honourable man, and your contempt for God is notorious…"

"I have no contempt for God, only the affluence of His Church."

"God and the Church are the same," Kirton warned.

Philip narrowed his eyes at the conceited ecclesiastic and squeezed the handle of his sword until his knuckles whitened.

"You may presume to know me, my lord Abbot, but I know the man beneath the mitre," he said coldly. "Edmund Kirton: adulterer, fornicator, dilapidator; believe me, God and the Church are not the same."

Offended by his defamatory attack, the monks crossed themselves and bunched together.

"His Holiness Pope Euganius dismissed the heretical charges against our Lord Abbot," the bailiff interceded bravely, poking a finger at the uncouth knight. "For shame that you should blaspheme in such a holy place!"

"Calm yourself," Kirton advised, raising his hand to diffuse the situation.

"Heretic!" someone dared.

"No... he is impulsive," Kirton countered.

The burning sensation in Philip's stomach and his anger subsided, but his threatening demeanour lingered until the abbot and his monks shuffled aside, allowing him to leave the Chapter House. Satisfied there were no assassins, Philip returned to the nave, which had become a haven for arriving nobility.

"The abbey is secure Your Grace," He reported to the duke.

Norfolk nodded limply and his son urged Philip to carry on as his father was too ill. Passing the gaunt-faced duke a sympathetic smile, he joined the guards, gathered in the rapidly filling nave and assigned them to their posts. Philip took up his own position in the sacrarium, close to the tomb of Edward the Confessor. Distressed by Philip Neville's impropriety, Kirton and the abbey hierarchy sullenly stood beside a lattice screen usually reserved for the few women permitted to attend a coronation.

Having spent Saturday night in contemplation of his kingship, Edward Duke of York eventually entered the great abbey through the west doors, and walked slowly up the nave, under a canopy of gold cloth perched on four lances. He was followed by several clergymen, swinging incense censers, his young brothers George and Richard, and his loyal lords. Forty Benedictines sang a Te Deum as he passed through the quire and on to the sacrarium. The smell of burning incense irritated Philip and he fought to hold back a sneeze. At the high altar, Edward stepped up onto a platform built over the green and purple mosaic floor. Here, he swore to protect the church, to do good justice, suppress evil customs and protect the rights of the crown.

Thomas Bouchier, the straight-faced Archbishop of Canterbury, came forward and made the sign of the cross over Edward's head, and he was undressed down to his undershirt for the unction. Assisted by William Booth, the doddering Archbishop of York, Bouchier solemnly anointed Edward's breast, shoulders and elbows with holy oil, while the choir sang the salomonen unxenunt. As the congregation watched in silence, Philip withdrew into the shadows, satisfied he had done his duty. Edward was redressed in a new suit of white and gold, saturated with glittering jewels, and a gold ring was rolled onto his finger. Finally, he was led into a chapel behind the altar, to the throne built by Edward I. Here, Archbishop Bouchier invited his nephew to sit on the historic wooden chair; its four feet carved in the shape of crouching lions aggressively guarding the Stone of Scone, captive symbol of Scotland.

Edward made himself as comfortable as his awkward size allowed, and the Cap of Maintenance was gently laid on his fair hair. Philip watched proudly while his cousin accepted the rod and sceptre of King Edward, and held his breath as the gold crown was lowered onto his head. The Duke of York faded into history, and King Edward of England, the fourth of that name, was born. The ceremony continued with the rendering of homage by the peers and the new King walked the short distance to Westminster Palace, under a canopy of gold cloth, held aloft by men of the Cinque Ports. Philip shadowed Edward's every move, his probing eyes and attentive ears symbolic of his suspicions. At the waterfront palace the king and his guests enjoyed another sumptuous dinner.

Once the celebrations were over Edward planned to bring order out of chaos, however, with an empty treasury and a government in disarray, new proposals would take time to implement. For the moment he was happy to put such thoughts aside and sway toward personal pleasures, a path greatly encouraged by his chamberlain.

Concerned by Edward's increasing isolation, Philip Neville decided to pay him a visit. Dressing in his finest livery he walked to the royal apartments in Westminster Palace, but was told to wait. Restlessly pacing the guarded corridor outside the king's bedchamber, he released a series of frustrated gasps loud enough for those inside to hear. Eventually the mitre-shaped door cracked open and William Hastings pressed his thin, pasty face into the narrow opening.

"Dear friend, His Majesty is busy and cannot see you today," he apologised. "Come back tomorrow."

Philip beseeched William to let him in, but the chamberlain was adamant.

"I cannot, we are discussing matters of state," he explained.

The agitated knight turned to leave when a young, fair-haired fellow yanked the door open from the inside. Barging past Hastings he tumbled out of the apartment holding his boots, his creased shirt hanging out over his hose. The inebriated youth staggered down the corridor, turned, and raised his goblet.

"To large breasted women everywhere!" he slurred.

"Why does the king surround himself with such fools?" Philip lamented.

"Who knows?" he laughed, weaving off.

Philip was about to storm away when he called back by a voice he recognised.

"Come in cousin!"

Spinning on his heels, he fumed at the half-dressed chamberlain. Forcing him aside he entered the royal bedchamber.

Shuttered windows and a garish, over-excessive use of red and green candles hurt Philip's eyes, and he was stifled by the heat emanating from a smouldering fire. Hundreds of shimmering lights scattered in clusters around the green and gold painted boudoir turned the deep red velvet of the embroidered coverlet, and its saeter, the colour of blood.

"Sire," he blushed, snatching the cap from his head, the

odour of stale food and perspiration complimenting the tawdry decor.

"Come," Edward responded lazily, kicking a buxom wench off the bed. "Up here."

Philip frowned at the half dressed figures sprawled across the divan, while the shapely young woman blithely wrapped a sheet around her naked, white body and danced into an anteroom. Discarding his sword belt, Philip eyed her perfectly round arse with an appreciative leer.

"Matters of state!" he muttered at Hastings as the chamberlain climbed up onto the bed, flicking a lock of hair from his forehead.

Hastings sank down into the soft bed beside his King, its cream sheets strewn every which way, and Philip reluctantly joined them. Sitting opposite, he leaned back against one of the rigged, wooden posts that corkscrewed into the velvet canopy overhead.

"You may have her," Edward said, noting his interest.

"No Your Grace, not after her wool has been beaten by my Lord Hastings."

"You were not always so fastidious," Edward chuckled, his voice wavering from an excess of wine. "My father told me of your adventures with two maidens, after the victory at St Albans."

"Sire, I have waited long," he whinged, the memory of that torrid night stimulating a sensation in his groin. "He told you that?"

"U'huh," he sniggered before sighing jadedly, "what is it you want, I am busy."

"With matters of state, no doubt," Philip repeated cynically, admiring the sensual touch of silk beneath his coarse fingers and noticing Edward's shirt, which lay open to the waist, exposing several ugly red lesions on his chest.

"That's none of your business!" he huffed, staring at his cousin.

"My lord, we must not tarry in London. The north is…"

Drawing his voluminous shirt together, Edward sat up and wagged a finger to stop him.

"The north... I am King now. I do as I please and answer to no one for the right."

"But Somerset is recruiting and Margaret conspires with the Scots, they will not rest until her husband is back on the throne."

"Conspiracies and assassins, you suspect our very souls of treachery," Hastings joked, easing his thin body back against the bedpost, one arm resting on his bony knee. "Good friend, I love thee dearly but are you now a necromancer who can foretell the future... Are you Merlin?"

Still angry with Hastings for keeping him waiting, Philip showed his exasperation in a simmering glare.

"Calm yourself cousin," Edward warned, noting his suppressed rage. "Richard controls the north and we have great confidence in his ability, do we not my lord Chamberlain?"

Hastings delicately sipped wine from a silver goblet and tutted at a loose thread trailing from the sleeve of his satin shirt.

"We do sire."

"Your Grace, a progress in the north would siphon support from Henry," Philip urged, looking at Hastings, daring him to interrupt.

"Do the people love me?"

"Yes sire, more than they did your father," Philip confirmed, the heat causing him to perspire heavily, "but they must also fear you."

"Why?" surprised.

"If they fear you, they will not betray you."

Hastings stifled a smirk and Philip's anger rose to a new level.

"What of Berwick?" he snapped, almost forgetting to whom he was speaking. "Margaret has handed it to the Scots on a plate."

"We will have Berwick back," Edward groaned. "There is no money for a war with Scotland."

"We are in great debt," Hastings added.

"Huh," Philip scoffed.

"Hear me!" Edward warned, infuriated by Philip's discourtesy to his chamberlain. "If you wish to go north, you have my permission. In fact..." glancing at Hastings for corroboration, "I give thee license to go!"

"Sire?"

"You shall take our felicitations to our most noble and loyal cousin, Richard Earl of Warwick," he decreed, "and thank him for his continued efforts on our behalf."

"But I am captain of your bodyguard..."

"I relieve you of that burden." Edward smiled, raising a hand as if to remove a curse.

Philip looked aghast as Edward plucked an apple from the pewter plate beside his bed and sank his teeth into its soft, bruised flesh. Looking up, Edward seemed almost surprised to see him still there.

"Your Grace, I..."

"I have given thee license to leave," Edward chomped, his mouth full of masticated apple, while Hastings wrung a wet towel into a bowl and wiped the royal fingers. "Go now and God speed."

Philip hopped off the bed, the odour of perfume-coated sweat offending him.

"May God preserve thee, sire." he announced, glowering at Hastings. "Will," he added, almost as an afterthought, glancing down at the partially concealed pot beneath the bed, "remember your position," kicking the metal bowl and spilling part of the foaming contents, "empty the royal pisspot!"

Backing out of the bedchamber, he bowed and slammed the door.

"Watch Warwick, my lord," Hastings said exasperated by Philip's insolence. "He refused to support your father's claim to the throne."

"I know. I stood beside him in Westminster the day they quarrelled."

"He is a master of deception," Hastings warned.

"I am mindful of my cousin's ways."

"What of Philip?"

"The abbot of Westminster complained to Lord Norfolk of his conduct during my coronation," Edward bemoaned, shaking his head. "What am I to do with him?"

"He could be dangerous."

"Not to me, Philip is loyal to the House of York," Edward insisted, trying not to laugh at his parting comment, "but his antagonism against the Church is a concern."

"He will not forget the past."

"If he does not, there is no future for him here. Now, fetch that woman back and find your own plaything," he purred, snuggling down and using a sleeve to wipe apple juice from his chin.

"But it was I who acquired her."

"For whom did you acquire her?"

"Why, for you sire."

Edward snatched his gold crown from the table and plopped it on his head.

"A perfect fit," he sighed.

Chapter 6

It took Philip Neville two weeks before he found his cousin, Warwick, besieging Alnwick Castle. After storming out of the council meeting in York, Warwick pursued Henry and Margaret, forcing them to seek sanctuary in Scotland. Like a hungry bear denied its dinner, he prowled the border country waiting for them to return. While Edward prepared for his coronation, Warwick and his brother Montague blunted a Lancaster-Scottish advance on Durham, before heading for Alnwick, home of the late Earl of Northumberland.

"My lord," Philip announced cheerfully, dismounting outside his grand pavilion.

"Welcome cousin," Warwick chirped kissing his cheek, before ushering him into his colourful marquee, set up near the town wall.

Philip arched his throbbing back and followed him inside, turning to dismiss his men as an afterthought. Falling heavily into a sheepskin-lined, X-shaped chair, Warwick watched Philip pluck several cushions from a pile, drop them on the rug-covered floor, and slump down.

"Wine!" Warwick demanded, snapping his fingers at a servant.

The boy forgot what he was doing and promptly obeyed.

"'Tis good to see you looking so, so healthy," he opened, noting Philip's tanned face, and raising a goblet in salute. "London must be buzzing with excitement. Tell me all the news, how went the coronation?"

Taking a gold goblet filled to the brim with red wine from the server, Philip eyed it tentatively.

"I see war has its rewards, my lord." He smiled, noting the heraldic crest on the cup, as part of the contents spilt, splattering his dusty hose.

"Why else do we fight if not for profit? That cup you hold once belonged to Hotspur himself."

"Then I shall savour its contents all the more."

"Drink your fill my weary cousin and narrate to me the events of Edward's crowning," he began, adding suspiciously, "and the reason you have come."

Philip downed the wine rapaciously, but with a horrified grimace.

"By the holy sepulchre, are you trying to poison me?" he gasped dragging a sleeve across his mouth, but refusing the server's effort to refill his vessel.

Warwick laughed and massaged his thigh out of habit, before waving the perturbed servant away.

"'Tis good to have you here," he laughed. "That is English wine."

"English wine? We make wine like the French make war," he declared, the sour taste causing him to shudder involuntary. "My lord, I have come at the king's behest, to offer you his gratitude for your continuing success," he announced. "How goes the siege?"

"Slow," Warwick lamented, looking over at a miniature of Alnwick Castle displayed on a long table. "They will succumb in the end, but it's taking forever. Time is not an issue, but the rumours from court concern me."

"What rumours, my lord? Tell me what you have heard and I will enlighten thee, whether it be truth or falsehood," he promised, the lengthy journey making his body heavy.

Crossing one booted leg loosely over the other, Warwick sniffed the contents of his nose back and eyed his fatigued visitor.

"It is said the king has the ear of Lord Hastings," he alleged, the hammering, digging and complaining of the besieging Yorkists, echoing in the background.

Philip bit the side of his forefinger, and the taste of dry sweat reduced the bitterness of the wine.

"True," he lamented, recalling how Hastings had made a fool of him in front of Edward.

"I also hear from one of my spies, that Edward showers his new friends with titles."

"Your informant is correct."

"Why does the king not call for me?" he asked,

fidgeting uneasily.

"You answer your own question, my lord," Philip said, wondering if Sir John Wenlock was Richard's spy. "Our noble cousin has sent me here with an offer for you: Warden General of the East and West Marches."

"Huh," he sniffed, "anything to keep me away from court, but when Alnwick falls I'll ride to London and my brother-in-law will pay for his overindulgence of our cousin," he promised, thumping a fist down against the chair arm. "Edward will rule England only through the Nevilles!"

"I'll go with you."

Philip's offer was followed by a moment of silence.

"Enough doom and gloom," Warwick sighed, shrugging his shoulders. "Come and see my cannon."

"Cannon?" Philip said excitedly a sharp twinge in his back forcing him to rise deliberately.

"Only one piece which we found abandoned by the Scot at Carlisle," Warwick chuckled, leaping from his chair and beckoning for a varlet to fetch his sword.

Walking out into the blinding sunshine, Philip squinted and turned to the earl.

"I fear cousin Norfolk will not see the year out."

"'Tis a miracle he has survived this long," Warwick remarked, buckling his belt.

"Yes," Philip agreed, crossing himself. "Is John here?" he asked referring to Warwick's younger brother.

"He is... somewhere," Warwick answered, looking around.

"Do we need armour?"

"No, we're out of range."

"Then after you, my lord."

A low, uneven earth wall, topped with timber had been thrown around three sides of Alnwick's perimeter. The ineffectiveness of the Yorkists' single cannon and two huge trebuchets showed on the faces of the listless soldiers, as they sat idly watching a dozen carpenters put together a third prefabricated catapult.

"Your men seem indifferent," Philip noted; the stench of unwashed bodies and horseshit, accentuated by the heat.

"They are debilitated by months of marching and fighting. 'Tis their wives and sweethearts they wish to be with now, not chasing the dregs of Henry's army," he revealed, holding a scented nosegay to his nostrils. "Only a few hundred lame dogs are keeping me out," he added, acknowledging his three bladesmiths as he passed their open forge. "Inactivity is turning our muscles to fat, some days I can't get out of bed until mid-morning."

"What news of Somerset?"

"His mistress has sent him to seek help from her uncle, the King of France," he sneered, referring to Queen Margaret. "But I plan to send my own ambassador to frustrate her plans."

"The French King will refuse your envoy, my lord."

"Charles is ill and his son, Louis, opposes everything his father favours."

"Somerset has a notorious reputation, you must send someone his equal."

"Lord Wenlock sails for Burgundy within the week."

"Wenlock," Philip gasped, trying to hide his feelings.

"The Scots are the problem," Warwick said, the nosegay muffling his angry tone. "The Bishop of St Andrews has persuaded Mary to help Margaret."

"Then the king must offer peace," Philip pressed, shaking his head.

"Yes, but will he do it? By St Paul, the sooner I speak to my cousin the better it will be for all of us!"

"We are wasting are finest soldiers, they should be better used."

"Perhaps against the French?" Warwick huffed, irritated by the heat and the smell. "It's always the French with you; you blame an entire race for one single act of barbarity."

"Yes," Philip countered, hurt by his eruption. "They murdered our men at Castillon, after they surrendered."

"We did no less at Towton."

"Charles will give Margaret men, money, and a fleet, and this war will go on," he replied, resenting the comparison.

Warwick ignored his emotional riposte and Philip calmed down.

Built on a hill above Alnwick town, the castle guarded a strategic crossing of the River Aln to the north. Lying between the castle's south wall and the town were a series of farmed fields, covered with tents and all the paraphernalia of a besieging army.

As they strolled leisurely behind the siege works, Philip was impressed by Alnwick's formidable walls and stout towers. The couldn't-care-less attitude of Warwick's soldiers confirmed his opinion that the siege was not going well.

"My lord, Alnwick will not fall to assault," he warned, observing the thick sandstone walls. "Only starvation or treachery will bring them to their knees."

"You have a high opinion of your military prowess."

"My lord, your machines have caused little damage, and your men are discontent."

"But I have a hostage." He grinned, irked by his cousin's conceit.

"A hostage?" Philip echoed his interest kindled. "Exeter?" he speculated, "Oxford?"

"No," Warwick said with a smirk, "though Northumberland's brother, Ralph, has offered to make his peace with Edward."

"'Tis bad enough we have the likes of Wenlock in our camp, but Ralph Percy? My lord, have a care, we will soon have more Lancastrians for us than against us," he warned, recalling the day Sir Ralph unhorsed him at the Coventry joust.

Shrugging off the insult to his friend, Wenlock, Warwick narrowed his eyes and clamped his lips together in a mean grin.

"You were jesting?" Philip smiled.

"'Tis no jest; Ralph Percy has offered to submit to the

king in exchange for retention of his lands."

"Then why are we fighting outside his front door?" Philip growled as the solitary cannon roared into life, making him jump. "By God's teeth!" he yelled, as a huge rotating stone ball arced over the space between besiegers and besieged.

Falling short, the gunstone splashed harmlessly into the Bow Burn, a tributary of the River Aln, which formed a natural moat protecting Alnwick's south and east walls. While the displaced foaming water settled, the garrison let out a cheer and shook their fists through the crenulations.

"You should not despise Lord Wenlock, for he is a good friend," Warwick said, flustered by Philip's offensive tone. "Can a man not make one mistake in his life?"

"Mistake?" Philip looked aghast, "He fought against us at St Albans."

"But he was with us on Towton field."

"Huh," Philip scoffed.

"And he fought the French."

"Under Henry's father."

"Did our fathers do no less?"

"Have no doubt, my lord, when the time is right, he *will* change his coat again."

"Nevertheless, he is a loyal friend, but come," his temper rising, "come and see my cardinal prize."

"We should take no prisoners," Philip muttered.

Warwick held his tongue, and with a look of menace in his eyes, he patted his cousin on the back, before steering him towards an overgrown path.

Richard Neville led his cousin along a narrow, tree-strangled track that sloped away from the Yorkist siege-works and opened out into a grassy clearing, six hundred paces from the camp. A solitary, buff-coloured hemp tent lay nestled in a leafy glade, close to the tumbling waters of the Aln. Due to wind direction and the rushing river, the sounds of war could not be heard.

"Only two guards?" Philip enquired, trying to guess who could be inside.

"Only two," Warwick reiterated, acknowledging the guards and raising the tent flap.

Smiling roguishly, he motioned for Philip to enter. As he bent he was unceremoniously shoved inside. Baffled by Warwick's behaviour and trailing laughter, Philip stood up and focused. Looking around the humid, cluttered little tent, his shoulders suddenly dropped and his mouth fell open. Seated at a small table, playing cards with two attendants, was Elizabeth Percy, trepidation radiating from her stunning blue eyes at the unexpected intrusion. Staring through the hazy light, Philip was rooted to the spot as Elizabeth slowly lowered her cards, and smiled.

Standing a little over five feet, with waist-length, auburn hair, Elizabeth Percy possessed two crowning glories: bright blue elliptical eyes and a bewitching smile, yet at nineteen she was considered past her prime for wedlock. Like her father, Thomas Lord Egremont, Elizabeth was obdurate, a trait she demonstrated by refusing all offers of marriage. When she rejected the third Duke of Somerset, Egremont thrashed her severely. Angered by his daughter's refusal to choose a husband, and irritated by her presence at Healaugh, he sent her to live with his older brother.

Philip Neville first met Elizabeth in the summer of 1458, at the Corpus Christi pageant, in York. Uninterested in wagons full of mummers, his wandering eye homed in on her across the busy market square. Seated in a stand with her uncle, the towering Earl of Northumberland, his wife, and the Archbishop of York, Elizabeth radiated an air of disenchantment. Pushing his way through to the Percy stand, Philip leaned nonchalantly against the steps leading up to the platform. The girl, whom he presumed was Northumberland's daughter, showed her boredom by a series of sighs and deliberate shoulder drops. Enchanted by her pale skin and exquisite features, he made his interest obvious. She returned his impertinent smirk with a superior pout, but a calculated cough from her aunt brought her attention back to the procession. The pageant finally ended with a prayer from a mummer dressed in white, playing the voice of God, and the crowd dispersed.

Northumberland led his party to St John the Baptist's Hall, headquarters of the Merchant Taylors' Guild, in Aldwark. Philip followed inconspicuously, or so he thought. Elizabeth spotted him trying to hide behind a fat woman, who constantly shooed him away, and his ridiculous ducking and diving tickled her. Suddenly Elizabeth slipped, twisting her ankle on the uneven street. As she fell Philip caught her in his arms, and in gratitude, Northumberland invited him to dinner. At the instigation of Lady Eleanor, Philip was seated on the top table, between her young son Henry, and her daughter. Elizabeth was sat on the far side of her cousin, but this arrangement did not prevent them from talking. During dinner, Elizabeth revealed her father's name and his connection with Northumberland, and the blood in Philip's veins froze. He knew Egremont well. Only the year before, he and his cousins had clashed with him and his retainers at Castleton, and beat them up.

When Sir Henry toasted the king, Philip raised his goblet and pretended to drink, but he was being watched by the archbishop. With the eyes of the prelate on him, Philip knew he was about to speak out against his disloyal act. As the archbishop put a hand to Northumberland's ear, Philip stood up and revealed his full name, and his kinship with the Nevilles. The hall went silent and several Lancastrian knights jumped out of their seats, ready to challenge him. Philip glanced uneasily at Elizabeth, who offered a smile laced with regret. Northumberland waved for his knights to sit down and advised Philip to leave. He responded with an apologetic bow and left.

Three weeks later, Philip received a letter from Elizabeth, asking to meet. Between July 1458 and June 1459, they met half a dozen times, but since the death of her father, at Northampton, they had not seen each other. For Philip it was eighteen months of heartache, anger and confusion. He sent many letters but received nothing in return. When Alexander brought word to him at York that his mistress wished to see him, he felt reborn. Forced to join the king before they met, he believed they were destined never to be together.

Now she was here, and all the anxiety and sadness that dragged at his heart for the past year and a half, vanished. To keep their secret Philip commanded her two attendants to leave. Fearing for their mistress's virtue, they refused. Not sure what to do he drew his sword, and in a rush of material, scattered cards and high-pitched shrieks, the two women ran from the tent. The guards outside, laughed as they cowered together tearfully lamenting their concerns and waiting for the inevitable screams.

Dropping his blade back into its scabbard, he fell on one knee, took Elizabeth's slender hands in his, and kissed them lovingly.

"Sweet Lady," he gasped, uncomfortable with his appearance. "Forgive my bearing, I've been in the saddle for many days…"

"I have longed for this moment, my love." she responded, nuzzling her sensitive face against his rough, unshaven cheek.

"My heart has been cold since our last time," he said woefully. "Why did you not answer my letters?"

"When my father was killed I sank into despair, for all his faults, I loved him."

"I knew nothing of his fate that day until it was over."

"And I never blamed you," she half smiled. "I know Warwick had ordered the execution of the nobility before the fight and I explained as much in my letters… I can only assume my messages were intercepted by my Aunt Eleanor," her voice trembling. "When my father died, she became over protective."

"Hush," he whispered, placing a finger gently against her soft lips and glancing at the narrow opening, lest the guards overhear. "If my cousin should discover our secret…"

"Alas I fear he knows," she interrupted, "What other reason would you be here?"

"Then my head is already on the block," he moaned, rising.

"My Uncle Ralph has offered fealty to King Edward. Warwick is mindful of this, yet he insists on keeping me here," she lamented. "And my poor cousin Henry is to be sent to the Tower."

"My lady, Henry cannot be set at liberty; he is destined to inherit his father's title," Philip explained, recalling the day at the Merchant Taylors' Hall in York, when young Henry Percy deliberately pushed his head forward, whenever he tried to speak to Elizabeth. "The Percys are one of the cornerstones of Lancaster's strength; if he is free the north will rise up."

"He is only a child."

"But one day he will be a man."

"Oh when will this end, when every noble family in England is destroyed?"

"I see you wear red and black," he sneered, "your father's colours."

"Do I not have that right, I am a Percy," she snapped, before softening her tone. "Oh my love, I am confined in this small tent with nothing but a wardrobe and a pot for my personal use," she cringed.

Philip looked around the cramped tent and frowned at its lack of furnishings. He loathed the Percys with one exception, and for her he would lay down his life.

"Edward surrounds himself with fools whose only interest is playing games," he revealed, recalling his last meeting with the king. "Now my cousin, whom I love like a brother, toys with my affections, what to do?" he fumed, knuckling his jaw.

"Richard's lust for power is strong and he will destroy anything in his path to achieve success… I pray for peace," she sighed, squeezing his hands, "yet I know deep down, it will never happen."

"You stir such passion in my heart that at times I cry out for an end to all this. But what trade shall I brook if peace should come? I have no money, no property, and I care nothing for politics. I have carried a sword since my eighth year, and know only how to fight," he explained. "When I think of peace it is with a subdued heart."

"'Tis sad when a boy is plucked from his family and sent to live with strangers, who teach him how to kill, when it would be far better for him to learn how to love," she said with a faraway stare. "When we were young and my father spoke to us of war, I watched his face and what I saw frightened me. I see that same look in your eyes, it is in the air you breathe, and the food you eat; without a war your life would be meaningless. You love fighting more than you love me, and the sad thing is… you don't know it."

"Your words are laced with bitterness, my lady."

"Oh Philip, pay no heed to me, I'm turning into a cynical old maid," she smiled, shrugging off her apathy. "Are your wounds healed?"

His mind suddenly drifted back to that cold Sunday on Towton Moor, and his eyes fixated on the sunlight filtering through the material of the tent. "Yes," he said thoughtfully. "I saw men fall like leaves from a tree on a windy day," he added morosely, unconsciously touching his left shoulder, "Thomas Markham died there."

"Poor Thomas," she offered, though she never knew him.

"Yes, poor Thomas," he echoed, resenting her apathetic comment.

Elizabeth edged closer and gently ploughed her willowy fingers through his tangled, greasy hair.

"'Tis rumoured the scent of blood is so strong, farmers refuse to work their fields," she said, staring into his haggard face. "And travellers fear to use the roads at night. Some have even seen dead soldiers wandering in the woods, near Tadcaster."

"Old wives' tales, when you're dead, you stay dead,"

he moaned, the sensation of her warm fingertips massaging his scalp, bringing him out of his transitory state, but her innocence caused him concern. "You are not safe here."

"I am to be sent up to London."

"London!" he gasped, a sense of dread gripping his heart, "that hotbed of treachery and infidelity, for what reason?"

"I am to be a lady-in-waiting to the Duchess of York."

"You will not go."

"Lord Warwick and the king's brother have been granted my father's estates. If I refuse they threaten to execute my cousin, Henry."

"I'll speak to Richard…"

"No! Richard wallows in my misfortune. Why would he allow us this time together, other than to humiliate me further? The Nevilles will never forgive my family for the past."

"This cannot happen," he growled, scratching his itchy head, confounded by Warwick's scheming. "I'll not permit it."

"You cannot stop it! Oh, if we met at Breckles Miln none of this would have happened. I waited an eternity for you, 'twas upon my return that my companions and I were taken. Alexander escaped with my brother John, but the rest of our men were slain and the women captured. Now I must go to London and pay homage to a king who loathed my father."

"Where is your Scot?"

"Close," she whispered, "he will not abandon me."

"'Twas not my fault, I was summoned to join the king and there was no one I could trust to send you word," he explained, attempting to absolve his conscious.

"None of that matters now, I have prayed for you to come and you are here."

"I see your sweet face in every cloud; every pool; every mirror. No matter where I turn your image haunts me, the only constant in my inconsistent world," he declared, taking her hands in his, careful not to bruise the soft skin.

A warm sensation spread slowly along Philip's abrasive fingers and up his arms, until his entire being bubbled with adoration.

"At night I relive our moments together until I am driven almost insane," he declared, "I would slay my cousin to set you free. You have but to command and it shall be done."

Her heart sank at his boyish exuberance and he watched despondency tone down her expression, forcing him to swallow hard to conceal his helplessness.

"If you find yourself in trouble in London, write to me and I'll come for you," he promised, resigning himself to the inevitable.

His impetuous proposal caused tears to form in her eyes, and her mouth to tremble. Drawn together by despair they kissed tentatively, lips barely touching. Exhilarated by the emotion, Philip slid his arms around her waist until he felt her narrow ribs through the material of her linen dress. She yearned for him to hold her tighter and pressed her body against his, to indicate her desire, and he happily complied. Standing on tiptoes, she wrapped her hands around his neck and they fused in a romantic meld. This first intense kiss in almost two years nurtured into something more passionate than Philip had ever experienced, and he cherished the moment. With her cool arms coiled around his hot neck, his skin tingled, yet he felt strangely calm.

After time without end, their lips parted as if by mutual consent and Philip's heart beat so loud, he thought they could hear it in Alnwick. Looking into her stunning eyes, he ran his tongue across his lips and enjoyed her taste.

"My Aunt Cecily is a good woman, she will be kind to you," he whispered, releasing her with gut-wrenching reluctance and smiling kindly. "But you will be as a lamb amongst the wolves at court. If you find yourself in danger send your Scot to me and I will ride like the wind."

"I can look after myself..."

"Do as I say," he barked, his anger directed at his cousin, Richard.

Elizabeth nodded bravely and the furtive lovers kissed longingly, once more until Philip grudgingly broke the bond. Drinking in the sweetness of her rose-scented perfume, he removed the banded veil and stroked her fine delicate hair, allowing the soft strands to tumble through his fingers like water.

"Farewell sweetheart," he sighed, and in the blink of an eye he was gone,

Anger and impotence clouded Philip's judgement as he pounded back along the trail, leading to the Yorkist camp. He sought, and found the object of his antipathy standing with a gaggle of nobles, three hundred paces from one of Alnwick's towers. In the midst of a heated argument with his brother and uncle, Warwick managed a sideways glance at his cousin.

Philip stood away from his quarrelling kinsmen and looked around. The ground between the castle and the siege works was speckled with the stumps of sawn-off trees, the trunks of which had been hauled away by Yorkist pioneers. The distinct rasping sound of two-handed saws was indicative of the trunks being cut into planks. These rough boards were being nailed together to form mobile palisades, which would be used by Fauconberg's bowmen to get closer to Alnwick. Lines of palfreys stood safely tethered in the shade, munching oats from a long trough, while a group of esquires practised under the scrutiny of an elderly master, who cursed their lack of effort.

Tiring of his brother's inflexibility, John Lord Montague left the group and stomped over to Philip.

"He wants everything his way," he complained, shaking his head, "as always!"

"And he'll get it," Philip scoffed angrily, "as always."

Sensing his petulance, Montague huffed and stormed away, leaving him to lament his antipathy.

While the council broke up, Philip used the heel of his

boot to work loose a stone embedded in the ground.

"If only that were Somerset's head," Fauconberg joked, creeping up and grabbing Philip's neck with one of his powerful arms.

"Better if it were the head of the king's new chamberlain, my lord," he choked, breaking his uncle's iron grip.

"Umbrage against one so highly placed." The partly-armoured Fauconberg asked, "What ails thee?"

"Why is the daughter of Egremont held prisoner?" he demanded.

"She's a hostage... a guarantee for her uncle's loyalty," Warwick answered, joining them. "What concern is it of yours?"

"Do we now make war on women?"

"Hah Uncle," Warwick laughed, joining them, "this from a man who would put all who oppose us to the sword. Do you have a soft spot for this maiden?"

"You have a soft spot in your head!" Philip scoffed.

"Nephew!" Fauconberg snapped, a man who hated disrespect no matter what the reason.

Warwick grinned behind his uncle's back, but the wily patriarch spotted him.

"Stop acting like a virgin on her first night! What is this all about?"

"Why, our kinsman has fallen for the daughter of Lord Egremont."

William Neville found his statement hard to digest and looked at Philip for an answer, but he stared down at the ground.

"A Percy," he cogitated, "'tis a lie!"

Philip's awkward silence turned Lord Fauconberg's disbelief to outrage.

"By all that is holy, deny this slander!" he insisted.

Philip stood speechless, forcing the aged warrior to thump his hands against his steel hips and push out his barrel chest.

"'Tis the truth," Richard pressed.

"What sorcery could force you to cherish the offspring of such a heartless bastard?"

"She has cast a spell on him," Warwick smirked, striving to sprinkle a little humour into the dispute, "she's a witch."

"Don't talk like a turd; she is no more a witch than your own good wife. Hah! For all her vile potions, she has yet to bear you a son."

Richard loved his wife, but her failure to produce a male heir broke his heart. Taken aback by the insult, he seethed inwardly and unconsciously massaged his old wound.

"And stop rubbing your leg, 'twas naught but a scratch!"

Philip was well aware of his cousin's personal anguish, but any sympathy he once felt was supplanted by resentment. He also knew Warwick's reputation for ruthlessly executing those who opposed him, and he began to worry. Perspiring heavily Philip sensed the nervous twitch pulsating below his left eye.

"How long has this been going on?" Fauconberg asked brusquely, "Weeks... months?"

Philip tried to think up a favourable response and stop the spasm under his cheek, but he failed to do either.

"By St Paul, do you know what this could cost us?" he groaned. "You will end it now."

"I confess my fault Uncle, but I cannot help the road my heart has taken. Don't blame Elizabeth for the sins of her father."

"Egremont was born evil," Fauconberg snarled, scratching his bushy beard and glaring at Warwick, who pouted like a chastised child, "a merciless cunt who would have murdered us all, given the opportunity. How long have you known?"

"Long enough," Warwick answered.

Stung by his reply, Philip's jaw fell open.

"Then you too are at fault."

"Your opinion of me is unimportant. I am Richard

Neville, Earl of Warwick, the most powerful man in all England and beloved by the commons. I answer to no one," he declared, his posture and tone oozing arrogance.

"You answer to the king!" Fauconberg barked, his wobbly jowls quivering.

"No, Uncle, you answer to the king! I have placed the crown upon his head, no one can better that!" he announced loud enough for those within earshot to hear. "I make my apologies to God and no other!"

Pivoting on his heels, the agitated earl stormed away barking commands to those he passed, while Philip stood waiting for his uncle to react. Stunned by Warwick's highly-charged almost treasonous statement, Sir William fumed, until his face took on a purple hue. Needing to vent his fury he aimed his armoured toe at a wooden bucket and lashed out, adding a gut-busting roar to the kick. The object of his wrath bounced over the ground in the direction of a group of archers sat rubbing beeswax into bow staves. Jumping up, the bowmen shook their fists at Fauconberg, who raised his hands ruefully. Recognising their chief, they sheepishly accepted his apology and returned to work.

"We all helped Edward take the crown..." Fauconberg explained, turning aside and coughing harshly. "Richard desires a dukedom, and will make a pact with the devil to get it. His star is rising swiftly, but his fall will be the more spectacular," he prophesied, looking at Philip. "If he was not my born nephew I would cut his throat for what he just said. And if you continue to offend those in high places, you will end up like your father."

"My lord, I must return to London," he said, "The king surrounds himself with faithless courtiers-"

"Edward has his father's strength and his mother's brain. He will be a powerful King. Our work here is almost finished. When we ride south the strength of the Nevilles will draw Edward away from those feckless fools who have attached themselves to his throne."

"We must not delay..." Philip hissed.

"Calm down," he warned, observing the distress in Philip's eyes, and waving away a bank of odorous smoke, billowing over from the archer's fire.

"I cannot," he stressed. "What will become of the Percy girl?"

"The daughter of Egremont is to join the Duchess of York's household. Her presence at court will help secure peace between our families. God knows we need it."

"Will she be safe?" he whined, stepping back to avoid the stench of hoof glue.

"My sister is a fair woman."

"All will know of my humiliation," he said, pacing to and fro, and biting his thumbnail, his anxiety un-assuaged.

"I am bound for Calais, so from me this indiscretion of yours will go no further, but I cannot answer for Richard, though I fail to comprehend your attraction for this woman. We killed her father at Northampton, and the Percys have long memories."

"As do the Neville's... 'tis our downfall."

"Take heed nephew, in the end she will prove no different."

"I sympathise Uncle, but my fate is in God's hands."

"Then I hope he looks kindly on you, considering the contempt you show his ambassadors here on Earth," he smirked, swinging his armoured legs and stalking away. "You know, the king will never consent to you marrying a Percy."

"Farewell!"

Fauconberg looked over his shoulder, waved, and continued on his way.

Philip glanced down at the trees sheltering the little tent and gripped the handle of his sword. He thought to run down, kill the guards and set Elizabeth free, but knew he would never get away with it. Shaking his head, he went off in search of his men; the siege of Alnwick forgotten as matters of the heart predominated.

Chapter 7

By the end of the second week of September 1461, the Earl of Warwick had taken Alnwick and Philip was back in York, where he languished in self-pity for several months. His cousin, Norfolk, died early in November and Warwick ordered Philip to wait for him at Middleham. Grudgingly he obeyed, spending much of that winter and spring helping to tutor the king's young brother, Richard Duke of Gloucester. With the advent of summer, Philip accompanied Warwick on several raids into Scotland. The resentment accrued against his cousin at Alnwick, gradually diminished, and at times, it was as if nothing had happened, but it didn't last.

Having secured troops and a loan from her cousin Louis, Queen Margaret crossed the Tweed and occupied Bamburgh Castle. Using bluff and dexterity she quickly regained control of northeast England. When King Edward heard French soldiers were rampaging through Northumberland, he raised an army and headed north. Greatly outnumbered, Margaret left Somerset in Bamburgh and fled back over the border. At Durham, Edward was laid low with measles and forced to turn the army over to his cousin. Warwick marched on Bamburgh and Somerset offered to surrender if his rights and property were restored. Warwick agreed, and on Christmas Eve the Duke of Somerset gave fealty to Edward. Warwick and his 'new friend' then rode to Alnwick, which opened its gates on 6 January 1463. By the end of the month, Northumberland was back under Yorkist control.

A few days before Somerset changed sides, Warwick sent Philip to Newcastle, to assist the new Duke of Norfolk in forwarding supplies to the army. Away from the action, Philip's temperament disintegrated; jealousy twisted his thoughts, and he cursed his cousin's machinations. Rumours of immoral behaviour in the royal palaces helped shred Philip's delicate emotions, and when he learned of Somerset's change of allegiance, he turned to drinking.

After two weeks of drunken debauchery, he sobered up and rode to Sheriff Hutton, Warwick's bleak residence north of York, accompanied by Robert Harrington, his new esquire.

On a cold January afternoon, the private hall in the south tower of Sheriff Hutton bore witness to a heated argument. Richard Neville was sat at the highly-polished dining table, a goblet of red wine in his hand, and a look of exasperation on his face. Recently returned from his labours in the north, he was looking forward to a much-needed rest, but it wasn't to be. His irascible kinsman cantered into Sheriff Hutton's frosted courtyard less than an hour after he arrived. Leaving his esquire to quarter the horses, Philip demanded to see the Earl. Informed of his arrival, Warwick groaned and gave a reluctant nod. The hunch-shouldered steward led Philip up the circular stairwell to the hall. Removing his gloves and cloak, he bowed respectfully to the Earl.

"'Tis good to see you cousin," Warwick lied, waving his steward out.

"And you, my lord," he responded, brushing down his wet hair and warming his bloodless hands in front of the roaring fire. "By St Paul I am fair frozen."

"I know why you are here," Warwick began cautiously, "but I am in no mood for a quarrel."

"I have not come to argue," Philip said, keeping his back to his cousin and rubbing his aching fingers, to restore the circulation. "I am sorry for your loss," he explained, referring to Warwick's mother, who had passed away recently.

"I shall miss her, though she was never the same after Wakefield," Richard sighed, crossing himself and looking at his favourite dog, Mongo; a huge beast lying on a rug in front of the hearth, soaking up the heat. "Let me speak plainly, I know the reason you are here," he repeated. "Somerset."

"He is the devil incarnate," Philip snapped, cursing his inability to control himself, "he will never be reconciled to

128

the House of York, not in a thousand years. Why has the king accepted his fealty?"

Richard placed his oversized silver goblet on the table, closed his eyes slowly, exhaled and opened them again.

"Edward believes he can win over the Lancastrian nobility," he answered, his words coated with fatigue.

"Then he is a fool."

Philip's offensive words rebounded off a score of old shields, set high along two of the whitewashed walls, before echoing up into the vaulted, timbered roof.

"I don't want to hear this," Warwick warned, wishing his cousin was anywhere but here. "The cold has infiltrated my very bones and I am worn out."

"My lord, Somerset is a traitor and should be chastised, not absolved and compensated."

"You're talking to the wrong man."

"Then speak with the king, he will listen to you."

"No, I am deliberately kept from court by my enemies."

"You must do something…"

"You don't understand the science of government…"

"I don't give a fig for the science of government!"

"Then you are a fool," Warwick hissed, hostility creeping into his voice.

"Yes, my lord, I am a fool… you sent me to Newcastle, and before the sweat on my horse's arse was dry, you and Somerset were carousing in the taverns of Durham, like old friends," he exaggerated, drawing his weapon from its scabbard and eyeing its polished blade. "This is the only government I know of to resolve disputes. I swear never to serve the Duke of Somerset, nor fight in any army he is part of. I would rather pledge allegiance to Louis of France!" he fibbed, laying the three-foot arming sword on the table.

Mongo raised his sleepy head and growled, but perceiving no threat to his master, he yawned and buried his huge head down into his shaggy fur.

"Have you forgotten Guines, and Somerset's promise never to fight you again?" Philip reminded him.

Warwick gritted his teeth to contain his rising temper. He held his own views on Somerset's change of loyalty, but kept them to himself. Standing, he walked over the green and blue tiled floor to the fireplace, spread his fingers toward the heat and looked up at the large, colourful tapestry above the mantle.

"I miss my sweet Anne," Richard mused, observing a woman at prayer in the weave, her angelic face reminding him of his wife."

The warmth of the fire and a strong odour of wood smoke, made Philip sleepy. Recalling his last meeting with Elizabeth, at Alnwick, he stared hard at Richard's back, his cheek muscles pulsating. Anger and heartache brought a tremor to Philip's lips and drew his eyes to the sword on the table.

"We must all make sacrifices to achieve final victory," Warwick declared.

"Have I not sacrificed enough?" he sighed, his attention once more drawn to his cousin's back, "my God I have nothing left."

"You must learn to forgive…"

"I cannot," he gasped, glancing at a wooden cross on the wall beside the door and massaging his temples with thumb and forefinger. "Can you forgive those who murdered your father and despoiled your property? Counsel Edward, my lord, warn him!"

"Enough!" Warwick growled passionately; evoking the image of his father's decaying head above the Micklegate, and forcing his eyes shut to rid his mind of the graphic torment that still haunted him. "I have come home to arrange for my father and Thomas to be reburied with my mother," he revealed, turning from the fire and knocking his goblet off the table out of frustration.

Mongo opened one eye, looked up and curled lazily down into a ball as the silver cup clattered across the floor, its contents marking the wall.

"Somerset has bored his way into Edward's affections, but the king does not answer to me… perhaps he has a plan," Warwick growled. "I don't know, but I'll not justify myself to a mere knight!"

"Somerset must be exposed for what he is."

"Dear God, spare me," Warwick yelled in desperation, using a napkin to dab wine from his hand. "Enough! I put up with your tantrums because you are my cousin, and you have stuck by me through thick and thin, but you push me too far."

As an indentured knight, Philip knew he could never challenge Somerset on equal terms. After years of loyal service to the crown, all he had achieved was the status of an armoured servant, but he would not be cowed. Seeking to calm the situation, Warwick slumped down onto a low couch, near the fire.

"'Tis not right that we argue," he said calmly. "Forget Somerset, his greed will bring him down."

Philip removed his blade from the table and sullenly dropped it into its scabbard. Snatching a face jug, he poured a cup of vernage wine, but his hands shook and the sticky liquid spilled over his fingers. Falling heavily into a narrow chair, opposite his cousin, he licked the sweet vernage from his hands and thought hard.

"My lord, Edward's father trusted Andrew Trollope and was betrayed, and killed. Somerset will do no less," he prophesied, examining the moulded face on the jug. "This looks like Lord Hastings," he sneered, turning the jug to show Richard the grotesque caricature.

"Somerset has been removed from the game," Warwick replied, ignoring his comment.

"No, my lord," he warned, "he waits for the right moment to turn his coat, though Edward is too indolent to see it."

"Hastings and Herbert distract the king with wine, women and song, and the governance of England is ignored."

"Hastings is your brother-in-law, can you not…"

"Marriage to my sister was the means to an end for Hastings," Warwick interrupted. "His influence over the king waxes, mine wanes."

Philip rubbed his aching fingers and huffed.

"William is a libertine, who covets every beautiful woman," Warwick revealed, planting another seed of anguish in his cousin's receptive brain.

Philip looked hard at Richard over the rim of his goblet.

"Every woman," Warwick emphasised.

"'Tis a lie," he pouted.

"I do not lie."

"Then why did you send Elizabeth to London?" Philip moaned, shooting out of his seat and pacing irritably.

"She is a Percy and as much an enemy to us as Somerset."

"I must go."

"No doubt you will ride to London, kill Somerset and steal her away."

"Have no doubt of it, my lord," he hissed, knuckling his forehead in despair.

"Then you are a fool."

"The Duke of Somerset will never fight Henry," Philip declared.

"Wait and see," Warwick advised as a wave of weariness swept over him and he struggled to shake it off.

"My lord, shall I have supper brought up?" his butler asked, entering the hall.

The delightful odour of food emanating from the butler's clothes brought Mongo out of his sleep. Lurching slowly up onto its thick hairy feet, the dog slapped his jowls and panted eagerly.

"Yes," he nodded, as Mongo followed him over to the table and nestled his body against his master's legs. "You will dine with me this night and return to Newcastle on the morrow, with a clear head."

Philip wasn't looking forward to the long ride back to Newcastle. Snow was falling heavily, and a strengthening wind whistled eerily through the twisting stone passageways, but he was obdurate.

"Me, a mere knight, dine with the greatest Lord in all

England?" he mocked, as a servant tiptoed in and retrieved the goblet from the floor. "No, I must go now."

"I could command you," Warwick said, grateful for his decision.

"You have that right."

"Leave if you wish, but you are not to go to London," he warned, rinsing his hands in a bowl of warm water brought in by a servant.

"If you say so, my lord," Philip smiled withdrawing.

As he descended the cold, dark twisting stairwell, Philip was already planning to disobey his cousin.

Despite the dangers of the time, the journey from Newcastle to London proved uneventful. Heavy snow and a bitterly cold wind kept most people at home, allowing Philip and his small band of retainers and servants a safe, if uncomfortable ride. The inclement weather slowed the pace and it was almost two weeks before nine bedraggled horsemen and a supply wagon trundled into the village of Islington, a mile from London. Moving on, they soon arrived at the ditch, surrounding the city wall. Clattering over Aldersgate drawbridge, the weary, frost-blown group entered the capital, watched by a warden and several apathetic guards. Drawing their horses to a halt, the party sat hunched and shivering in the saddle, while Arbroth nudged his rouncey towards a Franciscan monk, hurrying back to the warmth of his monastery.

"Good friar!"

"Yes my son!" the cherub-faced monk responded, keeping his face from the wind.

"Is the king here in London?"

"No, he is at Windsor!"

"My lord..." Arbroth said, turning to Philip and drawing the hood from his face.

"I heard," he rasped, his breath clouding white in the cold air.

"To Windsor?" the Scot asked, pulling his cowl back, while the monk hurried away.

Philip nodded slowly and waved his men on.

Steering his plodding palfrey toward St Paul's Cross, Philip Neville led the group out of London via Ludgate. Making their way along Fleet Street, their faces swaddled against the razor-sharp wind howling up the river valley, the horsemen looked apathetically at groups of listless beggars gathered together over smoking braziers outside St Bride's Church. Passing through the Liberty of the Savoy, they turned south at the Charing Cross monument and followed the Thames for twenty miles, until they saw the dominating chalk hill, on which Windsor Castle stood. Crossing the bridge to the south bank, the badly strung-out column forced their ragged horses up the steep slope to the off-white, heath stone gatehouse.

A red-faced captain of the guard, sheltering between the gates and the drawbridge, eyed the approaching visitors suspiciously. When they turned onto the drawbridge, he spat in disgust and tore himself away from the comfort of his shelter. Philip kept his face covered, but opened his black cloak to reveal the Warwick coat of arms on his surcoat. Keeping his hands inside his woollen coat for warmth, the captain nodded sharply and shuffled aside. The visitors rattled over the wooden drawbridge, spanning the overgrown dry moat into the lower ward. Philip's panting horse walked sluggishly around the circular Great Tower and up into the higher ward, its head drooping from exhaustion. Passing through an old narrow gateway, the party was met in front of the Royal Chapel by a guard armed with a poleaxe. Staring at the long-handled weapon, Philip felt a tingling sensation in his left shoulder.

"We seek the king," his esquire announced, his words steaming through the wet scarf over his mouth.

"Who are you?" the guard asked cagily.

Before he could reply, John Bouchier Lord Berners, the king's uncle and Constable of Windsor, appeared with William Hastings in tow.

"Let them pass!" Bouchier commanded, pointing at the guard.

Philip lowered his scarf and Berners greeted him cordially, but Hastings' smile had vanished.

"I am Sir Philip Neville, my lord."

"I knew your father," Berners said noting the condition of his men and horses. "Have you ridden far?"

"From Newcastle, My lord," his esquire offered.

"In this weather?"

"I must see the king," Philip announced.

"Then you are out of luck. His Majesty is on his way back from a meeting with the Earl of Warwick. He intends stopping in Oxfordshire, to hunt. But you are welcome to lodge here until his return."

Put out by his answer, Philip passed Hastings a disapproving sneer and thanked Lord Berners for his courtesy.

Hastings added his apologies and announced he was leaving.

"So soon?" Berners questioned.

"Matters of state, my lord?" Philip smirked, shaking ice from his scarf and cocking his head to one side, sarcastically.

"That's my business," Hastings snapped.

Philip offered a wry smile.

"You have made the king's chamberlain uncomfortable," Berners announced, watching Hastings walk away.

"The king's chamberlain has made himself uncomfortable, my lord," he countered, dismounting slowly and holding onto his saddle to relieve the pain rampaging up and down his spine.

"He is a most ostentatious fellow," Berners confessed, "and full of bluster."

"The king surrounds himself with many such fools," Philip declared.

"Too many."

The short, kind-eyed John Bouchier, his body wracked with arthritis, led Philip and his esquire to their rooms. Arbroth and the others were quartered with the garrison.

Assigned an apartment in the King Henry III Tower, a high D-shaped building on the south wall at the top end of the Lower Ward, Philip removed his damp cloak. While he stood thawing out in front of the roaring fire, he quietly cursed himself for disobeying Warwick's explicit orders not to go to London. Suddenly a sixth sense drew him to the window. Peering through the thin, distorted glass he spotted Hastings cantering toward the gatehouse.

"That's right, run," he muttered to himself, a derisive glare contorting his glowing face. "Cowardly knave."

"What are you looking at?" Berners asked, handing him a goblet of wine.

"There goes a man who has something on his mind," he chuckled, while a servant reinforced the fire with a huge log.

"He rides as if the devil was biting his arse," the constable grinned, joining him at the window.

"The craven dog," he hissed, gratefully slurping down the warm wine.

"Has he caused thee offence?" Berners asked, stunned by the strength of his antipathy.

"We were friends, once, but since he has been made King's Chamberlain, Lord Hastings has revealed his true qualities," he said, recalling that day in the royal bedchamber.

Philip had hoped to confront Hastings over the rumours concerning Elizabeth Percy, now he would have to wait for another opportunity.

"He came here last night and kept me waiting, while he preened himself like a peacock," Berners explained.

"Conceited little shit," Philip sneered, as Hastings and his party disappeared through the gatehouse.

"When you have bathed, join me for supper," he offered, edging back to avoid the strong smell of stale sweat emanating from Philip's clothes.

"Thank you my lord," he nodded, as his host left the room.

Shortly before eight of the bells, five thirty in the

afternoon, Philip disrobed and eased his foul smelling body into a huge, half-a-cask of steaming water. Sitting on a bed of soft sponges placed in the bottom of the luxurious tent-draped tub, he laid back and enjoyed a cup of wine from the castle vineyard and relaxed. While the hot scented water lapped over his pale scarred body, the aches and pains of his wounds diminished. Staring up at the ceiling, the fragrant steam invading his nostrils reminded him of Elizabeth's scent.

"Fear not my lady I will come for you soon," he hissed, tentatively touching the ribbed scar running down his left shoulder.

The wine gradually dulled his senses and when the water cooled, he was overcome by jealousy. Angry and suspicious, he eventually climbed out, dried off and dressed for supper.

For two days Philip explored the grounds of Windsor Castle, pacing the windswept walls, whoring with a village girl, and playing chess with Lord Berners and Sir Francis Talbot. By the third morning the frustrated knight had had enough. Throwing off his blanket, he leapt out of bed and woke his seventeen-year-old esquire by tearing the bedding from his pallet.

"Get up Rob!" he barked, "we're leaving."

"My lord?" Harrington mumbled, shivering from the sudden blast of cold air.

"Up lad," he repeated, leaving his esquire in a state of drowsy confusion.

Woken by the noise from Harrington's room, Francis Talbot, nephew of the late Lord Talbot, poked his head out of his chamber.

"May I go with you?" he asked scratching his head.

Talbot's father had died with Richard of York at Wakefield, and he was at Windsor hoping to secure a position in his son's household. His manor, near Ashby de la Zouch, suffered substantial damage when Margaret's hordes marched on London, and he was in financial distress. Philip had shared a dormitory with Francis when they were esquire's together, at Sheriff Hutton, and remembered him as a very private person. Francis joined the Yorkist army at Towton and was knighted by Edward after the battle. Talbot possessed a thin, pale face and a chin that jutted out just a little too far. A small pinched nose, underlined by a narrow moustache, made his eyes look too close together.

"Alright," Philip agreed, "but be ready to leave before sunrise."

"I have to pray…"

"Then you pray, but I'll not wait for you," he warned.

Hurrying down to the lower ward, Philip roused his men by yanking the blankets from their bodies and yelling at them to get up and saddle the horses.

Smothered in cloaks and furs, and with several fresh packhorses in place of the broken down wagon, the party was soon ready to depart. Thanking a bleary-eyed Lord Berners for his hospitality, Philip led his men out through the gatehouse as dawn broke. With their faces enveloped in thick scarves against the raw wind, they cantered down the slope and headed for Oxford through a landscape blanketed in snow. By early evening of the next day, they were splashing across the icy River Glyme and closed in on the great royal palace at Woodstock.

"Lo and behold!" Talbot gasped in relief, spotting the illuminated twin towers of the lodge through the trees, "We have arrived."

"Thank God! My bollocks are frozen to the saddle," Philip shivered, lowering the scarf from his face and shaking the water from his hair with a jerk of his neck, while the rest sniggered at his crude comment.

Woodstock Palace was a magnificent stone hunting lodge, built on high ground and contained numerous apartments, kitchens, workshops and a chapel. It was to Woodstock that King Henry II had brought his mistress, Rosemunde Clifford, to woo her.

Rubbing his chaffed backside, Philip sighed gratefully at the sight of the lodge and led his men toward its welcoming light.

"It will be good to see the king again," Talbot said.

"If he is here, but he has changed much since Towton," Philip warned.

"No one who fought at Towton will ever be the same."

"Stay thy horse stranger!" a torch-toting silhouette barked.

"Who addresses me in such a fashion?" Philip snapped, peering at the approaching shadow, unable to make out the face.

"Hugh Spooner, sergeant of the king's bodyguard!"

"Which King?" he sneered mischievously.

The shadow came to an abrupt halt, allowing the torch to drop, and Philip heard the familiar scraping sound of a sword being drawn from its scabbard.

"Come forward and declare your allegiance to King Edward, or die where you stand," came the warning.

Philip chuckled and nudged his mount on.

"Halt!" the shadow repeated with more urgency, barring their progress with its body.

"You would take us all on?"

"I would."

"Then calm thyself friend, I am Philip Neville: cousin to the Earl of Warwick and to His Grace, Edward, King of England."

Spooner was unconvinced and refused to move. With a grunt, Philip angrily wrenched open his cloak exposing the crest on his red velvet tunic. The sergeant retrieved his spluttering torch, keeping the point of his sword aimed at him. Curling his fingers around the hissing torch he raised its flickering light until he recognised the arms of the Earl of Warwick.

"Forgive me, sir," he apologised, stepping aside.

Philip nodded and waved his men on.

"Where is the king?" Talbot asked, dismounting and walking with the young sergeant.

"Hunting in Wychwood Forest," he replied, removing the hood from his head to reveal a smooth young face, closely cupped by a head of thick hair.

"I was told he was still at Middleham."

"We arrived here only yesterday."

Philip steered his horse over to a group of soldiers clustered around a smoking brazier, near the lodge entrance.

"I seek accommodation for myself and my men," he demanded, dismounting.

Those huddled around the fire eyed the strangers contemptuously and continued warming their hands over the flames.

"Well?" Philip frowned, mindful of their hostility.

"There's no room here," one of them declared, slapping his sides for warmth.

"Then find room!"

"My lord, every apartment is taken," Spooner echoed, housing his blade. "There is room at the George Inn, down in the village."

"To hell with the George Inn," Philip spluttered, leading Clovis by his bridle.

"Don't judge him unkindly," his esquire whispered to the flushing sergeant. "We have travelled many leagues to see the king."

Spooner offered the hospitality of his brazier and a bowl of hot venison stew.

"The king has many lords and knights with him, there is no room."

Harrington thanked Spooner for his kindness and hurried after his master, while the men slid from the saddles and led their horses to the stables, inside the lodge.

For the next thirty minutes Philip and his companions grumbled away their aches and pains over the glowing brazier. Powdery snow continued falling, reminding those who were there of Towton Field. They talked of how they would rather be fighting the French than terrorising fellow Englishmen. The conversation ended abruptly when a messenger came thundering up to the lodge.

"The king!" he announced, dismounting.

Pandemonium whirled around the brazier, as the guards fell over each other in their enthusiasm to grab helmets and weapons. Eventually they formed a ragged line and straightened their jacks. One lad, his sallet on back to front, tumbled out of the lodge and tripped. Plucking his helmet from the dirt, he plopped it back on his head and joined the line.

The king's return was heralded by a distorted fanfare of trumpets, accompanied by the crazed barking of a pack of slavering alaunts and greyhounds. Enveloped in thick furs, King Edward followed his mud-splattered dog-handlers, who had been dragged through icy mud most of the day. Edward's household retainers rode beside him, each one vying for the most prestigious position at the king's right hand. Bringing up the rear were the bodyguards, varlets and a cart laden with several dead animals.

Philip Neville wrapped the cold, wet scarf around his mouth and lingered near the sparking brazier with his men.

"A bountiful hunt, Your Grace?" Spooner grovelled, grabbing the decorated leather reins of the king's horse to steady the beast, while the barking increased.

"A fair day's work Hugh!" Edward yelled above the noise, removing his right leg from the stirrup and swinging it over the high cantle. "A hairy great boar almost had me, but I brought him down with a single arrow."

As he dismounted, the rowel of Edward's left spur caught in the stirrup strap, causing his horse to walk on and forcing him to hop several paces.

"Woah!" Spooner yelled, struggling to control the unruly palfrey, "steady."

Philip's quick-thinking esquire came to the rescue. Utilizing his ballock dagger, Robert Harrington came forward and knocked the spur up, freeing the royal limb. Embarrassed by the incident, Edward thanked the youngster for his presence of mind. Harrington bowed and rejoined his companions congregated around the brazier. The king looked over at Philip and his men with a curious eye, while the frenzied barking rose to an irritating pitch, and the dogs fought to break free of the leash.

"Shut them up!" Edward yelled. "And get them out of here!" he added, dismissing the hunting party with a flick of his wrist.

Removing his riding gloves, Edward rubbed his hips to relieve the pain that had plagued him for the past two hours, and strolled over to the heat source, while the dogs were dragged away.

Edward stopped at the brazier and looked at each of the men in turn. When he stared at Philip, he un-wrapped his scarf and threw back his cloak. Before the king could respond, Philip went down on one knee, grabbed his cousin's cold right hand and pressed his lips to the gold ring on the forefinger.

"Sire!"

"Cousin!" Edward said surprised, dragging him to his feet and embracing him. "Welcome."

Philip examined him with a concerned frown and noted his blotchy complexion, and slightly round face.

"My lord, 'tis good to see you well... but you have grown corpulent," he dared; the frustration of their last encounter forgotten.

Edward bent his knees and looked him in the eye, while those nearby stared, open-mouthed at his impudence. After a stony silence the king laughed raucously.

"When one is confined to bed, one acquires too healthy an appetite for there is nothing to do but eat. Now, leave your insults outside but bring your companions in. We will dine together tonight and you can tell me what business has brought you here in such weather," Edward said. "Lord Warwick told me you were in Newcastle, are you well?"

"Yes Your Grace, no Your Grace, I mean I am here to warn you not be deceived by those who pretend to be your friends," he said, looking beyond the king in an attempt to distinguish the dark, faceless figures of his escort.

"Deceived," Edward chuckled, confused, "by whom?"

The whinnying of a horse caused Philip to glance at a

group of mounted men, silhouetted against the tree line; one of whom nudged his horse towards a narrow shaft of pale yellow light beaming down from an upstairs window. A cloud of smoky vapour billowed from the approaching horse's nostrils, making it look like some mythical beast. When the horseman's face materialised in the weak light, a look of shock twisted Philip's features. Henry Beaufort, third Duke of Somerset, was younger than Philip, and slightly shorter, but he was a very athletic warrior. His dark piercing eyes, heavy brows and narrow lips were shadowed by half an inch of tightly-packed beard, as black as his heart.

When the duke dismounted, his boots crunched the snow underfoot and the hem of his long, mud-caked cloak dragged along the ground. Removing his velvet hat, Somerset slapped it against his hip and joined the king.

"I am wet through," he announced.

Stepping away from Edward, Philip threw the flap of his cloak over the left shoulder and drew his sword. Fearing for the king's life, several of his bodyguards came forward, unsheathing their weapons, only to be stopped by Edward's raised hand. Somerset reacted by grabbing the hilt of a concealed dagger from under his cloak.

"Put up your blade cousin!" Edward boomed. "Why do you draw sword against Sir Henry? He is captain of my bodyguard. Would you kill a man under royal sanctum?"

Staggered by Somerset's presence, Philip was unable to restrain his unbridled hatred.

"Sire, this man killed your father and murdered your brother," he spat angrily, lowering his blade and pointing accusingly at the duke. "Bastard!" he hissed, forcing the words through his gritted teeth.

"I had no part in that," Somerset countered, outraged by the unprovoked insult, "'twas Lord Clifford."

"'Tis easy to accuse a dead man, Your Grace," Philip scoffed.

"Believe what you will."

"Sir Henry has made his peace with the king," someone

volunteered.

"What sorcery is this?" Philip yelped, looking hard at the black faceless figures of Edward's escort. "Come forward and reveal yourself!"

"I am Anthony Woodville."

The twenty-one-year-old offspring of Lord Rivers, was a new associate of Edward's. Father and son had fought under Henry's banner at Towton, but soon after they saw the advantage of transferring their allegiance.

"Come into the light, if you have the balls," Philip scoffed.

A slender, fair-haired youth nudged his horse forward and dismounted.

"Ah, I remember you. You cried like a baby when we captured you and your family at Sandwich, and carried you off to Calais?" Philip leered.

Young Woodville flashed a look of concern at the king and anxiously bit his lips. Flabbergasted by Philip's verbal assault against two of his courtiers, but captivated by his confrontational stance, Edward held back.

"Your Grace, the Beauforts are bound to Henry by blood," Philip declared, as Woodville joined Sir Henry. "They will never serve the House of York!"

"Who are you to profess to know my mind, and speak to me in such a manner, and in the presence of my King?" Somerset demanded.

"Why you…!"

"Enough!" Edward snapped. "You are my cousin, but you go too far. I am prepared to absolve my father's executioner for the sake of peace, will you do no less?"

"My lord, I cannot forget the murder of my father so easily," Philip reused, anger causing his heart to pound against his chest.

Edward looked over at young Harrington, who pretended not to be listening. Scratching his wet hair, he discharged his frustration in a lengthy growl.

"Come," he hissed, overlooking Philip's crass comments. "You will sup with me this night, and we'll put the past behind us."

Rather than antagonise the king, Philip sheathed his sword.

"As you command, sire," he bowed, while the rest of Edward's party dismounted and followed him inside.

Somerset spoke discreetly with two of his men before throwing an arm around young Woodville's shoulder and leading him inside.

"Cunt," Philip muttered under his breath, bowing sarcastically as the duke passed him, the enmity on both their faces clear for all to see.

Most of those who followed Somerset in offered the irate knight their silent support. To these Philip responded with a knowing nod before rejoining his men at the brazier. Shaken by his impudent diatribe, and baffled by the king's lack of censure, Francis Talbot shook his head.

"You must cool your hot blood," he suggested. "Sir Henry is a dangerous man."

"Huh," Philip sneered, as the cart, laden with the corpses of several hinds and a boar, creaked and swayed through the gate. "All I need to compound my misery is for Will Hastings to show up."

"I saw the threat in Sir Henry's eyes," Francis warned.

"Don't worry about me..." Philip said, his words cut short by the head of a royal esquire poking out of the door.

"Philip Neville!"

"I am he."

"The king commands you to lodge here this night, and attend vespers."

"Vespers," he groaned, "what must I suffer for this King?"

"Be on your guard," Francis urged, placing a cautious hand on his arm.

Philip looked disapprovingly and Francis withdrew the offending limb.

During supper, Philip, seated below the high table, continually glared at Somerset whenever their eyes met. Having eaten his fill of veal and goose; overindulged on

145

imported fruit, preserved in sugary syrup, and downed far too much wine, Philip and Francis staggered up to their assigned bed-chamber on the first floor. Collapsing on the bed fully dressed, they were soon fast asleep. Shortly before sunrise, an explosion of noise shattered the stillness of the night. Waking with a jolt Philip instinctively reached for his sword, but the weapon was suddenly snatched away. Adjusting his eyes to the intrusive light, he groggily asked what was happening. Outside, confused voices echoed in the narrow corridors, and armed guards could be heard rushing about.

"What is the meaning of this?" Philip rasped, covering his face with a hand to protect his eyes from the glare of an invasive flambeau. "What's happening?"

"Take heed, my lords," came the gruff response, as a clutch of guards surrounded the bed. "Move and you die!"

With his blurred vision clearing, Philip attempted to defy the order, but Talbot held him in check with an arm across his chest. "Have you taken leave of your senses?" the Duke of Somerset barked, entering the crowded room attired in his bed robes. "Why would you murder a man who invites you to his table and calls you friend?"

Philip presented Talbot with a frosty smirk before replying.

"Don't mingle words, Your Grace. The very name Beaufort stinks of treachery. Tell me and tell me straight, who has been murdered?"

"No one, fortunately," Somerset answered, crossing himself, "but one of your men confessed that you, Philip Neville, did command him to assassinate our most noble sovereign, King Edward."

"Your Grace, this is an outrage," Talbot stammered.

"Who would confess such an untruth?" Philip asked passively, raising himself up, but forced back by the point of a sword levelled at his heart.

"Your own servant," Sir Henry crowed triumphantly, scratching his dense beard.

"Then bring him here and have him repeat his base accusation."

"The dog has taken his own life," one of the guards answered, with a knowing look.

"How fortunate," Philip scoffed, aware his life hung by a thread.

He knew Somerset had a good reason for joining the king. Being so close, he could lull Edward into a false sense of security and have him killed at his leisure.

"I demand to be taken to the king," he snapped, anxiety causing him to tremble.

"You demand nothing. The king has ordered you to be detained here," Beaufort revealed coldly. "Tomorrow you and your conspirators will be taken to London, for trial."

"Your vile plan with not work," Philip said, seizing the blade circling in front of his eyes, "you Lancastrian dung-heap!"

Squeezing the sharp point with his right hand Philip stared into the guard's surprised eyes, until he jerked the blade away, causing the steel to slice deep into the soft palm.

"You will show respect to His Grace," the swordsman warned.

"Kiss my arse," Philip spat, wincing at the pain. "I am mindful of your intrigues, Your Grace."

"This won't help you," Talbot groaned.

"Can you not see what he is doing?" Philip hissed, wiping his bleeding palm on the blanket.

"Take heed Sir Francis," Somerset intervened, "do not link your name with this assassin; he is for the block, but you are not implicated in this matter."

Francis glanced at Philip, who continued to stare at his accuser.

"I'll not stand trial, I guarantee it. I shall be murdered somewhere on the road, as my father was."

Talbot looked at Beaufort.

"You may leave," Sir Henry offered.

Philip shook his head as Francis shuffled off the bed,

and while he fumbled with his sword belt, Somerset's attention was distracted. Raising himself up onto his elbows, Philip eyed the three guards around his bed and tensed his body, but with a sword-point barely a finger width from his throat, he knew now was not the time for heroics.

"Fare thee well," Philip called, as his friend walked to the door. "Go to Lord Warwick and tell him what has happened here."

"You don't have to do anything," Beaufort countered. "You are free to go, if you leave now."

Unable to look at Philip, Francis turned and left. Outside the chamber he lingered a moment, hoping the courage to go back and help his friend might surface; it didn't, so he hurried along the narrow low-lit corridor cursing his weakness.

"What of my men?" Philip asked, easing his body closer the edge of the bed.

"Martin Rouse is dead, the rest are implicated in your treason and will be sent to London, in chains."

"What a fool I am," he muttered. "I should have killed you last night."

"You could have tried," Beaufort mocked. "Take his sword and the candles, and go!

The guard's picked up Philip's blade, grabbed the candles and left.

"You should not hate me, for I can show leniency to the stepson of my uncle," the duke said quietly, "we are related."

"I would sooner be a son of a bitch than kin to any Beaufort."

"Then you are a fool and you will die a fool, for I am the king's boon companion and captain of his bodyguard," he boasted.

"You are the fool, Your Grace, for you will never be reconciled to the House of York. Come, we're alone, declare your true reason for serving Edward and I shall die content."

"'Tis your mother I am sorry for. You will die and she will weep, as she did for your father."

Philip stared at Sir Henry until he was forced to look away.

"What a waste," Somerset sighed, leaving the apartment.

"Go to hell!"

Sir Henry turned and looked at Philip before slamming the door shut.

When he heard the key rattle heavily in the lock, Philip laid back and cursed his misfortune. Unarmed and in dark confinement, he felt alone and vulnerable. He knew he had to escape, but was troubled by what might befall Arbroth and his men, if he succeeded. With dawn set to light up the countryside, he made up his mind to go. Rolling off the bed he tip-toed to the window and looked down at the two guards stamping their feet in the frozen courtyard below.

"Hum?" he grunted, walking back across the room.

As he moved cautiously over the floor, a series of squeaks and groans from the warped boards raised his anxiety. Reaching the door he laid an ear to its rough surface and held his breathe. The sound of snoring told him the guard outside was fast asleep. Returning to the window, Philip rubbed icy frost from the glass with a fist and put his face to the cold pane. Craning his neck he was confused by the sudden absence of the guards. Forcing the window open sent a thick line of snow falling from the sill, which reminded him of his childhood, when he climbed out of his room and hid in the trees to avoid punishment. Expecting the collapsed snow might give him away, he leapt back. Nervously gnawing the inside of his cheek, he slowly pushed his head out but there were no guards to be seen, and the torches spread around the huge square were fizzing out, one by one.

Throwing the thick, knee-length cloak around his shoulders, Philip clipped the clasp under his chin and clambered out onto the sill, but the effort was much more demanding than it had been in his youth. Grabbing the window frame aggravated his bleeding palm, but a nagging thought that Somerset might want him to escape, supplanted the pain. From the window it was only a short drop. Looking around the courtyard, he drew a deep breath and leapt, hitting the ground with a back-jarring thump. Angered by his poor landing, Philip stayed crouched, leaving blood from his injured hand to form a strange pattern in the snow.

From the stables opposite, the sound of disturbed horses stomping among the straw worried Philip and he presumed Somerset might expect him to head for that locale. Allowing himself a crafty chuckle, he limped away in the opposite direction and disappeared amongst the closed workshops crowding the courtyard. Eager to prove his theory, he weaved through the individual shops. Near the stables, Philip ducked down and waited until a pale yellow hue splashed across the grey sky. His caution was rewarded when he caught sight of an indistinct shadow lurking inside the stables. Had he elected to ride, whoever was hiding among the horses would have pounced as he put boot to stirrup.

"Cunning bastard," he whispered, spitting and withdrawing quietly back through the workshops, "I'll have to walk out."

Leaving the lodge unchallenged, he made his way down to the tree line, expecting to be called back – it never happened and he considered himself fortunate.

Chapter 8

Philip Neville struggled through the cold inhospitable forest, distressed by the fate of those left behind at Woodstock. His faith that Edward would not condemn the innocent kept him going. If he had doubts he would have returned, or would he? Perhaps he was afraid to go back? To frustrate pursuit, he avoided roads, villages and bridges; a tactic that forced him to cross several fast-flowing streams, and traverse uneven fields carpeted in a layer of smooth snow.

In the clear sober morning after Philip's escape, King Edward shook off the effect of too much food and wine, and reflected on the alleged treachery of his kinsman. There had been no actual attempt on his life, only the confession of one, Martin Rouse, now dead; purportedly killed by his own hand. One of Somerset's men unearthed the conspiracy and informed his master. As captain of the king's bodyguard, Sir Henry arrested the 'so-called' conspirators without informing the king. When the plot was revealed to Edward, he pondered the fragile evidence and tried to fathom out why Philip would wish him dead. His biggest concern was how did Martin Rouse manage to slit his own throat? Francis Talbot's pre-dawn departure fuelled the king's suspicions. Edward dispatched Hugh Spooner to find his cousin, without informing the captain of his bodyguard. He also surrounded himself with his most trusted men, and took to wearing a sword.

Shortly after Spooner's departure, Edward sent detachments out in all directions to look for Philip. Standing beside Somerset, he announced– loud enough for all to hear – that his cousin was to be brought back alive.

"I will have the head of any man who causes him harm," he warned.

Somerset agreed, but offered Anthony Woodville a meaningful nod. Eight hours after Philip's escape, the royal hunting party dispersed. Edward, Somerset and young Woodville returned to Windsor; Robert Harrington and Philip's men, released against Somerset's protests, rode to York.

Zigzagging north, Philip Neville aimed for the town of Warwick, fifty miles from Woodstock. The temperamental knight senselessly threatened every sharp branch that tore his clothes. With each new tear or moment of anguish, he cursed Somerset with mounting intensity. For five long days and five longer nights, he endured the harsh wintry climate, walking the dark unfriendly forest at night and bedding down inside his wet clothes before dawn. Wiping his constantly running nose on the fraying hem of his cloak, he vilified Somerset's name to the trees. Frozen, miserable and depressed, he planned his revenge; each day a different scenario, but with the same result: Henry Beaufort was to be the anvil for his hammer.

Leaning against the trunk of a sycamore tree, less than a hundred yards from Warwick Castle, Philip Neville scratched his healing palm. Soaked to the skin, his hose in tatters; face overgrown with whiskers and hair a sticky mess, he looked more like a beggar than a knight. Crunching on a piece of raw turnip, he dragged a greasy sleeve under his red nose and released a shivery gurgle of satisfaction. Closing his eyes, he thanked God, while his stomach groaned hungrily. Rather than rush into a trap, he slithered over the wet ground and concealed himself in the ruins of an abandoned cottage near the river. For more than an hour he scrutinized the grey-brown, sandstone barbican, observing all who entered and left the castle. He knew his cousin was away, but hoped some friendly soul was home.

When the sun dropped below the horizon and the temperature plummeted, anaesthetizing coldness forced him to move. Rising with a painful whimper, he untied his hose and braies, dropped them to his knees and urinated against the crumbling wall. The steam rising from the fountain of piss brought a quivering giggle from his throat. Tutting as he dribbled down his leg, he blew on his frozen fingers and struggled to retie hose to doublet. With darkness closing in, he broke cover and walked cautiously up to the great fortress.

Built on a bluff overlooking the River Avon and the walled town of Warwick, Warwick Castle was the principal seat of Richard, Earl of Warwick. From here he controlled the Midlands, the 'heart of his empire' as he called it. The formidable gatehouse was guarded by two massive corner structures: Caesar's Tower, rising above the river, and Guys Tower, a twelve sided edifice to the northeast. A deep dry moat, excavated around the three landward sides of the castle, added to the defensive capabilities of Warwick.

When Philip approached the well-lit gatehouse, his torn, muddy cloak slipped from his shoulder and he yanked it aggressively back in place. Despite his shoddy appearance, the watchman on the drawbridge recognised the Neville livery. Stepping aside, he allowed Philip unchallenged access. Hobbling through the outer doors and under the vaulted gatehouse, he passed through a second set of doors leading into the courtyard. As he headed for the apartment block along the south wall, Philip spotted Warwick's constable and offered a weary wave.

"Good evening."

The double-chinned, middle-aged constable pulled the cowl closer to his chubby face, coughed harshly and hurried on without a word.

"Fuck yourself," Philip muttered.

Fatigue and hunger made it difficult for the trembling knight to open the door of the Great Hall, but he grunted and pushed until it moved. Stumbling inside he was greeted by a gust of warm air, and Hugh Spooner with four armed men.

"Shit," he hissed, slapping a hand to where his sword should have been.

"'T'was only a matter of time," Spooner said ruefully, leaning against the table, legs crossed and thumbs hooked nonchalantly over his belt.

"I knew something was wrong by the constable's

attitude."

"The king presumed you would come here."

"Yes, my cousin is no fool."

Conscious of his weakened condition, Philip shuffled over to the dining table. Pushing Spooner away he swung his legs over a low bench and eyed the platters of leftovers. Ignoring the guards edging toward him with drawn swords, he grabbed a cold pig's trotter from a bowl and ravenously tore at the fibrous meat with his teeth. Spooner silently motioned for his men to back off.

"What of my people?" he asked, angry with himself for falling into such a trap.

"They have been set at liberty."

"By whom?"

"By the king."

"And my horse, and sword?"

"I know nothing of your property, sir knight."

"And what of that dog, Somerset?"

"His Grace left for Windsor, with the king."

Philip emptied a bowl of bread ends onto the table and filled the vessel with red wine. Washing down a mouthful of pork, he exhaled slowly before spooning the tepid grease up with a chunk of wastel bread.

"Am I to die?" he asked, using a dirty fingernail to remove annoying of gristle from his teeth.

"No, I have orders to take you to Westminster."

"Come then," he chomped, wiping his slimy fingers and mouth on his wet cloak and indicating the door. "We must not keep His Majesty waiting!"

"You may rest here tonight, my lord, we can leave in the morning," Spooner offered, sensitive to his sorry state. "If you give me your word you won't attempt to flee?"

Grateful for Spooner's largesse, Philip nodded submissively and buried his head in his hands.

The young sergeant ushered his men out, and as the heavy door slammed shut, Philip opened his eyes, and looked around the hall. The dark panelled walls still bore scars of vandalism, and empty hooks showed where tapestries and portraits once hung. Damage caused by the Lancastrians after the Earl of Warwick fled overseas, following Ludlow. A solitary servant now entered the room and waited, ready to assist the weary knight.

"Have you heard from your master?" Philip asked.

"No m'Lord, nary a word," the servant replied, shaking his head. "Shall I fetch more food?"

"No, I'm too tired to eat. Where is the Lady Anne?" he sighed, forcing his fingers through the week-old growth of twisted beard covering the lower half of his face.

"M'lady is in mourning..." he revealed, meaning Warwick's recently deceased mother.

"Is she here?"

"No sir."

Philip wiped his nose on the badly stained sleeve of his doublet and ordered the attendant to fill a tub with hot water.

"And fetch the barber," he added, struggling to remove his muddy boots.

"He be sick, m'lord, and is taken to 'is bed," the servant announced, motioning for him to turn around, and taking hold of his boot heel.

"Get him up," he growled, unravelling the filthy, stained dressing around his left hand, and examining the raised purple scar running from thumb to little finger.

The servant pulled off Philip's filthy boots and took them away.

Washed, shaved and dressed in a fresh set of clothes, borrowed from his cousin's vast wardrobe, Philip felt rejuvenated. Rather than struggle upstairs to the apartments, he wilted into a cushioned seat next to the fire and fell asleep. That night, while strong winds howled and whistled around the exposed castle, and the fire ticked low in the grate, Philip slept the sleep of the damned. Nightmares of Castillon, Towton and the man with no jaw, trespassed into his unconscious mind, and he tossed and mumbled through the dark hours. The storm died out shortly before dawn and the troubled knight finally succumbed to a more peaceful slumber.

The crash of pots and pans from the kitchen woke Philip with a jolt. Stretching his limbs as far as he could, he yawned louder than was necessary and rubbed crusty sleepy dust from his eyes. A guttural snort cleared his nose back into his throat and he sat up, only to discover aches and pains he never knew; his reward for sleeping in a chair. Opening his bleary eyes he was shocked to see Hugh Spooner sitting opposite.

"What in the devil's name are you doing here?" he yelped, almost leaping up out of his chair.

"Good morning," he smiled.

"So, you don't trust me," Philip growled, "I gave you my word!"

Rising early, Spooner had attended matins before making his way to the Great Hall. Taking a seat he sat quietly until Philip woke.

"No, I have been to chapel," he replied, the smile draining from his face.

"You lie."

"I do not…"

"Huh," Philip scoffed, belching and making a face at the foul taste in his throat.

"I've ordered breakfast."

"Good," he yawned, as Spooner slapped his hand on the table behind him, a signal for the butler to bring the food in. "I could eat a horse."

Entering the hall at Spooner's signal, the smartly dressed butler cast a white linen cloth over one end of the long table and placed two settings on opposite sides. He was followed in by two servers carrying platters of eggs, cheese and toasted bread soaked in wine. Philip quickly washed his fingers and dried them on a towel, as his mouth watered in anticipation.

"How long have you served the king?" Philip asked, taking a small loaf of bread and breaking off a chunk.

"I was a soldier in Calais for two years. When Edward left with the Earl of Warwick, to invade England, I was one of those chosen to accompany him. I have been with His Majesty since we landed in Kent," the young sergeant explained, dabbing wine from his chin.

"Tell me, is he taken in by Somerset's fawning?"

"No."

"He's up to something," Philip sighed.

"Fear not the treacherous hand of Lord Somerset, the king will not be deceived."

After breakfast, Philip washed his face, cleaned his teeth and was ready to go. Wrapped in one of his cousin's thick, richly-furred cloaks, he walked out patting his stomach, and filled his lungs with cold fresh air.

"Thank you," he said pulling on a pair of supple riding gloves, and mounting a sprightly young palfrey brought for him by a groom.

"Trust nobody at court," the constable warned, casting a discreet eye at Spooner.

"I don't," he replied.

Impatient to be on his way, Spooner sat on his horse, deliberately provoking a pack of terriers and spaniels leashed to an iron ring near the gatehouse. The dogs reacted by jumping and barking aggressively. Philip shook hands with the constable and trotted over to the waiting escort.

As he passed the dogs, they barred their teeth and growled up at him. Philip jerked back by the reins and stared back.

"Shut up!" he suddenly yelled.

The dogs fell over each other and cowered together, whimpering at his outburst.

"I hate dogs," he grinned, aiming his horse at the inner gates.

As they crossed the drawbridge, fine icy sleet sprayed their faces, forcing the six men to draw their hats down over their eyes.

Escort and prisoner marched briskly through the Great Hall and out into the corridors of Westminster Palace, the soles of their leather boots thumping rhythmically against the flagstone flooring. When they entered the arched King's Cloister, Philip Neville glanced at the guards posted at every doorway, their distrustful eyes shadowing him as he passed by. Approaching a door guarded by two men armed with poleaxes, the group came to a sudden halt. One of the palace guards lowered his weapon across his waist; barring access to the king's chamber and demanded to see their authorization for admittance. Spooner removed a piece of folded paper from the wide cuff of his glove and handed it over. Pensively rubbing the area between his nostrils and upper lip with a forefinger, the guard scrutinized the pass. With a snort of disapproval, he returned the pass and rotated his poleaxe to its upright position.

Following Spooner inside, Philip drank in the garish, cluttered splendour of the king's privy chamber. Shivering with apprehension, he remembered the biblical tale of the lion's den and felt a sudden affinity with Daniel. Removing his hat, cloak and leather gloves, Philip moved to the fireplace, its heat welcome after the bitterly cold journey. Scratching his healed palm, he paced the room. Impatient to learn his fate, he nervously rolled the narrow, gold ring on the middle finger of his left hand, worn in memory of his grandfather.

Hugh Spooner revealed nothing of the king's intentions during the ride from Warwick, and at times Philip's imagination got the better of him. Several opportunities to escape opened up during the nights, but he gave his word, a pledge he now regretted. The sound of rapidly approaching footsteps drew all eyes to the door, and Philip's mouth dried. Anticipating Edward's arrival with trepidation, he almost exploded when Henry Beaufort entered. Suspecting a double-cross, he flashed a contemptuous glare at Spooner whose look of abhorrence was proof he knew nothing.

"What knavery is this?" Philip demanded.

Dressed in a long black velvet gown that reached

almost to the floor, a thick gold chain hanging loosely around his bearded neck, the Duke of Somerset scoffed at the flustered knight.

"Philip Neville what are we to do with you?" he said mockingly, shaking his head.

"Release me and confess your own guilt?"

"Leave us," Sir Henry commanded, "all of you!"

But, Your Grace, I have orders." Spooner pleaded.

"Leave now," he insisted.

Hugh Spooner jostled his men out, glancing apologetically at Philip.

"No one is to enter," Somerset warned, his intense stare intimidating the sergeant.

"I must protest…" he gasped, making a weak show of defiance before leaving.

Philip walked past Somerset and slumped into a high-backed wooden chair near the fire, pulling his crimson doublet straight. Resting his right foot on his left knee he drummed his fingers fretfully against the armrest, and refused to look at the duke.

"This place is never warm," Somerset mused, sitting opposite and pushing his hands towards the fire.

"How is my brother?" Philip asked, refusing to make eye contact.

"Michael is in good health, but he will never be reconciled to the House of York, and Lady Joan is distressed by your misplaced loyalty."

"Be mindful in your choice of words, Your Grace. My loyalties rest on solid foundations, unlike yours. Am I here to face trial?"

"If I had my way you would kiss the executioner's block, but the king has decreed otherwise."

"You are a treacherous knave," Philip declared, the dread that had plagued him since his escape from Woodstock, fading.

Aggrieved by the insult, the volatile duke jumped to his feet and threw his hands in the air.

"Why do you insult me with such ruthless

humiliation?"

"Don't confuse humiliation with revulsion, Your Grace. My father was murdered by your father, and my uncles were slaughtered at Wakefield, on your command," he countered. "Now your shallow uncle sleeps with my mother. Do you believe I could have any passion for a Beaufort, other than hatred?"

"I knew nothing of your father's death and I will swear to it on holy relics," Somerset proclaimed.

"Such an undertaking would be a waste of time," he scoffed.

"This is not about your father," Somerset announced, suddenly having an epiphany, "this is really about you."

"What are you talking about?"

"This air of outrage you convey, it's all about you," Somerset amplified.

"Hah," he scoffed, not sure what he was talking about.

"I saw my father cut down at St Albans without mercy," Beaufort said. "Yet I forgive my enemies. I gave fealty to Edward and he welcomed me. Now I am captain of his bodyguard. We hunt together and share the same women."

"The king is corrupted."

"If you believe that why do you continue in the service of one who has no more right to the crown than I have?"

Baffled by his words, Philip stared at the duke and rubbed his chin thoughtfully while a sharp pain in his knees forced him to uncross his legs.

"I serve my King faithfully," he declared. "That he travels a road more diverse than mine does not mean I will betray him."

"I served a king with all my heart, but he spent his days in religious contemplation and his mind in the clouds. If Henry should again take the governance of this country into his hands we will all be ruined," Somerset answered tactfully. "Edward is the only prince strong enough to unite us and re-conquer our French lands."

Philip anticipated Somerset might, if provoked, confess

his reason for deserting Henry, but his sycophantic responses only inflamed his patriotism. At his pledge of fidelity, Philip leapt to his feet and the abhorrence in his eyes burned deep into the duke's brain.

"'Pon my troth, what playacting; if I had my sword I would plunge it into your black heart from point to crossbar and wash my hands in your blood!"

"Would such an act release the hatred from your perverse soul?" he answered calmly, "I think not."

Philip sat down and the duke lamented the king's order that only palace guards were to carry arms during his attendance. Leaning forward, Philip buried his face in his hands and Sir Henry shook his head.

"'Tis fortunate the king has such faith in you, for I would not hesitate to end your miserable life here and now," he sneered contemptuously.

Philip lowered his hands and revealed a most sinister expression.

"If I live long enough to see your head rolling in the dust I shall die happy."

"You would not live a minute longer if I had my way," Somerset predicted.

Foiled in his attempt to discredit Philip at Woodstock, Sir Henry hoped he would accept his declaration as a loyal subject of King Edward. Having failed again, he knew he would have to eliminate this troublesome knight; unfortunately now was not the time.

"Shove your head up your arse!" Philip snapped, "Your Grace."

"Why you…" Somerset countered angrily, lunging out of his chair, only to be stopped by a knock on the door. "You took Elizabeth Percy from me, now the king's chamberlain has taken her from you," he hissed, the anger in his voice causing spit to dribble into his black beard, "and I hope it tears your heart out."

"She was never yours…" Philip bit back, as the door opened.

"The next time we meet bring your sword," Somerset

161

said, turning and smiling at the untimely interruption, "My lord Chamberlain."

"The king will see you now," William Hastings announced, surprised at Sir Henry's presence and bowing courteously. "Your Grace, I was not aware you were here."

Somerset could do nothing save respond cordially. Waving the two men out, he stared contemptuously as the king's extravagantly dressed chamberlain picked up Philip's cloak, hat and gloves, placed them in the crook of his arm, and beckoned him out.

As they walked quickly along the corridor Philip simmered over Somerset's deceit, and wondered if the whole world knew of his affair with Elizabeth Percy. Looking slyly at William Hastings he ground his teeth and narrowed his eyes. Since the coronation, Hastings' reputation and wealth had blossomed. He had been made a Knight of the Garter and granted the estates of three Lancastrian Lords, but marriage to Warwick's sister made little difference to his amoral behaviour.

Approaching a small, guarded antechamber leading off St Stephen's Cloister, the chamberlain suddenly put his arm out, forcing Philip to a stop.

"All I have done, I have done at the king's behest," he said, nodding at the guards, who stepped aside.

Without a word, Philip knocked his arm up and entered the apartment.

The king was seated behind a table with Hastings' younger brother Ralph, Keeper of the Royal Lions. They were busy discussing plans for the feast of St Edward, due to take place at the Tower on 18 March. Both looked up at the interruption and Philip bowed smoothly, while Hastings offered the king a sympathetic frown.

"You may leave us," Edward said, sitting back in his chair.

The younger Hastings, almost identical in looks and physique to his older brother, objected.

"You would be alone with him?"

"I have no reason to fear my cousin."

Bowing politely the two courtiers edged backwards out of the chamber, eyeing Philip suspiciously as they went. When the door closed, Philip fell on one knee and bowed his head, hoping for justice but fearing retribution. Edward pushed the papers away, and walked slowly around to the front of the table. Philip remained perfectly still and Edward lowered his large hand, every finger adorned with glittering rings.

"Rise Philip, you have nothing to fear."

Gratefully kissing the royal hand he slowly rose, arthritic pain shooting through his knees at the effort.

"Your Grace, I did not conspire against you, Somerset is a lying dog, I would never cause you harm," he spluttered, his inability to control his tongue forcing him to speak from the heart. "I swear it."

"Calm yourself, not once have I doubted your loyalty."

"But there are those who…"

The king raised a hand to cut him off but Philip would not be silenced.

"Why have I been hunted like an animal?"

Edward, his long, well-groomed chestnut hair spilling down onto his broad shoulders, moved away from the table and turned his back to his cousin.

"I trust you more than most, though I confess when your servant was murdered I saw treachery coming out of the very walls. If Somerset's men had found you, you would not be here now?"

Philip lurched forward to speak, but rocked back on his heels, allowing Edward to continue. "You judge Somerset by his past service to Henry," Edward explained, turning to face him. "But there is much to be gained by having him on our side."

"And much to be lost sire," he parried, unsure what to do with his hands. "On Towton field it was your wish never to see his face again."

Edward recalled his angry declaration that Sunday and tried to explain his change of heart.

163

"Yes, though twelve months have come and gone, and much has changed since that day. As long as Henry is at liberty my crown is in danger. Margaret covets a union with France as we speak, and fills her army with Scottish mercenaries."

"Fear not, Your Grace, Richard rules the north with an iron hand," Philip assured him.

"Yes, but for how long? My treasury is empty and the demands never end," Edward complained, shuffling among his paperwork and digging out several letters. "This: a plea from Calais for money to pay the garrison... this from the Mayor of London. I am forced to borrow more and more from foreign bankers," he sighed. "So I must inveigle those who once opposed me, if not for their fidelity, then for their influence."

Concerned by his tentative alliance with Somerset, Edward kept his misgivings to himself and always defended him in public. Thoughtfully tapping his front teeth with a thumbnail, he sat down in his chair.

"'Tis rumoured my cousin's army is dissatisfied," he said, turning and looking out of the window at the churning River Thames. "For the past two years the harvests have been poor and I am told complaints echo loudly, more so in Yorkshire."

"Take no comfort from scandalmongers, sire. Yorkshire may be for Lancaster, but the northern army is loyal."

"Loyal? To whom? Richard has made my army his own."

"The devil take the knave who has told thee such an untruth. Name him, Your Grace and I'll cut out his lying tongue."

"That's not important," Edward frowned, unimpressed by his rejoinder.

"The Nevilles have never betrayed you... and never will."

"A crown flourishes on treachery," Edward said, bidding Philip to sit. "Thus for the sake of peace, I am

164

forced to seek favours from old enemies."

Philip tried to comprehend his logic, when an uncomfortable thought struck him like a thunderbolt.

"The French?"

Edward's piercing blue eyes coupled with a portentous silence gave him his answer, and he puckered his brow disdainfully.

"You have no concept of politics," Edward scoffed, impatiently. "A treaty with France will force the Scots to abandon Lancaster, and cut off a good supply of manpower for Henry."

"But Louis is Margaret's cousin," he whined. "He'll never sign a treaty with us, unless it is advantageous to France."

"We'll see."

"Some would you kiss the devil's arse to keep their crown," Philip muttered to himself; his tone sprinkled with offence, as heat from the fire caused tiny beads of sweat to form under his hairline.

"Have a care for I have two hats," Edward cautioned, catching his snide comment. "One I wear as your cousin the other as your King, do not confuse the two."

Mistaking the sheen on his face for fear, Edward beckoned an arriving servant, bearing a tray of sugared almonds and wine, to wait. "'Tis a miracle such a cynical head has not been lopped off before now."

"I crave pardon, Your Grace. I am but a humble knight whose opinions count for little," he apologised, licking his lips and noting the taste of salt caused by a build-up of perspiration.

Edward frowned at Philip's insolent tone and feared for his cousin's life.

"I try to please everyone," he sighed. "If I had known what it was to be King I would never have taken the crown. Rather I should have placed it on the head of my royal fool," he added, anger creeping into his voice. "This audience is over!"

"Great sovereign," Philip urged, aware he had caused

offence.

"What is it, more conspiracies? Perhaps you suspect my dogs of plotting to eat me in my sleep?"

"No sire."

"Then what, speak up?"

"I…"

"Well?"

"Nothing, Your Grace," he hesitated.

"I command you!"

"Lady Elizabeth…"

"Elizabeth?"

"Elizabeth Percy," he said meekly, lowering his head, "she is one of your mother's ladies-in-waiting. I must see her."

Edward rose slowly from his chair and stood up straight.

Mindful of his legendary temper, Philip braced himself for the storm, but it never came.

"Why?" he asked.

Philip focused on a silver statue of St George slaying the dragon, set on a sideboard near the window. Aware of Philip's liaison with Elizabeth Percy, Edward shook his head and tutted. Offended by his reaction Philip smouldered and gripped his palms to re-route his anger.

"'Pon my soul," Edward scoffed. "You would condemn your King for putting his kingdom before all else, yet you wish to call on a woman whose father reviled my family with his dying breath, what hypocrisy!"

"Sire, my affection for Egremont's daughter goes beyond family dispute," Philip said. "But my loyalty to you is sacrosanct."

"The need for a treaty with France is paramount; and for it to succeed, I am willing to forget the past."

"You *are* King of France."

"I am King of Calais," Edward huffed, angry at the amount of English territory lost by his predecessor's incompetence. "Your request is denied."

"My lord?"

"She is affianced to Ralph Hastings."

Edward's revelation took his breath away and he struggled to make sense of it. In one cold, miserable month, Philip's whole world had disintegrated. The king was considering a treaty with France; the Duke of Somerset had become his intimate companion and his Lord Chamberlain, Hastings, planned to marry his young brother Ralph to Elizabeth. What had gone wrong, so quickly? He needed to get away, to think, and the impulse to go became overwhelming. With the woeful news of Elizabeth's betrothal numbing his senses, Philip made up his mind to disobey the king and seek her out. Had Edward commanded the marriage, had Warwick threatened her? Resentment, jealousy and confusion warped his judgment, and he wanted to yell out for emancipation.

Breathing deeply through his nose, he rubbed his face and asked permission to stay at the palace.

"You are a brave knight and Richard is in need of such men," was Edward's unsympathetic response. "You may stay in the palace tonight," he decreed, well aware that if Philip remained too long, he would cause mischief, but the excuse he offered was poor. "With Somerset here, I fear for your life."

"But Your Grace," he whined, "your life is in great danger. You are coveted by those who wear your colours and take your gold, but wait only for you to stumble. When you are down they will tear you to pieces like the jackals they are."

"For shame Philip, Somerset will not have me murdered, not yet. You don't understand the game of politics."

Philip remembered hearing this hogwash before, but said nothing. Observing his cousin's strained flickering eyes and anxious movements, and recalling the tension at Woodstock, Edward felt a pang of remorse.

"With Henry in Scotland, Somerset's greed has brought him to me. As long as I pay, he will be my devoted servant. I have little to fear from Henry Beaufort, for now."

"The Duke of Somerset will never serve..." Philip began, only to be cut off by a knock on the door.

"Ah William," Edward smiled, relieved as his chamberlain entered.

"Sire, Lady Grey is here," he announced bowing low.

The king curled an arm around his cousin's shoulder and led him to the door. "I have a son," he whispered in his ear.

"An heir?" Philip gaped.

Edward put a finger to his lips and lowered his voice further.

"No, Arthur is a bastard; his mother is wedded to another."

Philip looked at Edward and grinned.

"If this woman loves you, marriage will not prevent you from loving her," Edward said.

Concerned by his naïve comment, Philip aimed his chin at Hastings.

"Your son is not the only bastard, Your Grace."

"Take care of our friend, Will. Allow him the freedom of the palace, and set a place for him at table tonight," Edward announced, exchanging an expressive frown with Hastings.

"Don't send me away, sire," Philip protested, snatching his cloak and gloves from the chamberlain. "I beg you."

"'Tis for your own safety; there are many dark corners in Westminster."

The two men bowed and reversed out of the chamber.

As they marched quickly through the king's cloister toward the Great Hall, Hastings glanced furtively at Philip, but the gesture was spotted.

"What are you looking at," Philip growled aggressively, "My lord Chamberlain?"

"Nothing friend," he replied, a tremor in his soft voice.

"You call me friend yet you show me no more consideration than you would a dog," Philip scoffed. "After the coronation, you kept me waiting while you lay with a whore."

"I will always be a friend to you, Philip Neville, though you may not know it."

"If that be true why have you sanctioned your brother's betrothal to Elizabeth Percy?"

Hastings stopped abruptly, forcing Philip to backtrack several paces.

"To secure the Egremont estates for His Majesty," he explained.

"Then why did you leave Windsor in such haste?"

Hastings' mouth moved but no sound came out and Philip bathed in his anxiety.

Looking the ostentatiously attired royal favourite up and down, he suddenly lost all composure. Grabbing Hastings by the throat, he pinned his thin body against the cloister wall. As the back of his head hit the bare stone, a gasp of pain fled from his lips.

"To secure the Egremont estates," Philip spluttered, spraying spittle as his pent up anger exploded. "To secure the Egremont estates!"

The fear in Hastings' eyes goaded Philip on and he tightened the grip on his scrawny neck.

Several guards moved to intervene, but Hastings stopped them with an outstretched hand. Surprised by the ease with which he was able to raise the chamberlain off the ground, Philip relished the moment. With nothing to gain he relaxed his grip. William coughed and spluttered, and wiped the spit from his face.

"You are not worth the effort," Philip muttered, exhilarated by the fear he had inspired. "Phew, you reek like a whore!" he added, the stink of perfume abhorrent.

"Don't ever touch me again," Hastings barked, pushing him away and massaging his throat. "You dare lay a hand on the king's chamberlain…!"

"I dare…" he struck back.

The sharp creaking of a side door caused the anger in both men to ebb, and their attention shifted to two women exiting the room. One, a slender swan-necked beauty caught Philip's attention and he bowed his head as she

169

passed, his eyes fixed on her striking features. The other, a more mature woman, deliberately slowed the pace and looked vacuously at Hastings, who indicated that the king was ready to receive them. Observing her dour nod of acknowledgment, Philip resented their arrogance. When they turned the corner, he looked at Hastings.

"It is fortunate you are the king's boon companion."

"And you are fortunate the king shows such leniency, for I would not, my brother-in-law sent the Percy girl here, 'to be used as Edward saw fit'. I knew nothing of your affection for her until it was too late. That is why I left Windsor; I had caused thee offence. It was unintended and I am heartily sorry for it."

"Who was that?" Philip asked, ignoring his excuse.

"Elizabeth Grey."

"She is very attractive; what does she want with the king?"

Hastings straightened his ruffled collar and continued along the corridor, but Philip followed, pressing him for an answer.

"Why is she here?"

"Edward desires her."

"Edward desires every woman."

"He holds this one in high esteem, though she is ambiguous."

"Then he is a fool to pursue such a creature. Give her to me and she'll mew like a kitten."

"Don't let the king hear you," he warned. "I'll order an apartment prepared…"

"No, my lord, I'll not tarry in this place, 'tis better for me to go, lest I wake to find a traitor's blade poised over my heart… as I did at Woodstock."

Grateful for his decision to leave, Hastings made no effort to change his mind.

Heading across the muddy palace yard, they made their way to the stables. While Philip waited for his horse to be brought out, Hastings informed him of Warwick's desire for the king to marry a French princess. Philip laughed at his suggestion, but Hastings retained his equanimity and the laughter tailed off.

"I don't believe it."

"Why would I lie?"

Philip draped the cloak around his shoulders and pulled on his riding gloves.

"What of Burgundy? Does my cousin abandon his allies as easily as he abandons his friends?" he asked.

"He seeks to keep our allies, but to deny Henry and Margaret theirs."

"Does Edward believe Louis will honour a truce with the House of York?"

"Edward is willing to pay any price to keep Louis and Henry apart."

"I fought the frogs; they will never reconcile with an English King who claims sovereignty over a single acre of French soil!" Philip declared agitated by the chamberlain's confirmation of what he already knew.

"Edward is looking to the future, dear friend."

"What future is there for us with a French alliance?" he lamented. "And don't call me friend; you who took away that which was dearer to me than life."

Hastings heard of Philip's affiliation with Elizabeth Percy from courtly gossip, but did not believe it. Only now, when it was too late, did he understand. Silently cursing Warwick for his connivance in the affair, he lamented his part in Philip's misfortune.

"I have done what I have done for my King; should he command my life I would gladly offer it," he said bravely.

"Why not make that offer now?" Philip scowled, clipping the cloak beneath his neck and mounting. "One day you and I will meet in the lists," he warned, jerking the reins hard and turning his horse toward the palace gates, "until that day?"

Stung by the threat, Hastings stared at the bad tempered knight until he galloped out through the gatehouse.

"Have a care Philip Neville, you have more lives than a cat," he muttered, "but they're running out fast."

Chapter 9

Oblivious to the cold wind blowing into his exposed face, Philip cantered quickly along King Street in defiance of Edward's order. His destination was Baynard's Castle, the home of Edward's mother, the Grand Duchess of York. More a palatial residence than a castle, Baynard's stood between Thames Street and the north bank of the river, and was dominated by its tall waterfront towers. As the result of a devastating fire over thirty years before, an expensive rebuilding programme had enhanced Baynard's appearance and desirability.

The short journey from Westminster took Philip through the Liberty of the Savoy, under Temple Bar, over the odorous Fleet River and into London via Ludgate. As his palfrey's iron hooves echoed beneath Ludgates' Romanesque archway, he had second thoughts. Pulling back on the reins, he sat and pondered before digging in his spurs and steering the horse along Bower Rowe. Turning right before St Paul's, he cut down through a network of narrow streets, skirted a drunken brawl in Carter Lane, and turned south into Thames Street. Ignoring the traders, and several indolent guards on duty at the entrance to Baynard's, he dismounted in the courtyard. Jerking back his cloak, he handed the reins to a stableboy and made for the private apartments. At first he was refused admission by an inflexible guard, but the man was forced to swallow his pride when a maidservant leaned out of an upstairs window and ordered him to step aside.

"Come up to my lady's chamber!" she yelled at Philip, who cringed as her husky voice grated on his frozen ears.

Hurrying inside and up the stone steps, he knocked lightly against the door to Lady Cecily's private rooms and wondered how she knew he was coming. Removing his hat, he spat on his hands, flattened his hair and waited, his heart pounding at the thought of seeing Elizabeth again.

"Entrée."

Exasperated by the heavy, damp cloak constantly

slipping off his shoulder, he yanked it back and twisted the iron ring.

"Who is it?" Lady Cecily asked, squinting at the shadow standing in the doorway.

"'Tis me my lady, Philip," he announced, bowing graciously, "Philip Neville."

"Nephew? What a surprise, Sarah said we had a visitor."

Surrounded by four of her ladies-in-waiting, seated on the carpeted floor beside her chair, 'Proud Cis' pressed her face to within an inch of her embroidery loom and sewed off a short length of thread. Her ladies, meanwhile, acknowledged the caller with coy nods and flirtatious smirks. Looking at each of their pretty faces, he frowned at Elizabeth's absence.

As they continued to scrutinize him, he tried to ignore them. Under their intimidating analysis he could do little but stand red-faced, knees atremble.

"Well, are you going to speak or must I guess why you have come?" Cecily asked, tying off the wool and pushing her loom away.

One of her ladies covered the lower part of her face with a funnel sleeve and whispered to the others, and Philip knew his discomfort had tickled her. His mouth dried, his cheek twitched, and the urge to bolt for the door was strong; fortunately his aunt came to the rescue. With a sharp clap of her hands, she dismissed her giggling ladies. Rising delicately, they placed their sewing down on a low table and glided into an antechamber, smiling and curtsying as they passed the flushed knight.

"Ladies," he mumbled, jerking his head as he tried to salve his injured pride.

"These noble daughters act like children every time we get a male visitor," she said.

After the death of her husband, at Wakefield, the Duchess of York took an obsessive interest in her son's kingship. It was said she ruled Edward, and on occasion, would scold him mercilessly. In her late fifties, Cecily's days were dominated by a series of staid prayer sessions and long walks. She often lived with Edward, offering advice and maintaining a cheerful sense of humour, though she would not suffer fools. Attired in a long, black mourning dress, she addressed the son of her dead brother with heartfelt joy.

"My eyes are not so good, come closer so I can see you."

Philip obeyed and she reached out to touch his gloved hand. "You are like your father," she smiled. "He was my favourite, and I miss him. How are my dear sister-in-law, and your brothers?"

"Mother is in good health and Thomas, Thomas is Thomas," he grinned, kissing her hand and trying not to look at the faint hairs protruding from her chin. "I've heard nothing of Michael since Towton."

"And William…?"

"Who?"

"You heard," she frowned, "William Beaufort is nothing like his brother, or his nephew. He has no lust for power and he loves your mother, you should be happy for her."

Philip glanced out of the window at the churning River Thames below, and sniffed.

A shrewd woman, Lady Cecily sensed his hostility. She knew he detested his stepfather and spoke no more of him.

Removing his gloves and cloak, he draped them over a large, painted chest, close to the fireplace.

"You have not come to visit me, have you?" she asked, tucking several loose strands of grey, brittle hair behind her ears. "Why are you here?"

Philip knew better than to lie and bent down to examine the colourful, unfinished lion and unicorn figures, sewn on her loom.

"I would speak with one of your ladies," he said, turning to rest his arms on the dressed stone mantle above the fireplace, allowing the heat to warm his legs.

"One of *my* ladies?"

"Yes."

"Which one?"

"Elizabeth," he said clearly, before mumbling her full name, "Elizabeth Percy."

Raising her thin eyebrows, she stared at his back.

"For what purpose?"

Philip's courage evaporated and he struggled to answer.

"You must have a reason?" she pressed, puzzled by his silence.

Shifting his attention to the flames dancing in the grate, he failed to come up with a rational answer.

"Philip, if you wish to talk to me have the courtesy to look at me."

"I cannot say," he mumbled, glancing over his shoulder.

Cecily Neville was well aware of the gossip permeating the corridors of Baynard's Castle. Since Elizabeth's clandestine arrival in November, the rumours of a Neville falling for a Percy were rampant. Philip's demeanour told her they were more than just rumours.

"The Percy girl was brought here in great secrecy," she revealed, urging him to sit. "I did not want her here, but my son insisted," she continued, dabbing her grey, watery eyes with a handcoverchief.

"Is she within these walls?" he asked, indicating a preference to remain standing.

"Yes, but you must forget her, she is promised to another."

"Ralph Hastings," he simmered, the pinkish glow in his cheeks becoming stronger.

"Yes."

"Hastings," he repeated with a guttural growl.

"That family has done well by my son," she revealed, drawing her loom closer and squinting, as she tried to rethread the needle, "though I have some influence over Edward, I cannot always be with him."

"Why does he pursue this policy of gratifying knaves and traitors?"

"There are many fools in high places, but not all are as foolish as they seem," she exclaimed, stabbing the wool at the needle. "My son has his father's strength, but lacks his ruthlessness. Perhaps that'll come in time."

"Perhaps," Philip sighed, observing her feeble attempts to thread the wool, and shaking his head impatiently.

"Permit me," he offered, taking the needle from her and rethreading the wool. "I must go now."

"But you've only just arrived," she gasped., "Stay a little longer, we have much to talk about…"

"I cannot, I have a long journey ahead of me," he explained, passing her the threaded needle. "The king has ordered me north," he said, retrieving his cloak and gloves, before kissing the back of her heavily freckled hand.

"The weather is not fit for travelling."

"I'm staying at 'Le Erber' tonight," he said, referring to Warwick's great house off Dowgate Street, close to St Mary's Bothaw.

"Do you have funds?"

"Yes my lady," he fibbed; too embarrassed to tell her he was almost penniless.

"Then God speed you on your way."

"Farwell my lady," he bowed, closing the door behind him.

Lady Cecily shook her head expressively before returning to her loom.

Outside the apartment Philip waited, scanning the dimly lit passage in both directions. He hated to deceive his aunt, but he had no intention of leaving, not yet.

Philip came to Baynard's several times, when his Uncle Richard was in residence, but his unfamiliarity with the place confused him. Hesitant on which route to take, he could only guess where Elizabeth might be. Making his way along the dark, narrow corridor, illuminated by an occasional flambeau, he walked to the end and turned a corner. Coming across a spiral stairwell that disappeared down into the blackness of a lower floor, he stared into the coiling abyss. The aroma of freshly baked bread hit his nostrils and he released a gratifying groan, for he not eaten since breakfast. Miffed at reaching a dead end, he was about to retrace his steps when something made him stop. From beyond a tiny, arched door came the faint sound of feminine laughter. Resting an ear against the woodwork, he held his breath and listened.

At first there was silence, then a muffled giggle. Stepping back, he rapped his knuckles against the oak door. Receiving no response he struck harder and the patter of approaching footsteps made him step back. Seconds later a young maiden cracked the door open.

"Yes?" she scowled tersely, annoyed at the interruption.

Ignoring her blatant disapproval, Philip pushed his way in, deliberately squeezing past, the feel of her shapely body against his pleasant. When he saw Elizabeth Percy, seated on a low cushioned seat, his hostility withered. Her sweet concerned face forced his anger into retreat and the infatuation he once felt for her, bubbled to the surface.

"Philip!" she gasped, trying to make sense of his presence, while the book on her lap slipped to the floor.

He tried to believe that she was not to blame, but her wide eyes, quivering mouth and rigid posture, contradicted his logic.

"You are not permitted in here sir knight," the girl holding the door hissed, peeping out into the passage, before slamming it shut and wincing at the deafening bang.

"Hold your tongue," he commanded, without taking his eyes off Elizabeth.

"Hold my tongue," she blurted, putting a hand to her chest in exaggerated shock.

"Oh do shut up Catherine," Elizabeth groaned, turning to Philip. "Why have you come?"

"A strange welcome," he responded, "I want to know why you betrayed me... you to whom I spoke from the heart and hoped, one day, to marry. I deceived my family for you."

"Forgive me," she said softly, looking guiltily at the floor.

Rather than allow her shame to cause further embarrassment, Elizabeth ordered her companion to leave. The girl sullenly made her way to an anteroom, deliberately avoiding eye contact with the intimidating visitor.

Philip knew pleading would be useless, besides he was not one to beg, so he made up his mind to say what he had to say and leave.

"When I first saw you, you kindled a flame in my heart that I believed would last forever. Now that flame has gone out," he said, coldly, the memory of their last kiss, re-awakening the tingling sensation that left his lips sensitive for days. "And for what?" he sneered, shaking the blissful memory from his mind, "for Ralph Hastings?"

Elizabeth rose slowly and Philip couldn't help but admire her beauty. As she stood, the material of her pale, green dress clung to her body, and he remembered their intimate moments together. The fragrance of her rose water and lavender scent filled the room with a sweetness so overpowering, his emotions unravelled. If only he had defied his King and kept the rendezvous at Breckles Miln, or stolen her away from his cousin at Alnwick. He wanted to take her in his arms, but a sense of betrayal dominated and he lashed out with a verbal assault against her fiancé.

"Ralph Hastings!" he repeated, "that dancing bag of bones, that craven milksop, who grovelled with his brothers before Henry at Ludlow, begging for mercy! That gutless piece of…"

Distressed by his malicious outburst, she drew back fearfully. Sensing her anguish he ceased his fervent tirade and rubbed his face irritably. Elizabeth edged toward him, but he shied away.

"This is not my fault," she bemoaned. "My father and uncle are dead; my cousin is a prisoner, and my brother has fled to France. I am a pawn, to be used by powerful men as they see fit. The king has ordered this marriage."

Her plea revoked Philip's inflexibility, and his outrage mellowed. The urge to take her in his arms almost drove him insane, but pride held him back.

"But you are pre-contracted."

"Oh Philip, we were swept up in a wave of romantic ideals. We exchanged words in a field... there were no witnesses. We promised ourselves to each other... I am being forced into this," she whined, "by your cousins."

"Words?" he gasped, "mere words!"

Suddenly he had a thought, irrational in its inception, but one he believed might resolve the issue.

"Come with me now," he whispered; his heart pounding as he grabbed her hands and looked pleadingly into her eyes. "We will ride to the coast and take ship for Burgundy. I'll offer Philip my sword and we can live out our days..."

Her demeanour suddenly changed, but not in the way he expected. Breaking from his grip she shied away.

"No, I will not. The king commanded this marriage," she snapped, "Burgundy would turn us over to Edward the moment we stepped ashore."

Philip knew he had made a fool of himself and his face flushed with embarrassment. The look of abhorrence in her eyes answered the question that had nagged him for days. Fighting to regain his self-esteem, he wanted to cut her throat, but decided against such a radical course. Warwick and the king's chamberlain were to blame, or were they? Perhaps it was his fault. Had he been more forceful none of this would be happening, but her reaction obliged him to reconsider her avowal of innocence.

"The king cannot force you to wed. Tell him you are pre-contracted to another."

Her stony silence gave him his answer.

"Does Ralph Hastings know it was I who took your maidenhood?" he snarled, pacing to and fro, as hope turned to despair. "And if you marry him, I shall reveal it to the world!"

Hurt by the threat, Elizabeth was about to plead for his

silence, but decided against it. Smashing a cupboard with his fist, he turned and walked to the door.

"I hope I never see your face again," he snarled, before leaving.

Shaken by his parting caveat, she slumped into a chair and wept. Despite everything, she still held an emotional attachment.

Outside the apartment, Philip leaned against the wall and closed his eyes. Moulding his hands into fists, he squeezed so hard his body shook with rage, and the cloak slipped from his shoulder. With the pain of rejection stabbing deep into his heart, he yanked the cloak aggressively back in place.

"Dear Lord in heaven, have I sinned so much that you take from me the most precious thing in the world?" he moaned.

Lady Cecily presumed her nephew would not leave until he found what he came for. When her maidservant finally saw him scuffing his feet across the wet courtyard, she informed her mistress. Cecily sighed and continued with her sewing. Reaching his horse, Philip sensed he was being watched and looked back, forcing the maid to jump back from the window. Pulling on his riding gloves, he snatched the reins from the stableboy and hoisted himself into the saddle. With a last look at the second floor windows, he wheeled his horse to the right and cantered out of Baynard's Castle.

Taking the route up to the west of St Paul's Cathedral and the Bishop of London's palace, Philip had no intention of lodging at 'Le Erber'. Manoeuvring his palfrey along the loosely-gravelled Pater Noster Row, he turned into Panyar Alley, which led to Aldersgate via St Martins Lane. Once through the gatehouse he headed for Barnet and the Great North Road.

The ride to York was cold, miserable and thought provoking. A complex jumble of emotions, ranging from self-loathing to murderous jealousy, tormented him throughout the journey. Finally after ten days, he drew up before the Micklegate; its snow-capped battlements still bearing the lop-sided skulls of executed Lancastrian nobles. With the war far to the north, the people of York felt secure and during the day the gates were left open, allowing travellers and tradesmen unrestricted ingress and egress.

"We're almost home," Philip told his weary horse, gently jabbing its flanks with his spurs. The animal reacted to his tone and the stinging pain by trotting quickly through the inner gates and down Micklegate. Near the church of St Martins-Cum-Gregory, Philip failed to notice a clutch of Benedictine nuns from the Clementhorpe Nunnery, crossing the street. Forced to speed up, the nuns were not impressed by Philip's unchivalrous manners. Unable to see their exasperated faces due to the bindaes covering their heads, he bowed apologetically from the saddle and continued down to the River Ouze. When he reached the apex of the hump-backed bridge, an icy blast hit the back of his neck. Glancing over his shoulder he watched the sun drop behind the city wall and shivered.

"Brrrr... that felt like the devil'S hand," he told his horse, ducking his neck down inside the collar.

Finally trotting into the dark courtyard of Claremont Hall, Philip released a grateful sigh. Before he could dismount, the front door swung open and Gilbert, the spotty-faced servant who helped Michael escape from York after Towton, appeared holding a bronze lantern and a cudgel.

"Who's there?" the nervous teenager demanded, aiming a weak triangle of light into the courtyard.

There was no response so Gilbert raised the lantern and his weapon, and tried to make out the shadowy figure.

"Who is it?" he demanded, his voice both threatening and scared.

"Is thy mistress at home?" Philip growled.

Gilbert aimed the open side of the lantern up at the rider, and its feeble light revealed a grim, darkly bearded face.

"Master?" he questioned, not totally convinced.

"Calm thyself," Philip sighed, "It's me."

"Master!" he gasped.

"Where is my mother?" Philip pressed, perturbed by the servant's spineless manner.

"She's gone tah Seward House with Master Tom," he said, greatly relieved, "'tis only Arthur and me here."

"Where are my men?"

"Master Robert sent them tah their homes. He and Ashley are with Lady Joan. Arbroth, Dan'l and tha servants are at tha Talbot's."

"Good." He smiled.

"One of Lord Somerset's men came and told Sir William you was safe," Gilbert explained, lowering his head shamefully for daring to mention that name which Philip detested.

With his breath billowing white in the cold evening air, Philip asked Gilbert if he knew anything of Michael's whereabouts. The shivering servant drew his lank hair away from his spotty forehead.

"Scotland," he announced

"With his stepfather?"

Gilbert gave a grudging nod.

"I'm on my way to the Talbot's. I shall stay at Neville's Inn tonight. Send my clothes there."

The teenager acknowledged he understood by tapping his head, and Philip disappeared into the night. Moving with a tremulous gait and snorting raggedly, Philip's horse became a cause for concern. Dismounting, he stroked the palfrey's sweaty neck and ran his hands up and down its forelegs looking for signs of injury. The animal appeared sound, but he decided to spare the beast by walking the short distance to the Talbot town house, in Stonegate. Turning into Colliergate, Philip noticed a stark difference since his last visit. York had become a centre for the dispossessed. Hundreds of families – their husbands, fathers or sons killed in battle –filled the streets, seeking shelter and solace. Philip felt sorry for the numerous maimed soldiers loafing around. Having lost a limb, or two, been blinded, or gone insane, they propped themselves up against the shops, begging for food. He detested the abuse they received from children who knew no better.

"The king should come here," he muttered to his horse, tossing several coins onto a bundle of rags, "and see this travesty."

An emaciated hand emerged, grabbed the money and disappeared back inside. The influx of so many impoverished souls was a heavy burden on a city struggling to cope with high taxes, introduced to sustain the Yorkist war effort.

Aiming for the Minster church, Philip continued along Lower Petergate, glancing up at the gabled timber and plaster houses, jutting out over the street from both sides. A vile odour of rotting vegetation hung in the air like a noxious fog, and the lamentations of the poor echoed loudly. Near the intersection with Grape Lane – a narrow, dark thoroughfare, overgrown with bushes and stinking of urine – he was accosted by several prostitutes vying for business.

"Get back to the pox-ridden stews you were spawned from!" he snapped, physically pushing one of them away.

"That's no way tah treat a lady, mah lord," one buxom wench scowled, lifting her tatty dress above her knees. "Fancy dipping yer lance in 'ere, it won't cost thee much... mah wool is as soft as duck down!"

"I wouldn't let my horse have you, you rancid harlot!" he rasped, as a squealing pig darted between his feet, causing him to slip on the slimy gutter.

Regaining his composure, he dragged his horse away, while the whore's contemptuous laughter echoed in his ears.

The Talbot town house lay behind a narrow row of shops at the end of a lane, off Stonegate. Leading his palfrey into the courtyard, its shoes clattering loudly on the cobbles, he forced the stubborn animal into the stables with a sharp slap on the rump. Whinnying defiantly the horse trotted in, and Philip spotted Clovis. Squeezing past he stroked his velvety face.

"Hello old friend," he smiled, patting his neck.

The palfrey nodded and Philip left.

Walking to the front of the house, he removed his gloves and ran a tacky palm through the thick hair covering his chin. Snorting back a gobbet of phlegm, he made a fist and thumped the door several times.

A key rattled in the lock, the door swung open and his senses were swamped by the pleasant aroma of roasting pork and wood smoke. Philip offered the perturbed servant a cordial nod, but his frosty manner irritated, and he pushed him aside before crossing the threshold and following the sound of friendly laughter.

The Talbot house was a modest two-story, stone and timber abode, with low beamed ceilings. The downstairs rooms were filled with tapestries, paintings and religious icons, and lit by several iron chandeliers hanging from the beams. Despite its cluttered interior, the house exuded an unpretentious homeliness. Calling his friend by name, Philip was greeted with a stony silence followed by the sound of chairs scraping against wooden floor.

"Dan?" he questioned, catching sight of a face poking out from behind a door and disappearing.

"Sir?" his groom responded, sticking his head out a second time.

"'Tis good to see you," Philip grinned, removing his hat and cloak. "Unsaddle my horse and rub him down, and when you've finished, remove the bridle and blanket from Clovis. Who said you could ride him?"

"He needed exercise," Daniel explained.

"Then take him out. Don't ride him through the streets… is Francis home?"

"I am!" came the cheerful response from a room opposite. "I told them to leave your horse until they'd eaten. Come on through!"

Daniel dropped his playing cards and fell over himself to carry out Philip's orders, while the Talbot men laughed at his enthusiasm.

"Take a look at his forelegs!" Philip said as an afterthought. "I want him in good shape when he's returned to my cousin."

Stepping down into the small dining area, its shuttered windows closed against the elements, a gentle rush of warm air hit Philip's frozen face, and he was overcome with exhaustion.

"Francis," he smiled jadedly, taking his extended hand, "and Lady Margaret! 'Tis a long time since we met," he added, kissing her warm cheek. "You must forgive me, I've been in the saddle nine days, or is it ten?" he pondered, scratching his itchy neck, while Francis motioned for him to sit.

"Yes, the days pass so quickly," Lady Margaret agreed."

Short, plump and ten years older than her husband, Margaret's bright eyes, tiny mouth and deep dimples, gave her a pleasant, maternal appearance. Despite failing to produce any children, Francis loved her. He cherished her attributes; honesty, piety, rationale and a passion for all God's creatures. With never an ill thought for anyone, it was said Margaret Talbot could see goodness in the devil himself.

Easing his chafed backside gently onto the cushioned bench, Philip leaned back against the cold wall, and every bone in his body ached.

"You have my gratitude for taking care of my men," he said, his stomach gurgling in anticipation of food. "Is Arbroth here?"

"He's visiting a friend, at St Leonard's," Francis said, referring to the great hospital next to St Mary's Abbey, as he poured his friend a cup of warm mead sweetened with honey. "Have you been home?"

"Home, you mean the home of William Beaufort," he scoffed, instantly regretting his unwarranted rudeness.

"I prayed for you," Margaret admitted, ascribing Philip's antagonism to his mounting misfortune, "and God has answered my prayers."

"Since we heard of your escape and arrest, we have been much concerned," Francis revealed.

"Somerset has vilified my name with his lies," he retorted angrily.

"The king knows the truth," Lady Margaret said, deciding to withdraw. "I will leave you to talk."

"She's a good wife," Philip nodded, rising to his feet, as Margaret attempted to disguise her limp, the legacy of a childhood accident. "I have been on the road for more than a week with only my horse for company," he groaned, flopping back down, as raging pain shot up and down his spine, forcing him to constantly shift position.

"'Tis time you were married," Francis decreed. "You need a good woman."

Philip thought of his encounter with Elizabeth and clenched his fists until the knuckles almost burst through the skin. Francis knew at once that he had touched upon an inviolable subject. The tension broke when a servant came from the kitchen bearing a bread trencher filled with pork, carrots, leeks and onions, and placed it before Philip.

"A good woman," he scoffed. "Does such a thing exist in this world?"

"What has made thee so bitter?" Francis asked, concerned.

"I'm tired," he sighed, "oh the injustice of it all."

The aromatic flavour, steaming off the stew, sweetened Philip's senses and he attacked the trencher like a ravenous wolf. Between mouthfuls he unfolded the story of his secret affair with Elizabeth Percy, of her presence at Alnwick, and engagement to Ralph Hastings. This poignant tale spilled over into another concerning the king's complacency, which blended with Philip's grudge against William Hastings. Guzzling several cups of clarry, he talked of his adventures after Woodstock, and the aspirations of his cousin, Warwick.

The conversation continued long into the wintry night, with Philip gaining his second wind after more wine. Scrutinizing Francis's expressions, he felt ready to test his sincerity. As the last of the food was eaten, Francis indicated for a waiting servant to remove the bone box and clear the table.

Certain he could trust the nephew of the late Lord Talbot, Philip rinsed his hands in a bowl of scented water and spoke of his anxiety concerning Somerset's fidelity.

"I know he is just waiting for an opportunity to turn his coat, again."

"Perhaps he has changed," Francis replied, the duke's machinations at Woodstock fresh in his mind, "such a thing is possible."

"No, Somerset will lick the king's arse forever and a day, but in the end he will bite it."

"That may be, but Edward will not tolerate any criticism against him."

"They have become too close," Philip sighed, his glowing face twisting into a grimace, as he stared at Francis, but he was looking beyond his friend now, at something only he could see.

I wonder what twisted thoughts are bouncing around inside that mind Francis pondered, resting his pronounced chin in his palm, concerned by Philip's smouldering gaze.

Leaning across the table, Philip cupped a hand to his mouth and spoke softly.

"The bond between Somerset and Edward must be broken or we'll all suffer the consequences."

"Somerset will not break his oath of fealty," Talbot said firmly, disturbed by his malevolent tone. "Henry of Lancaster is finished and he knows it, or he would never have come over to us."

"Then someone else must do it," Philip whispered portentously.

Francis felt a sudden shiver run down his back. Observing Francis's apprehension, Philip yawned heavily and sat back.

"It is late... we shall talk on the morrow," he groaned, "when my mind is not so befuddled by wine."

"Yes," Francis half smiled. "You must spend the night here?"

"I cannot, my clothes have been sent to Neville's Inn."

"No, dear friend, while you ate, I sent one of my servant's to fetch your clothes," he grinned. "Margaret has prepared a room; you cannot disappoint her, besides you won't be welcome at Neville's Inn."

Philip knew he was right; Neville's Inn belonged to the Earl of Westmorland. Though related, that branch of the Neville family sided with Lancaster. After Towton their property in York was seized, but many of the old staff retained.

"I accept your offer," he yawned gratefully, while a servant held a candle, ready to escort him to his bedchamber, "goodnight."

"Goodnight," Francis answered, pondering his friend's unorthodox proposal.

Philip woke at dawn, to the first bell of the day ringing out from the Minster. Rubbing his watery eyes he lay on his back, regretting his late-night exchange with Francis. Too much wine mingled with good food, exhaustion, and the comfort of a warm fire, encouraged him to speak from the heart. Snorting to clear his throat, he cursed his inability to keep his gob shut. Stretching all four limbs and yawning made his joints ache, and he moaned. With a bladder on the point of bursting, Philip struck steel to flint and lit the deformed tallow candle perched on a stool. Rolling off the bed, he reached for the pot, pulled down his braies and ecstatically relieved the agony in his groin. Touching his left shoulder, he traced the hard, raised scar with a forefinger. The psychological pain of that day returned and he winced, before pushing the pot back under his bed, and shuffling over to the table in front of the window.

Plunging his hands into a bowl of icy water, Philip drew the liquid swiftly to his face. The freezing water hit his half-closed eyes and coursed down through his beard.

"By all the saints!" he shivered, damping his hair and using a piece of rag, dipped in sage and salt, to clean his teeth.

Reaching for the window, he drew the wooden shutters open, wiped frost from the glass and peered out at the darkness.

"I can't see a thing," he moaned.

Opening the chest, brought from Claremont Hall, he perused the contents by candlelight.

Limited for choice, he chose a satin shirt, covered by a short, high collared, black quilted doublet, with slashed wrist-length sleeves. Thick, black woollen hose, a leather belt, with sheathed ballock dagger and high boots were also picked out. Glancing at his distorted reflection in a hand mirror, Philip chuckled at his roguish appearance. As he left the room, he scratched his hairy chin and decided to find a barber.

Near the top of the stairs, he noticed a dim light flickering behind a curtain. Curiously dragging the heavy material aside he saw Lady Margaret kneeling before a small alter table, praying to a portrait of the Virgin Mary. Conscious of her privacy, he lowered the curtain and tip-toed downstairs.

Breakfast took place shortly before seven, and in almost complete silence. Francis seemed agitated and Philip assumed he must have spoken to his wife. Something was on his mind for his eyes rarely left his plate, but the urge to press him was curbed by Margaret's presence. Philip's chance came when she excused herself and hobbled to the kitchen.

"The cold weather causes her leg much distress," Francis sighed, watching her.

Licking his spoon, Philip placed it deliberately beside the pewter plate and rested his elbows on the table.

"Did you get your appointment?" he asked, his breath causing a cluster of candles on the table to flicker.

"Appointment?"

"You were seeking a position in the king's household."

"No," Talbot shook his head. "When I left you at Woodstock I was forbidden to see the king, but I must speak with him soon, my family is in need of funds." He frowned, pensively chewing a piece of bread.

"Have you thought more on what we spoke of last night?"

"No, I'm not sure I understood?"

Philip sat back and stared thoughtfully at his food.

"We must sever the bond between the king and Somerset."

"Do you have a plan?"

"Not yet."

"How many are involved in this… conspiracy?" Francis whispered, glancing over his shoulder, lest Margaret or one of the servants should hear.

"Only one… this must be kept between us, not even your good wife will know."

"Alas, I cannot be part of such a plot," Francis announced, shaking his head.

"But…" Philip gasped, shocked by his rejection. "I…"

"Fear not, I will never betray thee," he promised, placing a finger to his lips and lowering his voice further. "Do what you must but I cannot be involved. What will become of Margaret if we are discovered? I'm all she has. I beg you not to do this; give him the time and Somerset will dig his own grave."

Philip took a mouthful of bread, looked down and chewed slowly.

"Many old enemies seek to reconcile with the king," Francis declared, wiping his hands in a surnape. "Perhaps it is a good thing."

"Yes, Edward is afloat in a sea of old enemies and who is there to prevent him from drowning. Somerset," he scowled, "whose only loyalty is to the gold in his purse?"

"As it is for many," Francis affirmed.

"The king should not have sent me away," Philip lamented, taking a swig of wine and staring at the table.

With Francis out of the equation, Philip would have to deal with the Duke of Somerset on his own; a prospect that caused him grave concerns.

Chapter 10

Having failed to secure Francis Talbot's support to discredit Somerset, Philip forgot about the duke for the time. After paying a visit to his mother at Seward House, he left York on St Valentine's Day 1463, and rode to Sheriff Hutton. With Warwick away attending the reburial of his parents and brother, he put aside his animosity. At the end of March, Philip returned to York, where a visit by his stepfather angered him to such an extent he threatened to expose him. Philip's indignation was only mollified by his mother's empathetic voice urging him to say nothing for fear of harming the innocent. Taking Clovis from the stables, he bade his mother adieu, ignored Sir William, and rode to Sheriff Hutton, picking up his retainers en route.

While awaiting Warwick's return, Philip utilized the time by improving his esquire's swordsmanship. The nights, he spent whoring with a serving girl whose lame husband was in a constant drunken stupor. With his armour polished, swords sharpened and horses rested, Philip could do nothing but wait. Such a hiatus was dangerous for a man with so much on his mind. The few nights he was alone, he would lie in bed, concocting plans to bring down the Duke of Somerset; some feasible, others idiotic.

By early June, Warwick was back in the north, but at Middleham Castle, over forty miles west of Sheriff Hutton. Twenty-four hours after his return, a frantic messenger arrived bearing grave news. Ralph Percy had turned his coat and surrendered Bamburgh to Margaret without a fight. Dunstanburgh Castle quickly followed and, on 1 May Warwick's friend, Sir Ralph Grey, treacherously lowered Alnwick's drawbridge to the queen. Warwick's biggest headache was Newcastle, which had come under siege from a Lancaster-Scottish army. He immediately dispatched couriers with orders for his knights, retainers and tenants to rendezvous at Middleham.

The messenger sent to Sheriff Hutton found Philip in

the courtyard talking to Emma, the attractive, twenty-year-old redhead he'd been bedding. Warwick's unexpected return forced Philip to abandon his whimsical plans for Somerset's downfall, but the prospect of a fight buoyed his spirits. While he scanned the note from Middleham, Emma wrapped an arm through his and snuggled up close.

"Leave me," he commanded irritably, continuing to read.

She ignored his sharp tone and held on.

"Go to your husband," he snapped, pushing the clingy serving girl away.

"I'll go with you," she smiled. "I can cook and…"

"Your husband needs you more than I do…"

"My husband has his ale," she parried, her smile waning. "You told me you wanted me."

"I did, but now I am tired of you."

She touched his hand and he pulled it back as if she were a leper.

"I have debased myself," she hissed, half in anger, half in regret.

"Did I complain?" he asked impassively, "Did you?"

"Yes every time you called me…" she responded, turning aside, "but I put up with it because…"

"And I put up with your whining."

Choking with heartache, Emma tearfully fled to the kitchen, to hide her shame.

"Pack everything up and get ready to leave!" he yelled aggressively at his men, who stood pretending not to be listening.

Philip took no pleasure in openly abandoning Emma; after all she was good in bed, but with his men watching he dare not show weakness.

A small column of six retainers, four servants, twelve horses and a cart full of the accoutrements of war, was soon bouncing along the well-rutted road to Middleham.

"Mah Lord, ye have broken her heart," Arbroth said, riding beside his master.

"I did no more than beat her wool; there was no love in

it," he scoffed trying to convince himself. "Though her body was soft and her cunnis tasted sweeter than vernage wine."

"She loves you."

"A young woman's fantasy."

Arbroth faced front, but his wry smile spoke volumes.

"What?" Philip snapped.

"Nothing, mah lord."

Since the previous summer, Philip and Richard Neville rode together chasing Lancastrians and besieging their castles, but they had grown apart. The trust that existed for more than sixteen years had been replaced by suspicion and hostility. Philip would never forgive Richard for the way he revealed his affair with Elizabeth Percy, or for sending her to London. Lord Fauconberg made light of their childish mood swings, and his jovial down-to-earth temperament held their fragile personalities in check. When he died suddenly, there was no one to assume his sagacious mantle, and the rift between Warwick and Philip widened. Disagreements flared over the most trivial of matters, but when it came to serious fighting, they put aside their differences.

When Philip and his small band arrived before the magnificent castle of Middleham, in Richmondshire, they found the army marching out through the East Gatehouse and down the winding slope to the village. In company with his standard-bearer, and a dozen mounted knights and esquires, the Earl of Warwick trotted alongside his billmen, acknowledging those he knew by name. Spotting his cousin waiting to join the column, he nodded curtly before cantering to the front. Put out by this brusque welcome, Philip ordered his men to merge in.

Accompanying the Earl of Warwick was the king's youngest brother, Richard of Gloucester. Philip first met the young duke at Edward's coronation, and spent the winter of 1461-62, helping to hone his martial skills. Spotting the eleven year old riding alone several horse-lengths behind Warwick, he joined him and they conversed amiably. For Philip the terse encounter with his young cousin concealed an ulterior motive; he badly needed an ally at court, someone he could trust. The dark-haired adolescent came over as virtuous, honest and loyal to his family; though candid in his opinion of those he did not favour. Despite the disparity in their ages they got on well, until Warwick, concerned by their familiarity, sent a message for Philip to join him at the front.

The journey to Newcastle was as rapid as the slowest wagon. When the column crossed the Tyne Bridge and approached the buff-coloured, twenty-five feet high sandstone wall encircling the town, two men rode out through a postern gate in the south curtain wall. Dressed in Montague's red and black livery, they cantered down the hill waving their arms.

"My lord!" one of the horsemen began excitedly. "Lord Montague has saved us."

"When the enemy learned of his coming they abandoned their camps and fled," the second rider added.

"Fair news indeed," Warwick smiled, looking at Philip, who lowered his head disappointedly.

When they heard Warwick was close, the Lancastrian retreat turned into a race for the border, which did not stop until the Tweed was in sight. With safety so close they laid siege to Norham Castle, until recently, the Episcopal estate of Laurence Booth, Bishop of Durham.

At a council of war held in a humble tavern outside Newcastle, Warwick, Montague, young Gloucester and a dozen others were seated around a rough trestle table, too small to accommodate them all comfortably. The Earl, unusually, called for suggestions but none of his subordinates dared tender an opinion. With no one willing to speak up, Philip rose slowly from his stool and proposed crossing the Tweed. Warwick folded his arms across his chest and leaned his seat back against the rough stone wall. He guessed his impulsive cousin might suggest such a plan, but allowed him to continue.

"We must invade Scotland, only by burning and

pillaging the lowlands will we eliminate the threat to our border," Philip said enthusiastically, looking to end the year with a significant victory that he was part of. "Northumberland will never be at peace as long as we remain on our side of the Tweed. We must finish this once and for all," he ended, sitting down and looking smugly at the council for support, while the innkeeper and his plump wife went round the table filling a collection of poor quality cups with tepid ale.

Warwick refused the drink and stared at his brother Montague, who sat nodding his support for Philip's plan, while murmurs of approval were bandied across the table.

"Ah Philip: invade Scotland," he frowned, shaking his head. "It is that simple… and John, you of all people?"

"My lords, we are bound to Scotland by a truce," the young Sir William Stanley interjected, delicately stroking his goatee.

"There are more than a hundred Scots in the dungeons of Newcastle," Montague parried, sweat dripping from his chin, "taken in arms against us; so much for a truce."

"We should honour no agreement with those who shelter our enemies, my lord," Philip argued. "The Scots raid our villages, burn our crops and flee back across the border… we should teach them a lesson they'll never forget."

"No!" Warwick yelled banging his chair down heavily. "The king's council voted for an invasion of Scotland, but Edward overturned that decision after I left London."

The room went silent. Montague and Philip were dumbfounded and everyone waited for an explanation.

"And who was responsible for that?" Montague growled.

"Who do you think?"

"Hastings," Philip muttered, as if a bad taste had been excreted into his mouth.

"Yes Hastings, and Somerset, and all who sit safely at court. My hands are tied."

"But you have the king's authority to protect the border

by any means," Montague frowned, baffled by his brother's lack of enterprise.

"I have no power to march onto foreign soil. That right belongs to the king," he protested, rising from his chair and dabbing sweat from his forehead with a handcoverchief. "But I will ask him, again."

"That'll take more than a week," Philip whined; the heat trapped inside the tavern unbearable. "We can attack them and be home before-"

"No!" Warwick barked aggressively.

The dank smell rising from the rotten, ale-sodden reeds covering the tavern floor, caused Philip to sneeze several times and lose his train of thought.

"What of Norham, my lord?" one of his captains intervened, swilling the foaming contents of his cracked cup and considering whether or not to drink.

"It is rumoured the king is set to forgive Laurence Booth and return him to his bishopric," Montague sniffed.

"He will do no such thing. I have not forgotten how the good bishop seized Barnard Castle with both hands when I was forced to fly abroad," Warwick said, his voice full of bitterness.

Deliberately placing a foot on the seat of his chair, Warwick rested an elbow on the knee. "We march on Norham," he announced.

During the passionately debated war council, the king's young brother sat silently in the background. Using the nail of his right forefinger to push back the skin from the cuticle of his left forefinger, he pretended not to notice the bickering.

"Edward seeks a permanent treaty with Scotland," Warwick explained, for the benefit of his brother and cousin. "This constant fighting is a drain on our resources," he went on pacing the limited space between the table and wall. "We cannot fight France, Scotland and Lancaster at the same time. There must be another way."

"My lords, we should drive the Scots into the sea, execute Henry and burn Paris!" Philip flared acidly, shooting up from his stool and looking at each member of the council for espousal.

This time his more fanatical statement received only bewildered stares, forcing him to slump down, shrug his shoulders and pout like a chastised child.

The only councillor to side with Philip was Warwick's aggressive and greatly feared brother, Montague. Slightly taller than Richard and three years younger, John Neville was a strapping warrior, with a swarthy complexion, square jaw and dark, heavily-browed, untrusting eyes. Unlike Richard, he disliked intrigue, was unforgiving to his enemies and suspicious of those who burrowed their way into the king's favour. A far superior soldier than his brother, John lacked the refinement necessary to negotiate. Like Philip he was analogous in his opinions of those who changed sides to save their lives, attaint and execute them.

"Everyone is out for what he can get," Philip scowled, his foot twitching excitedly under the table, "without a thought for the common weal of this country."

"And you are not?" Warwick countered.

"All I have are my horses, my armour and a dozen loyal men. But what I have lost I will never forget," he added coldly.

Irritated by the humidity inside the tavern and aware of his cousin's phobic disposition, Richard fiddled with his sweaty Adams apple and tapped his right cheekbone thoughtfully, before turning to his brother.

"John, take the horse and reinforce Norham; I'll follow with the foot," switching his attention to Philip. "You return to York."

"My lord!"

"You will take our cousin, Richard, and continue his training," he added, nodding at the young duke.

"My lord, you will need every soldier you can get if you hope to take on de Breze," Philip warned, referring to Queen Margaret's most formidable general.

"I need men who obey me. I warned you not to go to London but you defied me and you have suffered for it.

Now you *will* return to York and stay there!" Warwick declared, louder than was necessary, catching the concerned eye of one of his retainers.

The man discreetly shook his head, a veiled indication for the earl to reconsider.

"Your Grace, you will stay with me," Warwick said, preferring not to leave the amenable young duke under Philip's influence. "Philip will have much to do in York."

"There's nothing to do in York," he grouched.

Taking a flat pouch, offered by the long-faced, short-bearded Sir William Stanley, Warwick tossed it on the table.

"That is a letter from the king," he explained, pointing at the leather envelope, "you will present it to the sheriffs... and see that they follow what is written therein."

Barely containing his anger, Philip snatched the satchel, jumped to his feet and offered a cynical "Gentlemen" to the assembly before leaving.

In bad humour, he deliberately barged past William Stanley, lacerating his knuckles on the rough unpainted wall. The pain brought his temper to the fore and he kicked aside a stool lodged in the entranceway, to keep the door open and allow fresh air in.

"Our cousin is on a road to self- destruction," Warwick warned his brother.

"Does that surprise you?"

"Stick with him and you'll be sorry," he cautioned, annoyed by Montague's touchy retort.

Once outside, Philip furiously lashed at the dirt with the heel of his boot, until he caught the ankle of his left instep on the sharp rowel of his right spur. Grimacing with pain he looked up at the bright sky and cursed his continuing misfortune. His private sulk was interrupted by the rhythmic pounding of horses' hooves, which also distracted him from the pain in his ankle. Shielding his eyes, he watched two horsemen ride up to the tavern and rein in their well-run mounts. Caked in a layer of fine,

199

brown dust both men jumped out of the saddles before their horses came to a complete stop. One took charge of the panting, foam-flecked animals; the other confirmed the Earl of Warwick's presence with a guard on the door. Slapping his faded tunic to remove some of the clingy dust, the messenger negotiated his way over the broken stool and disappeared inside.

"Good day honest fellow," Philip offered the horse-holder, flapping the flying dust away. "What's that all about?"

Wiping sweat-streaked dirt from his face with a sleeve, the second rider led the two horses to a nearby trough. Plunging his head into the murky water, he drank avidly. After a lengthy silence, broken only by the water bubbling around his totally immersed head, he jerked his face up, gasped and spouted a stream of dirty water from his pursed lips.

"Well?" Philip growled impatiently.

"The king is sending an embassy to France," he coughed, shaking water from his hair and drawing a hand across his mouth.

"Does the king seek to ally with the French?"

The fatigued messenger shrugged his shoulders, as refreshing water ran down his neck and soaked into his badly-soiled jack.

"We have ridden from Coventry with a message for my Lord of Warwick, I know nothing more," he hacked, shooing a group of children away from the skittish horses.

Philip hurried back inside the tavern to witness his cousin's delight at the news.

"You've heard?" Warwick sneered, as his captains bowed and left, relieved to escape the sweltering heat.

"Does this news please thee, my lord?" Philip called above the rustling of boots over the reed floor.

"It pleaseth me no end; if we seal this treaty, Henry's supply line will be cut."

"He has Scotland, unless…"

"We are for Norham!" Warwick blasted, slamming his fist down on the roughly hewn table in a fit of irritation, which toppled several cups and sped his subordinates on their way. "You are for York. By Christ's blood, will you obey my orders?"

"Yes, my lord!" he retaliated, his face flushed with humiliation.

Outside, a varlet held Warwick's twitchy stallion steady, while the earl left the tavern and hauled himself into the saddle, bellowing for his escort to line up. All was a blur as horses and wagons were dragged onto the road by cursing teamsters amid clouds of suffocating dust thrown up by so much activity. By the time the army formed in line, Montague had disappeared with the cavalry, taking Robert Harrington and several of Philip's retainers along, and leaving him feeling sorely used. Warwick and his dejected cousin, their horses face to face by the side of the road, bade each other a cagey farewell before turning away, Richard heading north, Philip going south.

Back in the sweltering, airless city of York, Philip Neville dismissed his remaining retainers and rode to the family home in St Saviours. His fractious mood was not helped by the news that his mother and Thomas were in Scotland, with Sir William. Muttering under his breath, he stomped up the stairs to his old room, fell on the bed and slept. Next morning he made his way to the Common Hall off Coney Street, to call on the sheriffs, accompanied by Arbroth. Despite wearing a light tunic, the heat made him sweat copiously. The stink of rancid waste decomposing in the gutters, forced him to cover his nose.

When he arrived at the Common Hall, Philip was told one of the sheriffs was sick and the other was at the council chamber on Ouze Bridge. Annoyed, he spun on his heels and marched back along Coney Street, pursued by Arbroth. The clamour of the crowds fuelled his aggravation. Traders yelled out of their open-fronted shops to advertise their wares; dogs barked; cartwheels clattered against gutters; babies cried, and a cooper cursed when his bellows boy brought the hammer down awkwardly, splitting his thumb. The din inflamed Philip's petulance and he deliberately barged people out of his way and insulted them if they reacted, leaving Arbroth to apologise.

At St Michaels Church, he turned down into Lower Ouzegate and headed for the bridge. With Arbroth surplus to requirements, Philip sent him to the poultry market, at Pavement, to purchase a goose for supper.

"And round up the others," he added, handing him a little money.

Arbroth was about to leave, when Philip growled at him to give up the pouch.

"And stay out of the taverns!"

"How do ye expect me tah find ower men if no in the taverns," he groused sarcastically.

"Do as I say."

Arbroth tapped his forehead and left.

As Philip crossed the bridge, the sound of laughter from below made him look over the side at a group of fishermen mending their nets on the river bank. Envious of their carefree life, he wondered what path he would have followed, had he not chosen the sword. Shrugging the pessimism from his mind, he approached the guard at the council building and showed him the leather pouch. Recognising the Warwick crest, the fellow grunted and shuffled aside. Taking the narrow stairs two at a time, Philip pushed the envelope into the face of the esquire of sword and mace, at the top. Again the emblem had an instant affect, and he stepped back, allowing Philip to interrupt a meeting between the sheriff and four aldermen.

"I am in conference here," the sheriff announced, the terse lisp in his voice, irritating.

Philip tossed the pouch onto the table, emblem down, and narrowed his eyes.

"Then I'll wait, my Lord Sheriff," he growled, rudely placing a foot on one of the empty chairs.

"By what right do you barge in here?" one of the

aldermen asked, twisting his neck and frowning disdainfully at the intrusion.

"Turn that over and you will see from whom my authority comes," he countered, pointing at the thin leather satchel; his threatening voice and frosty stare forcing the alderman to look away.

A second alderman, seated opposite the sheriff, casually flipped the pouch and recognised Richard Neville's heraldic insignia.

"The Earl of Warwick has no jurisdiction here," he dared.

Philip knew he was right, but was not prepared to show weakness.

"Speak again and I'll cut out your tongue," he threatened, standing straight and fingering the ballock dagger hanging from his belt. "Now leave us, all of you, with the exception of you my Lord Sheriff," he added mockingly, the trapped heat causing sweat to form on his face and trickle down his neck.

Insulted by the knight's blatant contempt, but fearing his temper the aldermen left the chamber in a flurry of rustling papers and glaring disapproval.

"Tradesmen," Philip muttered, as they traipsed past him.

"Those men are highly respected, and everyone is loyal to King Edward," Thorpe vouched, offended by his impudence.

"Yes, but while I fight, they stay here and grow fat."

"Without our taxes and goods, the king would not be able to fight his wars."

Philip scoffed at his explanation and introduced himself to William Thorpe. The silver-haired, middle-aged Yorkshire merchant, with a pronounced lisp and droopy eyelids, disliked holding office in such turbulent times. Nodding reluctantly while his unwelcome visitor sat on one of the vacated chairs, Thorpe watched Philip steer the pouch toward him.

"What is this?"

"Open it and see."

Untying the thong, the sheriff opened the worn, leather envelope and removed the letter from inside. Snapping the blood-red royal seal he unfolded the stiff paper. The vibration of his myopic eyes beneath one long, thick grey brow was a sign that he was studying the document. While he read, Philip sat back, tugged the wet collar away from his neck and watched his reaction.

Having perused the contents with an intense frown, Sheriff Thorpe rolled the letter into a cylindrical shape and jerked his heavy crimson gown of office out from under his backside.

"This should be given to the mayor."

"The mayor?"

"Yes... he has the authority to deal with this, or the chamberlains. 'Tis their job to sort fiscal matters, not mine."

"I am commanded to hand the pouch to you, my Lord Sheriff, and no other. Is the king's letter addressed to you?"

Having served in France under Warwick's father, William Thorpe was now happy to go with the flow. Lately he was feeling every one of his fifty years, and hated anything that might upset his delicate stomach. With his old comrade in arms dead, Thorpe assumed his son Richard regarded him as a confidant. The prospect of becoming embroiled in the dynastic dispute, showed clearly on his deeply-ridged forehead. Shaking his head, he unrolled the letter and re-examined its wording.

"Are you aware of the contents of this letter?"

Philip shook his head; he was more concerned why the windows were shut on such a hot day.

"It invites the good citizens of York to contribute a thousand pounds," he revealed, "to reimburse the Duke of Somerset, no less."

Philip's eyes widened and his jaw dropped.

"The money is to be taken to Durham," Thorpe continued, unaware of Philip's antagonism towards Sir

Henry Beaufort, "and handed over to Lord Warwick, who will forward it on to His Grace, the Duke of…"

"Somerset," Philip cut him off. "That black dog!"

"Black dog he may be, but he is The king's favoured pet," Thorpe said, with a hint of satisfaction at Philip's discomposure.

"When will the king wake up?"

"My Lord of Somerset has been much criticized of late," Thorpe explained, hoping he didn't notice his momentary display of pleasure.

Philip failed to hear the end of his statement, and the relieved sheriff decided to read out that part of the letter relevant to him.

"The bearer of this dispatch has the king's authority to arrange collection of the said monies, and escort it to Durham. To avoid suspicion he is to take no more than twelve armed men."

"The king plays games with me; he is aware of my intolerance for this… this Judas, and orders me to take him his forty pieces of silver," Philip hissed, banging his fists together. "And I am to haul it to Durham with only a small escort; a target for every outlaw in the forest!"

"This letter does not mention you by name."

"Richard, you arse," Philip groaned under his breathe, nibbling his thumbnail.

Sensing his mounting anger, Thorpe rolled the letter up and placed it on the polished table, trying hard not to gloat at his visitor's frustration, but finding the temptation too great.

"I have no love for Somerset, but I must obey this order," Thorpe declared.

"Yes we must all dance to the royal tune, though we detest the music," Philip mocked, watching the scrolled letter rocking on the uneven surface.

"I am to tell no one of your destination. You too are commanded to be silent on this matter," Thorpe added, his voice trailing away, lest he cause offence.

Philip put a hand to his forehead submissively.

"How long will it take you to collect such an amount?" he huffed.

"Two weeks, perhaps three. It is a great sum."

"Take four."

"Four weeks?"

"Four weeks."

"Lord Warwick will not be happy."

"Lord Warwick can go and…" he hissed, before calming down. "Lord Warwick will not know."

"What will you do?"

"I'll help clean up this pigsty you call a city. Are you aware there is a dead horse in the moat?"

Thorpe frowned at his impertinence and proceeded to defend his position.

"York is full of refugees and crippled soldiers. Our coffers are empty and the king constantly demands more money. It is the mayor's responsibility."

"No, my Lord Sheriff, you are accountable on matters pertaining to the running of this city," Philip countered, placing his elbows on the table and leaning forward.

"It will be hard to find this money," Thorpe whined, edging back to keep a fair distance between himself and his hostile guest.

"The Church has money," Philip smiled, thoughtfully rubbing the rough edge of his thumbnail against his bottom lip.

"I have no authority over the Church."

"I'm sure the dean will be happy to donate some of the Church's wealth."

"Archbishop Booth is in York," Thorpe chirped, attempting to remove part of the burden from his own shoulders.

"Then I shall pay His Grace a visit."

"He once showed great favour to Henry of Lancaster," Thorpe revealed, craftily stirring the pot.

"My Lord Sheriff, William Booth should have been banished ten years ago. Now he has the king's confidence, and his brother is his confessor, but one day they will pay for their sycophantic grovelling," he vowed, dabbing his sweaty face on a sleeve.

"You will not get the archbishop to part with money."

"We'll see," Philip said moulding his features into an amused grin.

"What do you need from me?"

"Ten of your most able soldiers."

"I don't think there are ten fit men in the city. Our best soldiers are with Lord Warwick, those that are left are mostly invalids, but I'll do what I can."

"Have them meet me outside the Minster gates tomorrow, after three of the bells."

Thorpe nodded and Philip thanked him for his courtesy, before departing with a polite bow. Although the mayor and sheriffs held the civic power in York, Philip's authority came directly from the king through Richard, Earl of Warwick, and Great Chamberlain of England. Warwick knew Thorpe would obey the royal wishes no matter how much he loathed them.

The next morning, shortly after the third bell of the day, almost 7a.m. ten miserable wretches stood outside the gates of St Peters Cathedral, near the south transept. Each man carried a sword and displayed the colours of the city: a silver shield with a red cross emblazoned with five red lions, on faded jacks. They knew Philip only by the Warwick arms on his scarlet doublet and muttered under their breath as he approached them, accompanied by two of his own men.

Bald Harry and Peter the pious were two adventurous west-countrymen, previously in the service of the Earl of Devon. When their master sided with Lancaster they offered their services to Warwick, who gave them to his cousin after the second battle of St Albans.

"Do you know why we are here?" Philip asked, arrogantly.

"No, my lord," the tallest of the group responded, leaning against the stone wall surrounding the Minster.

With his thumbs tucked into his belt, Philip nudged his

chin at the gates.

"We are here in the king's name, to ask the dean for a contribution. If he donates in good faith, all's well and good; if he refuses, we have the authority to seize jewels and plate to the value of the assessed amount."

"Tha dean will not permit armed men inside," the lanky soldier cautioned, removing his sallet and scratching his lank hair.

"If he summons tha church guard, there'll be a fight," the smallest warned, looking for support from his lofty companion.

"Then he'd better cough up," Philip said. "I'll cut off the ears of anyone who lays a hand on those carrying out the king's command!"

The York men were not happy at the prospect of a scuffle in the cathedral, or this antagonistic knight's unprovoked threat against the popular dean. All knew the story of Thomas à Becket's murder in Canterbury, in 1170, and no one wished to be part of such a damning scenario. Philip's man, Peter, had also expressed a lack of enthusiasm for the mission. Sensing their communal apathy, Philip had a rethink.

"You stay outside with the weapons," he announced, pointing at his two retainers.

The city men were unmoved by his offer, but he cared little for their opinions; he was here to do his duty.

"Harry, Peter, wait by the doors and let no one in, the rest of you leave your swords, and follow me."

As Philip pushed open the wooden gates, leading into the cathedral close, several church guards moved to intercept. Noting his livery they stepped aside, allowing the early morning visitors to proceed. Climbing several wide steps to the double doors, he glanced up at the lattice of wooden scaffolding clinging to the unfinished central tower, before handing his arming sword to Harry. Twisting the thick, black iron ring with both hands, he leaned against one of the weathered oak doors and pushed, but it failed to budge.

"Well, don't just stand there you codheads," he grunted, "help me!"

Several volunteers belatedly came forward and put their shoulders to the door, until it creaked open and a blast of warm air blew out.

"Tis a warning!" one of the York men gasped, stepping back fearfully as the perfumed air brushed his cheek.

"Silence!" Philip growled, scoffing at his superstition. "It's only incense."

Crossing the threshold, Philip looked up in awe at the incomplete central tower, while, from the direction of the Quire, choristers sang the Ave Regina Coelorum. The York men followed him cautiously into the holy sanctum, each man dipping two fingers in the water stoup behind the door, before dropping on one knee and crossing himself. Philip attempted to exert his hostile secular prejudice, but the spiritual influence of the Norman basilica was overpowering. The singing from the Quire rose in tempo and he struggled to remain detached, Leonel Powers' emotive music seeped into his soul until he was lost in another world, a world he was no part of. The striking harmony of the choir absorbed him totally and the mercenary reason for his presence in such a sacred place was forgotten.

Philip's mouth trembled and remorse slashed at his heart, but when the singing stopped abruptly, he came back to reality. Using thumb and forefinger, he tactfully wiped his eyes, making sure no one saw his moment of weakness. Twelve male choristers, dressed in full-length white cassocks, and ranging in age from fourteen to forty, filed quickly out of the Quire. Shuffling past Philip, the strict, rakish precentor offered him a contemptible sneer. Bewildered by the head of music's mute surliness, Philip ordered his men to search the Minster.

"If you find the archbishop bring him to me."

Lighting candles from one of the braziers used for heating the Minster, the guards dispersed, their footsteps echoing loudly in the cavernous cathedral.

Archbishop William Booth was not a difficult man to find, and though his advanced age and infirmities kept him more at his home near Nottingham, he had come to York to discuss the ongoing building work. When Philip and his men entered the Minster, Booth was attending an early morning conference in the Chapter House, with the dean, treasurer and several canons. Cupping a hand to his ear the archbishop listened attentively to the treasurer, when a knock on the doors broke his concentration.

"Enter!" he bellowed, fuming at having to stop his oration.

Surprised by the intrusion, Booth looked up as the doors opened and a burly, dull-witted Yorkshireman walked to the middle of the room.

"What can we do for you, my son?" He asked kindly.

The soldier snatched the sallet from his head and dropped it, the noise of the helmet bouncing over the tiled floor echoed loudly and seemed to go on forever. Overwhelmed at the presence of the archbishop and so many high status clergymen, sitting on cushioned, stone seats, built into the octagonal walls of the painted Chapter House, the soldier retrieved the object of his embarrassment.

"Well!" the treasurer snapped.

"Forgive me, Your Grace," the clumsy layman begged, falling to his knees and bowing his head. "A messenger from tha Earl of Warwick demands to see thee..."

"We cannot hear you!" the treasurer complained, edging out of his seat and curling a hand over his ear. "Get up and stand against the doors!"

The soldier shuffled back several paces before repeating his words.

"Where is this fellow who summons me in such a fashion?" Booth asked, as the treasurer frowned at the archbishop's largesse.

"Out there, Your Grace," he smiled, jerking his head.

"Then bring him in," the treasurer hissed.

"Calm yourself, John," William Booth said, waving his

210

hand slowly at the irate treasurer.

Suddenly an excited chantry priest burst into the Chapter House. "Your Grace!" he blurted hysterically. "There are soldiers in the church!"

"We know," the dean said, raising a hand. "Attend to your duties, there is nothing to fear."

"But..."

"Go my son."

The nervous priest bowed, turned and crashed straight into the precentor.

"I'm sorry..." he bleated.

"Walk!" the precentor barked, the collision almost knocking the book of song from his grasp.

"My Lord Archbishop, I am to take you to him," the soldier whinged.

"I'll go with this insolent knave Your Grace," the dean interrupted, rocking off his seat.

"No Richard. It is me he wishes to see," Booth said, edging out of his seat.

"Call the guards, Your Grace," the precentor pleaded.

"No... I want no violence here."

Struggling to put weight on his arthritic legs, the elderly archbishop defied all offers of help, but as he stood his sanctimonious smile dropped, to be replaced by an expression of pain. Using his crozier for support he gestured for the soldier to lead on.

Before leaving the Chapter House, William Booth glanced above the doors at the colourful painting of Walter de Grey, the excommunicated Archbishop of York. Limping and lurching painfully, he followed the deliberately dawdling soldier. Once in the beautifully painted, L-shaped vestibule connecting the Chapter House with the north transept, Booth's ears picked out the sounds of unusual activity. A brusque demand from somewhere high up was followed by the slamming of a door. Anxious pleading from threatened clerics, and muffled warnings of retribution bounced off the walls. When the archbishop appeared in the dusty building site that would one day be the rebuilt central tower, Philip was busy examining the fifteen life-size statues of English kings, which made up the choir screen. When he saw Booth's slothful gait and stooped posture, his tyrannical attitude mellowed.

Nearing his seventy-sixth year, William Booth was known and loved for his generosity and kindness to the poor. As Chancellor to Queen Margaret, he had been on such good terms with the Dukes of Somerset and Suffolk it drew him into conflict with the House of Commons. His support for the queen's favourites inevitably brought calls for his banishment. With Margaret's help, Booth was promoted to the Bishopric of Litchfield and Coventry. Five years later he attained the lucrative post of Archbishop of York, an elevation that bred resentment. After Towton, Booth dropped his royal sponsor like a hot coal and switched his allegiance to Edward.

Attired from head to toe in dark green, furred, William Booth drew up several feet from his visitor. With a heavy sigh he rested both hands on the carved, ivory handle of his crook. Philip folded his arms across his chest and stared at the old man's severely lined face.

"Good day, my son."

"Your Grace," he replied bowing respectfully, but prepared that if Booth should offer a hand, he would refuse to kiss it. "I am Philip Neville, and I am here on the king's business."

William Booth knew by his manner that this knight had little respect for his office and decided not tender his hand.

"What does our great King wish from the Church?"

"Two hundred marks, Your Grace."

"More money," he sighed, looking up at the incomplete central tower and wondering how much more it was going to cost to finish.

Noting the jewel-encrusted gold rings on several of the archbishop's arthritically deformed fingers, Philip sneered, his low opinion of the Church given credence by such vulgar overindulgence.

"Are you refusing, my Lord Archbishop?"

William Booth shook his head and tapped his forefinger against his crook, while the sound of desecration intensified.

"I have no authority to order the raising of monies here, though I will pass the king's wishes on to the dean and chapter. But call off your men, there is no need for sacrilege; the Church will pay that which the crown demands."

Unfolding his arms, Philip plunged a hand inside his doublet and produced King Edward's written authority and a note from the sheriff, which he handed to the archbishop. Raising the royal writ to within an inch of his face, Booth narrowed his heavily-hooded eyes and read the blurred script. While the elderly patriarch's twisted, grey brows quivered, and his thin blotchy hands shook uncontrollably, Philip nodded at a soldier standing in the background, indicating for him to round up the men and leave. Offended by the terse wording of the king's order, the archbishop rolled the papers together and thrust them back at Philip. Suddenly, something about this obstreperous knight struck him as familiar and the elderly cleric edged closer, eyeing him inquisitively. A memory stirred; he had seen this knight before, but time muddied his thoughts and, try as he may he couldn't recall where or when.

"This letter is for the civil authorities. It asks no money of the Church."

"Is the Church not part of this city?"

"Yes," he sighed. "Allow us time my impudent friend and the king will have his money," Booth said hoarsely, unable to satisfy his curiosity.

"You have four weeks, and it must be packed in a banded chest with lock and key."

The archbishop bowed his curved neck, causing a painful jolt to shoot down his spine, and his resilience softened Philip's austere attitude.

"Please sit, Your Grace," he offered a hint of sympathy in his voice.

William Booth could also be stubborn, and he refused,

preferring to rely on his crook for support. Philip's respect for the old man grew.

"Now I remember you," Booth said, opening his grey eyes fully and pointing a misshapen finger at him. "You were at the Corpus Christi pageant several years ago, and you refused to toast King Henry."

Philip was astonished at his memory, considering they never spoke that day.

"I remember," he growled, the thought of Elizabeth Percy and Ralph Hastings together stoking his ire. "I'll come back in four weeks," he added, turning and heading for the doors. "Forgive my men, they have only obeyed orders."

"Whose orders do you obey?" Booth called after him.

Philip stopped and bowed his head before leaving, the smoking incense irritating his eyes. "Why, the King of England's, Your Grace."

As Philip followed his men out, Booth made the sign of the cross at him and shook his head. Exhausted by his exertions, the aging prelate motioned for two priests to come and help him to the nearest bench.

Chapter 11

For twentyeight days Philip Neville waited for the chamberlains to collect the money. Archbishop Booth persuaded the dean to contribute, and he grudgingly handed over the Church's share, as did the various guilds and all those asked to cough up. Debilitated by the seasonal heat and frustrated by inactivity, Philip spent his time inspecting the city's crumbling walls and towers, or playing cards. Towards the end of the month, a courier brought a message to Claremont Hall from his master, Francis Talbot, stating he was back from Ashby and asking Philip if he would like to go hunting. He gratefully accepted and spent the next few days chasing buck and hart through the Forest of Galtres.

Once the assessed amount was collected, counted and bagged, the process of assembling an escort began. Philip asked the sheriff's they asked the mayor, and he provided a score of the most worthless soldiers available. From this motley collection, twelve were chosen and sent to the rendezvous point at St Mary's Abbey. Early on the morning of 30 July, a red coach, its doors adorned with the city arms, was dragged out of the abbey stables. The vehicle was secretly loaded with half a dozen coarse bags wrapped in straw, and a wooden chest reinforced with iron bands. The money, a mix of gold angels, half angels, nobles, half nobles, silver groats and half groats, amounted to almost a thousand pounds.

To avoid prying eyes, Mayor Thomas Scawsby dispatched his carriage to the abbey the previous night and urged Philip to paint over the crests. The mayor also suggested he leave the city by the abbey gate. A letter from the sheriff was given to Philip by the prior on his way back from prime: the second service of the monastic day, 4-45.p.m. Philip read the note while eating breakfast in the abbey guesthouse, located between the church and river. Philip was surprised to discover the note was from his cousin Warwick, instructing him to send word when he was ready to leave York.

Abutting onto the city's northwest wall, between Bootham Bar and the Ouze, and surrounded by its own high wall, St Mary's was an ideal place for a detachment wishing to slip innocuously out of the city. Philip ignored Scawsby's advice to paint over the emblems on the carriage, and the start was postponed until the first splashes of pale, yellow streaked across the night sky. The delay brought a gaggle of inquisitive Benedictines out to see what was happening. The black-habited monks sniggered, as half-a-dozen dull-witted soldiers struggled to attach a pair horses to the shafts. Philip, Francis and Arbroth sat on a low wall, observing the farce.

"You see," Philip said, shaking his head, "look at the fools they've given me."

"What's it all about?" Francis asked, sniggering when a horse shat on one of the men-at-arms' foot, "and why the secrecy?"

"Wine for my Lord of Warwick," he answered wryly, as daylight streamed over the horizon, and the mist hovering in the river valley began to dissipate.

"Huh?" Talbot frowned, watching a soldier drag his foot through the grass to remove the shit from his shoe, well aware he was lying.

Eventually order came out of disorder and the corpulent sergeant in charge turned to Philip and flashed him a toothy grin. The Benedictines nodded their appreciation for this comical interlude to their mundane lives, as the liturgical bell called them to the chapel for the third office of the monastic day.

"Get ready!" Philip yelled, jumping off the wall and turning to Arbroth. "You know what to do."

The Scot glanced at Francis, before passing his master a knowing nod and scurrying away.

"Where's he going in such a hurry?" Talbot wondered aloud, trying to listen in on their conversation.

"Well, I am for Durham dear friend; it should take us no more than six days," Philip announced, ignoring his comment. "Tell the sheriff to send a rider to my cousin... and remind him to get that horse out of the moat, it stinks to high heaven."

"God-speed," Francis offered, as the escort formed up around the coach.

Philip mounted his chestnut palfrey, Clovis, and Harry and Peter climbed up onto the driver's seat.

"I don't want this," he moaned, looking at the dark outline of St Leonard's Hospital, silhouetted against the rising sun. "There are many loose tongues in York."

"Fear not. I have never heard of outlaws attacking a wine convoy," Francis grinned, patting Clovis's neck.

"I hope you're right," he replied, tapping his forehead and nudging his horse on. "Farwell."

The sacks of coin destined for Somerset's purse were stacked on one of the seats in the carriage, and the chest, donated by the Church, lay on the floor wedged between the benches. Expecting an easy trip, the overweight sergeant chose to ride inside. Removing his tight-fitting helmet and sword belt, he stretched his stunted legs out over the chest and rubbed his fleshy hands together. The knowledge that his men would have to walk all the way to Durham made him fart and chuckle.

Suddenly the coach lurched forward accompanied by a creaking of leather, and the strained snorting of the horses. The unexpected jolt threw the sergeant on his side and caused him to strike his head against the door.

"Watch it you tosspots!" he yelled, poking his quivering face out the window.

The driver and his companion sniggered at the sergeant's reaction. With an evil sneer Harry removed his hat, rubbed his bald head and aimed the iron-rimmed wheels at the nearest hole in the gravel path. Out in front, Philip heard the fat man's angry protestations and looked back to see the vehicle rocking dangerously from side to side. Harry and Peter's unkind laughter brought a smile to Philip's anxious face. Shaking his head, he motioned for the convoy to follow him through the abbey gates and out into a huge expanse of open country, towards the distant forest.

For five days the coach bumped its way along the trail, wending a path through the colourful Forest of Galtres. The corpulent sergeant walked and wheezed alongside the coach, preferring to huff and puff than be shaken to pieces by the excessive bone-jarring he sustained whenever he sat inside. His men – six walking in front and five behind, used to the more routine tasks of guarding gates or patrolling the walls of York – treated the march like a holiday. Only Philip and the sergeant knew of the money; the rest believed they were escorting wine for the Earl of Warwick. If anybody was suspicious they didn't show it, the escort chatted and laughed, unconcerned by the possibility of trouble. That worry rested on the shoulders of the knight out front, the one who plucked them from a staid existence and forced them to march and sweat in the hot August sun.

Philip's men were not so easily taken in. Why would a consignment of wine weigh so much, and what was in the locked chest, but they asked no questions. Being the only mounted man, Philip always rode on ahead, looking for a suitable campsite, his eyes and ears attuned to any unnatural sounds emanating from the brush. Peter thought it strange that when they stopped for the night their usually convivial master sat apart, radiating an aura of moody detachment.

When the sun set on the fifth day, the company halted in a sheltered clearing a mile from Croft-on-Tees Bridge. The horses were unhitched from the coach, a fire lit and a guard quota set up. While the men prepared their food, Philip picked the youngest member of the group.

"Can you ride?" he asked.

"Yes m'lord," the boy said enthusiastically, nodding so hard his helmet slipped down over his eyes.

"Good, take my horse and ride to Durham. When you arrive, seek out the Earl of Warwick and tell him where we are."

"Where are we, m'lord?"

"Half a league from the bridge beyond the village," Philip growled. "Can you remember that?"

"Yes sir," he nodded, mouthing his words.

"Stay on the trail and you'll reach Durham in no time."

The teenager climbed into the saddle and Philip slapped Clovis's quivering rump, sending the palfrey cantering down the road in a cloud of dust and horseshoes.

"Slow down, god-damn you, he's not a hack!" Philip yelled, as the lad grabbed Clovis's neck and struggled to keep his short feet in the stirrups. "Young fool."

Those not assigned to guard duty removed their helmets and relaxed around the fire. The sergeant asked if he could take some of the men down to the village.

"No!" Philip growled. "We stay together."

Worried by his manner, Peter watched his master pace the camp. With his head bowed and hands behind his back, he seemed agitated, and Peter communicated his concern to Harry.

"He's like a wounded bear tonight," Peter warned, turning to the ale-swilling sergeant standing over the cookpot.

"A little rabbit my lord?" the sergeant called through the smoke, offering a bowl.

Philip stopped in his tracks, shook his head and continued pacing. The sergeant shrugged his shoulders and ladled an extra portion of overcooked rabbit and onions into the bowl, before squeezing in between Harry and Peter. Using a wooden spoon and a piece of stale maslin bread, he scooped the mixture rapidly into his mouth, an action that, when added to the heat from the fire, caused him to sweat profusely.

"Take your ease fellow," Harry gasped shocked by the way he shovelled his food down. "No one here is going to steal your fare."

The portly soldier grinned, drew back his lips and forced the masticated food through several sizeable gaps in his teeth. The brown mixture oozed out, bubbled down his chin and splattered his hose.

"You pig," Peter hissed, the vile performance turning his stomach, while his companions, seated around the fire, sniggered at the repulsive act.

With supper over and darkness capping in an invisible layer of muggy heat, the company settled down to sleep. To deter animals Philip ordered the fire kept going through the night. The sergeant, as always, slept in the coach, from where the sound of snoring interspersed with an occasional grunt, was proof of his insentient state. Eventually the camp went quiet, with only the shuffling of horses and the collapsing, hissing timbers of the fire breaking the silence. The guards stooped heavily; worn out by their unaccustomed exertions they tried and failed to keep awake. Philip sat on his haunches alone, his back against a tree, knees drawn up and head resting on his arms. He stayed awake for hours, watching the trees and listening, but his eyes grew heavy and his breathing slowed. Suddenly Philip's ears pricked up and his eyelids sprang open. A sharp rustling sound in the brush behind forced him to hold his breath and tense his muscles.

A weary moan broke the nocturnal stillness, and movement in the foliage made him to glance down at the sword lying by his side. Dark monk-like shadows materialized from nowhere, and flitted silently through the camp. When the ghoulish spectres bent over each sleeping form and cut its throat, Philip shivered. It was over in the blink of an eye, and every man of the escort lay dead or dying. When the carriage door scraped open, the sergeant, not sure if he was dreaming, muttered softly. His lassitude did not allow him time to wake and he was killed by the point of a ballock dagger thrust savagely into his heart.

Philip Neville remained motionless; he knew that by his actions, he was no better than those he despised. He regretted the killings but knew they were a necessary evil. This was the prelude for his revenge against the Duke of Somerset. A single dark shadow suddenly broke away from the group and came toward him. Drawing the woollen cowl from his head, the man waited as if seeking validation. Philip looked up but saw only the outline of a head crowned with wild hair, and assumed it was Arbroth. Receiving approval for his action in the form of a silent nod, the shadowy figure rejoined his companions.

"Fetch the horses," he hissed, to a nearby confederate.

Another shadow emerged from the trees, dragging two sumpters and several rouncies. The rest of the gang broke the wooden parts of the chest and transferred the money to bags. Flipping the hood back over his head to conceal his features, Arbroth helped load the sacks onto the pack horses. Philip focused his attention on the crackling flames of the fire, which, when added to the whimpering twitch of a dying guard, conjured up an impression of hell. He regretted the killings and quietly asked God to forgive him.

When the featureless wraith's vanished, the camp was as quiet as the graveyard it now assimilated. Only the nervous shuffling of the two coach horses, uneasy at the scent of so much blood, indicated any sign of life.

"It is done," Arbroth announced, returning to his master. "They're all dead."

"All dead?" Philip croaked, his voice faltering as he traced an invisible cross on his chest.

"Yes, mah lord," he underlined with an apologetic air, before crossing himself.

"But…"

"They are well known in the taverns o' York, mah lord. If one o' them was ever seen again, there would be doubt."

"Can you trust those dogs?" he sneered, detecting movement in the trees.

"No, mah lord, they are outlaws with a price on their heads, but ah have promised them half the money."

"Half the money?"

"Aye, they could kill us and take it all."

Philip knew he was right. "Half the money it is. Where do you go from here?"

"We'll divide it up later and separate."

"You know what to do," Philip reiterated.

The Scot jerked his head.

"Do you have it?"

Thrusting a hand inside his cloak, Arbroth produced a heavy, gold linked, SS collar, with attached swan pendant, looted from the Earl of Northumberland's house in York, after Towton.

"'Tis heavy."

"Put it in the sergeant's hand," Philip said standing up, his knees aching from being in the same position so long.

Turning to face the tree, Philip placed his hands against its thick, knobbly trunk and glanced up at the dark creaking branches overhead.

Arbroth snapped off the swan and wedged it in the dead sergeant's hand, while Philip anxiously awaited his return. When he heard him coming back, he sucked in a deep breath and turned his head.

"Do what you must, and do it quickly, before I change my mind."

Arbroth drew a narrow-bladed rondel dagger from his belt and held it poised.

"Get on with it!"

"Ah cannah," he whined, his voice full of misgivings.

"You piece of Scottish shit! You son of a pox-ridden Caledonian whore! You…"

Suddenly the blade stabbed hard into Philip's left shoulder and he gasped. The sharp point bored through his thin tunic and cut into soft flesh and muscle until it pierced bone. The power behind the blow pushed Philip's face against the tree, and as his feet slipped on the damp grass, he scraped his chin, nose and cheek on the rough bark, lacerating the skin as he fell.

"God-damn you why that side?" he groaned, as Arbroth placed a foot on his back and yanked his dagger free.

"Ah am sorry," he grunted, grabbing his feet and dragging him unceremoniously over to the fire.

"Master," he whispered, rolling him onto his back. "Lord Warwick's men will be here at dawn. Do ye want a blanket?"

"No. Go now… ride hard for Durham," he struggled with the words, spitting out dirt and grass, which had found its way into his mouth as he was hauled over the ground. "Wait for me there."

"The wound is bleeding, but 'tis no bad," he said, tossing several large branches onto the fire to deter inquisitive animals.

Taking a final look around, he nodded at his master, before vanishing into the trees.

"That's what you think," Philip moaned as his footsteps faded into the night.

The warm, early morning sun filtered hazily through the trees and birds chirped merrily from somewhere high up in the leafy umbrella. As Philip woke, the welcome sounds echoed inside his head, but his left arm and shoulder throbbed mercilessly. Forcing his eyes open he found himself face to face with a young, grey rabbit squatting only inches from his bloody nose, fearlessly sniffing the air. Once he was able to focus, Philip saw dozens more scampering about the campsite, unperturbed by the slaughter.

"They're all dead!" someone yelled.

The rabbits disappeared in the blink of an eye and Philip knew his long distressing night was over. Raising a hand for attention, he delicately rolled over onto his back and the bloody scabs on his face cracked and stung.

"What happened here?" an authoritative voice demanded, while the party dismounted.

"We were attacked in our sleep," Philip managed. "They were Somerset's men," he revealed, cursing his impatience.

The young esquire commanding the Yorkist detachment knelt beside Philip and gently lifted his head, while one of his men brought a linen wad.

The boy Philip had sent to Durham lost his way and it was past midnight before he arrived. At first light a body of mounted men-at-arms was assembled and dispatched to meet the coach. From the Croft-on-Tees Bridge, they saw a thin ribbon of smoke coiling skywards, and headed for its source.

"Is anyone else alive?" Philip spluttered anxiously, as he was helped to his feet and the last timbers of the fire collapsed into the dying grey embers.

"No," was the response, as the bodies were checked for signs of life and dragged to the side of the road, for burial.

"Something here!" someone announced, prising open the dead sergeant's unyielding fingers, "if he'll let go!"

"Bring it here," the esquire barked.

Holding the bloodstained ornamental pendant at arm's length, the soldier carefully avoided several corpses and handed it over.

The smooth-faced adolescent examined the bloodstained pendant; eager to impress his men he declared it to be a symbol of Lancaster.

"Somerset will pay for this!" he vowed, scrutinizing the well-crafted gold swan, while his men smiled at his zeal. "Can you ride?" he asked Philip.

"Yes," he nodded, the huge, black scabs covering half his swollen face, stinging with every change of expression.

Having robbed and hastily buried the dead, and dressed Philip's injured shoulder, the patrol set off. Looking back, Philip frowned at the stained patches of grass where his men had died, and tried to block out the vile deed. Leaving the mayoral coach at Durham, the esquire led his detachment on. Apologizing to Philip, he explained that the Earl of Warwick was away campaigning against the Scots, and his headquarters were now at Norham Castle, over seventy miles to the north.

After an agonizing five-day journey, the party clattered over the drawbridge and entered Norham Castle. Here Philip had his wound cleaned and dressed by one whose breath was as bad as his remedial skill. With Warwick absent, he could do nothing but wait and worry. Perched on a stony bluff overlooking the Tweed, seven miles west of Berwick, built of sandstone, Norham housed an inner ward, accommodating the Great Tower, Great Hall and kitchen, and an extensive outer ward. Access was from the west, via a well-protected drawbridge. A second moat and gatehouse guarded the inner ward. Norham's strategic position made control of this exposed border fortress critical for the English.

When Richard Neville marched from Newcastle to relieve Norham, six weeks earlier, the Lancaster-Scottish army broke their siege and fled; the Scots across the border; the Lancastrians to Bamburgh. Warwick retaliated by doing exactly what Philip had proposed: he invaded Scotland. The Earl expected to be back in a week, but heavy rains and the enemy's hit and run tactics dragged the campaign out. Warwick returned to Norham two days after Philip arrived, escorting a wagon train bulging with plunder.

Notified of the attack on the coach and his cousin's presence, Warwick boiled at the loss of so much money.

"Where is he?" he growled, trotting into the inner ward with the young Duke of Gloucester at his side, and drawing up near the Great Hall.

"Inside, my lord," a guard replied, holding the stirrup for him to dismount.

"Get out of the way you rascal!" Warwick snapped, slipping and falling against the unfortunate wretch, while his palfrey's nervous whinny echoed off the high buildings.

The red-faced soldier stepped back and the exhausted earl regained his composure. A servant, waiting in the doorway, now came forward and whispered something to Warwick, who looked surprised. As he entered the Great Hall, Richard Neville cagily acknowledged his cousin, standing on a raised platform at the far end, leaning against the high table. Removing his leather riding gloves, he tossed them on one of the long tables spread around the Great Hall, and walked toward Philip. Suddenly the earl found himself assailed by a groom, anxious to relieve him of his short cloak.

"Easy," he hissed.

"Pardon my lord," the groom bowed, folding the cloak over his left arm and withdrawing.

As his dusty boots scuffed across the orange and gold tiled floor, Warwick was watched by his anxious kinsman. Unbuckling his belt, Richard deliberately dropped the heavy bastard sword and its scabbard on a badly-scarred table, and opened several hooks on his light fustian doublet. Stepping up onto the diaz, he nodded at Philip, who came forward to kiss his cheek and bow his head. Warwick responded by taking a firm hold of his shoulders with both hands.

"It's good to see you, alive," he said mordantly, studying the black, dry scabs coating half of his face, the tension of their last meeting still fresh in his mind.

"I have failed, my lord," Philip apologised, averting his eyes from Richard's probing stare.

"'Twas not your fault, but that treacherous knave Somerset, who deceived us all with his false fidelity," Warwick declared, his tight grip causing Philip to wince, "though the king will have none of it."

"Then we must convert him."

"And how do we do such a thing?" he asked, catching sight of a bowl of candied lemon set out on the top table next to a jug and several cups.

"Go to London and speak to him," Philip suggested, noting his cousin's muddy, badly scratched boots, as he turned to pluck a handful of the desiccated fruit.

"That won't be easy," he frowned, tossing several pieces of sugar-coated lemon into his mouth and indicating for him to continue.

While Philip shook his head and dabbed his weeping, scabby cheek with a hand towel, Warwick spotted the gold swan pendant behind the bowl.

"Is this it?" he asked, chewing the sweet lemon and picking up the ornament.

"Yes," Philip nodded, as fine sugary powder showered

the Earl's greying beard.

"Where is the chain?" he asked, examining the craftsmanship.

Philip shrugged his shoulders.

"A symbol of Lancaster no doubt, but one that could have been taken from a prisoner and sold on… this is not proof."

"I heard his name called out."

"You did, in what context?"

"In what context?" he echoed, regretting his zeal. "I don't understand."

"Why would Somerset take money meant for his own purse? It doesn't make sense?"

Philip's eyes flickered nervously and he used his tongue to drum against the inside of his bottom lip. Puzzled by his evasive response, Warwick munched avidly on the candied lemon and blew a contented moan through syrupy lips.

"Your men died in their sleep; did you post enough guards?"

"Yes, my lord, four men were on watch throughout the night, they must have fallen asleep."

"All of them?"

"The Mayor of York gave me with twelve dotards, none of them fit for soldiering…"

"I was told they all had their throats cut, except the one in the coach, yet you live?"

Philip's face flushed and his torment increased as he strove to cope with this unexpected interrogation.

"My shoulder is cut to the bone," he countered. "Perhaps they thought I was dead!" he blurted indignantly, his voice echoing up into the high timbered roof.

Exhausted and short tempered, Richard gnawed on a piece of pith and eyed Philip's scabby face.

"How did they know?"

"My lord?"

"The men who attacked you, how did they know your route, and what you were carrying?"

"The road through the forest is well travelled," Philip explained, his attention drawn to a recessed door, which gave access to the Great Chamber. "And the wheels of the coach cut deep... any outlaw worth his salt could see we were carrying more than a few casks of wine."

Using his tongue to force a strand of stubborn lemon from his front teeth, Warwick stared at Philip's glistening forehead.

"You have lost the king's money!" he sniffed, bouncing the swan pendant in his palm, before tossing it casually on the table.

"I did not lose the king's money!" he stammered, looking apprehensively at the narrow door.

Warwick huffed and threw a hard piece of lemon at the cold fireplace.

"You should have let me go with you; it was I who advocated invading Scotland."

"Could one of your men have been in Somerset's employ?" Warwick asked, ignoring his comment.

"But they're all dead," he reminded him. "Only the boy I sent to Durham survived."

"Did you hear anything that might implicate His Grace?"

"The night was dark, I heard only whispers," he said hesitantly, his confidence rattled by Warwick's doubts.

"Yet you said you heard his name."

"I, I cannot recall."

"Do you have a fever?" Richard pressed unsympathetically.

"No, my lord."

Any faith Richard Neville had in Somerset's change of loyalty had gradually diminished over the months. Now he saw an opportunity to rid the realm of this Lancastrian leech, and gain from his downfall. Warwick planned to feed the fires of distrust by using the ambush as fuel.

"Henry Beaufort has outlived his usefulness," he declared, baiting his kinsman.

"Then we must..." Philip began, suddenly aware of his

tactics and drawing back.

"We use a letter," Warwick recommended, dangling the carrot.

"From whom?"

"From a friend," keeping his voice low.

"Hastings?"

"No," Warwick groaned, irritated by his impulsiveness. "We falsify a letter from Edward to me questioning Somerset's loyalty, and have it intercepted by one of my people."

Philip looked confused so Warwick embellished his idea. "I have one who spies for me and Lancaster though he believes I know nothing of his double-dealing ways. He'll leap at the chance to ingratiate himself with the duke, who will pay handsomely to read such a missive before it is delivered to me."

"Then we kill him," Philip jumped in.

"By God's teeth, you take to intrigue with a passion," Richard gasped, lowering his voice. "Somerset will be distressed by the king's suspicions and his own doubts will eventually force his hand."

Philip loved the idea. Pouring a cup of well water from the table jug, he waved away a server, who had tip-toed from the kitchen and was stood waiting.

"Are you in pain?" Richard asked, eyeing the dark, uneven crust coating half his face.

"Only my shoulder," he replied, massaging the injured limb.

"Then harken to my news." Richard smiled, licking the sweet powder from his lips.

"Ralph Hastings is dead?"

Annoyed by Philip's senseless interruption, Warwick drew a deep breath and released it slowly. "The king was set to join me for an attack against the Scots."

"And…"

"Let me finish," he warned.

Philip apologised in the form of a slight nod and his cousin continued. "On his way here he stopped off at

Northampton with his friend Somerset, but that most loyal of towns suffered greatly when Margaret's army marched on London three years ago. A local recognised the duke and spread the word. The townsfolk became ugly and tried to pull the duke from his horse."

Listening attentively, Philip signalled for the patiently waiting server to come forward and fill his vessel with wine. Grabbing the green, glazed flagon from a sideboard nestled against the wall behind the high table, the server glanced at the half empty bowl of candied lemon as he refilled Philip's cup.

"What's wrong fellow?" Warwick frowned, breaking his rhythm.

"My lord, forgive me. The steward will have me flogged for leaving his favourite delicacy out," he whinged, pouring the wine and slouching away.

"This steward has expensive taste, but I'll eat the rest; you may as well be flogged for a pound than a penny."

"Thank you, my lord," he groaned, as he withdrew.

"They demanded Somerset's head, but the king appeased them with a cask of his own wine." Warwick continued, "Thus distracted, Edward was able to smuggle his friend out. The duke is now on his way to Wales, for his own safety."

"My God, how close did the citizens of Northampton come to performing a great service, and how cheaply are some bought off?" Philip scoffed.

"That may be, but Edward stopped at Fotheringhay and there will be no invasion of Scotland."

"By Christ's blood!" Philip flared acidly, "we must finish that which the good people of Northampton began," he urged. "Somerset must not be allowed to enjoy his time in Wales."

"It's already begun," Warwick said.

Philip looked puzzled.

"The money from the coach," Richard smiled.

Gloating over Somerset's misfortune, Philip's mind raced ahead, weaving the tapestry of deceit that hopefully would end with the duke's downfall.

"Queen Margaret is at Bamburgh, waiting for a fair wind to carry her to France," Warwick announced changing the subject, "and Henry is hiding in the... Are you listening?"

"Yes, my lord," he lied, concerned by Richard's penchant for speaking openly of his plans.

Several servants now entered the Great Hall from the pantry and made their way to the high table, to await the Earl's pleasure. One deftly cast a cloth over the remaining sugared lemon.

"Are my men here?" Philip asked amused by a servant who stealthily removed the bowl from the table.

"No, they're with my brother, but the steward tells me some of his staff has lost their money on the dice, so I know that scruffy Scot of yours is here."

"Arbroth is a law unto himself, yet I would not trade him for a hundred men-at-arms," he grinned, as Warwick noticed the vanished bowl and glowered at the two servants, who stood at attention, refusing to look him in the eye. "How fares our cousin Edward?"

"The more he remains in the company of 'new men' the more he degenerates. Herbert and his brood of Welsh piss-heads dominate at court, turning everything to their advantage," he moaned, determined to pry Edward's cursory companions from the throne, once Somerset had been dealt with. "Are you aware Thomas has been appointed an esquire of the body to Margaret's young son?"

"Thomas, but he is no courtier," Philip gasped, shocked at the thought of his youngest brother under Queen Margaret's spell.

"Nevertheless he is with her at Bamburgh."

"My mother's husband is behind this," he spat, "the bastard!"

"Margaret is determined to get an alliance with France," Warwick revealed, watching his reaction.

"Yes, and she will find much support in that god-damned country."

"Fear not, Edward will counter her seductive charms by sending his own ambassadors to Louis," Warwick explained, meaning his brother, George Neville, King's Chancellor and Bishop of Exeter, and Sir John Wenlock.

"For what reason?"

"Do not speak of this to anyone, on your oath as a knight."

Philip offered a baffled nod and put his right hand over his heart.

"I swear it."

"Edward desires a treaty with France."

"I don't trust the French. Louis is Margaret's cousin; he's not called 'The Spider' for nothing." Philip exclaimed, pacing to and fro. "I must stop my brother."

"You are too late."

"What of Somerset?" Philip frowned deeply, a reaction that caused his facial scabs to sting.

"I will deal with the good duke. Return to York and wait until you hear from me," Richard said. "But before you leave, find your Scot and tell him to give back the money he took or I'll have him flogged until Michaelmas."

Philip bowed sharply and left, glancing suspiciously at the small side door as he went. Richard turned and brusquely commanded the servants to leave, except the one who first spoke to him when he arrived.

"Where is he?"

The servant jerked his head at the mitred door leading to the Great Chamber before being waved away.

Once alone, Warwick walked to the door and pushed it open. From the space beyond, a veritable villain emerged wrapped in a cloak as black as night. Lowering his cowl, exposed a head of dark, oily hair, pinched nose, sunken cheeks and narrow eyes, all the attributes of a violent character.

"My lord," he offered bowing low, his voice as chilling as his form.

"Was it his man who came to you?" Warwick

demanded.

"I cannot say, my lord," he rasped, a legacy from an old wound to the throat. "The night was dark." Aware of Warwick's enmity, he walked to the window and peered out. "The one who came to me kept his face hidden, but he could not disguise his accent," he sneered, wiping his nose on a greasy sleeve. "We were paid well to ambush the coach…"

"And murder every man?"

"My lord, I was promised protection," he croaked, concerned by Warwick's rancour.

"You will leave here in one piece," he scoffed, "though I would sooner hang you from the nearest tree."

"After we cut their throats, the others left, but I hid in the trees. I saw the man who hired us talking to someone," he added edging away from the window, as Philip strolled past on his way to the Great Keep. "But I did not see his face…"

"How could you see anything?"

"I see more in the dark than you see in daylight, my lord."

"Would you know the one who came to you?"

"No; we always met at night and he wore a hood. When he spoke he kept his head down. I tried to follow him once but he vanished."

With a satirical sneer, Warwick handed over a small bag of coins. The assassin snatched the purse and tied it to the inside of his coal-black cloak. Offended by his very breath, Richard drew back until several feet of space separated them, and he carefully gauged the rogue's answer to his next question.

"Where is the money from the coach?"

"I know nothing of any money, only that which we were paid for our work," he said, his twitching eyes betraying the lie.

"The work of the devil," Warwick growled, crossing himself. "Get out before I change my mind and have you boiled alive!"

When his sinister visitor left through the same door as he came, Richard wiped his hands on his hose, ridding himself of the man's foul odour. Stepping up onto the raised floor, he walked past the great fireplace and looked at the full-length tapestry covering part of the north wall. A slight breeze made the colourful, wall hanging serpentine gently from left to right, breathing brief life into the huge religious figures woven in the fabric.

"You may come out, Your Grace."

From a concealed alcove behind the over-sized tapestry, emerged a young lad, immaculately attired in cobalt doublet and hose, a short sword suspended from his belt. The boy's long, dark hair contrasted vividly with his pale features, making him appear sickly, but the image did not portray a true picture. For this eleven year old was Richard, Duke of Gloucester, the king's youngest brother, and he was no weakling.

"You heard?" Warwick asked, bowing to his diminutive kinsman, who had been escorted to his place of concealment by a servant.

Gloucester nodded and Warwick offered an unctuous grin. "Do you wish me to get rid of our fallacious cousin?"

"No, my lord, nothing I heard convinced me he is guilty of anything; Philip is loyal and we have need of such men. My brother's affection for Henry's cast-offs is his affair; *if* our cousin is to blame for losing the king's money, he will answer for it."

"But he has done murder and taken money that belonged to..." his words trailed away as if he said something he shouldn't have.

"To you?" Gloucester beamed, in boyish innocence. "Name one man in England who would not murder for money?" Rubbing his itchy nose on his sleeve the young duke continued, "I would not take the word of such a knave."

"Your Grace is wise beyond his years." Warwick smiled, stymied by his youthful perception.

Resting an arm on Gloucester's shoulder, the earl led

him outside, where his tutor and a group of esquires were waiting to continue sword practice.

Leaving the Great Hall, Philip went in search of Arbroth and found him behind the stables, playing dice with a company of plunder-laden archers, and winning.

"We're leaving, hand those over and pack up," he commanded, pointing at the dice, "and give them back their money!"

Arbroth passed the small, wooden dice to his master and grudgingly returned his ill-gotten gains to the grinning archers.

Following the ambush in the Forest of Galtres, Arbroth divided the money with the outlaws and rode off into the darkness. Satisfied he wasn't followed, he stopped to bury the money before heading for Durham, where he learned Warwick was at Norham. Retrieving his master's palfrey he rode north. With Warwick raiding in Scotland, Arbroth spent his time drinking in a Berwick tavern. When he heard Warwick was back, he returned to Norham and waited for his master.

Philip and Arbroth rode out through the West Gate and followed the road south.

"Did ah hurt ye, mah lord?" the Scot asked, looking apologetically at the veneer of black, cracked scabs coating half his face.

"Yes you son of a bitch," he growled. "Did you give back your ill-gotten gains?"

"Most of it, mah lord," he groaned, dragging the packhorse.

"Where's the money from the coach?"

"What money?"

Philip was in no mood for levity. Keeping his eyes fixed on the winding road ahead he breathed heavily through his sore nose.

"You are nothing but a thieving dog," he hissed, bouncing the six confiscated dice in the palm of his gloved hand.

Arbroth nodded and cleared his nose by turning aside, blocking the left nostril with his thumb and snorting out sharply through the right, before repeating the process with the other nostril.

"Ah wore mah horse oot riding to Durham, where they told me Lord Warwick was at Norham, so ah wore oot another."

"Where's the money damn your eyes?"

"Ah took two pounds for a new rouncey, and ah have sewn a few shillings into mah clothing."

"And the rest?"

"Buried."

"Where?" he pressed, shaking the dice.

"Ah cannah say, mah lord, but I'll take ye there when it is safe to do so."

Philip knew he would have to trust him, but faith in one so loyal was not an issue. When half the dice kept showing a six, he glared at his crooked retainer.

"How is it possible?"

"They're weighted, mah lord."

"Weighted?" he echoed, trying to judge the difference.

"With mercury, ah bought them from an old Jew in Constantinople, and paid a high price."

Unable to rid himself of the nagging pain in his shoulder, Philip handed the dice back.

"Here."

"Thank ye."

"Huh," Philip snorted, wondering why he had been drawn to the small door in the Great Hall. "My cousin is suspicious, he knew what I would do when he gave me this task," he revealed. "A noose hangs around my neck... and if I am not careful the crafty bastard will pull it tight."

"Ah am sorry ah caused ye pain."

"Forget it. Leave the money buried for now, we'll fetch it up when the dust settles."

"Have ah told ye the story of the Bruce's heart?" Arbroth smiled, leaning back in the saddle and resting a hand on his hip.

"No," Philip groaned, rolling his eyes, "but you're about to."

"When that great King of Scotland, Robert the Bruce, breathed his last, his heart was cut oot o his body, as he requested it should be afore he died. The heart was placed in a silver casket to be buried in Jerusalem, by the Bruce's most trusted knight, Sir James Douglas."

Philip sighed and Arbroth frowned at his disinterest.

"Go on," he hissed, shifting in the saddle.

"Sir James took a ship for Flanders with seven knights and thirty loyal men. When they landed they were told Alfonso of Castile was gathering an army for an attack against the Moors. Sir James was a fighter and when he heard this he hired a ship to take him on to Spain, so he could join Alfonso…"

"Is there a reason why you're telling me this?" Philip blew.

"No," Arbroth said, shaking his head, "'tis a good story, nothing more."

"Then talk about something else."

It took seven days to reach York, and when they neared the site of the ambush, guilt ate into Philip's conscience, forcing him to take a different path. As Clovis plodded on, his anguish intensified and he wondered if God was punishing him for his transgressions.

Chapter 12

With his mother away in Scotland, and Thomas with Queen Margaret, Philip resided at the family home in St Saviours. When he first arrived the two remaining servants timidly revealed that Sir William had forbidden him to use the house during his mother's absence. Pushing the cowering servants aside, he threatened to thrash them if they even looked at him the wrong way.

"Claremont Hall belonged to my father," he spat, stomping heavily up the stairs and stabbing a finger at his own chest, "one day it'll be mine!"

August was a swelteringly hot month, and the narrow streets of York, overshadowed by rows of crooked timber houses leaning precariously toward one another, retained the heat, breeding disease and a debilitating listlessness among the populace. Preferring to walk to his place of business, Philip avoided piles of rubbish left in the streets, and dodged pots of piss tossed out of windows. Worried by Warwick's suspicions, he moped around the city and nurtured an obsession that his cousins were deliberately keeping him at arm's length. Such budding paranoia only increased his sense of impotence and isolation. He missed the thrill of battle and was desperate to see action. Appeals were sent to the king and Warwick, but his requests were met with instructions to stay put.

By late September the sultry summer heat was almost gone and a refreshing, autumnal breeze blew through the city, removing the apathy and sickness. On 4 October, the feast day of St Francis of Assisi, a courier dismounted outside the council chamber on Coney Street. In front of the mayor, the city aldermen and Philip Neville, he announced that the king was coming to York on the first day of December. The messenger then handed over two letters bearing the royal seal; one for the mayor, the other for Philip. Snapping the dark, red wax seal, Philip read the note from his cousin with an air of excitement. As his eyes scrolled down the page, he unconsciously picked at the last scab on his nose, and his cheery countenance slowly faded. The letter commanded him to assist the civil authorities in securing lodgings for a number of lords and their servants. He was also empowered to choose a site, outside the city, suitable for housing several thousand retainers and soldiers. Between Philip, the mayor and the sheriffs, they were to clear a tract of land for tents and arrange food supplies. Farriers, bakers, cobblers, cordwainers bowyers, fletchers, cooks, bladesmiths, and all other craftsmen needed to sustain the king's retinue, were to be accommodated.

Philip did his best to carry out his orders, but civil authorities and the military rarely worked well together. The outgoing sheriffs were apathetic, the incoming pair inflexible. One morning, in late October, after weeks of bickering with the council, a perturbed Philip Neville plodded across the muddy fields, alone. Leaving Bootham Bar he followed the wide ditch that encircled the city, resenting his role of harbinger. His esquire, page and retainers were still with Montague, leaving him only Arbroth and two servants. With his mind a hotchpotch of contempt for his lot, and concerned over the arrangements for Edward's visit, he trudged on, oblivious to the water seeping into his boot through a tear in the sole. As he dragged his feet through the clinging mud, a cold wind rumbled over the river plain, throwing his hair into a tangled mess. Cursing his assignment, he rotated his left arm to ease the aching joint.

As Philip slogged through the heavy, viscous mud, he fretted; the mayor and sheriffs were still being disruptive. He would pick a campsite; they found objections. He asked for carts and carters; they could spare none. He called for tailors to repair tents; they sent four, and so it continued. With his frustration mounting and his boots sticking in the mud, he almost fell into the moat.

"Fuck it!" he swore, regaining his balance. "I hate this shit!"

Passing between St Giles Church and the Bawing

Tower, he turned the corner and followed the ditch east, to Monks Gate, when movement in the distance caught his eye. Two riders were cantering towards him, the foremost waving excitedly. Philip looked back to make sure he wasn't waving at someone else before responding, but with less enthusiasm. Recognising his friend Francis, he surmised his companion to be a woman by the way she sat in the saddle. Cloaked from head to toe and keeping several lengths behind Francis, she aroused Philip's curiosity, more so because Lady Margaret never rode a horse.

Coming closer the woman nudged her horse level with Francis and Philip looked harder. As the distance diminished, her hooded features became more distinct and his attention was transfixed on her willowy shape.

"Good day dear friend!" Francis announced breathlessly, leaping from the saddle.

"Good day to you," Philip slowly nodded, his eyes locked on the young woman as she drew her mud-flecked mount to a panting halt.

"Madam," he offered, tipping his head.

"Sir," she responded, with a slight nod.

"This is my sister, Isobel," Francis grinned, mindful of his interest. "Sister, may I present Philip Neville, cousin to the king of England, cousin to the Earl of Warwick, cousin to the Duke of..."

"Enough, dear friend, I have cousins coming out of my ears," he laughed, embarrassed by the endorsements, but more so at his own sloppy response. "Mistress Talbot." He bowed.

Sensing his face blushing and conscious of his mud splattered attire, Philip grabbed the bridle of her horse and kissed her proffered hand, his lips barely touching the soft leather of her glove.

"Your sister is delightful," he smiled, hating himself for yet another asinine comment.

"Thank you sir," she smiled, her pale cheeks glowing red from the cold.

Lowering the hood from her head revealed a crown of pale yellow hair, which cascaded in gentle waves onto her slender shoulders. Philip noted the thin, twisted gold circlet around her head and loose hair, symbolic of her virginity, and tried not to stare. Attired in a long, close-fitting, green velvet riding coat, the hood collar and cuffs edged with white ermine, Isobel Talbot exuded all the attributes of a refined woman that he yearned for. Fighting to contain his emotions he bit his tongue, lest he make a fool of himself again.

With an amused smirk, Francis explained how they had met Arbroth on his way to the Great Tower for a game of football. The Scot informed them that his master was making his rounds outside the city walls. Having flowered into womanhood, her seventeen-year old curiosity was aroused, and she asked her brother if she could meet his friend.

While Francis helped her dismount, Philip saw a window of opportunity. Tugging at his windblown hair, he licked his hands and tried to compress the matted mess to enhance his appearance. Glancing up he caught Isobel watching him from behind her horse and looked away embarrassed. Finding his behaviour amusing, she whipped a rebellious lock of hair off her forehead with a sharp twist of her neck, and smiled demurely over the saddle. Not sure how to react, Philip turned to examine the overgrown moat, but his face flushed and his throat dried up.

Francis came to the rescue by suggesting they walk on; an offer Philip gratefully accepted. Taking the reins from his sister, Francis placed himself between Isobel and Philip and led the way back to Monks Bar.

"I hear the king is coming to York," Francis said, as they strolled casually between the fifty-foot wide ditch and a row of cottages.

"Yes, but his visit is no secret," Philip revealed, smiling sheepishly at Isobel, "there is still much to be done, there's a dead horse in the moat and the streets stink of sh–"

"My sister is here for a week," Francis interrupted,

while Isobel cloaked a snigger.

Regretting his choice of words, Philip closed his eyes and wished the ground would open up, and swallow him.

"I would give anything to meet the king," she sighed. "I have never seen a king or queen."

"Then extend your visit?" Philip suggested, groaning at the way his mouth ran on before his brain engaged.

"Alas I cannot; mother is ill and our sister is too young to care for her."

"I am distressed to hear Lady Talbot is unwell," Philip pouted, annoyed with Francis for keeping such news from him.

"We keep our wretchedness to ourselves," Isobel said, crinkling her forehead as she fought to mask her concern.

Looking down at the trampled, water-logged grass, bubbling and squelching around his boots, Philip could not comprehend his sudden interest for this engaging maiden, who caused him to stumble over his words. Francis noted his clumsy remarks and caught their furtive glances, but he was at ease with it. Despite Philip's pig-headedness, he liked him and believed his sister would make him a good wife. Overcome by a sense of compassion Francis decided to banish his friend's discomfort.

"What news of Somerset?" he asked.

"I hear His Grace is much indisposed toward the king," Philip scoffed. "He sits in Wales, blaming Edward for failing in his promises."

"Fair news indeed, for I believe he set the ambush and planned your murder, but there is talk of the Earl of Warwick's involvement."

Philip went strangely silent. His cousin's suspicions and unpleasant memories of that night still tormented him.

"That should never have happened," he lamented, referring to the deaths of Harry and Peter, before losing his head. "By St Paul, Somerset will rue the day he-!"

Isobel was shocked by his unexpected outburst, and he regretted his terse eruption.

"Please accept my apologies," he begged, rubbing his

forehead out of frustration. "My work here is difficult, and I am constantly hindered by the city elders."

"Save your regrets," Francis smiled. "I am mindful of the burden you bear."

Philip was puzzled; to what was he alluding, his work in York, or his personal guilt?

"I hear the Duke of Somerset and Queen Mary are most intimate," Isobel said, referring to Mary of Gueldres.

Philip sniggered and nodded, but Francis was unimpressed by her immature comment.

"'Tis nothing but a rumour," he frowned, astounded by her effrontery. "You should not listen to idle gossip."

Huffing brusquely, Isobel lifted her dress above her ankles, to avoid the puddles of muddy water. "Why are you walking in all this mud?" she gasped, fighting a losing battle to keep her feet dry.

"I am charged with finding lodgings for the king," he boasted, as they arrived at the outer gates of Monks Bar.

"I do not envy you sir."

Taking the reins of Isobel's mare from Francis, Philip stroked its soft white face and tactfully edged closer, hoping to catch a whiff of her sweet breath. Cupping his gloved hands, Francis helped his sister to mount before hauling himself up into the saddle.

"You must dine with us this night," Francis offered, wiping his gloves on his hose.

Captivated by Isobel's allure, Philip nodded vaguely.

"Will you be joining us at St Martins?" she asked, "for vespers."

Bewitched by her persuasive smile and too busy observing that she did not shave her forehead, nor remove her eyebrows, as was the fashion, he unconsciously agreed; a reaction that confounded Francis.

"Close your mouth brother before it is mistaken for the gatehouse."

Snapping his jaws shut, Francis was about to reprimand her when she jumped in.

"Perhaps, you would escort me and my sister-in-law

around the city. I have not been to York since I was a child."

Stunned by her blatant perjury, Francis shook his head in disbelief.

"Yes," Philip gasped, besotted by her feisty charm, blithely handing her the reins.

"Good," she smiled, sitting straight.

"Good," Philip echoed, eying her breasts as they rose and fell beneath her cloak.

Taking hold of the leathers, Isobel clicked her tongue against the roof of her mouth, added a tender nudge of her heels, and steered her docile mare through the outer gates. Francis offered his friend a confused frown and followed in her wake.

Philip watched them disappear into the crowded city, and tried to make sense of the pounding in his heart and the stirring in his loins. Bright and breezy after meeting Isobel, he spun on his heels and followed the ditch back to Bootham Bar, indifferent to the mud splashing his hose, or the water squelching inside his boot. Before returning home he met the new sheriffs to discuss the burgeoning campsite beyond the walls. An elated Philip Neville oozed confidence as he unveiled final arrangements for the king's visit. The meeting went well, regardless of the usual objections and long faces from the council. That night Philip slept soundly and woke early next morning, with a huge grin on his face.

Alas, Philip's joie de vivre did not last. After attending vespers at St Martins le grand, in Coney Street, with Francis, his wife Margaret and his captivating sister, he returned with them to the Talbot residence for reresoper. For Philip the evening was a magical experience, enhanced by the aroma of Isobel's haunting perfume, which permeated the very air he breathed. The conversation was charming and Isobel flirted unashamedly with Philip, who became more and more intoxicated by her beauty and frankness. They laughed and talked the evening away, until Margaret stifled a yawn and Philip thought it prudent to take his leave. Thanking his hosts for their hospitality, he never once took his eyes off the object of his desire. With a buoyant farewell to all, he kissed Isobel's soft, warm hand and left with an understanding that they would meet three days hence.

Philip spent the next few days supervising construction of the tented metropolis outside the city, and checking security at the archbishop's palace, where the king was to lodge. He performed his duties with a spring in his step and a cheerful word to all. When Isobel and her sister-in-law failed to show at the appointed time, he stormed away, grinding his teeth and clenching his fists. He had waited outside the Minster gates, as arranged, and heard the ringing of two bells sext and none, (eleven a.m. and twelve thirty) his fortitude ebbing with each dull clang. Yet he stayed, pacing the busy thoroughfare and hoping the next face in the crowd would be hers, but she never came and his patience finally ran out. To make matters worse there was no message, no apology, nothing.

Returning to Claremont Hall with his emotions in tatters, Philip pushed aside the servant, who opened the door for him, and fell heavily into a chair in the dining area. Slamming his dirty boots on the table, he sat in silence, recalling how he had fawned over Isobel. Lady Joan's absence, Michael's association with Henry of Lancaster and Thomas's trip to France, began to vex him. With nothing to divert his mind he festered and called for a flagon of William Beaufort's favourite Riboldi wine.

"I cannot," the young servant cringed.

"If you value your worthless hide you'll do as I say and do it now!"

Torn between the mild displeasure of the absent Sir William, and the rage of his hostile stepson, the befuddled servant brought the wine. Leaving the jug and a cup on the table, he hurried away to the kitchen. Using a foot to drag the table jug closer, Philip, his hands shaking with rage, poured himself a cup of wine. Spilling part of the contents over his clothes, he cursed his misfortune, downed the imported Riboldi and refilled the cup.

"Lying bitch, fucking whore!" he vomited, each foul expression more pronounced than its predecessor, "Cunt!"

Wiping a blend of wine and spittle from his chin, he narrowed his eyes and scoffed at the idea of a woman betraying him a second time, then he remembered Emma, the girl he callously abandoned at Sheriff Hutton.

"Perhaps I deserve it," he groaned, snorting back the contents of his nose.

The more he tried to understand what had gone wrong, the more he languished in a pool of self-pity, exacerbated by the strong wine.

For the next week, Philip went round the city in a surly manner, shouting at those who failed in their duties, no matter what the excuse. With no word from the Talbot's he fought the urge to call on them. He knew he had fallen for Isobel too soon, as had been the case with Elizabeth Percy, and his wretched heart would pay the price. The only way to escape her all-consuming image was through work and drink. He enjoyed the mind-numbing qualities of Sir William's wine, which helped him sleep at night, while preparations for the king's visit pulled him through the days. Fearing for his master's sanity, Arbroth begged him to call on Francis, but he mulishly refused, though it almost drove him insane.

One late November morning, a messenger arrived in York and announced the Earl of Warwick would be paying a call on the city the following day. The mayor and council held an emergency meeting and argued whether or not Warwick had any legal right to stick his nose into their business. He hadn't, but rather than offend such a great lord they agreed to humour him. Shortly before mid-morning next day, Philip Neville, Mayor Thomas Scawsby, and a host of city officials were congregated near the Micklegate, awaiting the arrival of Lord Warwick. A cold north wind blasted through the barbican, forcing the dignitaries to huddle together near the wall. When Sir Richard Neville and his entourage showed up, the mayoral party bowed respectfully. Pleasantries were exchanged, horses led away, and the group traipsed up the icy steps into the welcoming warmth of the gatehouse.

"Gentlemen," Warwick smiled, taking a goblet of wine from a tray-bearing server. "His Majesty the King!" he declared, removing a glove and raising his goblet.

Jostling for space in the cramped, smoky first floor chamber, the York men, anxious to get the day over, echoed his sentiment and enthusiastically downed their drink.

Making a meal of the last few drops, Philip smacked his lips and placed his empty pewter goblet on the window ledge, before stepping outside and signalling for his cousin to join him. The rest of the group followed and was soon snaking its way along the narrow ramparts, heading for a small tower, where the wall turned obliquely north.

The western part of the city wall traced the natural contours of the landscape to the River Ouze. At the south bank, Philip led the dignitaries down a series of steps to the ferry, and they were rowed across the river. Disembarking at St Leonard's landing, on the north bank, they funnelled into a column and followed him up into the tower and out along the wall. Passing St Leonard's Hospital and St Mary's Abbey they headed for Bootham Bar, the second of York's four gatehouses.

"I see work on the Minster is at a standstill," Warwick huffed, addressing one of the sheriffs and frowning at the wooden scaffold encasing the central tower, "and the moat is full of shit," he added, glancing over the wall and shaking his head. "Why would the king want to come here?"

Dwelling on the last meeting with his cousin, at Norham, Philip remained silent but now he decided to speak up.

"My lord, a writ has been nailed to every church door, yet the butchers continue to throw offal over the parapet. There are not enough wardens to watch every stretch of wall."

"Always some excuse," Warwick sniffed.

"And the tower won't be finished for years," Philip added impertinently. "So there's no point complaining."

Warwick pursed his lips, breathed deeply and restrained his temper.

Passing through the tall, dimly lit gatehouse above Bootham Bar, the group stamped their feet and warmed their hands in front of the fire, before bracing themselves for the next stage of the tour. From Bootham Philip and Warwick drifted along the walkway together, followed by Mayor Scawsby, the newly elected sheriffs and six aldermen, each attired in his warmest winter garb. Guards were posted at intervals, each holding a banner bearing the city arms, while a dozen men-at-arms shadowed the delegation. Whispers of an attempt on the earl's life were rife so Philip thought it wise to take precautions. Warwick nodded favourably at the number of tents going up northwest of the city and told the mayor his preparations were impressive, but should be completed by now; Richard Neville was not one to give too much praise.

"The king's tentmaster is pleased with our effort, my lord..." one of the aldermen offered.

"The king's tent master," Warwick scoffed, cutting him off.

As they approached the back of the archbishop's chapel, between the wall and the north side of the Minster, Warwick stopped and looked at a cleared area marked out for a cavalry camp. Placing a gloved hand on either side of the wall, he leaned into the cruciform-shaped opening and peered out.

"Somerset will desert Edward before the year is out," he whispered guardedly.

Philip's face lit up and he edged closer to Warwick.

"The letter?" he asked, his breath blowing white in the cold air.

"The letter," Warwick echoed, careful to ensure the others were out of earshot.

"I pray for the day..."

"You pray?" Warwick laughed, before walking on, "you who have such little faith in God."

"If you believe that, my lord, you will be an earl for the rest of your days," he joked, aware of Richard's yearning for a Dukedom.

Taken aback by the slight, Warwick about-faced, stepped close enough to Philip for their noses to almost touch and grabbed the cloak under his cousin's neck.

"Perhaps I should take up the post of High Constable, for I know you plotted Somerset's downfall before we ever spoke of it," he said portentously. "Be careful in your choice of words and to whom you address them."

"'Twas a jest," he gasped, shocked by his overreaction, "nothing more."

"Huh," Warwick huffed, releasing him and moving on.

Disturbed by the incident, Philip straightened his ruffled cloak and followed, scuffing his boots and scowling at those behind, lest they gloat at his chastisement.

"What are those?" Warwick asked, casually pointing through the wall at a series of red stakes stuck in the ground at intervals.

"Pegs," Philip said scornfully, referring to the tent markers.

"I know what they are," Warwick bit, as they neared the Bawing Tower, a tall, D-shaped structure, built where the city wall elbowed back to the south-east.

Warwick's aggressive retort worried Philip and he kept his mouth shut for fear of drawing further humiliation on himself.

"Queen Margaret is in France, but she is not welcome there," Warwick announced, his tone less hostile.

"Who cares?" Philip muttered looking over the wall at the monks of St Mary's hard at work in Paynelathes crofts, an enclosed area to the north.

Conscious of Philip's fragile ego, Warwick frowned at him before acknowledging the shivering tower guards as they bowed.

"Whenever we trade words, you sulk like a spoilt child. Accept criticism and learn from it," he urged, turning to address the guards. "Keep warm lads, stay healthy."

"We have argued much these past years," Philip shivered.

"Yes, but you always swim against the tide. Forget the past, the Nevilles must stand together or our enemies will pick us off one by one, and destroy us."

"Louis of France is no fool," Philip warned.

"Louis fears Edward's prowess," Warwick explained. "And he has refused Margaret an audience.

"What of Burgundy?"

"Burgundy will give her gifts and listen to her tale of woe... but in the end he will send her away with nothing."

"I hope you are right, my lord, I don't trust the frogs."

Warwick raised his eyebrows at his response.

"You will need to secure accommodation for Edward's women," he announced.

"Edward's women, how many is he bringing?"

"Who know?" Warwick sighed, but he wants them close, so bear that in mind."

"More headaches," Philip sighed rolling his eyes.

The elderly Mayor of York dawdled a dozen paces behind Warwick and his cousin, resenting their flagrant disrespect for his office. When he quietly complained to one of the aldermen and caught Warwick staring back at him, he blushed. Fortunately, the earl did not hear his comment, but knew by his body language that he was aggrieved.

"My lord, we can go down here," the mayor grovelled, offering a bow, just to be safe.

"My lord, we are not yet finished," Philip protested, irritated by Scawsby's fawning, "son of a draper," he added under his breath.

"Will you never learn to curb that tongue of yours?" Warwick tutted, returning the mayora courteous nod.

A closet Lancastrian, the mayor muttered under his breath and bowed low.

"We'll go down there!" Warwick announced, pointing ahead to Monks Bar, York's third and tallest gatehouse, which gave access to the city from the northeast.

"As you wish, my lord," Thomas Scawsby accepted with a false smile.

Philip allowed his cousin to lead on and kept close in to the wall, hoping to avoid the cutting wind whistling along the ramparts and numbing his face. Coming across several rough timbers, bridging a decayed gap in the walkway, Warwick strode boldly on. Philip hesitated and smirked when he lost his footing on the icy plank and almost fell. Grabbing for the wall, Warwick performed a strange little jig to stop himself from falling, and banged his elbow. Stopping to gaze at a cluster of windmills on a mound out near Monks Bridge, Warwick struggled to conceal his agony.

"I hear from my agent in France that your brother Thomas is most intimate with Margaret's son," he growled through gritted teeth, as sharp pain pulsated up and down his left arm.

"My brothers have been blinded by the Beauforts!" Philip shouted above the wind.

"They must realise the error of their ways before it is too late."

Disturbed by the veiled threat, Philip clamped his stinging, cracked lips together and redirected the conversation.

"Will the king invade Scotland before Christmas, or wait until the spring?"

Fed up with Philip's obsession for attacking the Scots, Warwick refused to answer.

"York cannot support such a large retinue for more than a few days," Philip explained, peeping over the parapet.

"France and England have signed a treaty, and Edward plans to draw the Scots away from Lancaster without a fight. He'll use the threat of invasion to secure an alliance with Scotland. The king has no intention of crossing the border, whether Scotland complies or not; this is all for show," Warwick revealed, referring to the burgeoning campsite.

"My God, what a waste," Philip growled.

"Edward hopes to overawe the Scots by a peaceful demonstration, and force them to abandon Henry once and for all."

"Queen Mary is dying and her son barely off the tit," Philip declared. "The Bishop of St Andrews will use any truce for his own ends, and Louis *will* support him."

"Louis has promised that France will not aid the Scots. The bishop is mindful of this and will come over to us, if only for the benefits he'll receive…"

"I don't trust Louis or the Scots," Philip scoffed.

"You don't trust anyone."

"No, how many have betrayed us in the past."

Warwick knew his cousin was right, but the thought that he might have sanctioned murder and spirited away a thousand pounds, made it difficult for the earl to empathize with him.

"I hope you won't be as overprotective of the king as you were at his coronation?" he said, nursing his throbbing elbow.

"I take my duties seriously," Philip warned, as they arrived before the door leading from the wall to the first floor of Monks Bar.

Warwick removed a handcoverchief from inside his cuff and wiped his runny nose. As he pushed open the small, nail-studded door, Philip noted a sinister look in his eyes. Richard Neville could turn ruthless in an instant and Philip wondered what was in his mind. Thomas Scawsby hustled the rest of the party in and slammed the door, grateful the tour was almost over. After a brief exchange with the warden, the mayor led the group down the steep, narrow steps to the street below. With snowflakes blowing in the air, he hurried them along Ogleforth to the Minster gates. Entering the close they made their way to the deanery for a banquet, presented by the dean and chapter of St Peters to honour the Earl of Warwick's visit.

Chapter 13

Henry Beaufort, the fretful Duke of Somerset, was convinced Edward had betrayed him. Exiled to north Wales was, he believed, his way of removing him from court until a more permanent solution could be found. Also, very little of the promised money had materialized. Edward's Commissioners of the Exchequer raised the assessed amount and sent it to the duke, but between the Nevilles very little ended up in his purse. Now there was the letter sent by the king to Warwick and intercepted by one of Somerset's agents. When the duke read it, he trembled. The forged letter revealed King Edward no longer trusted him. Insecure and apprehensive, he decided to make his peace with the House of Lancaster, and rode to Bamburgh Castle. When King Henry learned of Somerset's return, he rode to Bamburgh, and in an emotional scene, he forgave his wayward retainer. With the aid of his cousin Philip, Warwick had completed a perfect job of deception.

The sheriffs of York and their sergeants stood shivering outside Micklegate, the furred hems of their long cloaks sopping up the mud. King Edward was due to arrive on 1 December, and for the past two days they came and waited, only to be told he was delayed. Finally on the 3rd, the feast day of St Lucius, eight royal musicians lined the wall of the decorated gatehouse and trumpeted a fanfare. An array of richly embroidered standards flying above their heads twisted in the delicate zephyr of a cold winter's morn. In a demonstration of loyalty, the sheriffs and their entourage bowed their heads at the king's approach. From within the walled city a mass of people, alerted by the baying clarions, let out a hearty cheer. Edward acknowledged the civic father's as he rode through the gates. The mayor had just finished cleaning up the city, having been forced to issue a stern writ forbidding waste from being thrown into the streets. Shop fronts received a coat of whitewash and beggars found themselves herded away from the king's route. Gutters had been scrubbed clean and horses banned in the main thoroughfares. Nettles and weeds were uprooted from the Micklegate and its adjoining walls, and the rotting horse was finally hoisted out of the moat.

As the procession made its unhurried way through the narrow streets, the crowds pressed forward, breaking the cordon of soldiers, to touch the king's horse or stroke the royal legs. The Earl of Warwick and his brother, Montague, waited for their cousin near the south transept of St Peters, while the mayor and his aldermen congregated behind, craning their necks for a better view. The ailing Archbishop of York, dressed in a purple cope and mitre for the Advent season, leaned heavily on his pastoral staff, supported by the dean.

Philip lingered near his cousins, staring up at the gargoyles on the parapet of St Michael's-le-Belfrey. Oh how he wished someone would take a hammer and knock their ugly heads off. As the red and blue quartered royal banner came into view, the cheering spread into the Minster close. When the king appeared, the noise rose to an ear splitting roar. Snapping out of his thoughtful trance, Philip watched his regal cousin – cloaked in a suit of red, white and blue velvet – wave at the prettiest maidens. Riding alongside Edward, in all his splendour, was William Hastings, and the king's banneret. Edward's youngest brother, Richard, Duke of Gloucester, and a score of knights in full armour followed. Each warrior held a lance topped with a colourful pennant, their highly-polished suits dazzling the audience. In their wake came a long line of mounted esquires, archers and men-at-arms, and the euphoria escalated, as people in the crowd recognised friends. Unconsciously nibbling on a sliver of loose skin on his cracked lower lip, Philip wondered how Edward had reacted to the news of Somerset's treachery.

Dismounting in front of the Minster, Edward led his nobles inside and offered prayers for his safe arrival. Later he and his companions went to the Hall of the Merchant

Taylors, where they were treated to a banquet before retiring to the bishop's palace. For two days there was feasting, dancing, laughter and much barefaced sexual activity, before Edward received the Scottish ambassadors. The conference went well, despite the news that Queen Mary had died, and a truce was agreed. A document was then drawn up, to be ratified at Newcastle in March.

With the departure of the Scots, Edward's council turned to internal squabbling. Warwick, his brother, and his brother-in-law, Hastings, were for an invasion of Scotland, regardless of any treaty. No mere neophyte monarch, Edward's confidence had grown over the past two years, as he now demonstrated by overruling his mightiest supporter. With Scotland and France tethered by treaties, Henry and Margaret would have nowhere to go. Once they were disposed of, England's future under a Yorkist dynasty would be assured.

During the king's visit Philip Neville kept a low profile, for a good reason. By helping to deceive Somerset he had piled all his resentment for Warwick, Hastings and Elizabeth Percy, as well as his brother's treachery and his father's murder, on the unfortunate duke. Not wishing to betray himself, he remained in the background. Invited to attend a royal council in the Minster Chapter House on the 5th, Philip said very little. When Edward complimented him on his work in York, he complained about the council's lack of commitment and money. The king promised to divert cash to the city's empty coffers. Philip thanked him and left, and Edward, smarting over Somerset's treachery, told Hastings to remind him not to call for his dreary cousin too soon.

In the north, winter days were cold and the nights colder. Philip spent the daylight hours teaching his recently returned esquire, Robert Harrington, the finer point of swordsmanship. In the evenings he drank or played chess and tables with friends. King Edward eventually left York for the midlands; Twelfth Night came and went, followed by Candlemass and St Valentine's

Day, and boredom chipped away at Philip's fortitude. Having learnt that Lady Joan had returned from Scotland and was at Seward House, he decided to pay her a visit. On 20 February, he rode south with Arbroth and several of his men. The cold, raw starkness of the season made the ten mile journey drag, and a sharp wind blew straight into his face, cutting his gullet like a razor.

Seward House was an impressive two-storey manor, boasting half-a-dozen bedchambers, hall, kitchen, latrine and private chapel. As he approached the house, Philip saw a solitary blackbird fly across his path and tangle itself in the bare branches of an oak tree. While the bird squawked and flapped its wings to free itself, he looked at the familiar muddy track ahead and was struck by a moment of melancholy. As a child he loved Seward House, but with his father gone and the family divided, such happy memories had been consigned to history. Finally untangling itself, the blackbird flew away and Philip's bout of sadness went with it.

When the bowing, grey-tiled roof appeared through a lattice of twisted branches, and he heard the distinct echo of wood being chopped, the image of his father teaching him to use a sword for the first time came to mind. The clatter of blunt wooden swords, the pain in his knuckles, and Michael tottering on his chubby legs before falling onto his face, was vivid. He could see his father scooping them up together and a smile cracked his expression. Positioning one boy on each of his massive legs in front of the blazing fire, George Neville would tell them of his adventures in France. Philip loved his exaggerated stories and couldn't wait to become a knight, but the sinister spectre of George Neville's murder fogged his blissful reminiscences, and his body went stiff.

"Mah lord!" Arbroth called out, breaking his abstraction. "The tavern?"

"Tend the horses first!" he snapped, dismounting.

Shaking the tension from his body, Philip watched his men climb down from their horses and lead them to the stables. Removing his gloves, Philip noted the stark, squalidness of the season and headed for the house. Deftly skirting the muddy puddles potholing the narrow path, he massaged his aching shoulder; damp weather always made his old wounds ache.

Standing before the front door, Philip shook water droplets from his cloak, drew a deep breath and twisted the cold iron ring. Opening the door carefully, he entered so quietly his mother, engrossed in a shopping inventory as she shuffled from the kitchen, failed to hear him. Tip-toeing behind her, while she concentrated on the list, he suddenly barked like a mad dog.

"No!" she screamed in terror. "By the holy relics, you are such a fool Philip Neville!"

Several servants came rushing out of the kitchen bearing ladles and carving knives and stopped suddenly. Throwing his head back he guffawed at their reaction.

"Will you ever grow up?" she hissed, placing a hand over her thumping heart and shooing the concerned servants away.

"One day," he sniggered, "perhaps."

Dressed in a long, green dress, divided at the waist by a wide leather belt, Lady Joan's long, greying hair, twisted into buns at the sides, was wrapped in a white linen scarf. Despite his childish antics, Joan Beaufort was delighted to see her eldest son after almost a year. When he kissed her cold cheek she held him tight and they remained poignantly locked. Her headdress reminded him of the horns of a bull, and he chuckled to himself. Sensing his amusement, she pushed him away.

"Your manners have not improved," she huffed, noting his heavily lined face.

"I'm sorry," he grinned, trying not to look at her horns. "Why didn't you let me know you were home?"

"I sent one of the servants into town this very morning," she explained. "You must have passed him on the road. But you are here now... come, come and sit with me."

During her time in Scotland, Lady Joan had been treated like a leper, due to her Neville connections. Several of Queen Margaret's courtiers spitefully aired their opinions of her family to her face, but she always responded kindly. When William Beaufort gently rebuked his wife for her leniency, she smiled and told him that kindness provoked them more than any abusive riposte. Returning from Scotland with several servants and two of her husband's retainers, disguised as drovers, Joan Beaufort preferred the serenity of Seward House to the hustle and bustle of Claremont Hall.

Seated near the fireplace in the small, dimly lit hall, mother and son conversed amicably for almost an hour, but when they moved to the table to eat, she spoilt the ambience by mentioning her husband, William. At first Philip ignored it, but when she brought up his attainder for treason, he reminded her of Somerset's attempt to have him arrested at Woodstock, and his hatred for the very name 'Beaufort' erupted.

"I woke in the middle of the night with a sword aimed at my heart. I have been accused of plotting to murder my cousin, the king, and forced to flee with nothing but the clothes on my back," he said angrily. "And one of my men was cruelly murdered to enhance the lie. The Beauforts must be wiped out!"

"William is not like his nephew," she bleated.

"Huh," he sneered.

Sensitive to his obsessive loathing for her husband's family, she tried to steer the conversation on a different path.

"Do you despise your brother for his loyalty to Henry?"

"No," he pouted, "regardless of his affection for an idiot."

His vindictive response grated and she reacted by calling him mutton-headed and blasphemous for supporting a usurper, who stole the crown from the head of an anointed sovereign.

Philip sat back in his chair; he had never heard his

mother speak with such passion. She followed up her malicious attack on her nephew by slotting Warwick's name into the diatribe and branding them both traitors for signing a treaty with France. Philip wisely remained silent during her tempestuous tirade and watched the angst build in her tearful eyes. Unable to eat, she left the table, hobbled towards the dying fire and poked the disintegrating timbers with a rod, rekindling the embers.

"King Henry is a good man!" she sobbed softly, dabbing her eyes on the wide sleeve of her dress. "You think him unfit to rule because he hates war and all the senseless killing it breeds, but you are wrong."

"I'm sorry, my lady," he lamented, knuckling his forehead in frustration.

"If William is attainted we lose everything," she whined, "I am sick of living on the edge."

"Edward would not take this from you," he said, meaning Seward House.

"No, but he would take William from me; and you would gladly hand him the axe to cut off his head."

Leaping up from his seat, Philip took several agitated steps back and forth.

"The Duke of Somerset left Henry for Edward, only to renounce his fealty twelve months later."

"But William is kind, and he gives me what your father did not: love and security."

"Love," he scoffed, "his brother murdered my father… and he now forbids me from entering my own house, but I have defied him and drunk his wine," he half laughed.

"Oh Philip you are so blinded by hatred you cannot see the truth," she sighed, shaking her head. "No one knows who killed your father."

"I know!" he spat, stabbing a finger at himself.

"And what is to become of your brothers; do they stand in Worcester's shadow?" she bemoaned, clutching the wooden cross hanging from her neck.

"If they are, 'tis no fault of mine," he huffed. "Blame your husband. He turned Michael from the Nevilles and inspired Thomas to go to France?"

"He did not!"

"No?"

"No, Michael asked Thomas to go."

"Nonsense!" Philip gasped. "Why would he do such a thing?"

"Michael is to be wed," she announced, the slightest of smiles complimenting her words.

"What?" he coughed. "I don't believe it, to whom?"

"The Lady Anne, daughter of Lord Audley's cousin. She is a lady-in-waiting to Queen Margaret. Michael asked Thomas to go and watch over her."

"That she-wolf is no longer queen," he growled. "It would be better for all if Michael had gone to France himself."

"Nevertheless, Thomas has gone."

Philip knew he would have to concede the argument or ruin this, their first reunion in almost a year. Sitting down at the table, he slumped forward, rested his chin on his open palm and poked a knife at the plate of bread and creamy spermyse, an herb-laced cheese, brought to the table by a young serving girl.

"I have three sons but no grandchildren," she hinted, watching his eyes follow her maid back to the kitchen.

Philip knew where she was going with this and pretended not to hear.

"How old is this cheese?" he mumbled, feigning an interest in the food.

With a mother's natural inquisitiveness she asked if he contemplated marriage; after all he was almost twenty-nine. Philip refused to meet her probing eyes and Lady Joan sensed his unease. She knew of his association with Elizabeth Percy and of her engagement to Ralph Hastings. Observing the emotional conflict in his eyes and his attempt to conceal it, she allowed the subject to die naturally.

"I want you to keep Thomas out of this," she urged, reaching across the table and touching his rough hand.

"It's too late; he is appointed esquire to Henry's son," he revealed pulling his hand away. "Michael and your husband have pushed him in, not I."

"William offered him advice and money nothing more, and Thomas jumped at the chance… he was not content at Cambridge."

"And what of his engagement?"

"Alas, that has lost its appeal," she sighed.

"He should have been sent to train for knighthood," Philip scoffed. "If my father was alive he would have commanded it."

"If your father was alive, Thomas would have gone into the Church. He has no desire to waste his life in this senseless blood feud that has consumed the better part of your life!" she snapped, the anger in her voice mellowing, as she noticed his flickering eyes and the way his hands shook while he bolted his food.

"You drink too much," she said sadly, a serving girl brought him a cup of wine.

"I drink to forget," he countered, making eye contact, before looking away guiltily and slurping the wine.

"I want you and Michael to be reconciled."

"Where is he?" he asked, slapping his lips together and wiping his mouth, first on a sleeve then, as an afterthought, in a surnape offered by his disapproving mother.

"With the king."

"Henry of Lancaster is not the king," he growled contemptuously.

Cursing his own intolerance, he apologised and tried hard not to react so fiercely.

"Oh don't apologise," she sighed, conscious of his hostile disposition, "nothing you say surprises me."

Shocked by her prescience, he allowed her to continue.

"I want you to go to Michael."

"What?" he gasped, almost choking on a piece of bread?

"I don't care how you do it, but go and see your brother and ask him to bring Thomas home," she implored, her

261

mouth drooping sadly. "I don't want anything to happen to him."

"He won't do it…"

"He will."

"He won't!" he repeated, raising his voice.

Sitting back in the chair, Philip massaged his chin and wondered if he could use such a meeting for his own ends. He knew he must tread carefully, for Michael was his equal when it came to deception.

"Will you try, for my sake?"

"No," he said firmly.

"Please."

"Alright," he moaned, shaking his head. "I'll try," he said submissively, believing Michael would refuse outright. "But I'll not go to him; we meet on neutral ground."

Philip went on to insist that if Michael agreed, he was to bring no more than six armed men and tell no one, not even Sir William. Wounded by his intimation, Lady Joan accepted her son's abrasive terms and promised to send a servant to Bamburgh with a letter.

"What if he should read it?"

"I'll send one who cannot read," she snapped, irritated by his mistrust. "Where and when?"

"Neville's Cross," he grinned, referring to an ancient family monument outside Durham, "one and twenty days hence… if he accepts."

"He will accept," she answered, running a thumb along her fingertips to work out the date, "the feast day of St Euphrasia."

Amazed at her memory, Philip smiled and continued eating. With business out of the way, mother and son conversed on more amiable topics. To please her he agreed to spend the night at Seward House.

Chapter 14

In the first week of March, news reached London that the Duke of Somerset was in Northumberland stirring the pot of rebellion. Warwick urged the king to hurry the ratification of the treaty with Scotland. His brother, Montague, was sent north to rendezvous with King James's envoys at Norham Castle, and escort them to York, not Newcastle as planned. The king promised to meet the Scots on 20 April, five weeks later than the original date. With so much hinging on the conference Edward ordered Philip to Middleham, where Warwick could watch him. Philip asked permission to go on a personal errand first. Grateful to keep as much distance as possible between himself and his irksome cousin, Warwick agreed.

Early one fresh, March morning, Philip Neville, Arbroth, his esquire, page, and several men-at-arms, emerged from beneath their damp blankets. After a hearty breakfast of bacon, bread and wine they decamped for the final part of their journey to Durham. As they cantered along the dark road, the sun nudged its dazzling forehead above the horizon, banishing the night and lighting up the countryside. Birds sang their morning song and the rising temperature evaporated banks of rolling translucent mist from the valleys. Six days earlier, Philip received a message from his brother agreeing to meet and consenting to his demands: place, date and number of retainers. Wary of his motive, Philip played along.

Neville's Cross was a tall stone memorial, erected by Sir Ralph Neville to commemorate the English victory over the Scots in 1346. Topped by a carving of Christ on the cross, the monument was sited on rough ground half-a-mile west of Durham. Philip and his men travelled the last few miles in apprehensive silence, their distrustful eyes searching the ridges and ravines for anything unusual. Attired in a padded blue jack, with arms and legs partly armoured, Philip rode his favourite horse, Hotspur.

Weighing fourteen hundred pound, Hotspur was a courser, much sturdier than a palfrey, and suitable for carrying a knight into combat. Purchased at Smithfield four years ago for the sum of forty pounds, the muscular, fifteen hands high stallion had the power of a battering ram in a charge.

Drawing his horse to a walk, Philip raised his right hand and held it in the air as a sign for those behind to curb their mounts.

"Be on your guard," he warned, scrutinizing the trees and bracken surrounding the monument.

The party remained in the saddle, waiting patiently and jerking their heads in at the clacking of a magpie, or the rustle of a rabbit. The wait soon began to fray Philip's nerves.

"What happened to James Douglas?" he asked Arbroth, referring to a conversation they had back in August.

"Uh?" the puzzled Scot frowned.

"Black Douglas," Philip emphasised.

"Ah dinnah think ye wanted to know."

A cold glare cut Arbroth's sarcasm and he cleared his throat.

"He died in Spain, fighting the Moslems. His body and the Bruce's heart were returned tah Scotland, for burial."

"Is that it?"

Before he could answer Ashley Dean's young ears picked out the faint pounding of horse hooves.

"There!" the boy yelped, standing in the stirrups and pointing north where the road cut through the ridge.

The Neville men instinctively closed in on their leader and Philip tensed himself. At first the others failed to hear what the eleven year old heard, but soon the rattling of steel and the thud of horses' hooves grew distinct. Six armoured knights abruptly rose up from behind the ridge and formed a line on its crest. The bright midday sun hit their highly polished helmets and breastplates, giving them a glittering aura of invincibility.

"Knights of the Round Table," the young page gasped in childlike wonder, his jaw falling open.

264

"They look ready for a fight, mah lord?" Arbroth warned, as they trotted slowly down the incline, visors closed.

"Then a fight they shall have!" Harrington spat, puffing out his chest and struggling to control his impatient palfrey.

Trampled and almost killed by a rogue destrier during his service as a page, Robert Harrington held a secret dread of horses. Sensing his unease, the palfrey grew skittish.

"Steady," Philip urged grabbing his bridle, as the six knights came to a halt two hundred paces away.

"Let me sir," the sixteen year old insisted, gamely drawing his sword, as a single horseman cantered forward alone.

"No," Philip cautioned, forcing his over-zealous esquire's blade down into its scabbard. "Stay here, all of you."

"But…"

"Do as I say," he insisted.

Harrington bowed his head reluctantly and Philip nudged his horse forward.

As the distance between the two knights diminished, Philip searched for something familiar in his opposite number. The armour he wore was polished to a mirrored finish, his closed visor stuck out like a duck's bill and the plodding horse he rode, dribbled bubbling foam. Recalling his last meeting with Michael, Philip anticipated another explosive clash, but an uneasy thought flashed through his mind. Could this be Somerset? Had Michael betrayed him? Nervously biting his lower lip, he looked around for signs of an ambush. With the gap between them shrinking, Philip's mouth dried and his left cheek twitched. When no more than a horse length separated them, both men tugged back on the reins and pushed their feet forward, bringing both horses to a halt.

Philip's eyes blinked apprehensively, he gnawed the inside of his cheek, and his right hand lingered near the pommel of his sword, but there was no reaction from the other chevalier. Using the back of his glove to dab perspiration from his eyes, he watched his counterpart raise his narrow visor, to reveal a pair of dark, menacing eyes and part of a healed scar running down his left cheek. His chin and throat were masked by the steel wrapper, but it was Michael and Philip breathed easier. Anger, frustration and sadness consumed both boys as they stared at each other. Michael's horse eventually broke the tension by stamping the ground with a foreleg and shaking its dusty mane, prompting Philip to speak.

"Have you come to fight?"

"Have you?" he retorted, holding his visor up.

"You wear full armour."

"We're in Yorkist country."

"You'll not be harmed; you have the protection of the Earl of Warwick," he lied.

"That arse," Michael mocked. "What is it you want? Speak plainly, for I am not a patient man," he coughed, trying to stop his visor from snapping shut, "to hell with this piece of German shit!"

"Our mother has concerns."

"Thomas?"

"Yes," Philip echoed, allowing a slight smile to draw up the corners of his mouth.

"Why have you asked to see me?" Michael frowned, leaning back in the saddle and glancing around. "Are we to be attacked?"

"I gave you my word," Philip growled, keeping a concerned eye on the five knights waiting in the background. "We're alone."

"They will only intervene if I smell treachery," Michael promised tugging the metal wrapper down as his visor dropped. "I see you have that god-damn Scot with you," he scoffed, forcing the visor up and acknowledging Arbroth with a curt nod, before leaning out of the saddle and spitting.

Arbroth returned his brusque greeting with an uneasy

dip of his head.

"Craven dog," Michael muttered.

"Forget him… Edward has won over the Scots and the French, I ask you to make peace with him before it is too late."

"The time has not yet come for this knight to abandon his King as others have," he declared, ramming his fisted gauntlet against one of the pins linking the visor to its armet. "Louis will never ally himself to an English King who claims sovereignty over any part of France," Michael said confidently. "Henry still has many friends. You see this horse? A gift," he said, patting the animal's sweaty neck.

"From Sir William?" Philip sneered, admiring his armour, but not showing it. "It's only a matter of time before we find Henry," he added, rolling his hand into a fist to emphasis his words.

"Why are we here?" Michael pressed the padding of his helmet so tight against his face the horsehair stuffing irritated his skin.

"T'was not my idea," Philip groused.

"Mother?"

"I would not be here but for her!" Philip explained, narrowing his eyes. "Our cousin Montague is going to meet King James's ambassadors at Norham and escort them to York," he explained, shifting in the saddle, a mixture of perspiration, leg armour and woollen hose chafing his thighs. "Henry is finished."

"Why do you tell me this?" Michael asked, well aware of the York-Scottish alliance.

"To show you the folly of staying with Henry," he revealed, conscious he could verify anything he told him from Lancastrian agents.

As he listened, Michael sieved out the irrelevant details and pieced together the important elements. His cousin Montague, would, at some future date, be guiding a party of Scottish envoys to York. If they could be attacked, and the Yorkists blamed, King James might be persuaded to postpone the Treaty, or abandon it altogether.

"When is this to happen?" Michael asked casually, removing his gauntlets.

"Soon," Philip replied, his heart hammering against his chest as he tried hard not to reveal too much.

"I think you are toying with me?" he smirked, tucking his gauntlets through his belt and pulling at the wrapper in an effort to cool his red, sweaty face. "You always did use too many words."

Philip's disappointment showed in his eyes, but rather than force the issue, he reined in his zeal. "France and Scotland have abandoned your cause," he sniffed, certain Michael had taken the bait, "but at least your dog has come home."

Michael knew Philip was referring to the Duke of Somerset.

"He's not my dog. I would have his head on a spear, for he has caused my King to lose heart. Now he has come back and his treachery is forgotten."

"Our Uncle Fauconberg is dead," Philip declared with a heavy heart.

"Yes," Michael sighed, lowering his eyes to conceal his sadness.

William Neville died suddenly in January, while campaigning against Alnwick Castle. Both boys loved and respected the old warrior who reminded them so much of their father.

"I'll miss him," Michael said staring into space and crossing himself. "Will you look to our mother's safety now Thomas has gone?"

"You pushed him to go," Philip snapped, "you do it! Where is he?"

"With the queen; she's set up court in one of her father's castles," Michael revealed, as sweat dripped irritatingly from his eyelids.

"The fool," Philip hissed, arching his back and rolling his head to relieve the pain in his neck.

Neither brother spoke of the women in their lives, nor

of their emotions; such feelings were always kept locked away.

In the background, Robert Harrington leaned towards Ashley Dean.

"They seem friendly."

"Why shouldn't they, they are brothers," the youngster said rubbing his nose.

After a period of profound discussion interspersed with frenetic outbursts over which side was right, the conversation between the two knights petered out.

"Well, I am for York," Philip announced.

"Look to our mother's well-being until King Henry returns."

"Stop deluding yourself."

Michael ground his teeth and breathed deeply through his nose.

Before they parted, Philip tried once to persuade him to drop Henry.

"No," he said firmly. "You chose your side, I chose mine."

"You picked the wrong side," Philip said, spotting concern in his eyes.

"I'll never betray my King," Michael sniffed, pulling on his gauntlets and nudging his horse forward. "Fare thee well."

Dragging his reins to the right, Michael jabbed rowels to horseflesh and cantered away, his armour clattering as he jounced heavily in the saddle. Before following his companions over the crest, he stopped, turned and raised a hand. He retained this pose until his brother returned his salute. At first Philip refused, but when he did, it was too late, Michael was gone. Philip knew his brother was too astute to be taken in by any scheme he suggested, but there were others, only too eager to pounce on such an opportunity. Confident he would disclose Edward's plans to his King, Philip rode hard for Warwick's residence in Richmondshire.

In the great hall of Middleham Castle, Philip revealed

details of his meeting with Michael to his cousin, unaware he was about to set off a powder keg. Outraged at his lack of discretion, Warwick berated him in front of his young daughters. The humiliated knight tried to calm him down, but the inconsolable earl would not listen. His bellowing voice echoed down the two twisting stairwells into the vast cellar and kitchen below, and the servants working there, cringed.

"We must cancel everything. I'll not risk my brother's life!" he roared, pacing to and fro. "What will I tell the king?"

"My lord," Philip pleaded, "if you cancel, you will pass up a chance to put an end to Somerset's meddling once and for all."

Warwick turned his back on Philip and glared over his shoulder, his narrow, piercing eyes penetrating deep as he failed to understand his distorted reasoning.

"His meddling!" he barked, clenching his fists. "What of yours?"

"Give me a company of soldiers," Philip offered, "let me shadow Lord Montague, and I'll guarantee no harm will come to him—"

"Somerset is no fool!" Warwick cut him off, his facial muscles pulsating angrily.

Locking his hands together behind his back, the brooding earl smiled sympathetically at his startled children. Jerking his head around he stared at Philip, while his wife, attracted by the argument, came in and guided her daughters out.

"I haven't seen my girls for months and now they find me in bad humour!" he fumed, pacing tensely; furious that Philip's drive for revenge may have spoiled Edward's strategy for knocking Scotland out of the war. "Tomorrow I am for London, oh what do I do?"

"I warned you Somerset would betray us," Philip whined in a low voice.

"Yes," he scoffed his own complicity in the affair foremost in his mind. "You told me, yet the money is still missing."

"Sire?" he sniffed, crinkling his forehead.

"Nothing," Warwick snarled, recalling his conversation with the odious assassin, at Norham. "I can't think straight."

"What shall I do?"

"Jump off a cliff," Warwick muttered, releasing a low hissing sigh, before closing his eyes and massaging his temples.

"My lord," Philip lamented, staring at the table, "is there a way back for us?"

Warwick placed his hands on his hips and looked at the floor, but was unable to answer.

"May I leave?" Philip asked, aware of his cousin's exasperation.

"Go," he said, waving him away. "I'll acquaint my brother with this news. When he leaves for Norham, you will go with him and share whatever fate comes his way. But I give thee fair warning, should John die and you survive, pray you never come before me again."

Philip left the hall with the earl's threat echoing in his ears. Next morning he left Middleham and rode to York.

After the rendezvous at Neville's Cross, Michael headed for Bamburgh Castle, on the Northumberland coast. Ignoring his stepfather and the Duke of Somerset, standing together by the entrance to the Great Tower, he dismissed his companions and clattered up the stairs to the second floor. Forced to leave Scotland, following the truce between Edward and James, Henry of Lancaster planted his standard on Bamburgh's imposing battlements.

"Is the king here?" Michael snapped at a passing esquire, bashing his visor open.

"Yes," he answered snootily, pointing at a guarded chamber. "He's in there," he said, adding under his breath, "for all the use he is."

"Good, now help me take this god-damn helmet off."

Removing his gauntlets and armet with the bungling

assistance of the contrary esquire, Michael slapped his breastplate to shake off the dust and rapped knocked on the door.

"Come!"

Entering the apartment, Michael went down agonizingly on one knee and bowed his head. Surprised by the interruption, King Henry closed the religious booklet he'd been reading and motioned for his visitor to come closer. With his greasy hair clinging to his puffy face like wet seaweed, Michael rose, the sharp pain in the back of his knees contorting his features. Rattling forward, he lowered his head a second time adding a graceful sweep of his arm.

"Your Grace," he offered.

Slumped in a narrow, high-backed chair, surmounted with green and crimson velvet cushions, Henry of Lancaster appeared lucid and eager to hear what he had to say. Since recovering from his second breakdown, Henry took little interest in his kingship. The pale, smooth-faced passive monarch dressed simply and spent his days studying theology, listening to music or praying. The governance of England he delegated to those unworthy of such a task. With an upraised palm and a calm smile, he invited Michael to speak.

"I see my Lord of Somerset is back," he opened, glancing at a well-armed bodyguard standing in the shadows.

Henry treated his sarcasm with disdain and asked him to explain his presence. With rampant fervour, Michael revealed the Yorkists' plan to escort a group of Scottish emissaries to York, for the purpose of ratifying a treaty. Intrigued by Michael's lively hand movements, Henry, aware of Edward's conniving with the Scots, listened as he offered a solution.

"Sire, my brother believes I have fallen for his transparent strategy. No doubt he is relating the news that he has deceived me, and how we will lead our men into a trap."

"Are you certain of this?"

"Yes sire, some of my own men overheard one of Lord Scrope's retainers in a Newcastle tavern, singing like a bird. Edward and the Bishop of St Andrews have agreed to a truce that will leave us out in the cold."

Amused by Michael's confirmation of what he already knew, Henry elevated his eyebrows, and placed his slender, well-manicured hands over his mouth to smother an impish smirk.

"You are too late, Sir Knight, Louis of France has renounced us. Thus we are here, and here we must stay. When the Earl of Warwick is ready he will bring a mighty host against us, and we have little with which to stop him," he sighed. "You must pray and pray hard, for we are all in God's hands now."

"Give me a hundred mounted men and I will capture my cousin, Montague," Michael proposed, ignoring his comment. "We'll show the Scots they cannot rely on Edward to protect them."

"We don't have twenty mounted men, let alone a hundred," Henry bemoaned.

"Then give me ten, sire."

"I'll think on it," he smiled, his legs twitching excitedly.

Rubbing his palms on the armrests, Henry thanked Michael for his continued loyalty, opened his book and politely waved him out.

Puzzled by his behaviour, Michael stood up straight and insisted on an answer, the oily helmet under his arm beginning to slip and annoy him.

"Your Grace?"

"I will think on it," Henry repeated, without looking up. "You must be tired after your journey, go to the kitchens and have some mawmeny, there's a woman from the village who makes it the old way, thick and spicy," he smiled, smacking his lips together. "And do not provoke our friend, Somerset. The good Lord has seen fit to bring him back to us."

"Then the good Lord is a fool," Michael hissed.

Shocked by his unwarranted blasphemy, Henry snapped his head up as if to scold him, but changed his mind. Pulling the cap down over his forehead and closing his eyes meant he had nothing more to say. Angered by his childish behaviour, Michael bowed sharply and backed out of the royal chamber, his armour clattering louder than was necessary.

"He's as mad as his grandfather," Michael barked at the guards standing outside the chamber, and stomped away.

In an apartment on the second floor of the Great Tower, Michael paced and raged at the four walls before throwing his helmet against the window, denting both the stonework and the armet.

"Mawmeny," he muttered. "Why the hell would I want to eat that shit?"

Pressing his lips together, he took several deep breaths and called for someone, anyone, to come and help him out of his steel shell.

Gravely concerned by Philip's poor judgement, the Earl of Warwick met his cousin, the king, in London. Edward listened to Richards's complaint but believed the enterprise should go ahead, provided the escort was increased. Warwick didn't like it, but agreed and sent his brother written authority to second part of the Newcastle garrison to his force. By midday of 12 April, Montague was ready to leave York. Five hundred archers and men-at-arms were gathered in the grounds of St Mary's Abbey, awaiting the command to form up. Also there was Arbroth, just arrived, with news to boost Philip's confidence.

Sensitive to his master's obduracy and fed up with his drinking and cheerless silences, the Scot rode to Ashby de la Zouch without telling anyone. When he arrived at the Talbot home, he found out why Isobel had failed to meet Philip back in October. That very morning, a messenger came to the Talbot town house with the news that Lady Julia was dying. Leprosy had decimated her body and she had only weeks to live. Happy to see Arbroth, Francis explained everything, weeping wretchedly as he revealed his mother was not expected to see the summer out. He also told him he would return to York after the funeral.

"Inform your master that my sister speaks of him with maudlin concern," Francis added.

Thanking him for his kindness and a small sack of food, Arbroth returned to York.

When he reached Claremont Hall, Arbroth learned of Montague's imminent departure, and galloped to the abbey. He found Philip sitting on his horse, examining the remains of an old Roman tower. Weaving his rouncey between clusters of chatting soldiers, he trotted over to the solitary knight. With thunder wrinkling his forehead, Philip was about to rip into his servant for disappearing without a word, but when the exhausted Scot unfolded his tale, he forgave him. Grabbing him by the neck, he knuckled Arbroth's scraggly hair.

"You're a rogue, but you have a good heart," he laughed, as a wave of optimism and verve washed over him.

"Calm yourself, my lord," he spluttered, pushing him off and acknowledging Robert Harrington and the others.

"Line up on the road!" a sergeant roared, waving his arms and opening a path through a group of archers, "we're leaving!"

As the fifth bell of the monastic day rang out the time, five hundred foot soldiers, and their supply wagons, assembled on a crumbling section of Roman road. While centenars led the army out through the abbey gatehouse, Montague's brother, George, Bishop of Exeter and Chancellor of England, galloped into the grounds with an armed escort. Dismounting, the highly-charged bishop glared at Philip, who waited near the gatehouse, watching the army tramp out.

"Be vigilant my brother," he urged grabbing the bridle of Montague's horse and continuing to glare at Philip. "Trust no one."

In his early thirties, George was the youngest of the three Neville brothers. His short dark hair, dimpled chin and long face revealed a forceful, proud disposition. Highly educated, he had a reputation for being an eloquent orator, but was despised by some for his meteoric rise up the ministerial ladder. As chancellor, he had been sent to St Omer to negotiate the treaty with France, and to guarantee trade links with Burgundy, a task he accomplished to Edward's satisfaction. In York to visit the ailing archbishop, he heard of his brother's assignment and rode out to wish him well.

Lowering his head reverently, John Neville listened while his brother prayed and made the sign of the cross.

"Dominus Vobiscum," he ended.

"You worry too much," Montague laughed, crossing his chest.

"'Tis fortunate someone looks out for your immortal soul," he frowned. "May God protect you in the days ahead?"

Concerned by the bishop's intimidating looks, Philip urged his horse out through the gates to avoid a confrontation.

Mounted on his beloved courser, Constantine, Montague teased his brother for his caution and bade him farewell. As he cantered through the gatehouse, the stern-faced bishop blessed the soldiers filing past.

"Gloria patrie et fillio et spiritui sancto!" he shouted after them, sketching an invisible cross in the air.

The last of the grizzled veterans bared their heads and crossed themselves reverently. Brimming with self-confidence, Montague soon forgot his brother's advice and rode several miles ahead of the column, accompanied only by four bodyguards. Fearing for his safety, Philip begged his cousin to stay close to the main force. Thick with trees and sprouting second growth, the Forest of Galtres encroached onto the main trail, funnelling the soldiers into a narrow, slow-moving line. If attacked, the Yorkists would be hard pressed to defend themselves in such tangled country.

"My lord, the Duke of Somerset is ahead of us with an army." Philip warned. "This enterprise is no secret."

"No thanks to you," Montague chided, before galloping recklessly away and throwing a cloud of choking dust into the warm air.

Despite orders to remain with the foot, Philip, mounted on Hotspur, and Arbroth straddling a dilapidated hackney, set off each morning to shadow Montague without his knowledge.

Five days after leaving York, Montague's army was camped near the village of Dipton, ten miles south of Newcastle. A light rain had fallen during the night damping down the choking dust and the men's spirits. As usual, John Neville rose before dawn, wolfed a hearty breakfast, attended mass and made ready to leave. With enemy scouts reported nearby, he decided to wear armour.

"Hurry up!" he bellowed at his bodyguards with a madcap grin, while in a nearby open tent Robert Harrington panicked to secure his master's leg armour by flickering candlelight.

"Sir John is in fine fettle this morning." Arbroth yawned, chewing on a slice of cold, tough beef, as Montague and his men mounted.

"We'd better move or he'll be in Newcastle before we're in the saddle," Philip hissed.   Arbroth wiped his hands on his leather jack and annoyed him by offering up his helmet.

"Leave it," Philip growled.

"We're close tah Newcastle. The man should be safe now," Arbroth surmised, tossing the armet to young Dean, who almost dropped it.

"The sooner we get there the better. If anything happens to him," he said, leaving the tent, as Montague cantered out of the camp, "I'm a dead man."

Arbroth swallowed a last mouthful of salted beef and drew his forefinger across his throat in a morbid allusion. Philip dryly thanked him for terrifying his page and rolled his arms out, allowing Harrington to fix the steel breast to the backplate.

"Hurry them up!" he shouted, at a gangly ventenar from Nottingham, who stood drilling wax from his ear with a finger.

"They've not finished eating, my lord."

"Then they go without. Get them on the road and make haste!"

The cantankerous, company commander discharged a thick stream of brown spit and yelled at his archers to move. Grunting as he hauled himself up onto Hotspur's back, Philip was surprised when the horse bucked violently, almost throwing him.

"Steady, damn you!" he cursed, using rein and spur to bring the animal under control.

Following his cousin along the moonlit road, he came to a fork in the road.

"This way," he indicated, taking the right branch.

After riding for only a few minutes, Philip jerked back on the leathers, drawing Hotspur to a halt.

"Hear that?" he hissed, tugging the gorget clinging to his throat, and twisting his neck.

"There," Arbroth whispered, pointing into the black trees.

Philip and Arbroth listened while a series of loud, incoherent shouts bounced from trunk to trunk. Both men were confused as to exactly where the sound could be pinpointed. Cries of alarm and the sporadic clash of weapons grew more distinct as the first grey light stretched across the sky, increasing Philip's concern. Unsheathing his arming sword he dug his spurs hard into Hotspur's flanks. The courser reacted with a painful whinny and bolted into the underbrush. Jabbing his heels in, Arbroth followed as fast as his hackney would go. Ignoring the low branches slapping his unprotected face, Philip lowered his head and charged on.

When Montague had reached the junction, he took the left fork and blundered into a well- prepared ambush. He knew he was in trouble when two of his bodyguards were cut down before they could draw sword. With only enough time to snap his visor shut, Montague found himself assaulted from all directions. In the narrow confines of the road, he lowered his head and held his breath, as a barrage of sword and mace blows pummelled his armour. Constantine shrieked and reared in abject terror, forcing Sir John to hold on for dear life.

Suddenly a lone knight thundered out of the trees, body bent forward and sword arm stretched back over his bare head. Seeing his cousin in trouble and with Warwick's warning ringing in his ears, Philip Neville burst into the shadowy clearing like a whirlwind. Yelling at the top of his voice, and unable to change course, he bore down on the two men attacking his cousin. With bulging eyes and smoky vapour misting from its dilated nostrils, Hotspur slammed into the nearest horseman, hitting him with the force of a battering ram. The shocked Lancastrian and his horse were bowled over. Both crashed to the ground so hard that several pins on the knight's helmet broke and his sallet flew off. Unable to extricate his trapped leg from his kicking horse, the fallen warrior made his body as small as possible. Turning his courser in a tight circle, Philip wedged his sword under his left arm and purposely steered Hotspur over the disabled knight's unprotected head. The courser's heavy, iron-shod hooves snapped his neck like a twig and smashed his face to a bloody pulp.

Dressed in a buff leather jack with several pieces of ill-fitting armour strapped to his arms, Arbroth trotted out of the underbrush. Shouting in his native tongue to terrorize the enemy and conceal his own fear, he leapt off his hackney, onto the back of a Lancastrian. Grabbing his collar, he dragged him out of the saddle. Before he could recover, the Scot drove a ballock dagger deep into his ribs, leaving him coughing up blood and gasping for breath. Finally free to manoeuvre, Montague unsheathed his huge bastard sword and used it with great effect, cutting down one opponent and spraying the foliage with his blood.

Stunned by the unexpected turn of events, and fearing the arrival of more Yorkists, the surviving Lancastrians fled.

Three of the enemy lay dead and two others stood nearby, heads bowed. Two of Sir John's bodyguards had also been killed in the brief melee and another wounded. Staggered by the ferocity of the ambush, Montague raised his visor and nodded gratuitously at Philip.

"Kill them!" he spat, pointing at the prisoners, embarrassed by his own stupidity.

While the captives were led away for execution, Sir John dismounted and tried to control his trembling body.

"Get this off!" he grunted, grabbing the sides of his helmet and looking at Philip. "And don't say a word."

"As you wish, my lord," he replied, as the horse he knocked down, stood up, shook its bloody mane, and slowly dragged the faceless corpse of its rider to and fro.

Arbroth helped the only uninjured bodyguard remove Montague's helmet and its constrictive wrapper, while Philip sheathed his sword and patted Hotspur's neck. The rising sun illuminated the carnage and Montague moaned at his heavily dented armour and tattered surcoat. Pouring a skin of water over his head, he downed a cup of wine and quietly thanked the Almighty for his survival. Newcastle lay only eight miles away, but he decided to wait for the rest of the army; his zeal for riding ahead, curbed.

A second Lancastrian ambush was foiled before it could be sprung, and a sedate John Neville hurried the army on to Newcastle. The Yorkists crossed the Tyne Bridge as the bells of St Johns church rang out the hour of Sext: 9.40a.m. Exaggerated rumours of Somerset's strength forced Montague to make a four-day stopover. During a council with the mayor and John Lord Scrope, Captain of Newcastle, in the castle's Great Tower, a messenger galloped in through the Black Gate. Leaving his foam-flecked mount untethered, he ran into the tower and stumbled up the stairs to the second floor.

Entering the Great Hall, the wheezing, sweat-stained

messenger sleeved perspiration from his glowing face and bowed to Lord Montague.

"My lord," he panted, filling his lungs with air. "Somerset has been reinforced. In a few days his army will number more than three thousand."

"How came you by such news?" Montague asked calmly, while Philip Neville stood at the window looking down into the courtyard below.

"From Sir Richard Croft, my lord," he spluttered.

"Do you accept this as reliable, my lord?" the pint-sized, pot-bellied mayor asked.

"Richard Croft is not one to exaggerate," Montague sniffed, waving the scout away. "I will need most of your men, my lord," he said with a purposeful frown.

"You would leave us defenceless?" the mayor quivered.

"Newcastle will best be protected if I beat Somerset in the field," Montague explained. "To do that I must have every man you can spare."

"As you wish, my lord," he conceded.

Despite Croft's estimate, Montague knew his army was far superior to Somerset's hotchpotch force. The majority were Sir John's own retainers and tenants, who had fought with him many times, and were led by trusted officers. Dismissing the mayor, Montague told Lord Scrope he would continue on to Norham. Looking at Philip, he received an approving nod from his cousin.

Next morning, Sir John Neville, harnessed in his beautifully crafted Italian plate armour, its dents hammered out and the steel buffed to a mirrored finish, mounted his courser. Wedged comfortably in the saddle hand on hip, he sat watching his army file out of New Gate, every soldier a specimen of Neville power.

"Heads up lads!" he chirped proudly. "When we meet His Grace, we'll give him a lesson in the art of war!"

The men gave a rousing cheer and chanted 'Montague, Montague' as they marched past.

Philip Neville was on the opposite side of the road

hunched over his horse's neck, in conversation with several knights. They spoke with concern of Somerset's reputed strength and legendary luck. With the enemy reported far to the north, Montague's knights decided not to wear armour.

"You are not dressed for battle?" Sir John called across to Philip and his companions.

"We are not yet engaged with the enemy, my lord!" he shouted back over the heads of the marching foot, before turning to his esquire, "conceited arse."

Arbroth and young Dean sniggered at his comment and received a flash of anger in return. To avoid a tongue lashing they quickly attached themselves to the column.

"Watch that cart!" Philip warned, as a four-wheeled wagon, containing his armour and weapons, and those of his retainers, lumbered past.

Robert Harrington was not happy; his horse had gone lame, forcing him to stay behind and procure a remount, a task he did not relish.

"Find a horse and join us as soon as you can," Philip said, turning his courser onto the road.

Harrington waved them off and sullenly walked back through the gatehouse, scuffing his feet.

The Yorkists headed north with confidence that they could beat Somerset no matter how many men he had. On 25 April, the feast day of St Mark the Evangelist, Montague found his opponent on Hedgeley Moor, drawn up across the ancient Roman road, nine miles northwest of Alnwick. Somerset blocked the direct route to Norham and Montague knew he would have to fight.

Despite reports from his scouts on Montague's movements, the Duke of Somerset was unprepared when the Yorkists appeared.

While Montague's archers and men-at-arms formed up for battle, his knights donned their armour. Without his esquire, Philip Neville's harnessing took longer than expected. Once he was encased in his steel shell, Ashley Dean checked every fastening. During the short stopover in Newcastle, Walter, his bull-necked armourer, had meticulously hammered out the dents in his armour and used a mix of sand and vinegar to scrub the steel clean of rust. Polished to a silvery finish, the metal was coated with lanolin grease to prevent the rust returning. A new linen tabard, bearing Warwick's colours, covered his breastplate and hid the gold Latin text etched near the top. The imminence of combat sent the blood gushing through Philip's veins, and an exhilarating dizziness he hadn't experienced since Towton fuzzed his brain.

"Today I face my nemesis," he revealed, while his armourer tightened the straps on his greaves, "at last."

"Lord Somerset is an exceptional warrior," Arbroth cautioned, offering him his padded helmet, "he has a terrible reputation."

"So have I," Philip bit back, the fear of fighting such an opponent causing sweat to bleed from his brow. "Leave it!"

"That'll do." Walter nodded, satisfied there were no loose buckles, ties or straps.

Taking the heavy belt and scabbard from young Dean, the Scot buckled it around Philip's waist at the point where the metal cuirass and the fauld met.

"You're as safe as ye can be," he sniffed, dropping the arming sword into its scabbard, before tying on his own limited protection; an eclectic jumble of scavenged arm and leg armour.

"When will I be allowed to fight?" the boy moped, passing the Scot his red-painted sallet.

"When ye are an esquire," he growled, rubbing his sandy hair in fatherly fashion and strapping on his helmet. "Don't be in such a hurry tah die."

Pulling on his gauntlets, Philip flexed the fingers, making sure the plates moved freely, and ordered his page to stay with the wagon. Taking a cup of ale offered by Arbroth, he saluted his retainers.

"God be with you!" he announced, tossing the empty cup at Ashley and joining his cousin.

"And with yew, mah lord," Arbroth responded, downing the tepid liquid before selecting a sword from the wagon.

Pleased with the balance of his chosen weapon, he led Philip's five archers and billmen over to the centre of the line, slashing at the air to test his blade as he went. The Yorkist archers and men-at-arms gathered in familiar groups to check each other's straps and swill ale.

Standing out in front, Sir John Neville and his few knights dropped to their knees and bowed heads. The entire army, numbering almost a thousand men, followed suit, with the exception of Philip Neville, who tiptoed away on the pretext of checking his horse. A flock of priests made their solemn way to the front to offer absolution and pray for victory. The army then stumbled its way through the Lord's Prayer.

"Get on with it," Philip muttered.

Almost as if someone had heard his comment, a final 'Amen' was declared. Nobleman and commoner alike kissed the ground or the crossbar of their swords in a personal appeal to God before rising. Philip whispered a short prayer, crossed himself and walked Hotspur over to his cousin.

Sir John and his knights shared a last drink of wine from the same silver chalice as a token of their fellowship, before mounting. Preferring his much heavier armoured destrier Charlemagne, to his jittery courser, Montague led his knightly companions forward, to get a better look at the enemy, arrayed on a wooded ridge several hundred yards away. Sporting a colourful surcoat adorned with his personal colours, Montague spoke briefly to one of his knights. The man jerked his bald head in the direction of his retinue and put on his helmet. His sergeant responded to the signal by shuffling his retainer further to the right, a manoeuvre that brought them in line directly opposite their opponents.

"Did you pray?" Montague asked Philip, as he rode up.

"Yes, my lord, but I don't need a priest's guidance to

do so."

Sir John tutted and shook his head, then laughed raucously at his irreverence, before taking a last swig of wine from the chalice handed to him by his varlet, who had to stand on a barrel to reach.

"My lord, allow me to attack their flank," Philip suggested, emphasising his proposal by curling his left arm out.

Montague looked at his friend, Sir William Stanley, and patted the neck of his warhorse.

"The ground is too open, they will see you," he said thoughtfully, before announcing with nauseating confidence. "No, we'll meet them head on and use the weight of our horses to smash a hole for the foot."

"They will not stand, my lord," Stanley added confidently.

Suddenly a body of mounted Lancastrians, concealed in a clump of trees less than fifty paces away, burst out of their hiding place and charged Montague and his knights.

"By Christ's blood!" someone gasped, "look out!"

"Stanley fumbled to unsheathe his sword and control his horse, but failed to do either.

"They won't stand!" Philip snapped at the panicking knight, turning Hotspur toward the enemy and drawing his blade.

Before he could get into action, the Lancastrians, led by Ralph Percy, wheeled their horses and rode back to their main line. Steadying his edgy horse, Philip lowered his sword and looked at Montague, who seemed confused.

Two thirds of the Lancastrian army now turned and marched away. Unable to see this manoeuvre, due to a line of trees, Percy, having returned from his pointless charge, rejoined his retinue and faced the Yorkists alone. Philip watched astounded as Somerset disappeared and Percy stayed put. Encouraged by this bizarre behaviour, Montague sent mounted prickers to ensure the duke would not return.

"Now, my lords," he yelled, with an evil leer, "we'll

water our horses in their blood!" Drawing a deep breath, he turned sharply in the saddle. "Are you ready?"

"Aye!" his men roared, shaking their weapons at the enemy.

Slamming his visor shut, Montague nudged his destrier into a canter. Keeping slightly in front of his knights he trundled forward, while a steady stream of arrows flew overhead, showering the distant foe. Lancastrian bowmen sent volleys of arrows back and took a steady toll of the Yorkist foot struggling to catch up with their knights. The thought that Ralph Percy might escape drove Montague to slap his steel greaves hard against the heavy metal flanchards protecting Charlemagne's sides.

Riding close to Sir John Middleton, his tawny and red tabard rippling in the breeze, Philip Neville steered Hotspur up the sloping ground, and aimed for the rampant lion standard of the Percys.

"You take a great risk!" Middleton shouted through his closed visor, referring to Philip's lack of head protection.

"Yes, but when death comes, I shall meet it head on!" he retorted, drawing his blade.

The Yorkist warhorses punched effortlessly through the Lancastrian line, scattering the defenders like chaff in the wind. With Somerset out of the equation, Philip had only one thought: to capture Ralph Percy. The first hurdle to his goal was a terrified youngster, who raised his sword in front of his face as if to hide behind its narrow blade. Incapable of unleashing his anger on such a pathetic specimen, Philip wedged his sword under the left arm, bent down, grabbed the boy by the scruff of his neck and tossed him aside. The reluctant warrior dropped his weapon and ran for dear life.

Circling Hotspur, Philip sought out a more worthy opponent, but while he vacillated, he became the target of others, more proficient in the art of warfare. Spotting the bareheaded knight, a clutch of Lancastrian men-at-arms moved in, hoping to capture him for ransom. Manoeuvring cautiously around Philip's gyrating courser, they closed in like a pack of wolves. Using rein and spur, Philip twisted and turned his snorting horse to keep them at bay.

"Throw down your sword!" a long-haired axeman demanded, swinging his weapon in the air.

"Go to hell!" Philip snarled.

"Gladly, after I cut off your god-damn head!"

"Try it, you pile of shit!" he countered, lifting his arming sword, and bringing it down hard, gouging the axe haft as his assailant raised it above his head to deflect the blow.

One intrepid billman crept in on Philip's blind side, grabbed the stirrup and tried to tip him out of the saddle. Sensing danger, Philip turned his horse, pressed his knees in and brought his blade slashing down. The point split the billman's forehead open and he staggered away. Hacking left and right, and jabbing his spurs in hard made Hotspur suddenly rear up on his hind legs, forcing Philip to grab the reins to stay on. Circling cautiously, the axeman was about to hamstring the courser, when the Yorkist foot arrived. Their timely advent forced the attackers to flee, leaving one of their number dying.

"Run you gutless bastards!" Philip yelled.

With his horse and leg armour splattered in blood and brain matter, Philip looked curiously at the Lancastrian writhing on the ground. A loud, unified gasp caused him to snap his head up. Men on both sides ceased fighting and stood mesmerised at the sight of Ralph Percy and his mounted knights charging down the slope.

Stunned by the spectacle of half a dozen armoured knights galloping in a straight line; no one dared look away. The heads of the snorting Lancastrian coursers and palfreys dipped and rose, and their thick, dark manes danced gracefully in the light wind. With lips drawn back, the horses bared their teeth and flared their nostrils aggressively. On they came bowling over their own men and stopping for nothing. Ralph Percy's beautiful courser sprang over a shallow gully, full of fighting men momentarily frozen in time. Several Yorkist archers put arrows to bows and aimed at the soaring horseflesh. With all four legs splayed out in a magnificent display of equine majesty, Percy's light-grey horse was struck in mid-flight, but momentum kept it going. To protect himself from the flaying hooves, a kneeling soldier rammed his halberd up, piercing the beast's exposed belly. The honed blade ripped open a three foot gash and brought the heavy warhorse crashing down. Thrown from the saddle, Percy hit the ground and rolled over and over. The fighting resumed, snapping Philip out of his distraction, and he quickly dismounted.

"Get out of the way!" he barked, abandoning Hotspur and searching for Ralph Percy.

A confused Sir Ralph staggered to his feet, only to come face to face with a bareheaded Yorkist knight.

With a caustic grin Philip pushed aside two men eager to capture his prize, and grabbed Percy's wrapper.

"Yield!" he demanded, aiming the point of his sword at the slits in Percy's visor.

"Who are you?" he spluttered, dazed by the fall.

"Philip Neville, we jousted at Coventry seven years ago!" he sneered. "Or have you forgotten?"

Percy raised his visor and swung his right arm up to knock Philip's hand away.

"Philip Neville!" he hissed, stepping back and swiftly drawing his sword, aware of his association with his niece, Elizabeth, "I'll submit, but not to you!"

"Then join your brothers, you craven dog!" he shouted, lifting his sword with both hands and smashing it down on Percy's oily helmet.

The blade clanged against the top of Percy's rounded armet and sheared off, but the strike snapped one of the securing rivets causing the visor to hang awkwardly over his eyes. Reeling backwards, Sir Ralph, his ears ringing from the blow, stumbled across the uneven ground pulling at his wrapper to free the damaged visor. Before Philip could follow, a band of soldiers ran between the two knights and he lost sight of his quarry. When they passed, he looked but couldn't see him. Men-at-arms and archers were running and shouting in all directions, and rider-less horses galloped across his front. Unsure who was friend and who was foe, Philip went on the defensive, twisting his body and pointing his sword at anyone who came too close.

"Where are you?" he whined, as sweat stung his eyes and the gorget pressed against his swollen red neck.

"I'm finished," one unfortunate wretch croaked, sitting in a pool of his own blood, trying to staunch the flow draining from a tear in his stomach, "I wish to confess!"

"Confess to Saint Peter," he scowled, stepping over the dying archer.

Philip Neville had more compassion for Percy's horse, which lay on its side, a stream of bloody foam oozing from its mouth. With every twitch of its legs, engorged entrails pumped from the courser's gaping stomach. He tried to block out the horse's dying whinny, but the agonizing shriek echoed across the moor, as if its very spirit was being torn from its throat. The death of Percy's warhorse signalled an end to the battle. Order came out of disorder and the sounds of combat were replaced by the screams and groans of the wounded.

Montague's army had triumphed and the Lancastrian survivors were on their knees pleading for mercy. With his surcoat splattered in gore, Montague was in no mood for leniency, and his men slaughtered a number of the wounded until their bloodlust was sated. Though brief, Hedgeley Moor had been fought with as much brutality as Towton. Severed limbs, heads, fingers, ears, pieces of broken bone and intestines littered the ground. The sickly, sweet stench of death, warmed by an April sun, offended the nostrils of the living, and gangs of men were soon at work digging pits for the bodies. Unable to get into action until the battle was almost over, Arbroth still managed to capture two of Percy's apathetic men and fleece them of everything but their braies. Groups of aggressive soldiers gathered around the surviving Percy knights and esquires, robbing them and arguing over the pickings.

Wandering the field in search of Ralph Percy, Philip Neville spoke to several prisoners, but no one had seen him since his spectacular leap. Intuitively drawn to a low rise, he sheathed his bloody sword and followed his instinct. Fingering sweat from his eyes, he slipped on pools of dark, congealing blood and kicked his way through thick gorse. Looking down into a narrow marshy gully, strewn with sharp rocks and tall grass, he spotted several archers stripping a corpse of its armour.

After refusing Philips demand to surrender, Ralph Percy stumbled blindly away from the fighting. Struggling to open his jammed visor, he tripped and fell into the ravine, smashing both legs on the boulders sticking out of the ground. Unable to move his twisted limbs, Percy's agonizing cries attracted a gang of Yorkist archers, who scrambled down into the gully and grinned as they stabbed the helpless knight to death.

"You bastards," Philip erupted, recognising his bloody tabard, "you've killed him!"

The bowmen stopped their gruesome work and looked up.

"His legs were broke, m'lord!" a boy, of no more than twelve apologised, pointing a bloody finger at Sir Ralph's dislocated limbs. "He would not have lived long."

"I had him first!" Philip pouted angrily.

"Do you have a piece, my lord?" a hostile archer bit back, referring to the custom whereby a nobleman would hand over a piece of armour to his captor, as proof he had surrendered.

"No," he shook his head. "Did he ask you for mercy?"

"No sir, his last words were strange," the boy explained. "He said something about a bird in his bosom?"

"Huh," Philip scoffed, spitting and turning away. "What's that supposed to mean?"

With the fighting over, the dead were quickly collected and dumped into pits, and the battlefield gleaned of everything useful. Montague's herald had walked the grisly field, booking the dead and making notes of those who performed well, and those who did not. Philip stood with his legs apart while his armourer and page carefully removed his harness. Young Dean did his best to avoid the slivers of sticky gore wedged in the creases, and Walter looked at Philip expectantly. When the boy's delicate fingers sank into soft brain matter lodged behind the poleyn, he leapt back.

"If you want to fight you'll have to get used to that," Philip grinned.

Ashley retched and Walter laughed.

Percy's death and Somerset's escape infuriated Philip. The time wasted seeking revenge could have been better spent, and he knew Montague's herald had seen it all. The nagging pain in his left shoulder increased his petulance, and when his page fumbled to remove the last piece of armour, Philip barked at him. Using all his persuasive skills, Arbroth had bartered his booty with an esquire for a pair of leather boots and some money. Watching his master shouting at the boy, he stroked the soft leather of his new boots and grinned.

Chapter 15

Having abandoned Ralph Percy to his fate on Hedgeley Moor, the Duke of Somerset joined King Henry. Appreciating Michael Neville's skill in battle, the king asked him to join the duke's retinue; he refused. Henry could have commanded him, but it was not in his nature. Three weeks later, Somerset left Bamburgh and marched south hoping to regain the initiative. Rather than risk the king's life, Henry was left at Bywell, a castle on the Tyne, with the inflexible Michael Neville.

Montague, meanwhile marched to Norham, picked up King James's ambassadors and escorted them to York. Without stopping he led his army back to finish Somerset. On 15 May he found him near Hexham, thirty miles west of Newcastle, and attacked. Defeated and badly wounded, Somerset concealed himself in a cottage and counted his life in minutes. Dragged from his hiding place, the detested duke was swiftly and unceremoniously beheaded.

Philip Neville escorted the prisoners captured on Hedgeley Moor to Newcastle. Having delivered his captives he was ordered to collect reinforcements for Montague's army. This ignominious task was his, courtesy of Montague's herald, who had given an adverse report of his performance at Hedgeley Moor. Though he disliked it, Montague had to be seen to be fair and punish his cousin. Philip was to scoop up all spare detachments and send them north. Regrettably he dallied, attending a horse fair at Ripon, and visiting Seward House. Rumours of an impending clash reached him as he dined with his mother.

Within the hour Philip was riding hard to catch up with his cousin's army. He arrived in Hexham Village on 22 May, alone and exhausted, by which time Montague was on his way back to York. He had missed it all: the battle, the pursuit, the executions and the glory, and it heartily sickened him. Staring at Sir Henry Beaufort's head, wedged on a spear in Hexham marketplace, Philip addressed the grisly relic.

"I would give my left arm to have met you on the field, my lord," he said, bowing from the saddle before riding away, the urge to beat up Montague's herald, strong.

Four days later, Philip trotted through Bootham Bar to find York in euphoric mood. The king had arrived in the city a week earlier, and fourteen Lancastrian nobles were having their heads lopped off in a thrilling public display. At Claremont Hall, Philip stripped off his sweat-stained clothing, and eased his aching body into a tub of hot water. Utilizing a block of white soap, he scoured a week's worth of grime from his foul-smelling flesh and placed a wet towel over his face. Lying back, he released a long, low sigh and brooded on lost opportunities. Forcing himself out of the scummy water, he dried off and put on a clean set of clothes. Pleased with his appearance, he paid his respects to his cousin, the king, who was so glad to see him he invited him to a banquet at the bishop's palace.

That evening, King Edward was seated on the high table with his two brothers, Lord Montague, and the sickly Archbishop William Booth. York's mayor, the Scots, and a host of noble men and women were crowded together on tables that radiated out from the top table. Philip spent a tiresome evening wedged between the sheriff and a conceited merchant, whose endless boasting irritated. The atmosphere was rowdy, the food and drink abundant, and the bizarrely attired royal fool made everyone laugh with a bevy of imitation Lancastrian heads, which he kicked around the hall like footballs. The music, juggling, laughter and dancing went on long into the night. Next morning, Edward and his council met in the Minster Chapter House to discuss the treaty. For his twin victories, Montague was awarded the Earldom of Northumberland. Philip, who was not present, received nothing.

By early June the Scots were heading home. Mopping up the dregs of Lancastrianism was left to Warwick, who suddenly found himself bombarded with requests from his cousin, begging to join him. Having missed Hexham, Philip harassed the earl to the point of distraction, but in the end it paid off. Grateful for Warwick's indulgence, Philip tried to smother his hostility towards Richard. To celebrate his good fortune, he treated his men to an evening at the Sign of the Boar, a bawdy tavern in George Street. Early next morning, he burst into their room, roused the men and commanded them to stay in York.

"If my mother's husband returns send word to me at once," he warned.

Arbroth drowsily scratched his balls and farted.

"You drunken knave!" Philip hissed, covering his nose with a sleeve. "Is one here fit to ride?"

Oliver, the son of a dyer, raised his hand, but hoped another would volunteer.

"Good, load everything we need onto a pair of sumpters, and saddle Hotspur," Philip snapped. "Be back here by the third bell."

Philip shook his head as the servant rose slothfully, pulled on a pair of shoes, and shuffled to the door. He knew speed was essential, Alnwick and Dunstanburgh had already surrendered to Warwick, and he was moving on Bamburgh. Fortunately for Philip, Bamburgh Castle was captained by Ralph Grey, one of Warwick's retainers who had gone over to the enemy. Excluded from King Edward's general pardon, Grey had no option but to defy his old friend.

"Hurry!" Philip hissed, slapping the back of Oliver's head as he slouched lazily past.

"Yes sir," he grumbled.

"You stink!" Philip declared, turning his nose up at the odour of unwashed bodies.

Philip caught up with Warwick's army as it crossed a creek near Warenford, fifteen miles from Bamburgh. While Hotspur drank avidly from a shallow pool, he rested in the saddle, watching a score of imported Flanders mares straining to drag a wagon across the sluggish stream. Dismounting, Philip handed his reins to Oliver and walked beside the wagon, as it lurched out of the water. Easily keeping pace with the heavily-laden vehicle, he drew his fingertips along the fifteen-foot, black banded cannon barrel roped to its bed. Having been on the receiving end of cannon fire in France, these fearful new weapons intrigued him, and he pestered the gunners for information. Hailing from Germany, the cannoneers failed to understand him and raised their hands in gestures of confusion.

"Stupid foreigners," he rasped turning to Oliver. "Inform Lord Warwick I'm here."

The box-faced servant dabbed his tacky face, secured Philip's courser and the two packhorses containing armour and supplies to a nearby wagon, and urged his rouncey into a tripling half run.

When the head of his army was less than five miles from Bamburgh, Sir Richard Neville sent his herald back to find out why Philip had not reported to him in person. The herald found the object of his search seated on the floor of a straw-layered powder wagon, sharing stories and a flagon of ale with several pioneers. The flamboyantly dressed messenger resented the knight's familiarity and offered a curt nod.

"Philip Neville, you are to attend Lord Warwick."

Blaming Montague's herald for having missed the battle of Hexham, Philip's demeanour changed in an instant and he flared acidly.

"By the bones of Saint Peter, then I shall attend him at once!" he barked, lurching forward as if to spring from the wagon.

Offended by his manner, the shocked herald rode back to the front of the column. Turning to his companions, Philip burst into laughter. His ale-sodden cronies followed suit, each trying to laugh the loudest, spurring the herald to greater speed.

"Friends, I thank thee for thy hospitality," Philip said, stumbling from the jolting cart and snatching the reins of his courser from his servant. "Fare thee well!"

Shaking the fuzziness from his head, he brushed the dusty straw from his hose, mounted, and cantered to the front.

"Good day, cousin," Richard announced at Philip's approach.

"My lord," he replied, bowing deliberately and sweeping his arm across his midriff.

"You approve of the king's guns?"

"Yes," he said pensively. "I remember the damage they did to our army at Castillon."

"But you are not so taken with my herald?"

"Messenger boy," he scoffed, craning his neck to glare at Warwick's herald, riding on the far side, his eyes firmly set on the road ahead.

"Davy Griffiths is a good man." Warwick frowned. "I have granted your request to join this army, so you will respect my herald."

Philip shifted uneasily in the saddle and offered his cousin a submissive nod.

"I am in a dilemma," Warwick explained, resting his hands on the high pommel of his saddle, and allowing his palfrey to plod on. "The king wants Bamburgh intact, but I'll not waste my men in a costly assault, and I cannot wait for the garrison to be starved out."

Philip drew a deep breath and the salty sea air made him cough. Glancing up at the blue sky, he snorted to clear his throat and noticed a flock of circling gulls spiralling in search of food. Their loud squawking irritated and he was forced to wait while the earl conversed with his herald. Flashing a look of disapproval at Philip, Griffiths snapped the reins and urged his horse up the Bamburgh road, escorted by the king's herald.

"I have been given these guns, yet I am commanded not to destroy Bamburgh," Richard explained, jerking his thumb over his shoulder at the artillery train.

"My lord, if you cannot use them, why are you dragging them along?" Philip gasped. "It makes no sense."

"Calm yourself," Richard growled, shifting in the

saddle. "Edward needs a wife and England a queen. Only when a male heir is born to the House of York will Lancaster's reign be over. I've sent Lord Wenlock back to France."

"You have someone in mind?" Philip asked, biting his tongue at the mention of Wenlock's name, lest he offend his cousin.

"Louis's sister-in-law, the Lady Bona, will make a fine queen."

"Edward won't permit you to meddle in his private affairs my lord."

"Perhaps, but he favours this Lady. She is young and attractive," Richard smiled, shielding his eyes from the sun's intense glare, "and Edward loves beauty above all things."

Despite Philip's veiled bitterness toward his cousin, they chatted cordially as the army lumbered on towards Bamburgh.

Warwick's herald soon came galloping back down the road, the wide sleeves of his red and gold tabard billowing as he struggled to keep his cap from blowing off. Raising an arm, Warwick brought the column grinding to a halt.

"My lord," Griffiths panted, pointing back the way he came, his blotchy face as red as his scarlet hose, "Ralph Grey says he will live and die in Bamburgh, and will only submit if he is included in the king's pardon!"

"Huh," Philip scoffed.

"How many men does he have?" Richard asked, casting a look of disapproval at his kinsman.

"My lord, I am not at liberty to say," Griffiths gasped, "my office forbids me from revealing anything I observe during negotiation."

Warwick turned sheepishly to his harbinger, and commanded him to ride ahead and find a campsite for the army. A small inconspicuous man touched his cloth cap, steered his rouncey out of line and galloped up the road, accompanied by the sergeant of tents, the master gunner and a small escort. With a growl of embarrassment that reverberated down the line, Richard Neville waved the column on.

Half a mile from the imposing coastal fortress, Warwick rode over to his harbinger and master gunner, who were stood on a small hillock holding their horses. After a great deal of head shaking and finger pointing, Warwick issued orders for his master gunner to place the three biggest guns as close to Bamburgh's south wall as possible. Warwick was then guided to a site five hundred paces from the castle, which he had earmarked for a campsite. The position was well chosen on slightly rising ground, good for securing tents and drainage. There was also ample pasture for the animals, abundant trees and several fresh water streams.

Sir Richard's grand pavilion, recognised by its immense size and colourful stripes, went up in the centre. A red swallow-tailed banner, bearing the cross of St George and the white bear and ragged staff, was hoisted on a pole beside his tent for all to see. Warwick's nobles and knights spent the next hour arguing over whose tent should stand closest to the earl's, while the ordinary soldiers cut down trees and banged together a series of shelters. Before sunset, two criss-crossing dirt roads, twenty paces wide, had been scoured from the lush green pasture. A myriad of conical, square and round tents covered the cleared ground, some painted with heraldic insignia or stripes, others plain. Armourers, ironsmiths, bakers, cooks, butchers, bowyers, barbers and brewers set up their carts in lines by the side of the tented streets. When word leaked out that an army was in the area, local farmers arrived, driving herds of bullocks and castrated sheep, known as werthers. Mobile taverns sprang up and musicians, jugglers, dancers and prostitutes were drawn to the site. In twelve hours, the camp had the appearance, atmosphere and smell of a small town. Once the tents were up, most of the soldiers walked to the nearest stream, stripped off their soiled clothes and leapt into the cold water to wash.

While the tents were being hoisted, Philip spoke to his

servant, who nodded and rode away dragging the packhorses. A quarter of a mile out, he came across a roofless stone cottage with no doors or windows. Dismounting, he appropriated the ivy-strangled hovel for his master's use, by tying his horse to a rusted, iron dog ring, and unloaded the sumpters.

Pleased with the campsite, Warwick sent his archers and a detachment of Burgundian hand-gunners to surround the castle on its landward side. His small cavalry detachment rode away to watch for any relieving force, and the master gunner arranged prepared his cannon. Rather than waste lives, Richard Neville was prepared to defy the king and batter Bamburgh into submission.

Built on a table of basalt rock, fifty miles north of Newcastle, Bamburgh was a formidable coastal fortress. The pinkish, sandstone Great Tower dominated the castle and surrounding area, affording the garrison excellent all-round vision. As a deterrent against assault, a moat had been dug out of the soil one hundred paces from the base of the south wall, while a tidal inlet protected the north side. Warwick had great confidence in his artillery and knew his three bombards and six smaller Ribaudekins and Serpentines could pound Bamburgh's walls to dust, but the king's order not to destroy the citadel rankled.

From Bamburgh's south wall, Michael Neville watched the vanguard of his cousin's army arrive. He was still there when the wagons, bearing Warwick's heaviest cannon, were brought to a point two hundred paces from the Great Tower and unloaded. Michael was soon joined by most of the garrison, who looked on portentously as Yorkist carpenters placed sloping wooden shields in front of their guns to protect them.

"We're in for it now," Michael warned, without looking at the soldier next to him.

"What are they doing?" he asked naively.

"They're digging their guns in," Michael explained. "When they're ready we'll be fucked."

While Somerset offered his last prayer, in Hexham marketplace, Michael Neville was out hunting deer for the king's table. When he returned, Henry had fled and fugitives from the battle were rifling the abandoned royal chests. Informed of Somerset's defeat and the king's departure, Michael rode away and spent the next six weeks searching for Henry. Unable to find him, he rode to Bamburgh Castle. When he entered the great fortress, Michael and the few men he brought with him were greeted by Sir Ralph Grey, whose nervous demeanour indicated a man under great stress. Grey gloomily informed Michael that he expected Warwick any day.

With nowhere to go Michael decided to stay, but he offered those who came with him a chance to leave before the Yorkists arrived. Surprisingly every man accepted his offer; these brave warriors were brusquely told to assemble near the Great Tower, where a quarter of the garrison and their families were waiting to depart. Late that afternoon, a small gate leading out of the inner ward was thrown open and more than a hundred men, women and children shuffled down the narrow, sloping corridor towards the Constable's Tower. Michael stood beneath the tower's lower arch, his mouth firmly closed and arms folded across his chest. Staring menacingly at every soldier in the column, he cursed them. Aware of his obvious disdain, the discomfited warriors looked straight ahead as they funnelled through the arch. Incensed by their decision to leave, Michael looked for those who had come in with him and escorted them down to the barbican.

"Ned, you gutless piece of shit!" he yelled in the ear of one.

The humiliated archer kept his head down and Michael booted him up the arse several times, but the abuse only sped him on.

"That's it, run you dogs, your mothers were swiven by hogs!" he shouted after them, "and your fathers are nothing but jackals!"

His words brought no reaction and when the inner gates

were closed behind them, Michael rushed up the steps and along the south rampart.

"Cowards!" he bellowed, leaning through one of the crenellations.

Looking around at Bamburgh's extensive walls and towers, Michael knew the garrison was too small to man the place effectively. Pounding the stone with a fist, he cursed the spineless exodus. When Warwick arrived the next day and a Yorkist naval squadron anchored off the coast, Michael rued his decision to stay. Every morning after breakfast, he paced the walls hoping to see King Henry's standard on the horizon, only to be disappointed. Shrugging off his frustration, he would wander across the courtyard to Ralph Grey's private chamber on the third floor of the Great Tower. Here, in company with Sir Humphrey Neville and Sir Roger de Gravett, he discussed their options, the choices shrinking with every passing day. Michael believed his superiors had little penchant for breaking out and even less inclination to fight.

"They will begin their bombardment soon," he warned one morning, while he and Sir Ralph watched Warwick's gunners positioning a bombard close to the south and south-west walls. "And when they do?"

"I cannot surrender," Grey said, shaking his head. "The king will raise a new army."

"From where, this is the only place still flying his flag?" Michael stressed walking to another window and looking out.

"He will come," Grey nodded confidently, biting into a piece of fruit and joining Michael at the window. "This is the last plum in Bamburgh."

"And who will lead them, my lord?" Michael growled focusing on the big gun aimed directly at the tower. "Somerset is dead, Margaret and our gallant lords are in France, and we have been left to face Edward's wrath."

Grey knew he was right, which increased his anxiety. Tossing the half-eaten plum out of the window he nibbled his lower lip like a nervous rabbit and watched the bombard being secured to its wooden cradle.

"We must break out and ride for Wales," Michael urged, grinding up a bubble of yellowish phlegm from his lungs, spitting it out and watching its descent. "Harlech is a better place to make a stand; we can slip out at night and…"

Grey frowned at his coarse manners and pointed at the curtain wall below.

"And what is to become of those poor devils?"

"If Bamburgh is surrendered intact they'll be pardoned," he replied, but Grey's dithering caused him to add angrily, "for us there is nothing, nothing but trial and execution. We must get away before it is too late!"

"Richard is your cousin, he'll not harm you. I have betrayed our friendship; you go… but I cannot."

"Then you go to hell and damnation!" Michael blasted, banging a fist against the rough stonework and causing a jolt of pain to shoot up his arm.

Incensed by Grey's apathy, Michael massaged his aching hand and stormed through the narrow entranceway, leaving Bamburgh's red-headed commander to ponder his fate.

Two days later, Michael's forecast came true. The sun reached its highest point and shone brightly down from a cloudless summer sky, its intensity reduced by a balmy breeze blowing in off the sea. In his private chamber, Ralph Grey and his subordinates sat at a table mulling over Warwick's latest summons, in which he threatened to stay outside for a year if they rejected his offer. Warwick added emphasis to his demand by promising that for every shot fired against the walls, a Lancastrian head would be cut off, but Grey still prevaricated.

Standing near the apartment door, unconsciously scratching a curious rash on his hands, Michael Neville thought of his fiancée, Lady Anne, and was only half listening to the inane conversation. Suddenly a distant explosion, followed by a whistling sound and a loud bang, shook the room and everyone scampered to the window.

Squeezing into the narrow opening, Grey, Sir Humphrey, and de Gravett were shocked at the smoking black cloud trailing from the mouth of the big gun aimed at the tower. Only Michael appeared calm, pretending not to show concern, but the bombardment had begun and his sublime austerity was a mask.

On the morning the Yorkist artillery opened up, Philip Neville rose before dawn and ate breakfast with his servant. With no orders, he mounted Hotspur and cantered to the main camp, a quarter of a mile away. Following a line of dying braziers set up to guide those moving around at night, he headed east. With dawn about to break, he was suddenly greeted by a dense cloud of fog filtering through the trees. Dismounting, he tied his warhorse to a sapling and wandered cautiously into the grey mist. The slow-rising sun was still too weak to evaporate the milky veil, and confused shouts of soldiers calling to one another added a dreamlike quality to the scene. Walking tentatively to where he believed the camp lay, Philip became disorientated. Looking for a familiar landmark, he peered into the dense haze and stretched his hands out. Edging slowly forward like a blind man, he cursed loudly when the toe of his boot rammed into a concealed boulder. Closing his eyes he bit his lower lip to re-route the pain.

"Fuck, shit and fuck!" he snarled, squeezing his fists. "Damnation!"

An echoing chuckle from somewhere in the mist inflamed his temper.

"Laugh again and it will be the last thing you ever do!" he threatened.

"If you can find me, I will gladly offer my head for you to cut off!" the answer came back, accompanied by the sound of someone running away.

Once the throbbing in his toes receded to a bearable level, Philip opened his eyes and saw a massive, dark shape looming out of the fog like the prow of a gigantic ship.

Spellbound by the ghostly apparition of Bamburgh's Great Tower coming toward him, he held his breath. The high volcanic outcrop on which the castle stood and his propinquity to it made the fortress appear larger than life. The strengthening sun was beginning to burn off the fog and, as it gradually dispersed, the Great Tower appeared to be moving. Looking down, Philip found himself standing on the edge of the dry moat that protected the south wall. Within bow range, he backtracked to a nearby gun emplacement. Fortunately the castle guards had no interest in this early morning sightseer, and they watched amused as he backed away.

Settling himself on top of a large powder keg, Philip shook his head at the size of the bombard and the damage it could do to Bamburgh's walls. Swinging his legs to and fro, he watched two sweating gunners force thirty-pounds of powder into the breach of the twelve-foot long bronze bombard, named 'Dijon'. This great piece of ordnance, which once belonged to the Duke of Burgundy, had been brought over from Calais. The powder was followed by a massive stone ball, hoisted into its mouth with the aid of nippers and a pulley. Dijon's barrel was encased in a wooden frame, or shooting cradle, and wedged securely to a mound of compacted soil by more than a dozen stakes.

To protect the cannoneers, a prefabricated slanting palisade was placed in front of the gun, with a square opening large enough to shoot through. This worked like an upside down drawbridge, which could be raised to fire the cannon and lowered for reloading. One of the gunners, a swarthy hulk with no neck and short, greasy hair, patted the crude bronze barrel and spoke affectionately to it in German. Philip grinned at his paternal fondness and yawned heavily at the amount of time needed to prepare the gun for firing.

Satisfied with their work, the gun crew sat and gobbled down a meal of beef, bread and cheese, and slept the morning away. At noon, Dijon and the other big guns – 'Newcastle' and 'London' – set several hundred yards apart, sent their opening salvo against the citadel. Startled by the terrifying noise, hundreds of blue-grey sparrows exploded from the trees. Screeching and flapping their wings wildly they dived low in formation before soaring out to sea. A cheer erupted from the Yorkist camp when three gunstones hit the castle, one after the other, cracking masonry and breaking off great chunks of pink-tinted, light brown sandstone. Archers kept the defenders down by showering anyone foolish enough to show his head with arrows.

When Dijon fired, a tongue of orange and yellow flame shot from its mouth and a thick, grey cloud of acrid smoke blotted out the gun and its crew. The opaque cloud blew back into Philip's face and a stink of rotten eggs forced him to turn away and cover his face. Unable to recoil, the shock split the cradle cosseting the gun barrel and almost knocked Philip off his perch.

"Sweet Jesus!" he spluttered, gripping the barrelhead.

"You go damned quick," a gunner warned him in broken English, pointing at the volatile contents nestled between his legs and imitating an explosion with his arms, "or boom!"

Philip leapt off the keg and squatted on the thick, soft grass behind the gun, splaying his fingers out for support. From this position he watched Dijon's crew prepare the bombard for refiring, a process that took forever. After hours of huffing and puffing, and no more than two shots fired, he grew bored.

"Bugger this," he hissed, jumping to his feet and stretching. "I'm off."

The pain of sitting in one position for so long was intense, and Philip hobbled away like a cripple. Once the agony in his knees abated he retrieved his patient courser and cantered over to Warwick's headquarters.

As he approached the earl's grand pavilion, Philip tried to show off. Drawing both feet from the stirrups, he leapt from his trotting horse. Half running, he handed the reins to a guard and tripped in front of a group of captains gathered around a low table. The red-faced knight was greeted by a tall, debonair warrior, whose brown leather boots disappeared up his arse.

"Will you take a wager sir?" the ostentatious fellow offered, assuming by the odour of bad eggs emanating from Philip's clothes that he was attached to the ordnance.

"I will not. My father was too fond of gambling and my family has suffered for his excesses," Philip replied, nodding at each member of the group he knew and taking a cup of wine from an obliging server.

Spitting to remove the tang of gunpowder, he whisked the liquid around his mouth and sent it jetting out through pursed lips.

"How long do you think those people can hold out?" the high-booted knight asked, jerking his chin at Bamburgh.

"No more than a week," Philip said, looking the fancy knight up and down, "by then our guns will–"

A thunderous explosion cut him off, and all heads snapped around as a huge ball burst from 'London's' gaping mouth. Arching into the air, the spinning gunstone smashed into Bamburgh's southwest wall near the Great Hall, with a sickening thud. When the smoke and dust cleared, a massive chunk of masonry slowly toppled from the battlements, revealing a long serrated split, and forcing Philip to revise his estimate.

"Five days," he declared confidently.

"I said five days!" a wide-eyed esquire claimed, rubbing his hands in anticipation of collecting on the wager.

"We'll see," the captain with the highest boots in the army sniffed. "You did not strike on the bargain."

"But, my lord…"

Sensing an argument, Philip walked off in search of solitude.

"Take care of my horse!" he called back, pointing at the disgruntled guard.

When the sun went down and the guns fell silent, a trumpeter called the night watch out to protect Warwick's pride and joy. That evening, Philip attended a late supper given by his cousin Warwick for his recently arrived brother John. Due to the temperate weather a trestle table had been set up outside, covered with linen cloths, and lit by torch and candle. Richard and his guests ate, drank and talked in the relaxed atmosphere, while a company of minstrels played in the background. Philip and his cousin, John Neville, the new Earl of Northumberland, sat opposite each other joking about things that made no sense. Laurence Booth, the recently arrived Bishop of Durham, seated next to Northumberland, grew increasingly irate at their perverse sense of humour and exaggerated laughter. Noting his displeasure, Philip raised a goblet.

"To the Bishop of Durham," he smirked.

The half-brother to the Archbishop of York was not happy. As one of Queen Margaret's favourites, Booth had gone over to the Yorkists after Towton. As a reward he was appointed King Edward's confessor. Caught corresponding with Queen Margaret, he lost his temporalities and was confined to Cambridge until early 1464, when he was released, much to the chagrin of the Nevilles. Passing near Bamburgh on his way back to Norham, Laurence Booth was invited to dine with the Earl of Warwick.

While the squirrel-faced bishop picked at his food, he regretted having accepted Sir Richard's invite. He knew Northumberland and his cousin were secretly laughing at him, but refused to react. Laurence Booth's mouth was rigid and his dark, baggy eyes drooped; proof he was suffering from some painful malady.

"Cheer up, my lord," the newly promoted Earl of Northumberland chirped, as Philip banged the base of his empty goblet down on the table.

"Sir, if you were in as much agony as I am, you would not be so humorous," Booth moaned, rubbing the small of his back for comfort.

"My Lord Bishop, a hot plaster spread with honey and

pigeon shit might ease your distress," Northumberland suggested.

"Only if he eats it," Philip stuttered, swaying into Sir William Stanley, who was appalled by his disrespect and pushed him away.

Booth shook his head but cringed when he saw Warwick's penetrating stare. Despite the invitation, he knew Sir Richard loathed him. After Warwick was attainted at the Coventry parliament, Laurence Booth seized his lordship of Barnard Castle, only to lose it back to Warwick upon his return to England.

Having drunk far too much wine, Philip's head spun and he felt sick. Leaning back, he looked up at the blurred stars speckling the clear black sky. A warm, gentle breeze kissed his glowing face and he tried to focus on his cousin John. Through flickering candlelight, he vaguely noticed Northumberland nudge Lord Scrope to get his attention, and point across the table at him. Philip closed his eyes and swayed in his seat grinning inanely.

"You are vulgar and insulting," Stanley complained, looking at Warwick for backing.

Richard turned away and Philip appeared momentarily sober. Turning to the lightly bearded, younger brother of Lord Stanley, he stared at him hard.

"Be silent!" he snapped, slurring his words. "You arrogant little shit."

"His brother sold land near London to the bishop, who plans to build a manor and park there," Northumberland whispered in Scrope's ear. "William wanted the land himself."

"Then why does he intervene?" Scrope asked.

"The Stanleys believe in the knightly code above all."

"They do?" Scrope gasped.

"Strong wine has befuddled your brain!" Stanley snarled at Philip, "so I'll ignore your drunken insults."

Offended by his tone Philip rested an elbow on the table, placed his chin on the fist and looked him in the eye.

"You owe your position to family influence, I fought to

get here."

"I won my spurs on Towton Field," Stanley parried, disturbed by the insinuation.

"Hah, your father came late to St Albans, and your gallant brother did no less at Blore Heath!" Philip said angrily, banging the table and rattling the silver.

"Enough gentlemen," John Neville groaned, signalling for a server to refill Philip's goblet. "Must we argue on such a night?"

"My lord, I love you like a brother, but I have a mind to slice off thy herald's head." Philip frowned, snatching the refilled cup and looking at its dark contents. "For he did cause me to miss the fight at Hexham and..."

"'Tis time you went to your bed," Warwick interceded, in an inebriated, but firm voice, his sagging head rising and falling in staggered jerks.

"As you wish, my lord," Philip sighed, bowing his head and extending his arms apologetically. "But I would love to have met His Grace in combat."

Struggling to stand, Philip lost his balance and fell off the bench. Laurence Booth shook his head and nodded his thanks to Stanley.

Winded by the fall, Philip tried to rise but collapsed back, giggling helplessly and Northumberland signalled for two waiting guards to help him up.

Hauled to his feet and lifted onto his horse by the men-at-arms, Philip slumped forward and vomited before being led away by his unimpressed servant.

"Fare thee well...!" he yelled, rocking in the saddle.

The next day, Philip Neville rose from his dishevelled straw bed with a pounding headache and a sickly gurgling sensation knotting his stomach. Dressing deliberately in a crimson doublet, brown woollen hose and knee-high leather boots, he fumbled to buckle his sword. After a little bread, he wound a piece of linen around his forefinger, dipped it into a mixture of ground sage and salt, and brushed his teeth.

"Oliver!" he bellowed, strolling out into the daylight

and spitting, only to regret his outburst. "Where are you?" he groaned, massaging his forehead.

There was no response so he slouched over to his tethered horse.

"Hello boy," he gasped, stroking Hotspur's soft face and spotting the desiccated vomit streaking his neck. "Oh God."

Apologising to his faithful warhorse, he bent forward and closed his eyes to counter the threat of vomiting. Straightening up he shoved the toe of his left boot through the stirrup, threw his right leg over the saddle and wedged his arse in the hard curve. Judging the time by the sun to be near mid-morning, he trotted to the Yorkist camp.

Dismounting near Warwick's grand marquee, he broke up a belch in his throat and insolently hooked the reins over the spear of an unimpressed guard. Glancing at the long table strewn with overturned goblets and fly-infested leftovers, he pinched the bridge of his nose and breathed deeply, before entering. A lingering odour of stale sweat, made worse by the heat, hit him, and he grabbed a tent pole for support. Regaining his balance, Philip found his half-dressed cousin seated on the edge of his bed holding his head.

"Good morning, my lord!" he announced.

Philip's over-zealous greeting rebounded inside Warwick's sensitive brain. Shocked by the mental invasion he raised his red eyes above his hands and shook his head delicately before burying it back into the sanctuary of his palms.

"Where is the bishop?" he whimpered.

"He left here early this morning, my lord," a waiting servant offered.

"Good," Philip muttered, "what are your orders?"

"Do as you wish," Warwick groaned, waving his unwelcome visitor away, while a bevy of agitated servants began clearing the table outside. "I don't care."

Philip bowed and left as several varlets came forward to dress the indisposed earl. Walking away from the marquee, Philip threaded his way through a brood of barefooted washerwomen, jabbering over tubs of milky water and scrubbing dirty clothes with lye soap. Without warning, one of the big guns suddenly opened its first salvo of the day and the shock made Philip jump. A shriek from Warwick's tent caused him look back, just as a pisspot flew out of the opening. The vessel bounced across the ground like a football, its unsavoury contents splashing several guards. Philip laughed until the pain in his head returned.

The queasiness in his stomach subsided as the morning wore on and he began to feel hungry. Taking a bruised Costard apple from a barrel, he sought solace away from the busy camp. Finding a shady elm he sat under its leafy canopy, ate the apple and dozed. He was eventually woken by a column of cavalry riding noisily passed. Yawning and stretching his arms, he strolled over to the nearest gun emplacement, located two hundred paces from the Bamburgh's Davie Tower, a D-shaped structure on the southeast wall, close to the barbican.

Ducking behind the protective palisade, he asked a hunched archer how the day was progressing.

"Wait and watch," he grumbled, holding an arrow to the hemp as he looked for a target. "Noise and dust, and piss and shit," the bowman whinged, "they won't show themselves long enough for me to shoot. Why don't we go in?"

"There's no breach, if we assault now many will die for nothing. Henry of Lancaster is finished, so don't wish your life away."

"Huh," the archer scoffed.

Crouched behind the rough ash and elm boards of the covering shield were half-a-dozen Burgundian hand gunners. Pushing in between them, Philip put an eye to a knot hole and studied the limited view.

"Bloody Frogs," he griped, aiming his words at the Burgundian's incessant yapping, which irritated his sense of nationalism. "Only Englishmen should be here."

"And the Welsh," a burly pioneer added in a strange dialect, leaning on his huge mallet.   "Fuck the Welsh," Philip growled looking menacingly at the pioneer and recalling William Herbert's attitude to him during Edward's first council, in York.

Incensed by his response, the infuriated Welshman hoisted his mallet above his head and smashed it down hard against one of the wooden wedges used to keep the ten-ton barrel in place.

"Bastard," he hissed, visualizing the splintered head of the wedge to be the noggin of this conceited knight.

"Each time they fire that fucking thing, my head resonates like the inside of a church bell!" the archer moaned, patting his ears.

Philip was about to respond when he was hit from behind.

"By all that is holy!" he coughed, as something fell on the back of his legs.

"Hello," the cause of his hurt offered, untangling himself from Philip's feet and resting on his haunches.

"Francis!" he gasped, "What are you doing here?"

"I'll tell you when we are in a better place," Francis Talbot smiled, crawling forward and peeking through a gap in the shield. "Will they come out?"

"No," Philip sniffed, "this is the last of them. They have no stomach for a fight; but that piss-head Ralph Grey refuses to submit. He prays we will go away but we shall stay here all summer if necessary!" he declared, shouting the final part of his statement at the battlements.

Stroking his new goatee with thumb and forefinger, Francis grinned at the gunners as they swore liberally in German while preparing their cannon for its next shot.

"What's that?" Philip enquired, noting the thin hair on Francis' chin, shaped into a V.

"You like it?"

"You look like a goat," he teased "an old goat, but come, let's find somewhere quiet," he added, eager to learn about Isobel.

Strolling back to the main camp, Philip snatched a jug of cider, a block of hard cheese and a loaf of rye bread from a tent used by the sick. Finding a spot amidst an assortment of sacks and barrels piled behind Northumberland's yellow and white pavilion, they settled down on the grass. A strong smell of excrement and the tang of unwashed bodies passing to and fro didn't bother Philip, but Francis was not so blasé. Lying on his side, head nestling in his palm, Philip nibbled on the cheese and grinned at his companion's delicate nature.

"We've dug plenty of latrines outside the camp, but these people are so idle they'll shit where they sit," he chomped, "you'll get used to the smell."

"I'll never get used to it," Francis vowed, breaking the tourte bread, before revealing the reason he left York without a word.

While Philip listened to the graphic description of Lady Talbot's death from leprosy, a shiver ran down his spine. Snatching the jug he took a mouthful of warm cider and swilled it to loosen the cheese stuck to his teeth.

"You don't have to justify yourself to me."

"My mother passed from this world fourteen days ago," Francis explained, sounding almost relieved. "Praise God her last moments were blessed by the attendance of her family. Margaret was like a daughter to her. She defied convention and held her hand until the last breath left her body."

"Amen," Philip said, crossing himself. "Did she suffer?"

"'Tis most peculiar; her suffering eased after our pilgrimage to the shrine of St Cuthbert. From that day she accepted her fate with dignity. Though in much pain, she seemed at peace."

"Strange," Philip mused, lying down and closing his eyes. "How is your sister?" he asked tentatively, swinging the conversation.

"Isobel?" he smiled, "she is well and speaks of you often, and with much affection."

"May I call on her, when we're finished here?" he asked warily.

"Isobel's heart is hers to give to whom she pleases," Francis said. "I believe she has chosen; you may open your suit when you wish."

Surprised by his response, Philip tried to conceal his delight, but his face beamed with boyish excitement. "How did you know where to find me?" he asked, his morale buoyed by the clement temperature, and the thick malleable sward cushioning his body.

"I rode from Newcastle with some of Lord Northumberland's retainers, and your own men. 'T'was Warwick's herald who pointed you out, though he did not look pleased when I mentioned your name; have you offended him?"

Philip opened his eyes and answered with a smirk, which quickly changed to a scowl.

"Where are my men?" he grunted, raising himself up one elbow. "I told them to stay in York and watch my mother."

"Foolish friend, do you think I would leave her alone?" Francis grinned, tossing a piece of mouldy cheese over his shoulder. "Arbroth would not come with us. Lady Joan threatened to beat him with a broom, but he was adamant."

"Good," he nodded his tone less abrasive as he lay back. "Arbroth is the only one who can defy my mother."

"He told me you were with Lord Warwick." Francis yawned. "Your esquire has charge of our men. We have not slept these past nights for fear Bamburgh would fall," he sighed. "Alas, I can barely stay awake." He yawned again, his weary voice trailing away.

Philip covered his eyes with a hand, but as he breathed through his nose he heard a shrill whistling sound. "I confess I have been angry with you, but I knew nothing of your sorrow, and I am heartily sorry for it."

"We keep our grief in our hearts, though at times it almost broke my sister's spirit," Francis droned sadly.

Squinting up at the cloudless sky, Philip tried to keep

his eyes open, but the bright sun brought out a natural instinct to close them. Francis continued to unburden the guilt he felt over his mother's death. Propping himself up, Philip took a long swig of cider and looked around. His companion's tedious monologue was beginning to bore and he wished someone would come and call for him. Eventually Francis fell silent; unable to sleep, Philip stood up and rubbed his damp arse.

"Are you awake?" he hissed, amazed anyone could sleep in the midst of all the hustle and bustle.

There was no reply, only the slow rising and falling of his chest and the heavy breathing of someone in a deep sleep. Laying a dry, mucus-encrusted handcoverchief over Francis' face to prevent his skin burning, Philip left. As he walked away, he imagined his friend waking to find the disgusting veil over his face, and chuckled.

Chapter 16

The slow bombardment of Bamburgh went on for three days, and Philip noticed his cousin Warwick growing more intolerant, while arguments between him and his subordinates increased. The damage inflicted on the fortress fed his anguish; the heavy guns were making progress, but King Edward's order not to destroy the castle was a constant worry. Huge blocks of stone had been shot off the battlements and deep cracks zigzagged erratically across the south and south-west curtain walls. Unbeknown to the Yorkists, the garrison was desperate for relief.

Besieging a castle was an uninspiring task, despite the temperate weather and bountiful supplies. Limited combat and the tedium of routine drained the enthusiasm of the most ardent soldier. To alleviate the boredom Philip Neville played chess, tables and dice, or hunted. One morning, whilst out riding alone, he found himself unable to shake a vision of a naked Isobel Talbot from his mind. The more he tried the more graphic her pale, shapely image dominated, until he could think of nothing but having her.

"I'm like a dog on heat," he shouted at the trees, while the blood surged through his veins and a tingling sensation gripped his crotch.

Cursing Ralph Grey for holding out, Philip lashed his mount and rode hard to expel the lustful thoughts shredding his sanity. Finally he drew back on the reins and brought his courser to a slow trot, patting its sweaty neck apologetically. Unable to block out the explicit picture of her nakedness, he decided to return to camp, find a woman and beat her wool.

Cantering into the Yorkist camp, Philip headed straight for the armourer's tent, leapt out of the saddle and promptly sought out the object of his desire. Edith was a large-breasted nineteen-year old lass of easy virtue, who knew what he wanted by the look in his eye and offered herself willingly. With barely a word spoken, Philip steered her into a small, vacant tent and satisfied his carnal lust. There was no love in the act, he pushed her down on the dry, yellow grass, pawed her long, curly hair aside, buried his face in her ample breasts and took her like an animal. After ten minutes it was all over. Releasing a gurgle of pleasure, he rolled off her quivering body and drew up his braies.

"You were hungry, my lord," she flirted, using her undergarments to wipe his essence from between her thighs.

"I was starving," he replied sheepishly, regretting his moment of licentious weakness, as he guiltily tied his doublet to his hose.

"What do I get out of it?" she asked, pulling irritating grass out from under her plump arse.

"The satisfaction of being bedded by a Neville," he grinned, dropping a coin into a cup of fermenting cider.

"The Nevilles have never satisfied me," she parried, tutting at her torn blouse. "I barely felt you."

"Nor I you, it was like swiving a cow."

"And how many cows have you swiven, my love?"

"Too many," he chuckled, pressing a second coin into her fleshy palm. "Buy another."

As he left and made his way to the Earl of Warwick's pavilion, contentment replaced guilt, and he bantered freely with those who crossed his path. From the direction he came and his cheerful manner, they knew he must have paid a visit to Easy Edith, the popular armourer's daughter.

"Did you breach her wall, sir?" a smiling centenar asked, as he passed him.

"Aye and it was easier than trying to breach that bugger," he smirked, meaning Bamburgh.

Entering his cousin's marquee, Philip found himself in the midst of a raging storm. In one of his pedantic moods, the Earl of Warwick was advocating an all-out assault on Bamburgh. His equally pernickety brother, Northumberland, refused to allow his men to be slaughtered in such a senseless enterprise.

Standing almost back to back, arms folded across their chests, both men refused to budge. Their subordinates shuffled awkwardly, trying not to make eye contact with either, lest they be accused of intent.

"Good day, my lords!" Philip announced an infuriating bounce in his voice. "Have we surrendered?"

"You'd better leave," Richard warned, his cousin's cheerfulness stoking his ire.

"There's an easy way to end this," Philip suggested, guessing the reason for the strained atmosphere.

The humidity inside the tent was unbearable and Warwick threw his arms up. "Suddenly everyone is a general!"

"Then harken to my proposal, my lord," Philip said, amazed at his own confidence. "If Ralph Grey submits, the game is be over."

"So?" Warwick hissed impatiently.

Anxious to hear more Northumberland ignored his brother.

"What's on your mind?"

"If a messenger can get in to inform him King Henry has been captured, and that no help is coming, he'll lose heart and surrender."

"Ralph Grey will not be taken in so easily," Warwick growled, "no sir."

Richard's pessimism added an irritated timbre to Philip's next sentence.

"Then tell him the king has granted his pardon."

"You must not," Lord Scrope intervened, stunned at his dishonesty, "this is not France!"

"Who cares?" Philip retorted. "You will have your victory, my lords."

"'Tis not right Richard," Scrope warned, "to promise pardon and snatch it away. You must not condone such perjury."

"Fool," Philip muttered under his breath.

"We should consider it?" Northumberland cut in.

"He won't believe it," Warwick pouted.

318

"Then tell him if he continues to defy the rightful King of England and we are forced to attack, every last mother's son will be put to the sword!" Philip snapped.

"Calm yourself cousin," Northumberland warned, placing a hand on his arm, "'tis a plan worthy of consideration. What say you Richard?"

Warwick put thumb and forefinger to his sweaty chin and deliberated, before nodding slowly. "Where do we find this messenger?"

"Here," Philip offered, pointing at himself, "I will go and tell him I have been sent by Margaret."

"Does he know you?" Scrope asked coming round to the idea, the terrible stomach wound he received at Towton, forcing him to sip a mixture of opium and milk to ease the pain. "He knew your Uncle Fauconberg well."

"We met once, but I do not recall his face, so I doubt he'll remember mine."

"His father was famed for his memory," Lord Scrope cautioned.

"Ralph Grey is not his father," Richard declared, reflecting on their past friendship.

"My lord, you cannot offer pardon," Scrope urged; his agony evident by his distressed posturing.

"I won't," Warwick promised.

"How will you get inside Bamburgh?" one of Northumberland's captains asked.

"I'll ride in," Philip declared, stunned by his own confidence, "through the gates."

"Ralph Grey is no fool," Scrope stammered through a sudden surge of pain, which forced him to grab a tent pole for support.

"What if he refuses to listen?" Northumberland pressed.

"Then I'll cut his throat."

"Hah!" Warwick half-laughed, wagging a finger at his brother. "You see, the same old answer."

"Should it become necessary, my lord," Philip emphasized, the need to empty his bladder forcing him to

319

cross his feet.

"'Tis worth the risk," Northumberland contemplated. "What do we have to lose?"

"Nothing," Warwick scoffed, staring at Philip.

"What if you are discovered?" Scrope groaned; his torment easing.

"Then my life will end there," he said, pointing in the direction of Bamburgh.

"Let's hope your plan works," Warwick smirked, "for your sake."

Philip looked at Richard, then at Northumberland and back to Richard, and wondered if his bragging made him appear as foolish as he felt.

"When will you do this?" Warwick asked.

"Tonight."

"Tonight?" Northumberland echoed.

"So soon?" Lord Scrope appended.

"Yes my lords, at sunset," he explained, the pressure building in his braies, making him believe his balls were about to explode. "If I don't go tonight my courage will wither and I'll not go at all."

"What do you need?" Northumberland asked.

"Two Lancastrian tabards, two palfreys and a sword, for I'll not risk my own. My father paid eight pounds for this beauty," he replied, tapping the handle of his sword. "Oh, and the freshest corpse you can dig up."

"A corpse?" Northumberland gasped, trading a confused frown with Scrope.

"Yes."

"You shall have all that you ask for," Warwick promised.

"My lord, I will also need some worthy sign that I have come from the queen."

"I have the perfect piece," Richard said with a glint in his eye.

Taking a towel from a servant, Warwick wiped perspiration from his face and neck, and tossed the towel aside. Lifting the lid of his ornamental jewel box, he fumbled inside and yelped jubilantly.

"Hah!"

Concealing something in his fist, he indicated for his cousin to come forward and open his hand. Amused by his behaviour, Philip played along. Staring him straight in the eye, Warwick slapped something cold into his palm and stepped back. When he opened his fingers, Philip was horrified to see a bloodstained gold swan. It was the same piece that had been wedged into the dead sergeant's hand on the night of the ambush. The sight of the bloody ornament brought back bad memories and he snapped his eyes shut. When he opened them the blood was gone and the relief made him urinate slightly.

"God speed," Northumberland offered, oblivious to the silent drama between his kinsmen. Raising a goblet of wine, he toasted Philip's courage and put his flushed cheeks down to the heat.

Warwick handed Philip a cup of spiced wine, and leered smugly.

"Meet me outside the fletchers' pavilion as the sun sets," he said coldly, raising his goblet, "success."

Disturbed by Warwick's suspicions, Philip downed the wine, bowed to his superiors and hurried outside to piss.

The sizzling summer sun descended slowly below the horizon and a fresh sea breeze rippled through the trees, causing the leaves to rustle. The soldiers spaced out along Bamburgh's ramparts, watched the flaming orange ball descend with mixed emotions. One pasty-faced youth, a billhook resting against his shoulder, poked a finger up his nose and bored away at the crusted mucus glued to his nasal passage. Standing alone on top of the west turret, one of a pair behind the barbican, he detested this time of day. For this sixteenyear old it was going to be another lonely night of tense vigil.

With daylight almost gone, a low rumbling drum, punctuated by distorted shouting, drifted over from the direction of Warwick's camp. The youngster propped his billhook against the battlements and looked out through the crenallations. Eager to learn the reason for such commotion he peered hard into the night, but all he could see were hundreds of twinkling lights that marked the enemy camp. Casting his eyes down to a point several hundred paces from the barbican, he scrutinized the slanting wooden shield protecting one of Warwick's bombards. Silent now, he knew when the sun rose the beast behind the shield would unleash more stones at the south wall, but he was satisfied nothing was amiss.

The drum however, continued to roll and several soldiers, curious to know what all the noise was about, joined the boy in the turret. Drawing his rust-stained sallet down, he quietly cursed their intrusion.

"Are they coming?" he asked, squinting into the darkness.

"They won't attack at night," a seasoned veteran confided, pinching the lad's bony shoulder to instil courage.

Suddenly the pandemonium in Warwick's camp intensified and a keen-eyed esquire leaned into the crenulations.

"Look there!" he yelled, stabbing a finger into the night.

Alerted by the drumming and the crowd gathering on the barbican, Sir Ralph Grey and Michael Neville had made their way up the steps to a narrow section of wall, connecting the west turret to the gatehouse.

"What's going on?" Grey demanded, not sure what he should be looking at.

"There, my lord," the esquire pointed excitedly, "horses!"

"Archers!" Michael bellowed spitting the rabbit leg he'd been gnawing, over the parapet and drawing his sword.

Eager to know more Michael looked hard, but could only make out Warwick's distant campfires. Knocking a soldier's dancing billhook from his face, he listened to an incongruous sound, masked by the monotonous drumming. "Silence!" he demanded, cupping a hand to his ear, "someone's coming."

One soldier thought he could hear the muffled pounding of horse hooves and added his warning to Michael's. Another quickly confirmed it and soon everyone between the south wall and barbican were straining their eyes to see.

"Horses my lord!" the sharp esquire repeated, stabbing a finger over the wall.

Suddenly a horse and rider materialised out of the inky blackness, and galloped up the lengthy ramp leading to the barbican, followed closely by another.

"Knock them down!" Michael barked, pointing where to shoot.

"Wait!" Grey countermanded, raising a hand and rubbing the fingers together in nervous uncertainty. "Shoot over their heads!"

A dozen archers and crossbowmen released a scattered shower of arrows and quarrels, and received a fusillade of abuse from a pursuing body of Yorkist foot.

Thundering up the ramp below the south-east wall, the lead rider jerked on the reins, bringing his palfrey to a halt before the outer gates. Furious with Grey for revoking his order, Michael turned on his commander. Staring into his dispassionate face, his eyes blazed disgust, but Ralph Grey was used to his tantrums and ignored him.

"You do as you wish, my lord," Michael spat, storming away, "I am for my chamber!"

Grey knew his men were waiting for a reaction, but said nothing. Making his way along the walkway to the front of the barbican, he called for torches to illuminate the area below.

"Who are you and what do you want here?"

"I am Geoffrey of Gloucester!" the horseman spluttered breathlessly. "I have come from the court of Queen Margaret. I seek sanctuary?"

"This is not a church... who is with you?"

"David Fitz Allan," he wheezed, throwing the flap of his cloak over his shoulder to reveal a mud-splattered, blue and white quartered doublet, the section over his left breast bearing a golden eagle with its wings spread, "an esquire."

"Where is the queen?" Grey demanded unimpressed by the man's arrogant posture, feet thrust forward, and hand on hip.

"France, my lord!"

"My horse's arse knows she's in France, where in France?"

"Um," he hesitated, "her father's chateau, near Commercy!" he replied, worried he might be offering a little too much information. "Kouer-la-petite."

"What's wrong with him?" Grey asked concerned by the way the second rider was slumped forward in the saddle.

Nudging his palfrey closer, Geoffrey grabbed the bridle of his horse, turned the animal and pointed to a three-foot arrow growing out of his back.

"I fear he is dead."

Sir Ralph vacillated, unsure whether to allow Geoffrey asylum or order his men to shoot him down. Raising a hand he blinked rapidly.

"Archers!"

"No wait!" Geoffrey pleaded, fumbling for the gold pendant around his neck and aiming it up into the shimmering torchlight.

The sceptical commander held his hand and looked carefully, "What is it you wish me to see?"

"I was told to present this to you by His Grace the Duke of Exeter!" he announced in his most convincing voice.

Unable to see the object from where he stood, Grey waved his hand up and down slowly, a sign for the archers to lower their bows.

"Open the gates!" he commanded, before leaving the barbican, "but stay sharp!"

Accompanied by several men-at-arms, Ralph Grey

324

walked rapidly back along the barbican. Descending the West Tower, he made his way up a narrow set of steps leading to the Chapel of St Peters. From here he headed across the courtyard towards the Great Tower to meet the stranger.

Bamburgh's thick, oak doors yawned open, the heavy drawbridge thumped down and the wooden portcullis clanked up. Geoffrey trembled uncontrollably as he nudged his palfrey through the gates and beneath the steel-shod points of the raised portcullis. Towing the second horse, he forced his fatigued palfrey over the drawbridge, through the inner doors and beyond a second pair. Those he passed eyed him suspiciously, but he kept his eyes down and trotted up the narrow torch-lit ravine, toward a smaller set of doors at the Constable's Tower. The sound of the Great Gates slamming shut reverberated loud and cold sweat trickled down his back. Hunching low in the saddle, he gnawed his cheek as he cleared the tower.

Trotting up the incline, Geoffrey turned left and rode through a small gate, which gave access to the inner ward. Desperate to conceal the fear threatening to empty his bowels, he dismounted near the well-lit Great Tower. Dragging the dead man from his horse he laid him gently on the ground.

"Your worries are over, my friend," he whispered, "mine are just beginning."

Removing his riding gloves, Geoffrey prayed Ralph Grey would not notice the nervous tic pulsating below his left eye. The trembling, foam-caked palfreys shook their heads, flicking salty froth in the air. A flying gobbet of warm sweaty foam hit Geoffrey in the face and he turned away in disgust.

An hour before Geoffrey of Gloucester rode up to the gates of Bamburgh Castle, Philip Neville was in Northumberland's marquee, trying on one tunic after another. A chest full of doublets and surcoats had been found at Bywell, and confiscated. After Philip's offer to act as messenger, his cousin invited him to come and take what he wanted, but he was too pedantic. This tunic was tight under the arms, another loose on the waist, a third too extravagant, but they all had one thing in common, a bad smell. Finally he chose a quartered blue and white doublet with a golden eagle in the square over the left breast, the colours of the dead Duke of Somerset. While Philip changed, the sun set and torches were ignited through the camp. Warwick's trumpeter blew for the night watch to take up its vigil. Outside Northumberland's tent, the dull rhythmic thudding of two palfreys racing up and down a stretch of pasture caught Philip's ear. Dropping a thin silk ribbon over his head, he glanced at the attached gold swan pendant and pondered on its notorious history. Shaking the memory from his mind, he swapped his arming sword for another brought from the armoury and threw a short woollen cloak around his shoulders.

"At least you smell like a Lancastrian," John Neville grinned, eyeing his costume.

"Thank you, my lord," Philip frowned, bowing and walking out.

"Trust no one," Sir John warned, placing an arm around his neck.

"I won't," he confirmed, heading off to meet Warwick.

The two galloping palfreys were steered across to the baggage park, where Warwick was in conversion with Francis Talbot and his herald. A fresh evening breeze rolled in off the sea cooling the sweat on Philip's face and blowing the foul air from the camp. Joining his cousin, he noticed the horses had been ridden almost to exhaustion. Their heads drooped submissively, their quivering bodies were streaked with white foam, and steaming pink tongues flopped loosely in their mouths; the poor beasts were almost broken down.

"They're all in, my lord," the rider panted sliding from the saddle and resting his hands on his knees.

Warwick dismissed him with an impassive nod.

"Bring it out!" he commanded, addressing a pair of

servants standing near a conical buff tent.

Slipping inside, they soon reappeared carrying a large sack. Watching the two men struggle with the awkward bundle, Warwick turned to a group of fletchers and cupped a hand to his mouth.

"Don't just sit there you miserable codheads, lend a hand!"

Busy gluing goose feathers to aspen arrow shafts by the light of a brazier, the fletchers divided their attention between the task at hand and the overworked palfreys. Several grudgingly obeyed; the rest ignored the summons and continued their work.

As the four men carried the unwieldy sack over to Warwick, an arm flopped out of the open end. The fletchers, unaware of its contents, dropped their end and leapt back in horror.

"Pick it up," Sir Richard growled.

Crossing themselves they nervously obeyed, running the sack the final few yards.

"Now take him out and put him on a horse damn your eyes!" Warwick snapped, irritated at the delay. "By St Paul, do I have to show you how to piss straight?"

Francis Talbot crossed his chest and looked on solemnly as the coarse sacking was drawn back to reveal a well-dressed corpse.

"Who was he?" Philip asked, pushing an inquisitive soldier aside to see.

"It doesn't concern you," Warwick frowned, irritated by his curiosity. "More light!"

Philip glanced at Francis, whose stony silence reflected his unease.

"Remorse for a man you've never met?" Richard grinned.

"No, my lord," Philip remarked sourly.

"Hurry," Warwick rasped, as the four men fought to lift the lifeless body, and hold it against the agitated horse.

The earl signalled now to a soldier waiting in the shadows and he came forward. Placing a hand between the dead man's shoulders, he prodded the area below the dead man's shoulder blades. Finding a soft spot, he removed an arrow from his belt and cold-heartedly stabbed its barbed point into his back.

Philip winced at his brutality and Richard stared at him, daring his cousin to speak, but he held his tongue.

"He raped and murdered another man's wife," Warwick's herald explained, as the soldier bowed and left.

It took an eternity for the four men to steady the jittery horse and lift, and wedge the limp body into the saddle, and even longer to jam his feet into the stirrups, and secure the reins to his dead hands. After much effort and the air thick with curses the grim task was finished.

"Now go and get drunk," Warwick commanded, dismissing the flustered men with a few coins.

Mounting the second horse, Philip gripped the leathers, patted the quivering palfrey's wet neck and felt its heaving ribs moving in and out against his legs.

"You have second thoughts?" Warwick asked.

"No," he said firmly, turning his nose up at the unpleasant sensation of warm horse sweat penetrating his woollen hose.

Several giggling pages now appeared and threw handfuls of wet mud over the legs of both men and horses.

"That's enough you fools," Philip complained, as it splashed his face.

"'Bon chance'," Warwick offered.

"My lord," he nodded slowly, believing his cousin expected him to fail.

Taking a length of rope from a guard, Philip threaded one end through a ring, hanging from the saliva-coated bit in the mouth of the second horse, and coiled the other around his left hand. With a rueful nod at Francis, he jabbed in his spurs. The palfrey snorted defiantly and bolted, pursued by a group of yelling men-at-arms and accompanied by the beating of a drum. Leaving the security of the camp, Philip headed for the distant black silhouette of Bamburgh.

Approaching the south wall, Philip Neville wanted to turn back, but knew it was too late. Winding the tow-rope tighter around his left hand, he dug his spurs in hard, urging the palfrey's to greater speed. Swinging east the two horses cantered past several gun positions and followed the wide moat. Dragging the reins sharply to the left, he forced his mount into a short gallop and both horses leapt the ditch, only to stumble on the far side. With spur and a prayer he kept control, and his palfrey staggered up the lengthy ramp towards the barbican. The animal's ragged breathing caused concern and Philip doubted he would make it to the gatehouse. Glancing up at the wall, he saw torches illuminating the battlements and hoped the guards couldn't hear his heart pounding.

Dragging the flagging second horse and its bobbing, lifeless baggage almost tore his shoulder from its socket, and he was desperate to release the rope, but with the gates in sight he held on. When he was close enough he let go with a thankful gasp. The twisted hemp slipped through the ring on the bridle of the second palfrey and both horses came to a shuddering halt. The impulse to flee became overwhelming, but he vacillated and before he could decide it was too late.

Geoffrey of Gloucester spat the vile horse sweat from his mouth and grimaced as he drew a sleeve across his lips. Watching a group of soldiers bearing down on him he tried not to show fear.

"You are either very brave, or you are a fool," Ralph Grey announced, offering his hand, while others eager for news gathered around.

"I am neither my lord," he replied, shaking the proffered hand, an act that tugged his cloak open enough to reveal the gold swan pendant, resting against his chest.

"Is that it?" Grey asked.

"Yes."

"This trinket has saved your life, but where is its chain?"

"His Grace was forced to sell most of his jewels to help the queen," he explained, stifling a yawn. "Forgive me, I have ridden far and I'm exhausted."

"Then you must rest," Grey suggested. "Sir Roger here will show you to your room. When you have rested, join me for supper and tell me why you have come to this God-forsaken place."

Geoffrey hesitated and Grey put his vacillation down to grief for his companion.

"I'll have your friend laid out in the chapel."

"Thank you my lord," he smiled gratefully, as the tall heavily moustachioed Roger de Gravett, escorted him into the Great Tower.

Nursing his aching left hand, Geoffrey looked back at Grey and accidentally collided with several women coming out of the tower.

"Have a care sir."

"Forgive me," he apologised, nodding.

Shrouded from head to toe in long dark cloaks, they ignored his contrition and continued on their way.

"Wretched women," he muttered, before following an amused Roger de Gravett inside.

Washed, rested and dressed in the same malodorous doublet, Philip Neville, alias Geoffrey of Gloucester, joined Ralph Grey in his third floor apartment.

"Welcome," Grey announced, while a blank-faced servant placed several candles on a table near the window. "The bread is stale but we have plenty of salt fish and wine. I can offer you nothing better for some knave has stolen our grain and the meat has soured."

"Thank you," Philip nodded, unbuckling his sword and propping it against the wall. "I'm so hungry I could eat a horse."

While a servant brought water and towels for the diners, Grey took his seat at the table. Drawing a chair out Philip cocked a leg over its low back and bumped it in close, and Sir Ralph recalled another who used the same method but thought nothing of it. A meagre meal of tourte bread and dried cod submerged in butter was brought out on three plates and laid on the table.

The strong odour emanating from the colourless cod offended Philip's sense of smell, but he knew he must play along. Dipping his fingers into a bowl of water, he dried them on a towel handed to him by a page. Noting the extra plate he looked enquiringly at Ralph Grey. Bamburgh's reluctant captain's face was dominated by darkly-ringed eyes, illustrative of his inner torment.

"We wait for Sir Humphrey," he announced, coming out of his trance-like state at the sound of someone plodding up the stairwell from the Great Hall below. "Have we met before?" he mused, pointing a pewter spoon at his guest.

"Perhaps," he replied, Lord Scrope's warning ringing in his ears.

"Perhaps," Grey echoed thoughtfully, the low light veiling Philips flushed face.

"Good evening gentlemen," Sir Humphrey announced, entering the chamber.

Four years younger than his distant cousin Philip, Humphrey Neville was suffering badly from haemorrhoids. Unable to cope with the illness, he gladly relinquished his authority as captain of Bamburgh to Sir Ralph Grey.

Washing his hands, the richly attired knight nodded guardedly at the stranger and stood behind his own chair until the stabbing pain in his arse subsided.

"You must be the one... who rode through Lord Warwick's camp..." he struggled, blowing and moaning to alleviate his agony, "to share our fate."

"Geoffrey of Gloucester," Grey smiled, introducing the two men, "Sir Humphrey Neville."

"My lord," Philip replied rising from his seat and nodding politely, before sitting back down.

"A pity your companion did not survive," Sir Humphrey declared, rocking on his heels and frowning at the meagre fare, "to come so far... only to fall at the last hurdle."

"Yes, most unfortunate," Philip echoed, concerned his tone might give him away.

Humphrey Neville delicately eased his backside onto a cushioned seat, gripped the edge of the table with both hands and breathed out delicately.

"Let us pray," Grey announced, clasping his hands together against his chin.

"Pater noster que es in calis, santificue nomen tuum, adventiate regnum tuum…" he began.

While Sir Ralph monotonously ran through the Lord's Prayer, Philip sneered at his misplaced morals. Sensing his remote cousin analysing him, he glanced at Sir Humphrey, but his heavily hooded eyes were closed.

"Et nominee patrie, et filis et spiritus sancti," Grey concluded, crossing his chest.

"Amen," his companions echoed.

"How is Her Majesty?" the younger Neville asked, stuffing a napkin down his shirt front and slicing the pallid cod with a knife.

"She is much troubled," Philip answered.

"Huh," Grey sniffed, resenting her for leaving England. "Are we abandoned?"

Philip failed to answer and Grey tried to comprehend his silence. "What am I to do?" he pressed, as the page approached the table, poured red wine from a table jug into three goblets, and withdrew.

"Throw yourself on the mercy of the usurper," he exclaimed, gulping a mouthful of wine to help him swallow the indigestible cod and his bold proposal.

"Is that it?" Grey spluttered, shocked by his response.

"The king will raise a new army," Sir Humphrey declared.

"From where?" Grey growled.

"Alas my lords; King Henry is taken," Philip lied, deliberately keeping his answers short and trying to appear downcast.

"Taken?" Grey gasped, suddenly losing his appetite

and pushing his plate away. "The king... is taken?"

Ralph Grey, his freckle-flecked face as pale as the fish on his plate, looked totally crushed by the news.

"The queen has failed to pull Louis away from Edward. For those still holding out there is little hope," Philip clarified, emboldened by Grey's dejection and Sir Humphrey's ominous silence.

"How are you acquainted with the queen?" Sir Humphrey wondered, pushing the cod around his plate. "I have not heard of you before today?"

"I am a merchant, related to Dr Morton through my mother, and schooled in several languages. The good doctor recommended me to Her Majesty," Philip bluffed, observing how Ralph Grey seemed to have aged twenty years in the last few minutes. "I tutor the young prince in French, Greek and Latin."

"I know that livery," Humphrey Neville said suspiciously, eyeing Philip's stained doublet.

"They are Somerset's colours," Grey revealed, staring into space.

"Are you Somerset's man?" Sir Humphrey asked.

"No, the queen sent me here to seek those who are left, and to inform them she is raising money for her husband's cause," Philip explained. "But that was before I heard His Majesty was being held prisoner."

"Where did you trade?"

"Bristol, my home is there," Philip replied, amazed at his own quick thinking. "My lord, why do you question me? I have come here at great risk to bring you news."

"We have to be careful," Grey interceded.

"The queen must be distressed at the recent executions," Sir Humphrey bemoaned, pushing his platter aside. "We have lost so many friends. We must break out or our names will be added to the list," he warned, tearing off a piece of bread and dipping it into the insipid butter, to improve its palatability.

"Her Majesty is inconsolable," Philip announced. "These past months have proved ruinous for our cause," he added, the urge to crow triumphantly held in check.

"My head is spinning," Sir Ralph hissed. "I cannot think."

Grey's fortitude had been completely shattered by Philip's news, and he sat hunched down in his chair like a frightened fawn.

"I shall retire," he said, rising slowly, "forgive me gentlemen."

Despite his treachery, Philip felt sorry for Ralph Grey.

"How came you by such wretched news?" Sir Humphrey asked, eating a piece of bread, spread with butter and mixed with rosemary and sage to alleviate the pain in his arse.

"I met King Henry's chamberlain, three days ago."

"Perhaps it is only a rumour," he gasped through his agony. "How does a merchant cross the channel and ride all this way through enemy country, with only one companion?"

Fighting to keep his nerve, Philip attentively shredded the sticky fish with his fingers.

"Our ship docked at Southampton," he began, unable to eat, "we have ridden hard, my lord. When we arrived at Warwick's camp, we hid until sunset, and while they ate, we charged right through them," he explained, almost believing his lies.

"You were most fortunate," he said, his strong breath forcing Philip to lean back, "t'was a bold feat."

"Yes," he echoed, "I was fortunate."

Peeved by the merchant's uncomplicated answers, the suspicious Humphrey Neville grabbed his goblet by its stem and rose slowly.

"I do not intend to be taken," he declared, bracing himself to counter a sharp twinge of pain. "Goodnight…"

"Goodnight, my lord," Philip replied, rising slightly from his chair and bowing, while Sir Humphrey shuffled painfully out.

Sitting down, Philip gathered his thoughts and watched an elderly servant limp over to the table and scrape the uneaten fish from three plates onto one. Stacking the platters in an uneven pile, he slapped his linen cloth against the surface of the table, scattering the crumbs. Hobbling over to a stool near the door, he sat and used a chunk of bread to spoon the leftovers into his mouth. Concerned by Humphrey Neville's doubts, Philip washed his tacky fingers, snatched up his sword and frowned at the munching servant on his way out. As an afterthought, the man jumped up and opened the door for him.

"Thank you, my lord," he nodded, closing the door after him. "Kiss my arse."

Michael Neville was no fool. Sick of Sir Ralph Grey's lack of motivation, he refused his invitation to join him for supper. Instead he stayed in his room, pacing like a caged tiger and spitting abuse at the walls. Glancing out of the narrow window he cursed the distant fires of his cousin's sprawling encampment and scratched his itchy fingers. He could try and escape, but there were still loyal men in the garrison, men like Roger de Gravett. Kind-eyed and sympathetic de Gravett was a chivalric knight with a passion for Henry of Lancaster that was almost obsessive. His wife, Lady Eleanor, refused to leave Bamburgh and vowed to share her husband's fate. Michael could not abandon de Gravett as easily as Somerset had abandoned him on Towton Moor. As for the other two, he felt no compunction about leaving them to their fate. Concerned by Geoffrey of Gloucester's presence, he could think of no reason why someone would risk his life for such a useless enterprise. The more he mulled over his arrival, the more he suspected treachery. With darkness shrouding his chamber, he felt the walls closing in. Buckling on his sword, he descended the low-lit spiralling stairwell to the next level and acknowledged the guards, before continuing down a series of straight steps to the vaulted ground floor.

Outside, the cool air wafting in off the sea, calmed his fiery disposition and he fingered the raised scar running down his left cheek without thinking.

"You!" he shouted at a passing soldier.

"M'lord?"

"Where are the strangers' horses?"

"In tha stable," he replied, surprised by the question. "Sir Roger has given orders-"

"What orders?"

"They're to be slaughtered m'lord, fer meat."

Michael indicated for him to move on and grabbed a handful of dry twigs from a nearby pile. Twisting the fibres together, he ignited them from a brazier and walked to the stables, located next to the inner wall between the Great Tower and St Peter's Chapel. Inside he found the smith scrubbing ingrained dirt from his hands.

"Are those their horses Master Hollins?" he asked, running his coarse fingers down the nearest animal's tacky neck.

The powerfully built ironsmith wiped his large hands in his badly-singed leather apron and nodded.

With a caustic huff, Michael lifted the nearest palfrey's foreleg, to examine hoof and muscle. Fearing the flame the horse let out a frightened whinny and shied away.

"Be calm," he whispered, holding the torch at arm's length, his reassuring tone soothing the troubled beast. "I won't hurt you."

Saddened by the thought that such beautiful creatures were destined for the pot, Michael gently stroked the palfrey's velvety, white blaze and sniffed its hide. The smell was strong and the necks and flanks of both horses were caked in salty foam. There was no doubt they had been ridden hard, and he slouched out of the stables disappointed. Spotting a billman squatting on a barrel and probing the holes in his shoes, he walked over to him.

"Where are the two men who rode in tonight?"

"One is with Sir Ralph."

"And the other?" he growled impatiently.

"Dead," the billman sniffed, wishing he'd left Bamburgh when offered the chance.

"Dead... why was I not told?"

The billman shrugged his shoulders.

"How?" Michael asked.

"Arrow in the back."

"One of ours?"

"Who knows?" he said, scrutinizing his shoddy footwear.

"Where is he now?" Michael pressed.

"Who?"

"The dead man you jackanapes!"

"In the chapel!" he snapped.

The urge to kick the uncouth soldier off his perch was countered by a stronger desire to validate his suspicions. Purposely cuffing the back of his head, Michael hurried over to the chapel.

Reaching the dark little church, set against the east corner of the inner ward, Michael pushed open the narrow, weather-beaten door, which creaked eerily on its badly corroded hinges. Thrusting his torch into the silent sanctuary, he tip-toed inside. A gust of wind made the burning twigs crack and hiss, and the smoky light played tricks on his eyes. He thought he saw something lying on the altar table but it was only a shadow brought to life by the sparking torch.

"Can I help you my son?"

The words spun Michael around.

"What the he…" he gasped, coming face to face with the chaplain, his pale features distorted by the guttering light of the candle in his hand. "What are you doing here?"

"Where would you expect to find a priest?" the hawk-nosed cleric countered, ruffled by his prickly tone. "Why are you here?"

Shocked at the appearance of the silver-haired priest, Michael was momentarily lost for words.

"I am here to pray for the soul of that unfortunate wretch," the elfin cleric announced, pointing his candle at the body lying on a board near the north wall.

"I… I also wish to pray for him, Father," Michael stammered, indicating the door. "Come back later, please."

337

"But…"

"Later, Father," he insisted, shunting him out and slamming the door.

Holding the torch at arm's length, Michael walked slowly up the aisle and along the windowless north wall, until he saw the unmistakable outline of a body. The dead man had been laid out on a plank, close to the east apse of the chapel, and covered with a linen sheet. Taking a deep breath Michael yanked the shroud down as far as his waist and unconsciously made the sign of the cross. Drawing the light closer he leaned over the body, allowing his eyes to do the preliminary work. The face looked old for such an elegantly attired esquire, and was crowned by a thatch of poorly cropped hair greying at the temples. Thrusting his fingers between the dead man's lips, Michael callously wrenched the jaw down, revealing a set of stained crooked teeth.

"Hum," he frowned, raising his eyebrows and dropping the torch into an iron bracket on the wall.

Shifting his attention to the hands crossed over the massive chest, Michael touched the calloused fingertips and his concentrated frown twisted into a sneer. The expensive, poorly-tailored doublet made him chuckle but he was not finished. Uncrossing the arms, he pinched the muscle down both limbs, from shoulder to wrist, and compared them. The biceps were solid, but the muscles of the right arm were much larger than those of the left.

"You are no esquire," he muttered, grunting as he rolled the body onto its side. "Now my friend, how did you die?"

Taking the torch from its holder Michael saw the crusted hole in the man's shirt where the arrow supposedly struck, but found only a tiny amount of dry blood. Guided by the dancing light he ran a hand up the man's backbone to the nape and looked closer. Then he spotted a dark contusion on the neck below the hairline. Shaking the sweat of anticipation from his eyes, he spread his fingers, pushed them into the corpse's greasy hair and traced the shape of the skull. When his fingertips hit a swollen ridge, he separated the congealed bloody curls from the lump, and brought the light nearer until the smell of singed hair forced him to draw it away. Michael's scepticism had reaped its reward. Here lay a simple archer killed by a blow to the head. He had then been dressed to look like an esquire and stabbed with an arrow for the purpose of deception, but there was more to being an esquire than a fine suit of clothes. Flipping the body onto its back, he refolded the arms and pulled the shroud back.

"Bastard," he growled, kneeling before the altar and crossing himself, belatedly remembering where he was. "Forgive me."

Leaving the chapel, Michael Neville hurried back to the tower eager to reveal his findings.

Chapter 17

Philip Neville slept badly, his mind an aerated cauldron of fear and regret. Long before sunrise he woke yet again, only this time he could not go back to sleep. Rolling off his low pallet, he struck a spark and lit several candles. Once dressed, he walked out into the corridor and down a set of circular steps to the first floor. A guard pointed him to the nearest latrine; a narrow chamber next to the tower chapel. Untying his hose and braies, he squatted on the rough wooden seat and while nature ran its course his apprehension increased. He was convinced Humphrey Neville suspected.

"Bastard," he muttered, sniffing the musty material of his doublet. "Phew."

A refreshing early morning breeze blew through the tiny, glassless window helping him finish his toilet quickly. Using a handful of linen rags to wipe his backside, he dropped them into the privy and watched as they disappeared down the chute. Returning to his room Philip looked out the window at the guards idling along the south wall, their dark silhouettes outlined by stuttering torchlight.

After more than an hour of pacing and nervous contemplation, a sharp rap on the door broke his train of thought.

"Yes?" he snapped, surprised by the interruption.

"Sir Ralph asks you to join him in the chapel for prayers," a muffled voice announced.

"Tell your master I'll join him, after prayers!" he answered sharply.

"As you wish," the servant sighed, before withdrawing.

Buckling on his borrowed sword, Philip returned to the window, rotated his aching left shoulder and scrutinized the ramparts below. If he had to get out, the south wall would be the logical escape route, but after calculating its height he doubted he could survive such a leap.

With the first beams of daylight fanning across the

night sky from the east, Philip sat on the bed and compared his fondness for Isobel Talbot with his loathing for Elizabeth Percy. The more he tried to shut out such frenetic thoughts, the more they dominated. His hunger for revenge against the woman who betrayed him eclipsed any attraction he felt for Isobel. In the past such anarchic reflections could lead to emotional exhaustion, which only alcohol could obliterate. But today that option was denied him; today he must keep a clear mind.

A second, more persistent knock brought Philip out of his preoccupation. When the servant declared breakfast to be ready, Philip took several deep breaths to steady his nerves, and left the deceptive security of his room. As he entered Sir Ralph's private apartment, Philip found his host staring out of the window, hands behind his back, a stance that indicated something was wrong. When Grey spoke without turning to face him, Philip went cold. Tensing his body he moved his right hand across his stomach to the cracked, wooden handle of the sword resting against his left hip.

"Good morning," Grey offered, his impassive tone underlining Philip's fear. "Each day I stand here and watch the sun rise. Do you know why?" There was no response. "Because I know, in the end, I must surrender myself to my old friend. So I drink in each new dawn and thank God and the Earl of Warwick for the privilege."

Philip remained silent, apprehension drying the saliva in his mouth and cooling the beads of nervous perspiration blistering his rutted forehead.

Turning deliberately, Grey extended a hand, palm up but his reproachful gaze was elsewhere.

"You have not met our guest," he announced, looking at the door behind Philip. "May I present Geoffrey of Gloucester; he arrived here last night to bring us news."

An obscure figure hiding in the shadows, edged out into the room. Sensing movement, Philip instinctively spun into a defensive pose, his right hand half drawing the blade from its scabbard. Grey was impressed by his reaction, which only confirmed that he was no mere merchant. No, here stood a trained warrior attuned to expect the unexpected and be prepared for it.

Outside, the sun eased above the horizon and its welcome day beamed in through the east windows, illuminating the features of the man moving out of the shadows, and Philip froze.

"Do you now stand by your story Geoffrey of Gloucester?" Grey scoffed, outraged at being taken for a fool.

"Who are you?" Michael Neville demanded in a threatening voice, while his eyes searched Philip's dumbfounded expression for a hint of why he was in Bamburgh.

"I have told you my name, why do you doubt me?" he insisted, twisting his neck to answer Grey, but keeping his eyes on Michael.

Mortified at coming face to face with his brother, Philip dreaded the consequences for them both.

"This is Michael Neville, cousin to the Earl of Warwick and one of King Henry's most loyal knights," Grey confirmed. "Last night he examined your companion. That man lying in the chapel was no esquire, slain by an arrow," Grey revealed, breathing heavily through his nose and pacing agitatedly. "He was an archer killed by a blow to the head... did you murder him?"

"No," Philip snapped, offering Michael a pained frown.

"What did you hope to gain by coming here with this bag of lies?" Michael demanded, edging around, to position himself between his brother and Ralph Grey.

Philip lowered his head and Michael expressively urged him to keep their secret.

"Every word that has come out of your mouth is a falsehood!" he barked. "King Henry is not taken, for if that were true Warwick would have told us, he wants Bamburgh intact. Henry will come and break this siege, so your attempt to make fools of us has all been for nothing."

"And you will die for nothing," Grey inserted, angrily

grabbing the back of his chair and calling for his guards.

Two heavy-set, bearded Scotsmen entered the chamber and waited ready.

"Take this dog to the Muniment Tower!" Sir Ralph screeched, muttering something about betrayal under his breath.

Philip was unceremoniously disarmed, grabbed by the arms and forcibly led away.

"You see!" Grey called after him. "You should have come to chapel this morning! Perhaps God would have answered your prayers!"

"God will not help you, you treacherous dog!" Philip shouted over his shoulder, refusing to look at Michael lest their affiliation be discovered, "no matter how hard you pray!"

"What will you do with him?" Michael asked, trying not to sound too concerned.

"He'll have a day to reflect on his actions, and tomorrow he will die," he said in a distressed voice, Philip's caveat ringing in his ears.

"We do not know who he is, or what he hoped to achieve by coming here."

Shocked by his statement, Grey searched his face.

"We know why he came here... a moment ago you counselled throwing him from that very window!" he gasped, pointing at the opening. "What would you have me do? Wine and dine him."

"I want his name!" Michael retaliated, the desire to wring Sir Ralph's neck for his insouciance, strong. "Give him to me and I'll rack the truth from his body."

"No, he was sent here by the Earl of Warwick. At sunrise tomorrow his head will be on the battlements for his lordship to see."

Michael turned and left, slamming the door.

"How dare you walk away from me?" Grey yelled. "I command here!"

Philip Neville was escorted to the Muniment Tower, the larger of two square blocks, built onto the south curtain wall, in front of the kitchens. Without a word he was thrown bodily into a basement room.

"You cunts!" he screamed, picking himself up off the stone floor, as the door was slammed shut and locked.

With no window and a single tallow candle for light, Philip sat on a low bench, the only piece of furniture. Regretting having dreamt up such a scheme, he punished himself by cursing his egotism and punching the rough walls of his prison. All this pointless self-injury achieved was a set of bruised and torn knuckles, which only increased his aggravation. To alleviate the tedium Philip bent his head, so as not to strike the low ceiling, and paced.

"What the hell is he doing here?" he spat, lamenting his brother's inquisitive nature, "stupid shit!"

When his posture brought on backache, he sat down and verbally assaulted Ralph Grey and Humphrey Neville.

"Fucking traitors, pair of dog's bollocks!" he yelled, massaging his throbbing hands.

With daylight unable to penetrate the damp, subterranean dungeon, Philip lost all sense of time, and his petulance rose. Would Michael help him, or would he have to fend for himself? Putting the notion of help aside he decided to escape on his own. First he needed a weapon; the bench might provide one, so he broke it up with several vicious kicks, but the rotten wood crumbled. Dejected he slumped down on the cold floor, his fortitude ebbing. The thick stone walls and solid door meant any escape would have to be made with outside help, so he prayed Michael would put kinship before loyalty.

As time went on, hope gradually turned to despair and he sank into apathy. The lonely silence was broken only by an intermittent plop of water, and the periodic dull thud of a gunstone hitting the curtain wall. He tried to conjure a mental clock in his mind and gauge the time, but without daylight it was impossible. Unconsciously touching the swan pendant resting against his chest evoked images of that notorious night in the Forest of Galtres, and he shivered. Memories of Towton and Hedgeley Moor also came to mind, and he closed his eyes. Heightened by the propinquity of his incarceration, his past transgressions began to suffocate.

Philip's melancholic thoughts were interrupted when the heavy oak door was unlocked and cracked open. At first nothing happened; then a tray bearing a jug of cider, a small loaf of black bread, and an onion, was pushed in. Shielding his eyes from the strong light, he blinked to readjust and focused on the tray left near the threshold as the door was slammed shut. Blowing his nose between thumb and forefinger, he wiped the mucus on the wall before stooping to pick up the tray. Examining the food by low candlelight, he reeled back from the rancid smell, but hunger overcame his pride. Biting into the soft onion offended his palate and he spat it out. When he attempted to wash away the vile taste with a mouthful of warm bitter cider, he lost his temper and threw the lot against the door.

"I am to die, and all you offer me is this, this shit!"

"Do you want a confessor?"

"No!" he yelled, "I want something to eat!"

"Then eat your boots!"

Having eaten very little since the previous day, the groaning in his empty stomach grew louder and Philip rued his moment of anger. Dropping to his knees he ran his hands over the stone floor, his fingertips blindly skimming the foul-smelling straw and dirt. Stirring up the ancient dust added a clingy dryness to his throat and brought on a coughing fit, but a thin line of light, penetrating under the door, allowed him to retrieve some of the scattered food. The onion had disintegrated and the cider spilt, but the bread was so stale it remained intact.

"God-damn it," he cursed, plucking the loaf from the grime and sitting with his back against the wall.

Wiping off the worst of the muck, he nibbled the fusty bread and the bloody scabs on his knuckles cracked open, causing him to regret his self-inflicted torment.

As he gnawed on the coarse loaf, he sighed woefully

and suddenly bit on something hard.

"By all that is holy!" he shouted at the door, spitting the bread into his hand. "Am I to be poisoned?"

Lifting the candle, he drew the masticated mush to his face and studied what appeared to be a tiny cylinder of wood. Looking closer, he found it was a scrap of rolled paper, which had been folded tight and pushed into the bread, and the hole sealed with blackened fat.

"What the...?" he frowned.

Presuming the note was from his brother, he unrolled it carefully. When the crumpled square lay open, he tried to translate its smudged text by muted candlelight.

As he read, Philip's anxiety turned to relief. Michael had indeed sent the note; he could not allow his brother to be executed. The message was brief and to the point, urging him to wait, and warning him to destroy the note. Gasping his relief, he touched the paper to the candle, causing it to burn fiercely. As the fiery mass floated to the floor he reduced it to a pile of black ash with the sole of his boot, before resting back against the wall. All he could do now was to wait, but with the prospect of freedom in the offing waiting wouldn't be so hard, though he resented his inability to take charge of the situation.

With nothing to do but sit and watch the candle flame feed on the acrid, tallow fat, Philip's intolerance eventually returned. Darkness fostered his angst and the invisible plopping sound began to play on his nerves.

"Hurry up," he growled, massaging his sore knuckles, "for God's sake."

A muffled thud beyond the door caught his attention, and when the thin rectangle of light beaming under the door was extinguished, he sat upright. Picking up a shard of the broken jug, he crept forward and made ready to strike. A key clattered in the iron lock and clunked heavily; the door swung open and torchlight flooded the dungeon, forcing Philip to cover his eyes.

"Geoffrey of Gloucester," someone scoffed, "you arrogant shit-head."

Edging tentatively out of his cell, Philip saw the guard lying face down in an expanding pool of blood. His skull had been split open, and blood from the shattered cavity flowed into the gaps between the flagstones.

"Get out of the way," Michael growled grabbing the dead man's feet and dragging him inside. "The fool would not be bribed."

"You took your time."

"'Tis fortunate for you I came at all," he grunted. "Would you rather we did this in daylight?"

Philip found an apology hard to employ and offered a simple nod of appreciation.

While his rescuer sprinkled straw over the bloodstained floor, Philip watched in apathetic silence. Satisfied, Michael slammed the cell door and locked it, before leading the way up out of the basement. Reaching ground level, he drew a bundle from a tiny alcove and threw it at his brother.

"What this?" Philip asked, uncoiling a brown woollen habit.

"You could have gone out through a passage in the well, but that way is too well guarded, you have only one choice."

"And that is?"

"Wait and see, now put it on."

Michael peered into the night, looking for an opportunity to slip across the courtyard to the ironsmith's forge opposite, but a group of soldiers, between him and his objective, forced him to rethink.

"How do I get out?" Philip pressed.

"Through the gates."

"Through the gates? Impossible. Lower me over the wall."

"The walls are too well lit," he hissed. "Keep your voice down."

"I'll take my chance."

"I will not," Michael said, slipping out of the tower door and taking a roundabout route to the forge.

Wrapping the habit round his body, Philip flipped the hood up over his head and hurried after his brother. Keeping to the shadows, Michael led the way past the kitchens to the chapel.

"Fuck it," he gasped, stopping at a corner, only to have Philip slam into him and jar his back. "Do you want to get us killed?"

Irked by his carelessness, Philip flattened himself behind one of the buttresses of the chapel's south wall, and held his breath.

"Wait," Michael hesitated, as a guard ambled past.

"Scent?" Philip whispered, sniffing his perfumed hair.

"Soap," he snapped, flicking his wrist to continue.

Bending low, both men covered the final few yards to the forge undetected.

"No, not in there," Michael warned, putting an arm out to stop him rushing inside. "Go round the back."

In an unlit area between the forge and chapel, a four-wheeled cart stood parked, its low sloping sides bowing under the weight of two huge destriers. A faint shaft of light shone across the courtyard from an upstairs window allowing Philip to see that both animals had been slaughtered, and their hooves and manes cut off. Mystified, he blinked vacantly at Michael, who smiled back with his mouth but not his eyes; those remained fixated on the horses as he spoke.

"Get inside."

"What?"

"Take off your boots and that necklace," Michael commanded, looking around guardedly. "And climb into the belly of that one," he added, pointing at the destriers, "hurry."

Philip gaped at the fly-infested remains of the two warhorses, but activity in the courtyard added urgency to Michael's voice.

"Bustle damn you, before we are undone."

"How do you expect me to fit in there?"

"The insides have been cut out," Michael retorted

angrily, glancing around, to make sure no inquisitive eyes were watching. "Move it."

Philip shook his head, took off his boots, his belt, and the ornamental collar, and grabbed one of the cart wheels. Hauling himself up caused the bed of the vehicle to groan under the extra weight, and Michael nervously scratched his itchy hands.

"It won't work," Philip whinged.

"Sweet Jesus, hurry."

Pulling the woollen habit tight, Philip gripped the thick stomach skin of the nearest horse and wrenched it open, but the sweet, sour stink of decay invaded his nostrils and kicked his head back. "By Christ's blood!" he choked, smothering a retching cough.

"Quiet," Michael urged, anxiously squeezing the hilt of his sword. "Get in."

Philip lay on his side and tentatively backed his body and feet into the warm, slimy hollow, the pungent stench making him gag.

"Quickly," Michael insisted, picking up a pole and using it to lever the destrier's forelegs apart, an action that caused a swarm of flies to drone frantically.

"Do you want to take my place?" Philip hissed, half in, half out.

"'Tis your choice: the horse or the rack?"

Filling his lungs with fresh air, Philip forced himself in until the fractured bone shards stabbed painfully into his back and shoulders. Dropping the pole, Michael tugged the thick hide over his brother's torso. Despite every effort Philip's knees would not go in.

"Fuck it!" Michael growled, punching the dead horse.

"Ouch."

Before rescuing Philip, Michael bribed the butcher's son to help him clean out a horse. The fifteen year old was thick in the head but strong in the arm and between them they hacked out bone, and scraped away the insides, until a sizable hole had been excavated. The offal and bones were loaded into several sacks and prudently dumped over the north wall. Before washing the vile matter from his body and changing his clothes, Michael commandeered a group of soldiers to help him hoist the two horses onto a cart.

"I can do no more," Michael declared roping the animal's front legs together and throwing a sack over its belly to conceal Philip's protruding knees. "Take this," he whispered, slipping a dagger through the destrier's abdomen, where he assumed his hands to be. "The skinners will come and ditch the carcasses outside. Wait until they leave before making your move."

"What if they take them for meat?"

"They would not dare. These were Sir Humphrey Neville's pride and joy. They've been slaughtered to prevent them falling into the hands of our goodly cousin," Michael explained, picking up the discarded boots, belt and collar. "From here you're in God's hands."

"Then I am doomed for I am beyond His good grace," Philip joked, but Michael had already left.

Inside the dark cramped belly, the world closed in on Philip Neville as he struggled to attain comfort. The hot malodorous horseflesh compressed his foetal-positioned body and restricted his breathing to such an extent he thought he would suffocate. Sweating copiously he shifted to relieve the sharp pain in his neck, but the sawn off rib bones dug in, exacerbating his agony. Each time he moved, the slurping sound of liquefying flesh and the incessant flies tickling his face, added a new dimension of fear. Suddenly the contents of his stomach erupted. With nowhere to go, the glutinous vomit flowed back in his face. Spitting out lumps of partly digested food, he pushed the tangy bisque away with his tongue.

The cadaver's warm fluids seeped through the woollen habit permeating his clothing, and searing pain drilled into the back of his knees.

"God help me," he gasped, as his trapped left arm tingled with pins and needles.

When he felt something crawling over his face, his imagination ran amok. In his distressed mind he saw maggots eating his flesh, and the thought terrified him. Gripping the dagger he was on the verge of cutting himself free from his mouldering refuge, but changed his mind at the last moment. In an attempt to banish such lurid thoughts he closed his eyes and attempted to replace them with more pleasing imagery. Unfortunately any interlude, no matter how appealing, could not survive long in such a horrific environment, and reality shoved them aside, leaving him once more in illusory terror.

After a long period of mental and physical torture, Philip sensed movement outside. The bad-tempered dialogue of men who disliked their work became more distinct and he no longer felt alone. With his anxiety in retreat, the acidic odour of vomit and sweat, mixed with the stink of putrid horseflesh, caused him to spew a second time. Looking through the thin matting he noticed a faint, flickering orange light coming closer. Minutes later, the rattle of a horse being attached to the shaft and the harsh cursing of the skinners, allowed him to exhale and spit out the bitter bile. Suddenly the vehicle jolted sharply and he feared his decomposing coffin might fall off, but the cart rumbled forward and he stayed on. The two skinners turned the wain and it bounced heavily down the narrow passage leading to the Constable's Tower, and beyond. The rasping of the steel-reinforced portcullis winching up and the grinding of the Great Gates yawning open made Philip's heart race.

"What a waste," one of the skinners grumbled, prodding the two horses with his stave.

"Fair bit of meat on 'em," his friend griped in a strange dialect. "Pity tah let 'em rot."

"Don't stray too far," came the warning from one of the guards up on the barbican parapet.

"Ave no fear of that friend," the skinner dragging the hackney responded.

Philip carefully pushed a hand out and raised the

351

sacking slightly for a better view. Having the use of only one eye, he caught sight of the portcullis groove in the stonework, followed by the thick wooden planking of the great gates, and finally the barrel shaped belly of a guard gesturing them on.

"Get that pestilence out of here!" the guard scowled, the stench offending his nostrils.

"You'll be eatin shit soon my fat friend."

"A pox on you and yours!"

"Pig," the skinner jeered, while his companion squealed like a hog, "there's enough fat on you tah keep us going for a year."

"Fucked up idiots," the guard snarled, as they guffawed and hurried on their way.

Once through the well-lit outer gates, darkness closed in. Lowering the matting, Philip drew back his sticky hand and reduced his breathing.

The cart tipped forward and trundled speedily down the ramp. Philip was on the verge of yelling out when the vehicle suddenly juddered to a halt. Using poles to force the destrier off, the skinners heaved and swore. Fearing discovery, Philip forgot about the flies droning in and out of every facial orifice and tried to free his trapped arm.

"Push, you shit-arse!" one of the skinners gasped.

"This one's a fat bastard, like you," his companion strained, struggling to obtain leverage. "Get...off...tha...fucking...cart!"

Philip listened to their competitive banter until he felt himself moving. Warm vomit dribbled down his neck and the furious buzzing of trapped flies almost drove him insane. Closing his eyes he rotated his tongue to push stale spew and dead flies from his mouth, but the effort was thwarted when the destrier he was in slid off the cart and hit the ground with a bone-jarring thud. The horse took most of the impact but the shock forced a whimper of pain from Philip's lips.

"What was that?" one of the skinners hissed nervously.

"Nothing," his friend whispered.

When they pushed the lighter horse off and it crashed onto the other, a distinct moan was heard and the two men exchanged worried glances. Sweating profusely, Philip curled the fingers of his right hand around the dagger. The superstitious skinners crossed themselves, tossed the poles away and ran the cart back up the ramp to the security of Bamburgh's well-lit barbican.

Philip listened as the great oak doors slammed shut and the portcullis rattled down, before breathing easily. Pushing a slimy hand out of the destrier's stomach helped the precariously balanced top horse to slide off. The tormenting flies annoyed him to such an extent he pressed his face into the gash, and for the third time, he spewed. With little left to bring up, he groaned at the painful knotting in his stomach.

Exhausted by his ordeal, Philip found enough strength to wrench his tingling left arm free and grip the dagger with both hands. Turning the blade he deliberately sliced the thick skin between the destrier's tied legs, but bone prevented him from expanding the cut. Wiping dead and dying flies from his mouth, he forced his sticky face out through the slit. Grunting and heaving helped his head and neck break free, but his shoulders failed to breach the narrow opening. Looking up, he saw the torches along Bamburgh's south wall and heard the guards talking. One more effort would free him from his loathsome cocoon, but not before he could sever the rope binding the animal's forelegs.

Stretching himself Philip began sawing the hemp. His shoulders ached and sweat stung his eyes, but he persevered. When the fibres began to fray he sawed harder until the last strands parted and he was able to slide out. Struggling to his feet, he felt like a drowning man coming to the surface. Smothering a cough he filled his lungs with fresh air, breathed deeply and rubbed his legs to revive the muscles. Pulling the tacky hood off his gluey hair, Philip discharged a final omelette of flies and stomach acid. Tearing off the wet habit as if it were infested with fleas, he used it to wipe his face before tossing it away. Removing his wet stockings, he limped back to the Yorkist lines, accompanied by distorted laughter from beyond Bamburgh's walls, and he wondered if it was aimed at him.

Reaching the sleeping encampment, Philip went directly to the Earl of Warwick's pavilion. Near the entrance he was approached by two guards and asked for the watchword.

"How the hell should I know?"

"What are you doing here?"

"I am Philip Neville, you fools," he snapped, his temper rising.

"Lord Warwick has retired for the night," one of the guards said, recognising him.

"Then wake him up!" he snarled grabbing the man by his jack and pulling him close.

Shocked by his reaction, the second guard went inside to rouse his master.

"My lord," he whispered, gently shaking the snoring earl, "Philip Neville demands to see you, but he doesn't know the watchword."

"Tell him to go away," he mumbled, half asleep.

"I fear he will not leave until you see him."

Richard Neville had had a difficult day and did not appreciate being woken. Cursing the guard, he tumbled out of bed and reached for his robe. When he accidentally stepped on Mongo's tail the hairy hound growled, and Warwick apologised. Rubbing his bleary red eyes, he shuffled out from behind a partition and fell into a low chair. Folding the silky material of his gown around his exposed legs, he stroked his stubbly chin and sniffed disapprovingly at his unwelcome visitor. Barefoot and with his clothes a foul-smelling, bloody mess, Philip was in bad humour. Several yawning varlets appeared behind their master, ready to wait on him.

Eager to return to his bed, Warwick signalled for wine, and indicated with an agitated huff for his kinsman to speak. Philip grabbed the proffered cup, took a swig, swilled the wine around his mouth and made to spit, but with nowhere to jettison the vile cocktail he was forced to swallow. Wetting his lips he began narrating an edited version of his pithy adventure.

"My lord, the plan almost worked," he began, brushing off a fly stuck to the embroidered eagle of his tunic. "Ralph Grey believed me, but Humphrey Neville was not–"

"My scheming cousin?" the earl interrupted, meaning Sir Humphrey, his heavy eyes and lined face making him look much older than his thirty-five years. "Hah."

Philip took another mouthful of wine and swished it around his teeth to eliminate the sour tang.

"This morning, I found myself arrested."

"Humphrey?" Warwick guessed, raising his eyebrows.

"No," he said. "T'was the dead esquire, he deceived everyone, everyone but my brother," he added with a sneer, "suspicious turd."

Richard's ears pricked up and he leaned forward, hungry for more news.

"Michael is here?" he asked, refusing a goblet of wine. "Why would he allow himself to be trapped in such a place?"

Philip shrugged his shoulders.

"Who knows, but for him I would not be alive, he killed one of the guards and helped me get away."

"First he betrays you," Warwick said, surprised, "then he helps you?"

"Yes, no, he did not know me at first..." Philip stammered, scratching his tacky hair.

"You boys have a tendency for killing your own men," he muttered.

"My lord?" he frowned, wiggling a finger in his ear to clear it of gunk.

"Nothing," Warwick scowled, eyeing his cousin up and down. "So all the rotten apples are in one basket, but how have you ended up in such a sorry state... did you come out through a guardrobe"

"No, I've been inside a dead horse."

"A dead horse?" Warwick gasped, as Philip's sticky hair and rank clothes drew a swarm of nocturnal flying insects into the tent. "Where is the pendant?" he asked, swatting away an annoying fly.

"I no longer have it."

"Well it was a plan worthy of a better end," Warwick declared, sitting back and crossing his legs. "But fear not, Mr Cobb tells me his guns will open a breach any day now; then we shall avenge this insult."

"What of my brother?"

"What is your wish?"

"Clemency."

"From me?" Warwick smiled. "You have it, but I cannot answer for the king," he added, gently rubbing the sides of his mouth with thumb and forefinger. "Go now, we'll talk later."

"And the archer, my lord?"

"The archer?"

"The corpse I dragged into Bamburgh?"

"Forget him, he was set to be hanged," Warwick yawned. "Dead or alive he served his purpose," he ended, releasing a throaty groan and waving him away.

Philip bowed, and walked barefoot back to his billet.

Chapter 18

Philip Neville spent the next few days recovering from his ordeal. He bathed, though he failed to rid his body of the lingering odour of decay; he fornicated, and he hunted. His failure to coerce Ralph Grey into surrendering and his concern for Michael irked his conscience, but rather than crucify himself over such sentiments he kept away from his cousin. Warwick did not call for him, and he sensed something wasn't right; he knew Richard and his cousin's reticence troubled him.

Shortly before noon on Wednesday 4 July, the feast day of St Odo of Canterbury, Philip and several companions returned from a hunting trip to find the camp in festive mood. A large crowd had gathered in front of Warwick's pavilion and were toasting him with jugs of ale. Intrigued, Philip dismissed his party and handed the reins of the packhorse with a bloody hart slumped over its back, to one of his servants.

"You there!" he yelled, at a dancing barber as he vaulted out of the saddle, "what's happening here?"

"They've surrendered!" the barber sang, forgetting the lathered folding blade in his hand as he skipped away in celebration. "Bamburgh is ours!"

"Come back you fool!" Philip commanded, eager to know more, but the man was already lost in the crowd.

While Philip was in the woods, teaching his page to stalk a hart, a shot from 'Dijon' hit Bamburgh's Great Tower with such force it smashed through the stonework, causing considerable damage to the apartment beyond. Around mid-morning, the castle gates opened and a herald rode out seeking an audience with the 'merciful' Earl of Warwick. A short time later the command to cease fire was relayed to the Master Gunner, and the Lancastrian herald walked out of the grand pavilion, with Warwick. Removing his narrow, blue hat which came to a point at the front, he bowed graciously to the earl.

"God bless you, most noble Lord," he grovelled, before riding back to Bamburgh.

Warwick gestured for his waiting captains to join him inside.

"They are finished," he told a group of centenars, before following his subordinates in to inform them of the terms offered.

The centenars passed the news to their men and cheer after cheer rent the air, followed by a chant of 'Warwick, Warwick, Warwick,' which resonated loudly throughout the camp.

With mixed emotions and a detached nod, Philip allowed his men to celebrate, while he sought out Francis Talbot. Finding his friend, the two men went to Northumberland's marquee. They found Sir John Neville sitting astride an oblong chest, sipping verjuice: a blend of crab-apple and grape. The earl greeted his cousin with a sombre frown, while his servants packed.

"My lord?" Philip said cagily.

"It's over," Northumberland moped.

Not yet," Philip disagreed, "Henry of Lancaster is still at liberty."

"Until he is taken, the fires of Lancastrianism will smoulder on," Francis added, expressively.

"Yes and many of those who eat at our table today would join him tomorrow," Philip warned. "And don't forget Margaret, that she-wolf will use all her feminine wiles to draw Louis away from Edward."

"Louis will not help her, not now," Northumberland said. "When Harlech falls our swords will go blunt, our armour will rust and our great horses will be put out to pasture."

"No, my lord," Philip pouted, pacing irritably through the clutter, angry for having missed Hexham. "You put your sword away and let your armour rust, I will not. This is not over, no sir."

"I'll miss all this," Sir John sighed, ignoring his

outburst and reflecting on the comradeship, and excitement of the past.

"Remember Pocklington?" Philip smirked; referring to the Percy manor near Stamford Bridge, the site of a brawl fought nine years before, between the Nevilles and Lord Egremont.

Northumberland recalled the incident with a wry smile and Francis looked puzzled.

"We've been fighting the Percys for years," Philip reminded his friend. "We met them this day, over two leagues from York and thrashed the shit out of them."

"The dogs ran for their lives," Northumberland chuckled. "Did you see the look on my father's face when we rode into Middleham with Tom Percy in tow?"

"Yes." Philip smiled, but the thought of Sir Thomas's daughter, Elizabeth, made him press his lips together and snarl through his nose.

"Good days," John nodded, a faraway look in his eyes, "great times."

"We knew our enemy back then," Philip said, sniffing the sleeve of his crimson doublet for any lingering trace of the dead horse.

"Oh how I shall miss it," John mused.

"You have a wife and son waiting for you my lord," Philip reminded him, thinking of his own scattered family.

"'Tis true," he nodded, "I am fortunate, but there is nothing more stimulating than to cross swords with an opponent in battle. I will never forget that emotion."

"For me there is nothing to go back for," Philip whined, "I'm an indentured knight with no future. While the likes of Herbert and Wenlock…"

"What of the army, my lord?" Francis interrupted, sensing Philip's rising antipathy.

"The men will be paid off and return to their homes, to gather the harvest," Northumberland explained, looking at Philip and sliding off the chest. "Come, we shall join my brother," he added, shaking the pessimism from his mind and rubbing his hands in anticipation of plunder. "They'll be coming out soon."

Philip knew that when the Lancastrians marched out of Bamburgh, the Yorkists would pour in like a horde of vandals, and loot the place of everything but its stones. Shrugging off his despondency, he followed Francis and Northumberland out into the bright sunshine.

Bamburgh Castle had suffered from Warwick's destructive fire for more than a week. Huge buff-coloured sandstone chunks had been shot off the south wall and an assailable breach yawned invitingly. The discontented garrison had little stomach to fight on for a lost cause, despite Ralph Grey's passionate overtures. With every gunstone tumbling down more of the curtain wall and food supplies dwindling, morale sank to its nadir. Dejected by his superior's indolence, Michael Neville made several attempts to get out after his brother's escape, but failed. When the mysterious Geoffrey of Gloucester vanished from the Muniment Tower, whispered allegations were directed at Humphrey Neville. De Gravett told Michael of the prisoner's escape, and he played his part like a true Neville, pounding his fists and threatening to hang all involved. Michael agreed with de Gravett that Sir Humphrey must be implicated, a criticism exploited after he confessed a sudden desire to surrender, but Grey refused to act on their prejudice.

When the fatal ball from Dijon hit the Great Tower, its weight crushed in the ceiling above Sir Ralph's private chamber, burying him under a heap of rubble. Knocked unconscious, he was unable to prevent Sir Humphrey from usurping his authority. Gathering the few knights and esquires, Humphrey Neville called for a vote: fight on or yield. Considering the hopelessness of their situation, and the widening breach in the south wall, they elected to submit. Grey's own herald was sent to ask the Earl of Warwick for terms.

While the herald prepared to leave, Michael Neville, the only one to vote against surrender, stormed away frantically seeking a last way out.

"With such cowards in charge 'tis a miracle we have held out this long!" he yelled at Sir Humphrey, before heading for the Great Tower, "gutless knave!"

Despite his kinship with Warwick, Michael was well aware of his cousin's reputation for bloody revenge, and believed an example would be made of him for his loyalty to Henry. Looking out of his apartment window, he ran a forefinger up and down his raised facial scar and brooded on his dilemma. If he surrendered, would Philip help, as he had helped him? For more than an hour he fretted and cursed Humphrey Neville, until a shout from the barbican distracted his attention: the herald was returning. Shrugging off his anxiety, Michael made his way to the courtyard, hoping Warwick had rejected Sir Humphrey's offer to surrender.

The herald cantered back to Bamburgh, accompanied by Warwick's herald and a distant roar from the Yorkist lines – a sound that told the troops hugging the walls that the earl had agreed terms. Humphrey Neville and Roger de Gravett joined the crowd clamouring around the heralds as they rode up into the inner ward. In the absence of the garrison commander, Sir Humphrey pushed a way through and grabbed the reins of the Lancastrian herald's horse.

"What did his lordship say?" he pressed optimistically. "Hurry man!"

"My Lord of Warwick offers clemency to you, Sir Humphrey," he revealed, struggling to control his excited mount.

Michael stood quietly in the background, as the herald looked forlornly at de Gravett. "To you, Sir Roger, he offers nothing, nor to the traitor Ralph Grey. Nothing but trial and execution," he added, with sadness in his voice, for he respected the dejected warrior standing before him. "The rest of you are free to leave with the clothes on your backs, and nothing more!"

The crowd dispersed and a relieved Humphrey Neville rounded up his retainers. De Gravett slumped down on a step near the entrance to the Great Tower, and dropped his head into his hands. Not listed for mercy or trial, Michael knew Warwick well, but unlike Philip he had no love for his Yorkist kin. During his short time at Sheriff Hutton, he hated Richard's harrying of the young pages and often defied him. Shortly before giving up his brief career as a page, he stole his cousin's favourite sword and buried it in St Helens churchyard. Grinning at the memory, his face suddenly lit up. Offering de Gravett a cheerless farewell, he hurried into the tower.

Bamburgh's heavy portcullis cranked up, its great gates were thrown open, and a sullen procession of men and women filed out. Shuffling silently down the long ramp, they headed over to the sprawling, tented city that had mushroomed from Warwick's original camp. Borne on a litter by four servants, the unconscious Ralph Grey knew nothing of Sir Humphrey's actions. Roger de Gravett looked for Michael before leaving but failed to find him. Approaching a large black bombard, de Gravett did his best to avoid eye contact with its smug crew, but as he drew level the gunners jeered and raised cups of ale in derisory salute.

When the first refugees entered the Yorkist camp, groups of soldiers rushed over to search them, a task they performed with brutal delight. Warwick and Northumberland received Sir Roger's cowed submission, while Philip and a clutch of knights stood talking of the fate that awaited those like Sir Roger.

"My lord!" one of Warwick's captains implored, as several men-at-arms tore a poor woman's dress down to her waist in their frenzy for plunder.

"Let them go George. They have waited for this," Warwick said, the damage his guns inflicted on Bamburgh forcing him to ignore the chivalric code.

When Humphrey Neville arrived with his small retinue, Warwick acknowledged his Westmorland cousin's decision to surrender, with an expressive nod and a pass.

Sir Humphrey responded with a pained, courtly bow before leading his entourage away.

"So much for his promise to cut off a head for every ball fired," Philip scoffed.

Regardless of Richard's earlier assurance of clemency for Michael, Philip believed he would renege. Studying the face of every Lancastrian male entering the camp, he was prepared to protect his brother.

"My sword is at your service," Francis offered, anxious to make amends for his apathy, at Woodstock.

"No, I must do this alone," Philip said firmly, glancing at his own men, waiting eagerly for the order to advance on Bamburgh.

Secretly relieved by Philip's refusal, Francis watched as Ralph Grey was brought in and laid on a nearby cart. Drifting in and out of consciousness, Sir Ralph was in no condition to object when a group of archers ran over and stripped him of everything but his shirt and hose.

"What will happen to him?" Talbot wondered, his voice laced with compassion as he glared at the archer's shameful conduct.

"Gentle friend, this soldiering is not for you, you should have become a priest," Philip smiled, patting him on the shoulder. "You are much too sensitive."

"'T'was my mother's earnest wish, though my father would not hear of it," he sighed. "But this is not soldiering; I don't have the stomach for such unchristian behaviour."

"You must harden your heart, for if we show weakness they will not obey us," Philip explained, continuing to search for his brother in the crowd.

"What's to become of him?" Francis repeated, frowning at the returning archers.

"He is for Doncaster," Lord Scrope interrupted, eavesdropping on their conversation. "The king has ordered that he be sent to the Earl of Worcester, to be tried for treason."

"Worcester…" Talbot shuddered, crossing himself, and touching the silver cross round his neck to his lips. "May

God grant him a swift death?"

"A coach!" the cry went up, followed by a warning from Northumberland, who stepped out in front of his men and unsheathed his sword.

"You may do as you wish with the common women!" he bellowed, "but if any of you lays a hand on a lady, I'll cut it off!"

The dilapidated coach, its yellow paint flaking off in sheets, and the windows curtained by faded, green material, trundled down the ramp and bumped its way over the uneven ground. Drawn by a score of heaving Lancastrian men-at-arms, the vehicle creaked to a halt in front of Warwick and his brother. A nod from Sir Richard was enough for one of his esquires to draw back the tatty curtain, revealing half-a-dozen concerned faces.

"Ladies here, my lord," the esquire announced with a cheeky grin.

Warwick, the sun flashing off his richly bejewelled satin doublet, acknowledged their status with a bow and a sweep of his hand.

"I am Richard Neville, Earl of Warwick and Chamberlain of England, welcome to my camp. You will be treated with every courtesy at my disposal," he decreed, looking at the panting, sweating bearers slumped around the shafts. "If you wish to leave, I will give you horses for your coach and an escort."

Led by Sir Roger's wife, Eleanor de Gravett, and still wearing their indoor slippers, the women were helped from the coach by several esquires. The men who had drawn the coach were prodded to their feet and roughly searched before being permitted to leave.

"Thank you, my lord," Lady de Gravett replied, curtsying.

Warwick nodded at each of the six ladies as they filed past him on their way to his marquee. Eleanor de Gravett, a tall, very pale woman in her early forties, moved as if in a trance. Holding a crucifix to her thin lips she looked straight ahead, mumbling a prayer for her husband. As the

364

Bamburgh ladies passed him, Philip noticed they kept their heads down, all except one who wore a veil over her face and walked with a superior air. Folding his arms across his chest, Francis turned to speak to Philip and was shocked by the hostility blazing from his eyes. His friend was staring hard at the women, his mouth compressed so tight his cheeks pulsated. Stepping forward Philip turned and walked backwards, keeping pace with the women, and scrutinizing the profile of one in particular.

"Stop!" he commanded.

The young esquire leading the group, promptly obeyed and the ladies instinctively huddled together, their frightened eyes exhibiting a communal fear.

"My lord?" the esquire objected, looking to Warwick for support.

Intrigued by his cousin's conduct, Warwick did nothing.

"Havoc!" Northumberland suddenly yelled, charging towards Bamburgh.

"Havoc!" his soldiers echoed, racing after him.

Oblivious to the start of the 'free for all' Philip moved into the circle of bemused women. Targeting the superior one, her features obscured by the veil of her coned hat, he placed a finger to his lips and glared at the esquire until he stepped aside. Standing before her, thumbs hooked loosely over his belt, Philip's cold accusing eyes burned through the opaque muslin curtain, forcing her to look away.

"Yes, my lady, hide that face," he said ominously, "are you ashamed to speak to me?"

"A strange request from one who wished never to see me again; no Philip Neville, I've done nothing to be ashamed of," she answered proudly. "Ask of me what you will."

Slighted by her hauteur, Philip lunged forward and those watching thought he was about to use his head as a weapon, but he drew up sharply at the last moment.

"Step out madam," he demanded, standing aside.

"But we must stay together," Lady Eleanor protested,

silently beseeching Warwick's help.

"I will go with him," she said, grasping Lady de Gravett's hands to allay her fears. "This knight will not harm me."

Admiring her confidence, Philip pointed to a small conical tent.

"This way, my lady."

"What's going on?" Warwick asked joining Francis, as his cousin headed for the tent used by his Burgundian allies.

"'Tis the Lady Elizabeth, my lord…" he replied, as the esquire herded the rest of the women away, "I think?"

"The Percy girl?" Warwick mused, relishing the storm about to break. "She's the reason my cousin hates the whole world."

Yanking aside the flap of the blue and yellow tent, Philip looked back and saw Warwick talking to Francis.

"Good day, Lady Elizabeth!" Richard called out.

Returning a contemptuous sneer, Philip directed her inside and pulled the flap down so hard the structure shuddered against its centre pole.

"Has she married that fool Hastings yet?"

"Not to my knowledge, my lord."

"Then prepare to be entertained."

The tiny claustrophobic Burgundian tent reeked of stale sweat, exuding from a pile of fusty, unwashed jacks left on the ground. An invisible cloud of trapped, clammy heat exacerbated the smell, but they had privacy. Hoisting a sack on top of a box, Philip offered his reluctant guest a seat, she refused.

"Why were you in Bamburgh?" he asked, trying to understand what the future sister-in-law of King Edward's chamberlain, was doing in an enemy stronghold.

"Why were you?"

Surprised by her retort, he gnawed the inside of his cheek and frowned. Conscious of his volatile temperament she drew the translucent veil from her face.

"I was on a pilgrimage to the shrine of St Cuthbert,

366

with the Duchess of York," She explained.

Removing the veil exposed Elizabeth's beautiful, white face and an unseen force gripped his heart and squeezed it until the pain became unbearable. The silky tone of her sweet voice washed away all that had gone before and his brusque pessimism faded.

"Durham is many leagues from here, how did you end up there?" he asked, the aggressive lines ploughed across his weathered forehead dissolving.

"Lady Cecily permitted me to visit my Aunt Eleanor, in York. When we arrived at her home, I was told she had gone to Topcliffe. On our way there we were set upon by Sir Humphrey Neville's men. Our escort fled and we were brought here. Sir Humphrey knew my father and expressed his regret. After that I was treated with kindness and allowed to continue my journey, but before we could leave your army arrived."

"You should have come out earlier, we don't make war on women, especially one affianced to a key member of the king's household," he said mockingly, his eyes brazenly analyzing her shape beneath the cream, linen dress hugging her body.

"The Neville's despise Lord Hastings and would take great pleasure in humiliating him," she answered discomfited by his sarcasm and obvious attraction.

The thought of how quickly she took up with Ralph Hastings turned Philip's stomach.

"Fear not; the Hastings have the king's protection," he shot back dramatically, peeved by her collective, if somewhat accurate bundling of all Nevilles.

"When your guns began knocking down the walls, we women were placed in a tower for safety; 'twas there I met your brother."

"You met Michael?" he groaned. "My God, my shame is an open book."

"You don't understand; we spoke only a few words," she explained. "Nothing more."

"My cousin has revealed our intimacy to the world, and

William Hastings has destroyed it," he hissed, shaking his head. "How did you know I was in Bamburgh?" he asked, belatedly, "I came in the night and called myself by another name."

"I was told two strangers had ridden in. I was curious so I left my room," she began. "You passed so close to me I felt your breath on my cheek." He looked confused and she continued. "I was the 'wretched woman' you ran into near the tower, though you did not know me."

"Ah." He smiled, recalling the incident.

"Lady Eleanor told me you had escaped, I knew Michael must have helped but I kept your secret."

"Do you want my gratitude?" he scoffed.

"No," she countered, his tone stoking her ire.

"What happened to my brother?"

"I'm certain he got away, but I beg you, speak for Ralph Grey," she pled. "Beseech your cousin to spare his family the humiliation…"

"Grey is a traitor and Worcester will have his head off before the week is out," he snapped, galled by her misplaced concern.

The powerful scent of Elizabeth's perfumed body oil, sweetened by the trapped heat, supplanted the unpleasant odour and totally absorbed Philip's senses. Though he tried to deny it, he still loved her, but her betrayal muddied his emotions.

"Worcester is a vile creature," she lamented.

"Was your father no less?" he hit back, instantly regretting his hurtful rejoinder.

"My father paid for his crimes at Northampton."

"As Lord Hastings will one day pay for his?"

"I loved you once," she declared. "But you have changed, you are without compassion."

"You loved me?" he sneered, shaking his head. "You say this, yet while I bared my soul to you at Alnwick, you were thinking of another."

"You are wrong."

"Am I? I'll wager you had a good laugh at my expense

at Baynard's Castle."

"I did no such thing."

"And while I fought for my King, Hastings sat at court plotting to steal away that for which I would have laid down my life."

"You don't understand," she bemoaned, "you think too much like a soldier."

"Better a soldier than a craven coward!"

"And what is a soldier? A mindless animal that kills without compassion and cares nothing for those he leaves behind. I pity you. Now this is over where will you go, what will you do?"

"Keep your pity, madam," he snapped; her provocation and the humidity causing sweat to run freely down his face. "I have already found another to take *your* place, and it was as easy as putting one foot in front of the other," he fibbed.

"Oh Philip, the king is fond of you," she began, her voice tender and sweet. "Forget the past or revenge will eat your heart out, and you will never know anything but hatred."

"I seek satisfaction for the wrongs done to me, only then will I be content."

"What of the wrong you have done? No Philip, you will always be angry with someone."

While she spoke, he watched as a dewdrop of perspiration formed under her chin and trickled down her soft, white neck, leaving a glistening trail before disappearing into her cleavage. Lowering his eyes to her breasts rising and falling beneath the material of her V-shaped neckline, he ran his tongue appreciatively over his salty lips and breathed deeply.

"I have wronged no one," he pouted, detecting a hint of cinnamon.

"There is talk at court."

"Talk," he scoffed dabbing his wet face on a sleeve. "The king's court is nothing but a hotbed of treachery and infidelity, where fools gather to gossip like shrews."

"But the rumours…"

"What rumours?"

"There are those on the king's council who blame your cousin for the Duke of Somerset's downfall."

"Lies," he exploded, "lies, invented by traitors to discredit the Nevilles!"

"In my heart I know you would never be party to such deception," she calmly revealed.

Her trust in his innocence degraded him, and for a moment he despised himself.

The rising humidity inside the tent made Elizabeth light-headed. Moistening her lips with her tongue, she deftly brushed a hand across her mouth and Philip sighed at her all-consuming beauty. Lewd images formed in his mind and the urge to throw her on the ground and run his hands between her damp thighs intensified. Perspiration made the thin dress cling to her body and he visualized his tongue exploring the sweetness of her cunnis. The need to plunge his head into a bucket of cold water and douse the sexual fire burning within became paramount. Drawing a deep breathe he decided to end the reunion before he lost control.

"Now Bamburgh is ours, we will ride to London and rid the king of those deceivers skulking around the throne."

"You will not harm my fiancé," she warned.

"And who will stop me?" he gasped, impressed by her courage.

"The Nevilles will not be called to London," she countered, offended by his malicious crowing. "It is the king's wish that you be kept away from court; why do you think you are all here, so far from London?"

"You know nothing, so keep your mouth shut!"

"I know the truth," she dared.

"You cannot begin to conceive the power of the Nevilles," he boasted, making a fist to emphasis his next sentence. "We *will* come to London soon and break the spell Lord Hastings has cast over our cousin."

"My God, you truly believe your family is above the king," she said, stunned by his declaration.

"One day, William Hastings and his brothers will kneel at our feet," he bragged, "and beg for mercy, as they did before Henry, at Ludlow!"

"I won't listen to this," she snapped, staggered by the threat and drawing the veil down over her face before hurrying from the tent.

"Stop!" he yelled, drawing his sword and pursuing her out.

Elizabeth spun on her heels ready to spit venom, but sunlight glinting off Philip's blade alarmed her.

"No," she cried, covering her face with her hands.

Deliberately stretching his sword arm back, Philip brought the weapon swinging across her forehead. Believing her life was about to end, she closed her eyes.

Shocked by what they were seeing, the Earl of Warwick and Francis Talbot watched, dumbfounded. The point of Philip's arming sword sliced through the air and the swish of its razor-sharp edge cutting close to her tiny eyebrows, forced Elizabeth to pray. After a prolonged moment of dread, she exhaled, but couldn't understand why there was no pain. Daring to lower her trembling hands, she blinked and tears coursed freely down over her cheeks. Shock caused her legs to shake uncontrollably and she slumped to her knees. The flimsy muslin veil broke free and floated gently to the ground. Philip had merely used his sword to separate the veil from the coned hat. Ramming the sword into its scabbard, he stomped over to his cousin.

Several of Lady Eleanor's companions rushed out to help Elizabeth, and Philip glowered as they passed him. Grabbing a ladle of water from a leather bucket, he poured the warm contents over his head and blew heavily. Shaking the excess from his hair, he hurled the bucket as far as he could.

"All will know of your deceit!" he bellowed out of frustration, while Elizabeth was led to the earl's grand pavilion. "Putain!"

"What was that?" Warwick asked.

"He called her a whore, my lord," Francis coughed, embarrassed by Philip's disrespect.

"You have made an enemy of Ralph Hastings," Warwick smiled, impressed by his swordsmanship.

"Ralph Hastings made an enemy of me!" he retorted angrily, as Elizabeth stumbled into Warwick's marquee.

"You must learn to control that hot blood of yours," Richard smirked.

"And you, my lord, must revive Neville influence at court, and do it quickly!" Philip warned, as water dripped from his chin and soaked into his dusty tunic. "Or we'll all suffer the consequences."

"Calm yourself!" Warwick warned.

Philip jabbed his hands to his hips and released his aggravation in one long growl. Warwick raised his eyebrows at Francis, who met his expression and suddenly rued his sister's attraction for this self-destructive knight.

"Come, we must away to Bamburgh," Warwick declared, turning to a varlet holding his saddled palfrey. "Bring him!"

"My lord!" the varlet replied snappishly, running the horse over.

Warwick mounted up and galloped off towards Bamburgh, escorted by his herald. Philip and Francis followed on foot, alongside Warwick's fuming bodyguards, who had been forced to wait.

"We'll be lucky to come away with a dog bone," Talbot lamented, panting to keep pace.

"We will not lose out," Philip promised; the raging pain in his heart undiminished. "Have a little faith."

Chapter 19

The Earl of Warwick cantered into Bamburgh's inner ward, housing the kitchens, stables, great hall and chapel, and felt a sense of relief. Despite the partly tumbled down south curtain wall and cracked towers, the interior was intact. Dismounting near the Great Tower, he instructed his friend, Lord Scrope, to stop the looting.

"Finish it now boys!" Scrope barked, leaning nonchalantly against the entrance to the tower, watching his overloaded retainers carry away plunder. "And remember, one third of everything you take is for Lord Warwick's Marshal, and a further quarter for the Church!"

Scrope's words were received with angry jeers, and his men flouted the order by hiding items under their clothes.

Philip Neville and Francis Talbot entered the castle on foot, shortly after Warwick.

"What will you do?" Francis puffed, trying to keep pace with his more athletic companion.

"I mean to search every corner of this god-damn place," Philip vowed, heading briskly up the narrow path towards the Constable's Tower.

"Then I shall offer a prayer for your success," Francis promised, turning off and making his way up the narrow steps, leading to the chapel.

Philip explored the inner ward from top to bottom, but found no sign of his brother. Daniel, his strong-armed servant, lowered Ashley Dean down the well inside the Great Tower, and the boy scurried along its hidden passage, to no avail, Michael had vanished. Exasperated, Philip decided to return to camp and speak with Roger de Gravett. Commandeering an emaciated rouncey from its new owner, an enraged ventenar, he leapt on its dusty bare back.

"Move you fools!" he bellowed, whacking his heels against the feeble beast's bony flanks and forcing a way through the mass of soldiers criss-crossing the courtyard. "Get out of the way, god-damn you!"

Sitting alone in a small tent, de Gravett failed to react when Philip entered; he just stared at the ground. A promise of personal intervention at his trial garnered not a single clue from the disconsolate knight.

"The last time I saw him was when our herald returned with Lord Warwick's offer," he sighed, without looking up. "I haven't seen him since."

"Where could he be?" Philip whined, massaging his chin pensively.

"I don't know," de Gravett said woefully, raising his head to look at Philip and opening his eyes wide. "Geoffrey?"

"I pray Worcester will show you mercy, my lord," Philip offered, sad for deceiving such a kindly knight.

Sir Roger knew Worcester would be as ruthless as his reputation, and dipped his head gratefully. Miffed by de Gravett's answers Philip shook his head and left.

While he stood outside in the hot sun, speculating on whether or not Sir Roger was lying, the looters began drifting back from Bamburgh. The majority toted armfuls of junk: kitchen utensils, rugs and bundles of women's clothes; others were happy to have acquired a pair of boots or a piece of armour, which they could barter. One individual crowned himself 'King of fools' and wore a pisspot on his head, held a ladle in one hand, and a large wooden spoon in the other. All had one thing in common: their complaints against Warwick, for confiscating the best of their haul.

Putting his anxiety aside, Philip greeted his men as they returned with Francis.

"Have thee found good fortune, Davy my lad?" he asked.

"I have sir," his stocky retainer piped up, showing off a silk shirt and a crossbow.

"How did you escape the keen eye of the marshal?" he asked winking at his esquire.

"We tied everything in sheets and tossed it over the north wall," Harrington revealed, with a caustic grin, "then we walked out and picked it up, as you suggested, my lord."

"What of the earl's share… and that of the Church?"

"We have contributed, my lord," one of his two archers beamed, showing off a pair of silver candlesticks.

"We gave them a bag of pots and pans," his page chuckled, sporting a shiny sallet that dropped down over his eyes muffling his voice.

The thought of getting one over on his cousin brought a smile to Philip's troubled face and helped him forget his concerns for the moment.

"We have more than enough," Talbot exclaimed, slapping one of Philip's soldiers heartily on the back as he struggled to drag a heavy sack through the thick grass; the jingle of silver bringing a satisfied grin to his face. "Did you find what you were looking for?"

"No," he lamented, his cheery demeanour fading.

"Fear not, Michael has the devil on his shoulder," Francis said, opening the sack and looking inside. "He'll be far away by now… this is good stuff."

"I must speak to Ralph Grey," Philip said, as a group of billmen emptied their sack on the grass and cursed Warwick loudly.

"Then make haste for he will be on his way to Doncaster soon."

"I know."

"He'll tell you nothing," Francis warned, snatching a golden chalice from one of his men. "What reverential beauty," he declared, fingering its jewel encrusted rim. "From where did you acquire such a fine piece?"

"From tha chapel, m'lord," the bearded, heavily browed archer answered guiltily.

"Stealing from a church? You'll not go to heaven," Talbot tutted before turning to Philip. "What will you do if he refuses to talk?"

"I'll wring his neck!" he promised, heading for the cart.

Warwick left his brother and Lord Scrope to oversee Bamburgh's security, and rode back to the camp alone.

Irritated by the extensive damage to the south wall, he was out to make someone pay. The obvious scapegoat was Bamburgh's cataleptic captain.

Shortly before Warwick returned, Philip approached the wain containing the unconscious Ralph Grey. Dressed in a blood-splattered linen shirt and hose, everything else having been filched, he lay mumbling incoherently. Philip looked on benignly while a balding, portly surgeon shook his head and prayed for his patient's survival. Concerned at the extent of Grey's injuries, Northumberland had commanded the physician to keep him alive long enough to stand trial. Unable to climb into the cart to examine him, or obtain a sample of urine, the fat, sweating short-sighted surgeon nervously cut Sir Ralph's arm to bleed him. As Philip stared at the badly injured knight, the perspiration of impatience blistered his forehead. In an attempt to bring him around, he suddenly yelled his name. Grey's only response was a throaty rasp.

"Wake up Ralph!" Philip repeated, shaking the cart violently, "You son of a bitch."

"Please, my lord," the physician whined, swirling the small amount of blood around in a bowl. "He's oblivious to everything."

Surprisingly, Philip relented and used a sleeve to wipe the sweat from his cheeks.

The dry lacerations on Grey's swollen face, dark bruising round his eyes and mouth, and the tight bandage swathed about his head, made him look grotesque. Aware of the fate awaiting him, Philip felt a twinge of compassion.

The rest of the surrendered Lancastrians had been robbed, pardoned and sent on their way; only Grey, de Gravett and the ladies remained. The four litter bearers, who carried their unconscious captain over from Bamburgh, were also detained, and stood cowering beside the silver-haired garrison chaplain. Returning from Bamburgh, the Yorkist soldiers gathered in groups, drinking and joking as they displayed or swapped their plunder. It was this scene that greeted the Earl of Warwick when he arrived and dismounted outside his tent; the thunder on his face a clear indication that someone was in for it. Taking little notice of the euphoria, or the groom who took his reins, Richard Neville barged through the crowd and headed straight for the cart.

Placing his gloved hands on the warped side of the wain, he looked across and acknowledged Philip with a single word, "cousin".

"Wake up Ralph, God damn you!" he barked, spraying a fine, almost imperceptible film of spittle at his former retainer.

"My lord, I beg you," the surgeon objected weakly, trying to examine the blood. "Your brother told me to preserve his life on pain of forfeiting my own."

Warwick's intense scowl brushed aside the pot-bellied doctor's pathetic objection and Philip grinned as he ducked below the cart, his saggy jowls wobbling fearfully.

"You have caused me to defy my King and Bamburgh is knocked all to pieces!" Warwick yelled. "I must explain my actions to His Majesty, but you, old friend, alas you will answer to the Earl of Worcester."

His grim words had the miraculous effect of stirring Grey out of his tormented slumber. Half opening his dark, puffy eyes, he struggled to comprehend where he was, before snapping them shut and turning his face from the intense sun.

"Come here, Father," Warwick commanded, flicking a finger at the chaplain, "if you please."

Leaving the hypothetical security of the four servants, the elfin cleric walked over to the cart, stepped onto one of the huge wheel hubs and laid a bony hand on Sir Ralph's arm.

"Tell him," Warwick demanded, "quickly!"

"My son, you were badly hurt when the roof of your chamber collapsed. Sir Humphrey has surrendered Bamburgh and we are all in the Earl of Warwick's hands…" he hesitated, but a threatening scowl from

Warwick persuaded him to continue. "You are to be sent for trial and…"

"Enough," Warwick growled.

"God bless you," the priest whispered, making the sign of the cross before a guard lifted him off the wheel.

"Forgive me, Father," the man-of-arms grunted, shooing him back to the four terrified servants.

"You were a fool to betray me Ralph," Richard chided. "Why?"

"Why?" he moaned, blinking rapidly and using his tongue to moisten his dry lips. "I served Edward faithfully, for what? To be made Constable of Alnwick, while one less worthy was placed above me."

"Others have received far less," Warwick sniffed, glancing at Philip, who huffed in agreement, "but remain true."

Grey moved his head slightly.

"Was it your wife who persuaded you to betray us?" Warwick pressed, goading him into implicating his spouse.

"No, Richard, I have danced with the devil," he sighed, regrettably. "Now I must pay the price, as my father's father did before Agincourt," he explained.

"And pay you shall, though it pains me to see an old friend go to the scaffold."

"Be careful you do not end up in the same place, my lord," Grey warned, as searing pain shot between his temples forcing him to close his eyes. "My boys," he gasped, his voice trailing away, "my poor boys…"

"Your family will not suffer for your treachery, I give you my word," Warwick promised his tone less harsh, "rest easy."

When the thunder raging in his head subsided to a bearable level, Ralph Grey turned his face and opened his swollen eyes, only to see a familiar face looking down at him.

"Geoffrey?" he managed weakly, surprised to see him. "Who are you…?"

"Philip Neville," he revealed, resting his chin on his

hands.

Realization hit the injured knight like an archer's mallet and a knowing smile raised the corners of his bloody mouth.

"Yes... I see it now," he mused, recalling the way Geoffrey threw his leg over the chair at supper. "Philip Neville?" he whined, with a faraway stare. "Michael, is your brother?"

Philip answered by narrowing his eyes and Grey delicately tweaked his neck for comfort.

"I've been a fool," he stammered, "but you almost convinced me to open the gates."

"Where is my brother?" Philip asked.

"Michael? Michael is dead," he gasped closing his eyes and whispering the name of his wife, Jacquetta, before slipping into painless oblivion.

"The devil take thee for the liar you are!" Philip yelled angrily, before looking over at Richard.

"Do you want the dead exhumed?" Warwick half smiled, "or will you have me torture the priest."

"He's not dead; de Gravett saw him this very day," Philip countered, banging a fist against the side of the wain, raising dust and causing Grey to flinch unconsciously. "Where is my brother?"

There was no response, so Philip looked back to his cousin for an answer.

"Leave him dead," he advised.

"But he's not dead," Philip frowned, failing to grasp his meaning.

"If he is not, your meddling will sign his death warrant."

Philip rolled his left hand into a fist and knuckled his cheek.

"I must know."

"Then you're a fool."

"Perhaps."

"I have left a door open," Warwick said, "the king would not want him brought to trial."

"My lord, I must speak with de Gravett."

"Then do it quickly for I am finished here."

Philip nodded and hurried away, watched disapprovingly by Warwick.

"You stubborn…" the Earl muttered.

"My lord," Bamburgh's Chaplain interrupted, approaching tentatively. "What will you do with those poor creatures?" he asked, pointing at the four quaking servants.

"I have no time for such cringing cowards," he scoffed; offended by the way they huddled together like frightened sheep. "Get them out of my sight."

"Thank you, my lord," the priest grovelled, bowing his head.

The cart bearing Roger de Gravett and an insentient Ralph Grey, eventually left Warwick's camp and headed south. An hour later, Philip stood near a line of tethered warhorses watching the coach leave with the Bamburgh ladies. Observing the dust cloud thrown up by the wheels, a wave of despair washed over him.

"There goes my heart," he sighed woefully, scuffing his boots and slouching away, "bitch!"

By mid-afternoon, the prickly wind that had been dry-blasting the area for almost two hours dropped to a gentle breeze. Philip and Francis joined the Earl of Northumberland and his knights for a final meal, set out on a trestle table in front of his empty marquee. In a subdued atmosphere the diners devoured platters of oysters and bream, washed down with perry, a fermented pear juice. Philip told Francis how his grandfather had been implicated in the Southampton plot of 1215, along with King Edward's grandfather, and Sir Ralph Grey's, while servers replaced empty plates with full ones. While Philip endeavoured to absolve his grandfather's tarnished reputation, he thought of Elizabeth Percy. Seeing her again had reopened his emotional wounds, and relegated his concern for his missing brother.

"What will you do now?" Northumberland asked him, scooping a slippery oyster from its shell and plopping it into his mouth.

"When we ride to London I'll seek out Ralph Hastings and throw down my gauge," he snapped.

"I speak of your brother," Sir John slurped, creasing his brow impatiently.

"I don't know, my lord," he replied apologetically, drawing a long bone from the fish and trying to shake the malaise from his mind. "De Gravett knew nothing."

"My lord?" the pocket-sized Lancastrian Chaplin interrupted, presenting himself at the table. "Forgive me…"

"What do you want priest?" Northumberland scowled. "Do you spy on us?"

"No sire," he said fearfully, looking over his shoulder at the castle. "My church is there… I am here on an errand."

"What errand?"

"I seek a knight who goes by the name Philip Neville."

"Have a care, my lord," one of his captains laughed, "or he'll report you to the bishop."

"Why do you seek this knight?" Philip enquired, grinning at his companions and poking the fish bone between his teeth.

"Can you not see he is much troubled?" Northumberland chuckled, wiping his hands on a towel and tossing an empty oyster shell into one of two refuse voiders on the table.

"I have something for him," the silver-haired priest explained, as the shell missed the bone box and hit the table, causing Northumberland to tut.

"I am Philip Neville," Philip offered.

The chaplain looked confused and hesitated.

"He is, Father, truly," Northumberland attested, winking at Scrope while a server picked up the shell and dropped it into the voider, "and he badly needs to confess."

Philip rolled his eyes at his comment and the ecclesiastic produced a soft, brown leather purse.

"I was told to give this to you by one of Lord Grey's servants."

"What is it?" Philip sniffed, taking the pouch, his curiosity aroused, "and why me?"

"I don't know," he said, ogling the bountiful fare spread over the table.

"Why did you not bring it earlier?" Francis asked, taking a pinch of salt from a large, dragon-shaped silver salter, and sprinkling the grains liberally over his bream.

"I was to wait." The cleric drooled.

Philip tugged the drawstrings open and tipped the contents into his hand.

"Who gave you this?" he demanded, shooting out of his seat, but keeping the item concealed in his palm, "and where is he?"

"Calm yourself," Northumberland warned.

"Where is he?" Philip pressed.

"He took the road west," the startled chaplain answered, pointing in the direction.

Slipping the object back into its pouch, Philip looked over at his cousin.

"Michael is away," he gasped, slumping down and tossing the purse on the table.

"Praise God," Talbot said, crossing his chest.

"How?" Northumberland asked, staring at the cleric, whose hungry expression caused the earl to motion for a server to bring a plate.

"He was one of the litter bearers who brought Sir Ralph to your camp, my lord," the sallow-faced priest explained, grasping the proffered plate and seizing several salted herrings, and a fillet of bream. "You were but a few paces from him," he smiled, the aromatic fish causing his mouth to salivate and his stomach to rumble.

"Hold that man!" the words boomed out.

The diners suddenly found themselves surrounded by a dozen of Warwick's guards, their drawn swords a warning not to resist.

"What is the meaning of this?" Northumberland demanded jumping to his feet, while his guests looked at each other bemused.

"Bring him here!" Warwick barked ignoring his brother's tantrum and shooting a gloved finger at the quivering chaplain seated on a stool, set to take his first mouthful.

One of the guards stepped behind the cleric, shoved a sword in the small of his back and jabbed him over to his lordship.

"You dare threaten a man of the Church!" John Neville bellowed.

"Hold your tongue," Warwick snapped, turning to the priest. "Now Father, acquaint me with that which you have acquainted my brother."

"My lord, this is an outrage!" the chaplain spluttered, wincing at the sharp pain in his back.

"Aye Father, these are Godless times," Warwick agreed with a sinister leer.

"You go too far," Northumberland warned, throwing his napkin on the table.

Keeping one eye on his brother, Sir Richard pressed his hands to his hips and spoke in a most intimidating voice.

"Tell me what I want to know and tell me now, or by God I'll have you taken to the Great Tower and thrown off."

Philip watched the trembling priest squeeze his hands together and turn imploringly to Northumberland for help, but he was powerless to intervene. Philip continued to stare at the chaplain until the threat in his dark piercing eyes forced the petrified cleric to huddle close to Warwick.

"My lord, if I talk will you protect me?" he quivered.

"If you don't, I'll have your body thrown to the dogs," he promised, his patience waning.

"My lord!" Northumberland snarled, banging a fist on the table. "This is not right."

"One of the servants–" the priest began, only to be cut

off by the astute earl.

"By Christ's blood," Warwick gasped. "Davy!"

"My lord!" the smartly costumed herald shouted, cantering forward, his palfrey's cloth-covered chest, flanks and rump decorated with the Neville coatofarms.

"Find William Stanley and tell him to ride west, somewhere on the road he will come upon four men, I want them brought back!"

The herald bowed from the saddle and trotted indolently away.

"Hurry man!"

Davy Griffiths dug his spurs in hard, turning a lazy trot into an urgent canter.

Forgetting the priest, Warwick mounted his horse and rode back to Bamburgh. His guards sheathed their swords and jogged after him.

"I'm going," Philip announced in a highly agitated voice.

"Be wary of Richard," Northumberland urged, resuming his seat, infuriated at his brother's conduct.

"I'll go with you," Talbot offered, swinging his body away from the table.

"No. If you leave all we have will be lost," Philip warned, referring to the booty.

"What of that?" Francis asked, pointing at the purse.

"That? That has brought me nothing but misfortune. I never wish to see it again."

"What will you do?" Northumberland asked.

"Look for my brother," Philip answered pulling a pair of worn, leather riding gloves from his belt, "with your permission?"

Northumberland nodded and Philip left.

Attracted by the commotion outside Northumberland's pavilion, Ashley Dean ambled over to the table and waited in the background. Receiving an instructive nod from his master, he ran to fetch Hotspur.

Climbing into the saddle, Philip looked at the priest sitting on a box, shovelling fish into his mouth with a spoon. Jerking the reins aside, he bequeathed him an acrimonious glare before spitting and galloping away.

Philip rode hard for almost two miles before drawing his panting, chestnut stallion up. Bending to the side, he looked down and examined a series of fresh horseshoe indents cutting across the road, and patted his horse's sweaty neck. Loud voices somewhere ahead forced him to stand in the stirrups. Stretching his neck he saw a dozen mounted men, galloping haphazardly over the undulating countryside five hundred paces away. Dashing between clumps of thick-leaved sycamore, swaying elm and twisted oak, they waved and shouted at each other, acting more like drunken fools than soldiers. Spotting the top half of a man above the brush, several horsemen broke off and swerved towards him. Philip waited until they were close enough to see the silver stag's head badge on their red tunics.

Recognising the lone horseman by his livery, the first rider pulled up abruptly.

"Have you found them?" Philip demanded.

"Yes, my lord, we have them all!" he wheezed, while his excited horse cantered in tight circles, shaking its head.

"All but one," the second rider corrected, pounding breathlessly up beside his companion.

Philip's body stiffened and the sweat on his face turned cold.

"He went back that way!" the other horseman revealed, poking a finger in the direction of Bamburgh.

"Then go after him," Philip growled.

As they rode away he turned Hotspur and cantered back to camp.

"Stanley!" he fumed closing his eyes and looking up at the sky, "you bastard!"

When Grey's herald returned to Bamburgh with Warwick's terms for the garrison's surrender, Michael Neville knew he would not be on the list for mercy. Finding one of Sir Ralph's servants he offered a rose noble, if he would allow him to take his place as a litter bearer. The suspicious servant took the proffered coin, placed it between his teeth and bit into the metal before accepting. Michael swapped his fine leather boots for the servant's worn, flat-toed ankle boots, and his light doublet for a coarse, yellow tunic. After stuffing his stocky frame and big feet into the tight-fitting jacket and shoes, he hurried across the courtyard to the kitchen. Using grease and flour he camouflaged his facial scar and hacked off most of his hair. Concerned he might still be recognised, he walked outside, grabbed a straw bonnet from a carter and plopped it on his head. Tugging the frayed brim down over his eyes, he picked up a corner of the litter and helped lug his unconscious captain over to the Yorkist camp. Michael Neville did his utmost to stay inconspicuous, despite the seams of his tunic splitting. His hard work paid off when Warwick unwittingly dismissed him with the others.

After leaving Warwick's camp, the three servants made it clear they were going home.

"We are for Harlech," Michael growled menacingly, forming his hands into fists. "And we stay together."

The varlets looked at each other, hoping one amongst them might find the courage to speak out. Despite Michael's comical attire, they knew his reputation and grudgingly agreed. To get as far away, as quickly as possible, Michael paced them hard. At first all went well, but when they heard Stanley's cavalry, the three servants leapt up waving their arms.

"Shit," Michael swore, thumping one of them hard on the head and sprinting off as fast as his tight shoes permitted. "Cowardly dogs!"

Satisfied he hadn't been seen, he tossed his hat away and reduced his zigzagging run to a limping walk.

Using the thick underbrush for cover, Michael found himself being forced back towards Bamburgh. Reaching a point overlooking the tidal inlet, running below the castle's north wall, he scrambled up the shaft of a leaning elm. The climb produced so much sweat he slipped back several times, badly grazing his arms and thighs. Securing his feet on a stubby branch, he wrapped an arm around the gnarled trunk and contemplated his dwindling options. To the north lay a wide expanse of open country, to the south Yorkist foot were beating the brush, while Stanley's cavalry closed in from the west. With the fortress blocking any escape to the southeast, Michael felt trapped, but there was a chance. At the base of Bamburgh's north wall, between the castle and beach, a narrow trail wound its way to the coast. If he could get past the fortress without detection, and lay low until sunset, he might slip through the Yorkist lines and escape. The dull thud of Stanley's approaching horse broke his concentration and forced him to move. Leaping from his roost, amidst cracking branches and showering leaves, Michael landed with a graceless thump. Bending low he tore a new path through the tall grass towards the Tower of Elmund's well, Bamburgh's far north-western point.

Reaching the high-rising dolorite rock on which the castle's foundations had been built, Michael stopped to rest. Despite the scratches to his face and hands, caused by his chaotic run through the coarse underbrush, and his throbbing toes, he felt safe. Hiding among the thick foliage sprouting from a long-abandoned square tower, he dabbed sweat from his face and caught his breath. Astute ears now took over from tired legs and he listened to Yorkist soldiers arguing in the west ward. A cool breeze blowing up the inlet revived Michael's sagging spirits, and he cautiously hobbled down to where the bedrock and beach met. Using the aslant rock face for cover, he inched his way along the stony trail, below the north wall. Angry with himself for not separating from the servants earlier, he mourned his lack of a weapon.

Halfway to his goal, Michael sensed movement up on the wall and the echoing voices beyond grew louder, causing panic to set in. Spotting a natural cleft in the rock, he forced his stocky frame in. The jagged rock tore his tunic and drew a rattle of frustration, but he persevered until he was in wedged tight. Poking his head out in response to the distinctive tinny rattle of horse furniture, his heart sank. A dozen of Stanley's men had reached the inlet and were splashing through the shallows towards his hiding place.

"Down there!"

The words from the parapet condemned him and he knew it. Snapping his head up, Michael saw a figure balanced precariously on top of the north wall, pointing down at him. Having climbed up to urinate, a Yorkist soldier noticed something bobbing among the rocks. Yanking up his hose he yelled the warning. Several crossbowmen ran up to the wall and began shooting in an attempt to prise the fox from its lair. A shower of short, steel-tipped quarrels zipped over Michael's head, clattering harmlessly off the rock. The poorly aimed crossbow bolts and Stanley's approaching cavalry forced him to abandon his refuge.

"Fuck it!" he spat, ducking and diving below the wall, shadowed by the crossbowmen above, "you shit-heads!"

Restricted by an incoming tide, Stanley's men dismounted and clambered over the rocks in half-hearted pursuit. Reaching a point below the Constable's Tower – a tall square structure jutting out from the main wall – Michael found a warrior in crimson doublet and black hose, barring his way.

"You!" he gasped, eyeing the white bear and ragged staff badge over his left breast, a hand resting on his right knee, to help him balance on the slanting rock face.

"My horse is back there," Philip Neville announced, indicating the way with a jerk of his chin. "Take him and go!" he urged, waving a hand for the crossbowmen on the wall, to cease shooting and for Stanley's men to wait.

"Go where?" he hissed, distressed by his predicament, "into the sea?"

"Kill the dog!" someone shouted from the top of the Constable's Tower.

Both brothers snapped their heads up and saw the grim visage of Davy Griffiths staring down.

"Finish it!" the short, blond-haired herald commanded, a brutal austerity underlining his words.

"He's unarmed!" Philip retorted angrily, struggling to maintain his footing on the near vertical slope, while a score of curious faces popped up along the wall between the tower and Great Gate.

Philip's response was followed by the swishing sound of a sword somersaulting over the battlements. The Neville brothers watched the weapon hit the sand, point down, burying half the blade.

"Give Lord Warwick what he wants and he will show mercy!" Griffiths offered, resting his hands on two of the rough merlons, while his wispy hair rippled in the breeze.

Stunned by the suggestion, Philip wrestled with his conscience; he understood his meaning, but if he agreed, he would condemn himself.

Suddenly Michael released an angry roar and leapt for the sword. Grabbing the wooden handle he drew the blade out of the sand, lifted it up to his face and eyed the fluted steel before testing the point against his thumb. When a thin line of blood broke the skin his sense of helplessness evaporated. Now at least he could die like a warrior, but he had no intention of dying.

"What's he talking about?" he sneered.

"Who knows?" Philip huffed, extracting his arming sword from its scabbard.

"You know," Michael said ominously, narrowing his eyes. "What have you done?"

"Michael Neville, you have rebelled against the true King. Lay down your sword and you will be taken before Sir John Tiptoft, High Constable of England, for judgement!" Griffiths decreed. "However, as a knight of the realm Lord Warwick offers you trial by combat!"

"Wait!" Sir John Middleton wheezed, making his way out onto the roof of the tower.

While Northumberland's retainer regained his breath,

having raced up three flights of stairs, a gust of wind forced him to clamp a hand over his velvet cap. "This is not right," he spluttered.

"Fear not Sir John, at least we shall rid ourselves of one of these troublesome fools," Griffiths retorted, his cold-hearted response causing Middleton to shudder.

In a corner of the tower roof, a crossbowman, wearing the blue and white colours of the Duke of Burgundy, crouched cranking the handles of his crossbow. Suddenly the metal stirrup slipped from under his foot and the weapon shot from his grasp. Cursing loudly in his native language, the Burgundian retrieved his crossbow and examined it for damage.

"Bâtard stupide," Griffiths growled, the noise of the weapon clattering to the stone floor distracting him.

"Pardonne moi, Mon Seigneur," the Burgundian apologised, bowing his head.

"What's going on here?" Middleton frowned, trying to understand why Griffiths was alone on the roof with a Burgundian.

"Sir John, are you loyal to the king?" Griffiths asked calmly.

"Yes!" Middleton hissed, his frown more pronounced.

"Does that loyalty extend to Lord Warwick?"

"Who are you to question my allegiance? I fought beside his lordship on Towton Field, and stood by his father at St Albans!"

"But you serve his brother."

"So what!" Middleton snapped, agitated by the herald's patronizing tone.

"You are not to speak of this to Sir John," Griffiths advised, brushing dust from his gorgeous tabard.

"Do not presume to give me orders?" he warned, pointing at his own chest. "I cut off the Duke of Somerset's head!"

"Forgive me my lord," Griffiths apologised. "Philip Neville shows contempt for authority and openly insults the king's officers."

"Then you must kill them both, for if one survives, he will begin a legacy of revenge that will hound you to your grave," Middleton predicted.

Griffiths appeared disturbed by his words and Middleton continued.

"Edward would not sanction this. Philip is of his blood, and is a most loyal subject."

"Yes, he loves the king..." Griffiths sighed, his attention drawn to something stirring below, "as do we all."

"Then stop this-"

"I cannot," he said, looking over the side. "I fear it is too late."

Middleton scoffed in disgust and left the roof.

As he disappeared down the stairs, Griffiths passed the crossbowman a knowing nod.

On the shrinking beach below the final act of the drama was unfolding. Sidling down the rocky slope, the Neville brothers had reached the sand and were less than twenty paces apart. Like two Roman gladiators they were here for the entertainment of the crowd, and like those ancient warriors, they knew it would be a fight to the finish. Michael edged slowly to the side and his movements were mirrored by Philip, until both were mechanically circling each other. Suddenly Philip's indecisiveness vanished and he surged forward.

"Run past me," he gasped, his feet sinking into the crumbling, white sand. "And take my horse!"

"No!" Michael barked, bounding toward his brother, "but I will end this quickly!" he promised, his dark narrow eyes focused on Philip's raised blade as he tried to guess where the blow might fall.

"You think so," Philip puffed, noting his sweat-stained, tatty tunic and badly cropped hair.

They were barely an arm's length apart when Philip grunted and brought his sword scything diagonally across his opponent's face. Michael brought his weapon up defensively to parry the powerful strike, and countered by curling his blade so the point would cut Philip's face open from cheek to jowl. Fortunately the loose sand gave Philip the time needed to turn and cross his sword. When the heavy weapons clashed, he saw pure hatred blazing from Michael's cold staring eyes.

"I am not so easily disarmed these days," Michael boasted, hand on hip as he paced back and forth, breathing heavily.

"We'll see," Philip spat back.

"I have been taught by Pierre de Breze," he bragged, referring to a close friend of Queen Margaret, "the best swordsman in all France!"

"This is not France," Philip retaliated, baring his teeth like an angry dog.

Michael raised his sword and kissed the crossbar.

"Come for me brother," he taunted, goading him with his free hand, "if you have the balls!"

"I'll ram this sword so far down your throat you'll be shitting steel for a week!" Philip scoffed, slashing at his head.

Michael jerked back to avoid the strike, but Philip twisted his wrist altering the angle at the last moment. The unexpected change brought the sharp tip of his sword in contact with Michael's upper left arm, tearing the tunic and gouging the flesh. The momentum of the swipe, combined with soft sand, unbalanced Philip and he slewed away.

"You craven dog!" Michael yelped, slapping a hand to his injured arm. "I'll kill you for that!"

"Try it!"

With blood pumping from the three-inch gash and staining his sleeve, Michael gritted his teeth and leapt at his brother. Unprepared for such a move, Philip went down on one knee and instinctively raised his weapon. The blades clanged together and scraped apart with a sound that set Philip's teeth on edge. Forcing Michael back used up considerable energy and, with a guttural gasp, he staggered to his feet and rested his hands on his knees.

Philip's old shoulder wound began to ache and irritating sweat ran down his face. Recovering quickly, Michael lowered his bullhead and bounded forward; before Philip could react, the top of Michael's hard head crashed into his stomach. The weight behind the charge bowled Philip over and he toppled back. Following in, Michael scooped up a handful of loose sand and flicked it into his brother's face.

"You bastard!" Philip hissed, as coarse grains adhered to the sensitive membrane of his eyes, momentarily blinding him.

"Hah!" Michael yelled, waving his sword at those on the wall.

Attracted by the echoing clash of swords, more and more spectators made their way onto the north wall. Stanley's dismounted men, squatting on the rocks, watched the swordplay with keen interest. Many believed the fight was over plunder and wagers were rife; most gambled on their own knight but a few backed the thickset fellow with a bad haircut and faded yellow tunic, charging around the beach like a rampaging elephant.

With his opponent blind, Michael Neville saw his chance.

"I'll open your entrails!" he vowed, lunging forward.

Philip barely saw the distorted shape coming at him, but he clearly heard his triumphant crowing. Intuitively sidestepping, he raised his weapon defensively in front of his face.

Accelerating like a runaway cart, Michael gripped his sword with both hands and brought its diamond shaped blade down heavily on Philip's left shoulder. At the last moment, the blow was deflected by the crossbar of Philip's arming sword, and the point of Michael's redirected weapon dove down and struck rock. The steel tip hit the hard whinstone with such force that sparks flashed and the vibration jarred his hands, causing him to cry out and veer away.

"So much for Monsieur de Breze," Philip spat defiantly, thwacking Michael on the back, as he veered past.

To prevent him from again using sand as a weapon, Philip hopped onto the sloping bedrock and rubbed the last specs of grit from his tingling eyes. The razor-sharp rock almost penetrated the soft soles of his knee-high boots, but he felt safe.

"Oh…" Michael groaned, stretching his throbbing back.

The Neville boys forgot their kinship as they circled and attacked each other, sprinkling an ever weakening display with acerbic insults. Both bled from numerous cuts and their bodies ached from successive blows, which left them bruised and sore. Wilting under a searing sun, sweating copiously, and with his feet suffering from the serrated rocks, Philip tripped and staggered back onto the draining sand. Fatigue, thirst and injury slowed the combat to an aggravating tempo for those watching. Unable to continue, they finally sank to their knees and rested over the pommels of their swords.

"You wear our father's ring," Michael gasped, spotting the gold band on the middle finger of Philip's left hand.

"It belonged to our grandfather," he drooled, "an honourable man, dishonoured by a Lancastrian King."

Michael knew he was right but could only scoff in response.

"Why don't you swim?" Philip suggested, jerking his head at the sea.

"No!" Michael coughed; the pain in his ribs staggering his sentence. "You betrayed me, after I saved your life… for that–"

"You god-damn hog," Philip cut him off, wiping a mixture of blood, spittle and sweat from his mouth with a shaky hand, and glancing at the men in the tower. "I did not betray you. Throw down your sword," he urged, "and I'll speak to the king."

"No, he can go to hell," he panted, glowering up at the tower. "Eternal damnation on the House of York and all sons of bitches who serve it!" he added angrily.

"You're already up Shit Creek, don't make it worse," Philip warned, hoping his cousin would come and put an end to the contest.

"How can it get worse?" Michael scoffed.

Using his sword as a lever, Philip tottered to his feet and searched for one last ounce of energy. The sharp pain in his ribs, caused by a clout from the pommel of Michael's sword, fogged his concentration and he briefly thought of Isobel Talbot, but her pleasant image was quickly supplanted by that of Elizabeth Percy. Shaking the conflicting pictures from his mind, he bemoaned the fact that if he should die this day, he would die a most unhappy man, having never bedded Isobel. Lamenting his timidity, he vowed that should he survive, he would ask Francis for her hand.

With his attention in the clouds, Philip reacted tardily when Michael suddenly pounced. Leaping back to avoid the unexpected assault, Philip caught his heel on a concealed root and fell. Unable to check the speed of his charge, Michael tripped over his flaying feet, tumbled down the bank and rolled into the water. Both brothers lost their swords in a moment of comical mishap. Philip's landed several yards away; Michael's flipped over a grassy sand dune.

Standing in the shallows, Michael wiped his face and sprayed a fountain of salt water through pursed lips. Spotting a three-foot section of splintered mast, floating close to the beach, he splashed through the water. Grabbing the timber he waded ashore sneering at Philip, who rummaged around on his hands and feet like a blind dog. When Michael saw sunlight glinting off a metal object lying close to Philip's outstretched fingers, he shuddered. Calculating he would reach the sword first, Michael dragged the driftwood up the beach and hoisted it above his head.

Sensing danger, Philip rolled onto his back, but stinging sand particles and searing sun blighted his vision.

"It's over," Michael grunted, hauling the worm-eaten

timber high.

Suddenly he froze, his body trembled uncontrollably and water dripped off his chin. A memory of Castillon, eleven years ago, when they fought together against a horde of Frenchmen, curtailed his rage. With the echoes of that desperate battle bouncing inside his head, Michael unconsciously lowered the mast as far as his chest. The thought that Philip had betrayed him quickly slammed the door of compassion shut. Filling his lungs with air, Michael lifted the greasy wood above his head, but again he hesitated. Movement in the Constable's Tower caught his eye, and as he looked up he heard the unmistakeable hiss of a crossbow bolt just before it slammed into his chest.

"Finish it!" Philip yelled, as the shadow blocking the sun vanished, "for God's sake."

When nothing happened Philip rubbed his eyes and blinked to clear his vision. Looking around he saw the shimmering shape of a sword in the sand. Rolling onto his stomach, he reached for weapon and jumped up. Posing defensively, he waited for the next assault, but it never came. Examining the dark rocks and mounds of yellow, wind-burnt dune grass, he narrowed his eyes but there was no sign of Michael. Putting a hand down the back of his collar, he tried to brush annoying sand from to his tacky neck, but only made it worse. While he contemplated his next move, the adrenalin of combat diminished and the agony of his wounds intensified. Several deep lesions on his arms bled profusely, countless minor cuts, mixed with sweat and sand, stung, and when he touched the discoloured swelling on his left cheek, he winced. Unable to find Michael, he lowered his sword and frowned up at the tower for an answer, but the sun's intensity forced him to look away.

"Where are you?" he hissed, twisting in all directions.

As he headed down to the water, accompanied by ominous silence from the north wall, Philip sensed something was wrong. While he staggered along the beach, blood from a deep gash above his left elbow ran down the sleeve of his tunic, coursed between his fingers and dripped off the tips, marking his route. Reaching the shore he stopped and anxiously rubbed his face. The cold water lapping over his boots, and the wind cooling the sweat on his face felt pleasant, but what he saw froze his blood. Michael lay on his back drifting out to sea, one arm twisted around a length of broken mast, and a crossbow bolt growing out of his chest.

"You stupid bastard!" he yelled, forgetting his injuries.

Dropping his sword, Philip leapt into the sea and forced a way through the dense water, but Michael's body was caught in the current. Being a poor swimmer he went as deep as he dare, but swirling undercurrents and soft sand conspired to drag him off-balance. Up to his chin in freezing water, Philip came so close he could see Michael's yellow tunic washed pink with diluted blood. Stretching a hand out in desperation, he suddenly lost his footing and went under. With salt water gushing into his mouth, he panicked to regain his balance. Spluttering to the surface, he wiped his eyes and extended his fingers that extra inch, but Michael continued to drift. With the soles of his boots struggling to grip the soft bed, and his waterlogged doublet dragging him down, Philip knew he had reached his limit. He finally turned back and withdrew to the shallows, hacking up gobbets of salty snot. Standing in a foot of water, Philip fell to his knees and smashed his fists into the sea until the pain in his ribs forced him to stop.

Physically exhausted, he hung his head and allowed his arms to flop limply in the water. Fighting to hold back the tears threatening to pour forth, he denied those who would rejoice in his brother's demise, the satisfaction they yearned. Drawn to the body coasting out to sea, Philip turned and raised his hands to his mouth. With wet fingers entwined before quivering lips, he looked up at the clear, blue sky and mumbled a prayer for the salvation of Michael's soul.

"Misereatur tui omnipotens Deus et dimissis peccatis tuis, perducat te ad vitam aeternam… Amen."

Lowering his hands, he bit hard into the knuckles of the two forefingers, before snarling an angry postscript, "And you would have cut out my entrails, you fool!"

Philip plunged his head under the water, to rinse the sweat from his face and hair, and tottered to his feet. Snorting to clear clogged nostrils, he brushed back his wet hair and stumbled along the beach, despair clawing at his heart. Glancing up at the Constable's Tower, he stopped and focused on Davy Griffiths. Grabbing the white bear and ragged staff badge sewn over the left breast of his sopping doublet, he stared hatefully at the herald, who deliberately avoided making eye contact. Philip's attention remained fixated on Griffiths, until he finally met his demonic glare. When their eyes locked, Philip ripped the emblem from his doublet and thrust it at the herald.

"You bacon-face cunt!" he screamed, drawing out the last word as long as he could bear the pain. "I will kill you," he promised, pointing at him.

Recalling Middleton's warning, Griffiths failed to respond. Screwing the badge up, Philip threw it passionately to the ground, and used the heel of his boot to grind the emblem into the sand. When he looked up the herald was gone.

"You can run," he spat, "but I'll find you if it takes the rest of my life!"

Retrieving and sheathing his sword, Philip dragged his waterlogged boots up the beach, leering menacingly at those still watching from the wall. As he trudged back to his horse, he heard Stanley's cavalry mount up and ride away.

"Show's over," he scoffed.

Reaching his patient warhorse, tethered to a tree near the barbican, Philip took out a wet handcoverchief and used it to bind his bleeding arm. Delicately fingering the expanding lump on his cheek, he flinched before resting his rough chin on the soft, velvet saddle cover. Closing his eyes, he agonised over the final moments of Michael's life. Warwick's ironic advice to leave him dead came to mind, and he cursed his pig-headedness. Hotspur twisted his neck and gently nuzzled Philip's shoulder, bringing him out of his distraction. Massaging his throbbing shoulder, he shaded his eyes with a sticky, bloody hand and scanned the mass of water.

"Where are you?" he groaned, tracing his probable route.

Finally he spotted him, no more than a speck on the surface, bobbing in a north-westerly direction.

"The Benedictines will give him a decent burial," he told his horse, believing Michael would wash up on Holy Island, five miles away.

Philip's saturated doublet and hose clung to his body and water squelched uncomfortably in his boots. With great reluctance he untied the reins and led Hotspur away.

"They killed my brother," he lamented, coughing up and spitting out a bubble of bloody phlegm. "God have mercy on his soul."

Hotspur shook his head up and down and snorted.

Placing a foot in the stirrup, Philip hauled himself into the high chair of his saddle. Coiling the leather straps around the bloodstained fingers of his left hand, he gently nudged Hotspur's flanks. A light breeze wafted through the trees, rustling the leaves and he thought he heard a voice in the wind. Drawing his horse up, he looked out to sea once more, but there was nothing, nothing but the low rumbling of waves rolling ashore and the hiss of white water dissolving on the sand. Turning away he took a deep breath, and the nutty fragrance of almonds emanating from the gorse was drawn into his nose. As he steered Hotspur back to the Yorkist camp, the Earl of Warwick's colourful standard in the distance turned his sorrow into hatred. Staring at the banner, he cursed the name of Richard Neville and swore vengeance on those who had brought his brother's life to such an untimely end.